CONQUEST II

The Drowned Court

O sea bird
white upon the tide.

best wishes,

Tracey.

December 2017
Ambialet.

CONQUEST II

The Drowned Court

Tracey Warr

IMPRESS
BOOKS

First Published 2017
by Impress Books Ltd
Innovation Centre, Rennes Drive, University of Exeter Campus,
Exeter EX4 4RN

Typeset in Garamond by Swales & Willis Ltd, Exeter, Devon
Printed and bound in England by Short Run Press Ltd, Exeter, Devon, UK

British Library Cataloguing in Publication Data
A catalogue record for this book is available from the British Library

ISBN: 978-1-911293-08-8 (pbk)
ISBN: 978-1-911293-09-5 (ebk)

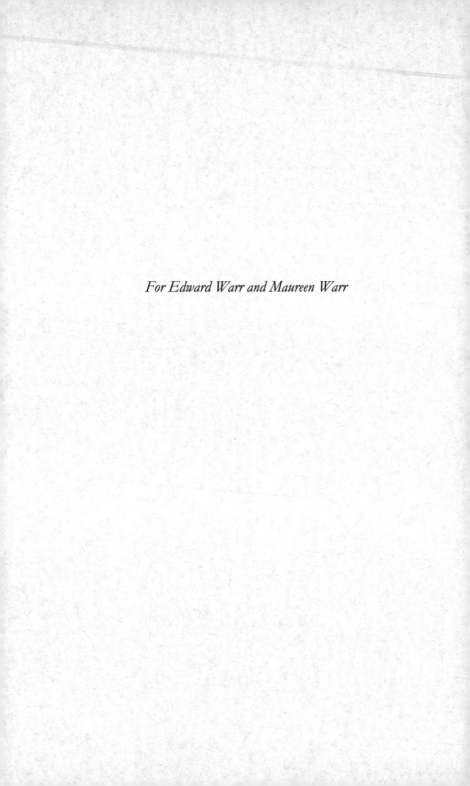

For Edward Warr and Maureen Warr

CONTENTS

Cast of Characters

Main Characters

Benedicta, a nun at Almenêches Abbey, Normandy; sister of the Flemish knight, Haith

Henry I, King of England and Duke of Normandy; youngest son of William the Conqueror

Nest ferch Rhys, wife of Gerald FitzWalter, the steward of Pembroke Castle; former mistress of King Henry; daughter of the deceased Welsh king of the south-west kingdom of Deheubarth

Secondary Characters

Adela, Countess of Blois, Meaux and Chartres; sister of King Henry; mother of Thibaut de Blois and Etienne de Blois

Amaury de Montfort, lord in Normandy; nephew of the Count of Évreux; ally of King Louis of France and enemy of King Henry of England

Amelina, Nest's Breton maid

Bertrade de Montfort, former queen of France; former countess of Anjou; sister of Amaury de Montfort

Cadwgan, King of the Welsh kingdom of Powys

Elizabeth de Vermandois, Countess of Leicester; wife of Robert de Meulan; mistress of William de Warenne

Etienne de Blois, Count of Mortain; Countess Adela's son and King Henry's nephew

Gerald FitzWalter, husband of Nest ferch Rhys; steward of Pembroke Castle

Gruffudd ap Rhys, Nest's brother; claimant to the former Welsh kingdom of Deheubarth, now ruled by the Norman king, Henry, under the stewardship of Gerald FitzWalter

Haith, Flemish knight in the service of King Henry since childhood; brother of the nun, Benedicta

Henry FitzRoy, Nest's illegitimate son by King Henry

Isabel de Beaumont, daughter of Elizabeth de Vermandois and Robert de Meulan

Juliana, King Henry's illegitimate daughter; married to Eustache de Breteuil

Mahaut, daughter of Count Fulk d'Anjou

Orderic Vitalis, a monk at the monastry of Ouches; a historian

Owain ap Cadwgan, Prince of the Welsh kingdom of Powys

Petronilla de Chemillé, Prioress and then Abbess of Fontevraud Abbey in Anjou

Richard de Belmeis, Sheriff of Shropshire; formerly Nest's tutor and clerk at Cardiff Castle for the Montgommery family, who were convicted of treason in 1102

Robert de Bellême, Lord of Alençon and Bellême; head of the Montgommery family; dispossessed by King Henry of the earldom of Shrewsbury for treason

Robert FitzRoy, King Henry's illegitimate eldest son; betrothed to Nest's foster-sister, Mabel FitzRobert

William *Adelin*, heir to the English throne; son of King Henry and Queen Matilda

William *Clito*, son of Robert, former Duke of Normandy; nephew of King Henry and Countess Adela; claimant to the Duchy of Normandy and others

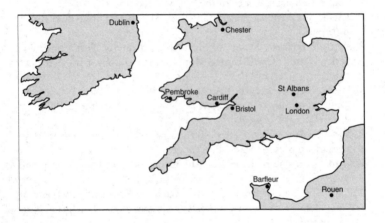

Map of Ireland, Wales and England

Map of Normandy and northern France

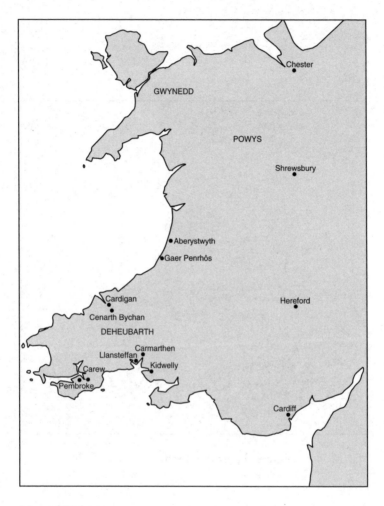

Map of Wales

Part One

1107–1109

1

Perplexing Parchments

'Read it to me one more time,' Amelina said.

> *Yr wylan deg ar lanw, dioer*
> *Unlliw ag eiry neu wenlloer,*
> *Dilwch yw dy degwch di,*
> *Darn fal haul, dyrnfol heli.*

I delighted in the roll of the Welsh on my tongue, like the tide coming home again to the beach. I sighed at so many years of forcing my mouth into the alien shapes of Norman French. 'O sea-bird, beautiful upon the tides.' I translated the Welsh for Amelina.

> White as the moon is when the night abides,
> Or snow untouched, whose dustless splendour glows
> Bright as a sunbeam and whose white wing throws
> A glove of challenge on the salt sea-flood.

'A gull,' Amelina pronounced with satisfaction.

'Obviously!' I said, instantly regretting my exclamation as I watched her pleased expression dissipate. 'But the question you must help me with, Amelina, is who placed this on my writing table?' I tried to mollify her. 'Who managed to get past all the castle guards and into my room?'

'Perhaps that person was already here, Lady Nest. Perhaps it was Gerald.' All her speeches to me for many weeks had been aimed at encouraging the tentative affection growing between myself and my husband. The threads holding Gerald and I together were fragile, and we were still weaving them carefully, warily, between us.

I shook my head. 'It's in Welsh.'

'Gerald speaks Welsh.'

'Not like this. The poem is sophisticated.' My husband is a Norman. A sympathetic one, but a Norman nonetheless.

'Then he paid a bard to write it for him.'

I shook my head once more, smiling at her stubborn desire that such a romantic gesture should come from my husband. Gerald's military strategies were often brilliant, unexpected, but in matters of the heart? No, he was tiresomely straightforward in that regard. 'He is not a romantic,' I said. I picked up a pinch of aniseed spice from a bowl on the table and chewed thoughtfully on it.

'The King?' she said hesitantly, always unwilling to bring his name up since the pain I had suffered at his abandonment. King Henry was capable of such a gesture, and he had given me many poems in our time together, but he did not send this. 'It's in Welsh. A Norman would send a poem in French.' I shook my head again, trying to wipe away the warm memories of Henry. 'Throws a *glove of challenge* on the salt sea-flood, Amelina.'

'Owain ap Cadwgan,' she exclaimed, bringing her fingers swiftly to her mouth as if to instantly silence it, as she voiced the name of the Welsh prince; the name that had been in both of our minds since I first picked up the mysterious rolled parchment left on my desk.

'Yes, it must be.' I had been betrothed to Owain long ago, before the Normans came and killed my father, stole our lands, stole me away to a Norman upbringing and the Norman court.

'He broke into a Norman castle for you once before,' she reminded me. 'He could do it again.'

'I can't feel so pleased with that now, Amelina,' I said, sharply, making her expression fall again. 'Now that I have Norman babies to protect.'

'Will you tell Gerald, then? Have the soldiers make a search of the castle?' She stood and moved behind me to brush my hair.

'It's too late for that. Whoever left this here is long gone.' Keeping my head still for Amelina's ministrations, I peered down to look once more at the poem, the stiff roll held open between my splayed thumb and fingers. Amelina finished braiding my black hair into two thick plaits. She swung them over the front of my shoulders and leant to pick up the garnet and gold hair jewels on my desk. I rolled the poem carefully and tied the silk ribbon back around it. If this was from Owain, it came too late. I had hankered for him once, when I was a child, a miserable hostage in a Norman stronghold. If Owain had rescued me from Cardiff Castle *then*, years ago, as he had promised to do, my life would have been different. I could have been a happy Welsh wife, a Welsh queen, but that chance had vanished. I was married to a Norman, to Gerald, and my small sons were half-Norman. I must negotiate amidst those complexities every day. 'It's too late,' I said again to Amelina. 'Owain can only mean trouble and pain now.'

She glanced at my face, then focused back on fitting the jewels to the ends of my plaits. She moved to the chest at the foot of my bed to find a head veil.

'But I can't betray Owain to Gerald either.'

Amelina was back with a fine, translucent veil in her hand. She grimaced sympathetically and tied the short veil in place around my head with an embroidered blue band.

'Or make Gerald doubt his trust in me,' I told her.

She frowned to show that she mirrored and fully understood these complications. 'Ohhhh, and who-ooo was her true love?' She trilled the refrain of a Breton love song from her homeland and smiled at me sardonically.

I ignored Amelina's humour. 'We will say nothing of this poem,' I decided. 'Owain cannot have been here himself. He paid somebody to bring this parchment into the castle, to leave it in my room.' When I was a girl, I was naive enough to think that Owain was planning to rescue me for my sake, to help *me*, but I know better now. I was merely a symbol for *all* these men to fight over, as hounds squabble over a bone in the courtyard. 'It's a challenge to Gerald,' I said, 'and I will not deliver it.'

Amelina waggled her head from side to side. 'But it is a beautiful poem of love too,' she said eagerly.

'I should burn it,' I said, as I slid it into my jewelled casket and closed the lid.

Downstairs, at the hall table, my husband waited for me with more perplexing parchment: King Henry's invitation. 'What does he mean by it?' Gerald asked.

I did not answer immediately. We both knew what Henry meant. I took my seat beside Gerald, carefully arranging the folds of my favourite blue wool gown around me. I suppressed a smile at the ceramic plate centred on the long table before us. It showed two kissing birds standing in water, and had come as a gift with the King's invitation. I reached over and took Gerald's hand, moving it away from the King's letter, forcing open his palm, and pressing my own to his. He lifted our hands to his mouth and softly kissed the back of mine, his pale blue eyes upon me. I smoothed the fair curls from his forehead.

'I am not invited,' he said.

I shook my head. There had been no mention of Gerald in King Henry's invitation to me to attend the betrothal of his eldest bastard son, Robert FitzRoy, and my foster-sister, Mabel Fitz-Robert, in Cardiff. It was deliberate. Everything Henry did was deliberate.

'He wants you to go alone.'

I nodded.

'And you will go?'

'I must,' I said. 'He commands it. He is our king.'

He dropped his gaze and a muscle moved in his jaw. 'He is King of you.'

'Not anymore, Gerald,' I whispered, bringing my mouth close to his ear. 'You are my lord, now. You will always be my lord.'

He swallowed. 'He wants you to himself.'

'Perhaps, but he will not have me. I must go for the sake of my foster-sister, Mabel.'

He nodded, not looking at me.

'Please Gerald, try to trust me. Trust us. I love you.'

He smiled an unconvinced smile at me. 'I do. I do trust us, Nest.' He touched the garnet jewel at the end of my plait, slid his thumb up onto my hair.

'I will be perfectly safe travelling with Haith,' I said. The King's knight had arrived the previous evening. 'I will leave Amelina here to take care of the children.'

Gerald looked surprised. 'You will not take your son to the King?'

'He does not command it.' I tapped the King's letter with the back of my hand. Whilst my youngest son, William, who was one year old, was Gerald's, my eldest two-year-old son, Henry, was the King's son, but he only knew Gerald as his father. The fear that the King would demand I give little Henry up to him to be raised at court had been my first flinching response on reading the invitation. Yet the King's letter made no mention of my boy and I had no intention of handing him over. If the King asked it of me, I would fight. I knew the King's other mistresses had all been obliged to give up their children to the royal nursery, but now Gerald and I had left the court, were safely in Wales, nothing would make me return little Henry to Westminster. If the King came here to Pembroke Castle with an army I would hide my son with the Welsh rebels in the mountains. Little Henry was mine and I was adamant that he would not go to the Norman court.

'No.' Gerald was thinking slowly. 'But surely, Nest–'

I interrupted him. 'I will *not* take little Henry to Cardiff. He stays here with us, with you. And *you* will never give him up, if you wish to keep my love.' I looked at him fiercely.

He gazed at me earnestly. I saw every day that despite little Henry's paternity, Gerald loved him almost as much as I did. 'I give you my word, Nest,' he said. I smiled to myself. If Gerald gave me his word my son had the best protection I could provide for him.

2

Resolved

There were very few roads in Wales and no other route to travel to Cardiff. I swayed in the saddle with the knight Haith at my side, enjoying the spring sun, and tried not to think about how I was travelling the same road I had first taken after my family and household were massacred at Llansteffan. I had travelled this road to Cardiff Castle as an eight-year-old hostage of the Normans.

The first day of this journey, Haith and I were forced to ride hard to reach our overnight resting place at the small monastery of Llantwit, outside Neath, before twilight closed in around us. We left Pembroke later than planned since Haith, as was his habit, had overslept. Today, however, feeling guilt for yesterday, he was up with the lark and we left early, riding at a leisurely pace. We would reach Cardiff well before nightfall.

Haith had raised an eyebrow when he learned at Pembroke that I had no intention of bringing the King's son with me to Cardiff, but he said nothing. Had Henry merely neglected to command it? He was never careless, although he might give that impression if it served him. Then did he leave my son with me as a gift, as an apology for abandoning me? I would learn his intentions soon enough, when I saw him. I tried to ignore my nervousness at the thought. 'Is the King well?' I asked Haith. He and Henry had been companions since childhood and Haith was fiercely loyal to his friend and master.

'Yes, lady. Now war is over in Normandy, King very fine.'

The Flemish inflections in Haith's speech had never improved in all the years I had known him, in all the time he had been speaking French at Henry's court. I sometimes thought he did it on purpose, to make himself appear a little silly, to conceal his intelligence. I sighed, thinking how the mere prospect of Henry, although he was miles away yet, immediately turned the air and all to intrigue and deceit.

Misinterpreting my sigh as a response to his mention of war, Haith said, 'King's brother is prisoner now in Salisbury. Queen visits him. Says he's content.'

The road was pitted with holes and cracks from the recent winter freezings and my reply had to wait while I steered my horse carefully around one particularly large fissure. 'Poor Robert.'

'Maybe he is happier as comfortable prisoner than as Duke,' Haith suggested.

I glanced at Haith. The sun lit his thick blond hair, turning his head leonine. He was always trying to put a positive angle on everything the King did, even when there was nothing positive to make of Henry's actions. 'Maybe.' Undoubtedly that was also what Henry told himself about his brother, now that he had usurped him as Duke of Normandy. 'Will the Queen be at Cardiff?'

'No. She prefers no travel. Likes to stay in London with children.'

'They are well, also? William and Maud?' I referred to the royal children, the legitimate ones. Henry's nursery in Westminster teemed with his other children too, the children of his legion of mistresses, of which I regretfully, stupidly, had been a member. His legitimate daughter, Maud, was five, and the heir, William, was three years old now. I had attended the Queen at their births.

Haith beamed at me. 'Very well,' he said. 'And you, lady? You happy home in Wales? With husband?' He glanced at me and looked away quickly. He knew my history and it offended his decency, his kindness.

'Yes,' I told him. 'I am very happy, Haith.'

'Excellence,' he said. We were riding past a copse thickly carpeted with new bluebells. Haith laughed, let go his reins and threw his long arms wide, as if about to embrace the arrival of spring, and I laughed with him. 'Why not?' he declared. 'You should be. You should be happy, always.'

After two days on the road from Pembroke, I longed to take a moment of respite before having to confront the King and the court, but knew I could not have that comfort. We rode through a huge encampment of merchants clustered in front of the long castle walls. They jostled one another, calling out their wares to us. I steered my horse through the gatehouse of Cardiff Castle and into the familiar bailey.

There was the hall where I had lived with Lady Sybil Montgommery and her family of four daughters for nine years. There was the well where I had drawn water every day and plotted to send Amelina to the Welsh King Cadwgan and his son Owain, hoping for rescue from my Norman captors. There was the motte towering above us, where I had often climbed to reach the tower and look out across the land and sea, longing for my freedom. There was the path to the postern gate where I had waited one moonless night for my betrothed husband, Owain ap Cadwgan, who told me he would come for me, he would take me home to my own people. But he never came.

I shivered, remembering how I had waited for Owain in the dark, waited all night until the cockerel crowed for the rising sun.

'Lady.' Haith held out his hand to help me dismount.

I needed no directions. Every inch of this castle was engraved in my memory, in the habits of my muscles. I brushed dust from my skirts and walked slowly to the great doors of the hall, trying to collect myself. Despite the familiarity of the castle, it seemed changed, smaller, where once it had seemed vast to me, when I arrived here as a distraught child. The impression of change was also brought about by the great crowd crammed into the castle for the King's court. Although his full retinue would not be here, many remaining at Westminster with the Queen, nevertheless there were hundreds of bustling people: servants, mewsmen, houndsmen exercising their charges, stableboys, a scribe with a stack of wax slates in his hands, cooks' assistants, water carriers.

Inside the doors, the hall was no less crowded, but here were both the King's formal court – his *curia*, and his *domus* – his personal household of chamberlains, stewards, butlers, scribes and marshals, all those with nearness to the King. It had been so long since I had been at court that, at first, I felt overwhelmed with this amorphous mass of chattering colours, furs and silks, unable to discern its individual shapes. The ostentation and luxury assaulted me after two years of relatively plain living with my husband at Pembroke Castle.

I looked around at bishops in their finest copes, chaplains and clerks, gloriously clad noblemen, ladies with small dogs and monkeys on fine chains. The King's favoured hounds wound their way around human and table legs. Dishes and jugs clattered. Rowdy soldiers and young sons of the nobility receiving their education at the King's court, those who formed his *familia*, his household knights clashed drinking horns and goblets, laughing loudly with each other. Orphaned heiresses, as I had once been, were bedecked with their best jewels, their hair loose and lustrous, hoping that either the King would favour them with a splendid (or kind) marriage, or turn his eye on them himself. The King had been away in Normandy for a considerable time and many people doubtless hoped to gain some satisfactory decisions from him. Despite the discomforts of travelling to Cardiff, as many as could get here were crammed into the castle. Each sat with their own agenda burning for the King's attention, but politely camouflaged by a façade of mere leisure. Their tension was heightened by Henry's strategies. He knew the art of manipulating hopes and fears.

I took a deep breath and allowed myself to focus on the centre that all these people swirled around. Henry sat at the High Table with his eldest son, Robert FitzRoy, on his right-hand side, and my dear foster-sister, Mabel, on his left. Robert was sixteen years old and had grown into gangling manhood since I had last seen him. Mabel was not conventionally beautiful, but at fourteen, she had the benefits of youth. She had the looks of her father and mother, moon-faced and a little buck-toothed, but to me she was as beautiful as the sun. I could not suppress an enormous smile of affection as our eyes met. I sobered my expression and curtsied to the King, my neck bent, my eyes on the toes of my blue riding boots.

'Lady Nest!' His voice was warm, honeyed, and my body responded to it. I was angry already and I had not even looked him in the face yet.

I rose from my curtsey and looked at him. His hair was blue-black, his dark eyes were avid, brimming with humour and intelligence. Remorse, apology, self-blame for his abandonment of me – those were alien concepts to him. I held his gaze. I was no longer a stupid, innocent girl. I had learned my lessons.

'You are greatly welcome here, to your old home,' he gestured to the hall, 'for this very happy occasion.' He gave me a formal welcome and I knew our real joust would come later.

I glanced at Mabel again and saw she was happy enough. Robert FitzRoy would make her a good husband. Like me, he had been fostered with Mabel's mother, Sybil de Montgommery, and he and Mabel knew each other well. 'It is, indeed, a very happy occasion,' I said. Mabel's father, Robert FitzHamon, had recently died from an old battle injury. Her mother had failed to produce a male heir, so the King had concentrated FitzHamon's vast patrimony, all of it, into Mabel as sole heiress, and given her to his illegitimate son.

'You have had a long journey, Lady Nest. Please, take your ease. We look forward to conversing with you further, later today.'

'Thank you, Sire.' I curtsied again, swept my gaze along the table, saw the thinning orange-grey hair and smile of the one person I recognised: Richard de Belmeis, my old tutor. It was he who had betrayed the Montgommery family and now he benefitted greatly from their fall, since the King had made him Sheriff of Shropshire and of all the former Montgommery lands on the Welsh borders. I did not respond to his smile.

'This way, my lady.' A servant gestured to the stairs at the right side of the hall. Those stairs had been riddled with treacherous holes and rottings when I lived here as a child, but now they were in a good state of repair. I followed the servant up to the first floor, through the room that had been de Belmeis' study and my schoolroom, relieved to find that the vitrine of locusts he had kept there was gone. The servant led me down the hall to the small chamber that had once been mine. My travelling chest was already at the foot of the bed.

'You travel with no maidservant, my lady?'

'No, my maid remained at home to take care of my children.'

'Should I send a girl to you, my lady?'

'No. It's not necessary.' I glanced at the jug of water and the clean linen on a small table close to the fire. 'I will fend for myself.' I needed some time alone and could not tolerate a stranger primping and probing at me, taking gossip about me back to the other servants and, in turn, to their mistresses and masters.

The servant left me to look around at the bed and its hangings, which had not changed at all, at the same view from the small window, the crackling fire in the same hearth, the same *aumbry* on the wall with its shelves now empty. I pulled off the white leather gloves, which the King had given me as a gift years before, and set them on the table. I rarely had occasion to wear such finery now. Looking at them, I tried and failed to not remember those times. When Henry abandoned me, I had wanted to discard everything he had ever given me: the clothes, books, jewels and tapestries, but Amelina remonstrated with me, kept things secreted away where I could not see them, until the time when I could bear to encounter them again without erupting into a welter of misery and rage. She was right. It would have been profligate to throw away such things. I loosened my cape fastening, letting it drop from my shoulders onto the bed. I unpacked my fine glass beakers from their wrappings and placed them on the *aumbry* shelf where they had formerly stood, in my previous life here. I smiled to myself, delighted that they had survived the dangers of yet another journey and continued to bear witness to all the passing times of my life. There was a light tap on the door behind me. Was Henry here to test my resolve so soon? I turned to see Mabel in the doorway, and she rushed into my embrace. 'I'm so glad to see you, Nest!'

I kissed her face. 'And I, you. But where is your mother?'

Her eyes instantly welled with tears. 'Gone,' she said bleakly. 'The King commanded my mother's remarriage to Jean, Sire of Raimes, in Normandy. My mother says he is a very minor lord. She thought she would meet you today, but the King … .' She sat on the bed, beside my discarded cloak, looking glum.

Mabel's grandfather, Roger de Montgommery, had been one of the most important nobles under Henry's father, William the Conqueror. Mabel's uncles, Hugh, and then Robert de Bellême, had been Earls of Shrewsbury, but the family was rebellious, arrogant, and Henry had brought them down spectacularly, five years ago. Henry attainted all the Montgommerys as traitors, and it was Richard de Belmeis, their erstwhile servant and my tutor, who had betrayed them, who provided the damning evidence. Mabel's uncle, Robert de Bellême, lost the earldom and fled to his lands in Normandy.

'Is there anything you need, Nest? Where is Amelina?'

'I left her in Pembroke with my sons. She sends you her love. I know my way around my old home well enough to manage ably without her for a few days.' I kissed her cheek. 'I am so very pleased to be here, Mabel. To see you betrothed to Robert.'

Smiling, she touched a fingertip to the vestige of a tear beneath one of her eyes, rose and left me to my memories.

I hesitated at the top of the stairs that wound down to the hall, garnering my courage to face Henry. I held out my arm and twisted my wrist to and fro, admiring the repeating bird's foot pattern that Amelina and I had embroidered in gold around the cuffs, neck and hem of my fine dark blue gown. We had been stitching for two weeks and the result was pleasing. I had sketched the imprint of the kite's foot in the sand at Llansteffan and Amelina and I had then copied it in stitch. The kite was a magnificent regal bird, biding its time, hovering and soaring on high winds and I had adopted this claw-print as my emblem, my secret sign to myself of adherence to my Welsh heritage. I was wearing my best jewels, including the small silver cross that Gerald gifted to me. Looking down at my slippered foot held in the air, about to take the first step, I reminded myself: I am a royal Welsh princess and the wife of Sir Gerald FitzWalter, castellan of Pembroke Castle. That was who I would take serenely into the hall, into the King's presence, to face all his court. I was *not* the King's discarded mistress, abandoned pregnant without so much as a note. I was not her.

Every step of those stairs was loaded with memories for me: hiding in the window embrasure set deep in the cold stone, overhearing the Montgommery family secrets, telling them to Gerald; one dark night, slipping surreptitously down these steps, and out to the postern gate, to wait for Owain ap Cadwgan who never came. I paused, half-way down, closed my eyes briefly, to dispel the memories and focus my mind on the present challenges instead. The sounds of the hall rose up to me: crockery clattering, a barely discernable lute drowned out by the buzz of voices, and a woman's high-pitched laughter. I opened my arms wide and touched the two sides of the cold stone tower with my fingertips, as if bathing in the noise spiralling up the stairwell. In truth, I had grown a little bored with the humdrum days at Pembroke Castle. I smiled to myself and proceeded down.

'Lady Nest!' The King was standing close to the bottom of the staircase. Had he been waiting for me? He took my proferred hand, wrapping his other arm closely around my waist. I locked my body into a mute resistance, which he ignored as he pulled me into the crowd. 'Here is the Vermandois!' he exclaimed, coming to a halt before Elizabeth.

Elizabeth had been my great friend in the years I spent at court, before I married and returned to Wales with Gerald. She looked a little different, grown into a woman in the three years since I had last seen her. She had been a child-bride, a mere eleven years old, married to Henry's leading counsellor, Robert de Meulan, who was forty years older than she. Since she had slipped from child to wife so fast, so early, she retained child-like qualities as she grew into adulthood. So much had been foist upon her in disregard of her own desires that now she felt she could do whatever she liked. I had often feared the outcome of her recklessness. She took my hands, smiling warmly. Henry did not remove his arm from my waist. 'I'm taking her,' Elizabeth said to him defiantly. Elizabeth and the King were great friends, which in part explained her success in recklessness, yet they had never been lovers, which had always struck me as odd considering Elizabeth's beauty and youth and Henry's usual inclinations.

'Of course!' he said, pulling a comical face at us both. 'For now, you are.' He released my waist with a sly caress, and moved off to speak with William Warenne, Elizabeth's lover, who smiled a greeting to me over Henry's shoulder. Elizabeth swung my hands and I looked down at our clasped hands in disorientated surprise, too slowly processing my feelings at Henry's sudden proximity and now his sudden absence again. He slipped so easily back into treating me with familiarity and instead of feeling angry at that, I was ashamed to find myself pleased at it.

Elizabeth drew me to the edge of the hall and a cushioned window seat, where we could find a little quiet in the hubbub. 'How are you, darling?'

'Well. And you?'

She rolled her exquisite, turquoise eyes dramatically, jerking her head in the direction of Warenne.

'So, still?' I asked.

'Oh yes.'

'And your husband?'

'Meulan is over there.'

I followed her gesture to look at her husband whose lined face and bent, pained posture spoke eloquently of his age and his years of solid service to the King.

'He has not been well lately.'

'I am sorry to hear it.'

She plucked at the sleeve of my dress. 'An unusual design, Nest,' she said, studying the golden march of the bird's foot around my cuff. 'You have a whimsical dressmaker. Still, you look gorgeous!' She leant closer. 'You had a boy?' she whispered.

'I had two boys.'

She shrugged. 'Yes, but you had Henry's boy.'

I nodded, reluctant to speak of it. 'This will be a fine marriage for Robert FitzRoy and Mabel FitzRobert.'

She ignored my attempt to change the subject. 'Does he look like Henry? Has the King told you what he will bestow upon him? Lands or title, I mean.'

'No.' I was shocked to recognise the avarice of the court in her expression, a craving that she and I had joked about when we perceived it together before. Unlike her, I had not arrived at the King's court at Westminster as a child. I learned to swim there as an adult. I was saddened to see that what had been play for her was now hardened into endeavour. Seeing that I could not deflect her from the subject of my son, I used the pretence of another face I recognised in the crowd to move off. 'Let's speak more later,' I called back to Elizabeth.

'Lady Nest! How delightful to see you.' The soft, smiling, young woman holding her hands to me in artless welcome presented a stark contrast to Elizabeth's hard glint. How on earth did Sybil Corbet survive the court? Protected by the King, I supposed. Such a warm welcome, coming from one of Henry's other mistresses could be taken as sarcasm, preparation for competitive verbal battle, but coming from Sybil, I knew it was sincere. She was slight despite having borne Henry several children. I knew from gossip that she was still his mistress and she was, as usual, pregnant. I had been at the birth of her first child and felt a real affection for her. Her simplicity was probably what appealed to Henry. It was a rarity amidst the self-seeking complexities of his court. Sybil made him laugh and relax and she was not inclined to jealousy. She was his respite from kingship. Henry was a loyal philanderer. He had kept Ansfride as his mistress for many years, but Sybil had come to Henry as a young girl and outlasted us all.

Looking over Sybil's shoulder, searching for the black head of the King, I was startled to recognise Bernard de Neufmarché and his wife Agnes. I had only met them once before, soon after I arrived at Cardiff as a child hostage, when I laid a curse on de Neufmarché, the murderer of my father and my half-brother, Cynan. I cursed that de Neufmarché should be hunted down by the Dogs of Annwn, who ran with the ghastly Wild Hunt. I cursed that the Dogs would gnaw voraciously on his innards. De Neufmarché was an aggressive Norman lord from the Conqueror's generation. He was nearing old age now and his muscles were turning to lard. His grotesquely battle-scarred face looked as if it had been cupped by the searing, fiery hand of a demon. Silently, I repeated the curse in my head and Sybil's cheerful expression fell, seeing something horrid in mine. 'What is it, Nest? You look as if you have seen a ghost.'

'Yes. I have remembered ghosts and I see a ghost walking,' I said in a fierce whisper, turning my gaze back to Sybil.

Sybil dropped my hands. 'Are you well?'

I forced a smile to my face. 'Yes.'

'Lady Nest.'

I turned to confront de Neufmarché's wife, Agnes, and was relieved to see she had only her two children with her, and her husband remained at a distance from me, on the other side of the hall.

'Lady Agnes,' I greeted her politely. 'And your children?'

'Yes, this is Mael,' she said, introducing a dark-haired young man of fourteen or so, 'and Sybille.' I judged that her daughter was about six years of age. Agnes was half-Welsh and the granddaughter of the former king of all Wales, Gruffudd ap Llewellyn. She had been forced to the marriage with de Neufmarché and had made no bones about her bitterness when I met her years before. She was in her early thirties now. Judging by the raddled lines of her face and her overly thin frame, the marriage had not improved for her. I smiled to her children, but was saved from further discussion with Agnes by the start of the betrothal ceremony.

I avoided Henry's glances, focussing on Mabel and Robert as the bishop blessed them. Mabel's pale brown hair was dressed with colourful threads and flowers. She wore a dusky pale red gown that suited her. Robert's resemblance to the King was visible in his stocky build and dark hair. When the ceremony was over, there was no avoiding the King. He came straight for me. 'My darling Nest,' he said quietly, taking my hand.

'Sire.' I took my hand back. 'I am glad to see you well.'

He stood too close, talking intimately to me as if we were not surrounded by a hundred people. 'Thank you. I am so *very* glad to see you, Nest. How is my son? And how is your life in Pembroke?'

'Henry is a fine boy, and Pembroke and my husband suit me very well.'

'Shall we walk in the gardens, Nest, and talk of old times?'

'I would rather not, Sire,' I told him. 'I fear I might catch cold.' The harshness of the stare I gave him did not match the mildness of my words.

His mouth curved. 'My stubborn Welsh beauty,' he whispered. 'How I have missed the coming and going of those dimples.'

I tried to keep my emotional confusion – and my dimples – from my face. It was all about the thrill of the chase with him. If

I had thrown myself at him during my time at court he probably would have left me alone. I was irritated to find myself feeling again the intense draw of him.

The evening's feast passed quickly in a flow of superficial conversation, an endless procession of delectable dishes, and beautiful music and poetry that nobody listened to. The men in the hall were growing raucous. I excused myself, kissing the top of Mabel's head as I passed behind her and murmuring against her hair: 'Do not drink too deeply, Mabel. You should retire soon.' I knew she would take my advice. I felt the King's eyes upon me but did not look in his direction.

In my room, I undressed and stood gazing into the fire in my shift, my fur-trimmed cloak slung loosely around my shoulders, my feet bare on the fur rug. I looked at the door latch. I could tie a ribbon around it to secure it shut. He would accept it if I rebuffed him, although he would try again certainly but it was best to face this, to deal with it. My initial excitement at the court had soon passed and already I longed to be at home in the calm certainty of Pembroke Castle with my husband, Amelina and my boys. There was a tap on the door. I had set a jug of wine and my two glass beakers on the table, ready for him. 'Enter.'

Henry too was dressed for bed, his calves bare beneath the fur-trim of his cloak and the edge of his nightshirt, his feet in glinting, embroidered slippers. He set his candle on the table.

'Sire.'

'Nest!' He opened his arms wide. The sight of the black hair curling on his chest, exposed by his loosely tied nightshirt, brought a flood of memories. I remained where I was. He pulled a face at me. 'You are cross with me.'

'Not anymore.'

'I treated you appallingly, my sweet Nest. And looking at you now, what an idiot I was.'

'No, Sire. You acted as you always do,' I said tartly.

He frowned, taking a step closer, opening his arms to me again.

I stepped around him to the wine jug, pouring a beakerful and holding it out to him. 'Will you take wine with me, Sire, to celebrate the expansion of your realm, and the betrothal of your son and my foster-sister?'

He raised an eyebrow, took the beaker from my outstretched hand.

I poured a small amount of wine for myself and breathed deep and slow, trying to stay calm. I sat on one of the two stools at the table, thinking I was probably safer seated than standing, where I could be embraced. I did not ask his permission to sit before he did. Since he had come into my bedchamber I decided he had allowed me to behave towards him as a man, rather than a king.

Henry sat down on the other stool and contemplated me. I ran the pad of my thumb along the engraved pattern of my beaker, looking at him. We always used to talk politics together, and I fell back now onto old habits, knowing he would find it hard to resist discussing his concerns and strategies with me. 'You have Normandy under your command now, Sire, after such a long struggle.' Henry had recently returned to England as Duke of Normandy, as well as King of the English. Rule of Normandy was a prize he had hankered after for six years: to rule the same domain as his father, William the Conqueror.

'Yes, and it is my endeavour now, Nest, to rule this new combined kingdom as well as I am able: England, Normandy and Wales.'

I tried not to visibly flinch at his inclusion of Wales in the list.

'But you would not believe, Nest, how swiftly my enemies begin to gather against me.'

'How?' I asked. 'They have no one to follow in your stead, with your brother imprisoned. He hasn't escaped?'

'No. Robert is secure in Salisbury. My opponents in Normandy gather around his infant son, William, claiming him to be the *Clito*, the rightful heir to Normandy.'

'But he is a small child?'

'No older than my daughter, around five years old.'

'This is no serious threat to you surely, Sire.'

'Not yet,' he said grimly, 'but de Bellême, de Montfort,' he counted them off on his fingers, splaying the palm of his hand towards me, 'Prince Louis of France, the Angevins, the Count of Flanders, they are all intent that my nephew, William *Clito*, will soon be a threat to me, given time.' He closed his outstretched hand into a fist and then relaxed it again, replacing it on his knee.

'Surely they crave peace now, and your good rule.'

Henry raised his eyebrows at me. 'Come, Nest. I think you know something of de Bellême, having lived in his sister's household here for so long. I think you know that peace cravings are not high among *his* longings.'

I nodded my agreement. 'You did not take the boy captive?'

He stared into his wine, frowning. 'You hit the nail on the head, as usual, Nest. It was foolish of me. I should have brought my nephew back to England, raised him here at the court. It was a mistake to leave him in Normandy.'

'Then why, Sire?' Henry did not often make such mistakes.

He shrugged. 'I was elated to have finally won the duchy. I felt pity for my brother, despite all his failings, and for my small, bewildered nephew. I did not want to appear a monster.' He sighed heavily. 'I don't know, Nest. I'm not sure what my motives really were. At that point, I was not averse to the possibility that I might rule Normandy as the boy's regent, but it didn't take me long to realise that would only bring anarchy to the duchy and make it impossible for me to control both England and Normandy. I left William *Clito* in the charge of Helias de Saint-Saëns as his tutor and guardian. I thought Helias was loyal to me, but it seems he may join de Bellême and de Montfort, use my kindness to my nephew against me.'

'How do you know all this, whilst you are distant from it?'

'My sister, Adela,' he said, looking up from his wine glass. 'She keeps me well informed. She has eyes and ears everywhere.'

Yes, so I could imagine. The redoubtable Countess of Blois, Henry's younger sister, Adela, was devoted to him, to his interests in Normandy. Henry did not underestimate or undervalue women as many men did. He knew and trusted to women's capabilities: his sister Adela, his queen Matilda. He knew women very well, but that did not prevent him from acting without compassion and compunction if he felt he had to.

'You will manage it,' I said. 'You are smarter and stronger than all of those who are against you.'

'I'm grateful for your confidence, my love. I have sorely missed that.'

I pulled myself up from the comfortable familiarity that had begun to seep into my limbs and mind. I sat up straight in the chair, put down my beaker, pulled my cloak tighter across my chest, feeling its dark fur stroke my jaw. Suddenly I regretted that I had challenged myself like this, left my hair uncovered, my feet bare. Perhaps I was no match for him after all.

'How is the Queen, Sire?' I asked. I had been in service to Queen Matilda and fond of her, before I became Henry's mistress.

'She is well but has decided she is done with heir-producing.' He gave me a wry smile, which I ignored. I was surprised to hear him say this. The Queen had suffered badly with both her pregnancies and childbirths, yet one son and one daughter were scant security for the throne of England and the duchy of Normandy. Intrigued to know his view, I was tempted to keep talking with him but knew I must be firm with myself.

'I am glad to see you well, Sire, and wish you success in all your actions. I fear I am tired now after my long journey from Pembroke and my husband.'

He let out a short, exasperated breath. 'It's like this, is it? Cold. Empty small-talk. I have to win you all over again?'

'No,' I said staring at him, feeling my fury rising. 'You do not have to win me all over again.' I enunciated each word. 'I am not available for winning all over again.'

'Nest …' he wheedled.

'Henry, I'm serious.' He made an irritated sound. I refilled my beaker and not his, putting the jug back down with more force than I had intended. I sat back and took a deep swig, my hand shaking on the beaker, my eyes holding his.

Henry lay his head to one side, as if to say: I see, I see this is your attitude. 'Nest. My dear Nest. What is it you want? An apology? I apologise for abandoning you. There was a small matter of a war in Normandy and then three kingdoms to rule.'

'I do not need your apology. Now,' I added quietly. Part of me wanted to berate him, to throw my past hurt and fury at him, but I knew that was a way in for him, and I had no intention of giving him a way in.

'Nest … .'

'Henry, I am happily married to Gerald. I am happy in Wales. Leave me be. If you cared for me, leave me be.'

'I am most reluctant to do that, Nest. You know I cared, care for you.'

'I am asking you to be kind to me, Henry. To behave with love to me. Because you did once love me.'

'Do still,' he said, leaning forwards, his nightgown taut across his parted knees, his eyes liquid, black.

He meant it. I knew that. He loved me. And Sybil Corbet, and his queen, and countless other women. I did not want that love and all the pain that came with it. I smiled thinly. 'Good night, my lord.' I stood, my stool screeching against the stone.

He stared up at me for a while. 'Very well.' He stood. 'You did not bring our son with you to Cardiff?'

'No.'

There was a long silence. 'I am leaving reluctantly, Nest.' He hesitated at the door, his expression mirroring his words.

I said nothing and he closed the door behind him. He would go in search of Sybil now. I subsided onto my stool, poured more wine with a shaking hand, trying to ignore the empty goblet that Henry had left behind.

3

A Conundrum

Sister Benedicta sat in the library of Almenêches Abbey in Normandy, reasoning with herself, trying to decide how serious a sin spying against Robert de Bellême might be. She wanted an end to war, she told herself. She wanted her brother out of harm's way. The day when she had waited for news of Haith from the Tinchebray battlefield, when King Henry of England fought his own brother, the former Duke Robert – that had been the worst day of her life. It was worse, even, than the day when she had first been separated from Haith, when she was six years old, when she had been thrust into and contained in the cloister forever. Was it purely the personal need for her brother's safety, she asked herself, or a more socially spirited yearning to end war that had got her into this bind?

It had been both reasons. She nodded quickly to herself, looking around to see if any of the other nuns were noticing this animated argument going on inside her head, but there were only two elderly sisters in the library this morning, and neither of them were paying her any attention. One had her nose almost touching the page of a book as she strained with old, rheumy eyes, to read. The other had given up such a struggle long ago and slept peacefully, her crucifix awry on her chest, her cheek resting on a curled, pale hand. Benedicta noticed how the thin skin of the sleeping nun's hand slipped and bunched as if that gauntlet was too large now for the shrinking bones beneath, how it was splotched with large brown age spots, and wrinkled with ninety years of prayer.

Benedicta resumed her inner debate. *That* was how she had got herself into this: a combination of personal *and* selfless desires – for Haith's safety and for universal peace. But … was it honest? Clearly not. It was not honest to spy on one's fellow nuns, to listen at doors, to pass on information, to participate in underhand plotting. Yet, King Henry, Haith's lord and longtime friend, was a better man than the man she was seeking to spy on, de Bellême, and besides, it was extreme fun. However, if what she was doing was so righteous, why had she not told Haith about it? He would object on the grounds of *her* safety of course, but perhaps, too, on the grounds of her honesty.

Exasperated with herself, Benedicta threw her hands up in the air, but brought them back together again smoothly in demure prayer when the short-sighted nun suddenly looked up. Reassured, the elderly nun returned to her pages. Benedicta, at thirty-six, was still young; the cropped hair beneath her wimple still pale gold. Yet, she reflected, she would be like these old, dozing nuns before too long: her sap dried up, worn out by days and days of doing nothing. Well, nothing except praying. Other people's business does not concern me, she chanted silently in her head. To say this sentence at least ten times over, every day, was the penance the Father Confessor had given to her,when she had obliquely confessed to the sin of great curiosity. Was that six or seven times she had said it so far today?

Benedicta dipped her quill in the ink again, finishing her latest report to Countess Adela of Blois, King Henry's sister. She had written down what she had been able to glean about the comings and goings of the King's enemy, Robert de Bellême. There was plenty of well-informed gossip about him here at the abbey since his sister was Abbess and his niece was the Prioress.

This spying had begun as an innocent game between Benedicta and Haith. Their mother had given them identical copies of a psalter and, when they were separated – she to a nunnery, he to Henry's service – they had written to each other in cipher using that psalter. Just for fun. Gradually the game had grown more serious. Henry became king and was set about with enemies to guard against. Benedicta, by chance, was well placed at Almenêches, a nest of Montgommerys, the enemies of the King.

Benedicta never had anything of real significance to tell Haith and so she had thought nothing of their game, but since King Henry had taken over the Duchy of Normandy, things had grown more serious again.

The King himself had written to Benedicta in a flourishing hand, on very fine parchment, and accompanied by the impressive royal seal. 'You would do me a great service,' he wrote, 'if you would keep my sister, Countess Adela de Blois, informed on all matters pertaining to Robert de Bellême. Your great learning and intelligence have come to my attention, Sister. I know that your aid will be invaluable to me.' The King told her not to mention this task to Haith, not to worry him, and to destroy the letter. Reluctantly she had done so. She was flattered by the King's attention and trust but assumed any information she had would always be of little import. But, gradually, she found herself embroiled in more and more lies. She did not tell Haith that she was corresponding with the Countess. Worst of all, she was deceiving the Abbess, her great friend.

She knew her motives for spying were complex. There was a pinch of vanity; she was good at it. There was a dollop of vengeance; she wanted to damage de Bellême. A few years ago, he had set the abbey ablaze, destroyed her life's work in the library, almost killed her. Benedicta enjoyed the irony that he had wrongly accused her *then* of spying, and now she was actually enacting his accusation against him. She shook her head at herself. All profoundly irreligious. Still, she could not stop spying. It was an addiction. She would need to confess it again – circumspectly, vaguely, of course – and do further penance for it. 'Thereby my latest report is concluded, honoured Countess.' She ended her letter to Adela de Blois with her own elaborate signature. Her quill was pressed into the tiny bowl of the final full stop when she was startled by the Abbess's voice close behind her.

'Sister Benedicta.'

Swiftly, Benedicta covered her writing with the inky cloth that she used to blot spills and blotches. She rose to greet the Abbess, blocking the older woman's view of the desk.

'Mother Superior, greetings.' She bowed her head.

'Will you come to my chamber, Sister. I have received a letter from a great lady, the Countess Adela de Blois, and I need to consult with you on this matter.'

Benedicta flushed a hot, uncomfortable red. Why on earth would the Countess write to Abbess Emma? Had she decided to expose Benedicta, decided her spying was despicable? She could read nothing in the Abbess's serene face. 'Of course … of course, Mother Superior. I will come right away.' Swiftly, she bundled her guilty letter into her chest, turned the key in the lock, and followed the Abbess from the library.

In her chamber, the Abbess gestured at the comfortable chair next to the crackling fire, opposite her own seat. Despite the spring weather, it was still chilly in the dark interiors of the abbey. Benedicta pushed the abbey cat from a cushion and sat down, disregarding a swirl of cat hairs; there was no need to be particular about her rough black habit. The Abbess's demeanour was friendly, as usual. Surely she would not be like this if Benedicta's hypocrisy had been revealed? They tended to drop formalities when they were in private together. Benedicta was the Abbess's confidante in fact, which was why, sadly, she was such an effective spy. She felt the frown at her hypocrisy might crack her forehead in two if she did not desist from it soon. She had made her bed. She must lie in it.

'Are you too warm, Benedicta? Too close to the fire? You are quite beetroot-hued!' The Abbess laughed kindly.

'No, no! Your fire is a delight after the frigid library!'

'Ah, yes. I am afraid that is true,' the Abbess said ruefully. Her father had established the abbey and now her brother, de Bellême, should be responsible for ensuring the nuns continued well-endowed with funds, but there was no sign that he acknowledged any such responsibility, and so they had to make do. Benedicta and the Abbess had spent years writing begging letters to all and sundry, to raise the funds to rebuild the ancient abbey that de Bellême had so recklessly reduced to ashes during the war between King Henry and his brother Robert, the former Duke.

'The Countess of Blois has written to you?' Benedicta began tentatively, shifting nervously in her chair.

27

'Yes.' The Abbess flourished a rolled parchment with a broken wax seal hanging from its short red ribbon. 'She has an extraordinary request that concerns *you*, I'm afraid, Benedicta.'

'Concerns me?'

'Yes. She requests that I give you leave to travel to her at Chartres. She says she has an important mission she wishes you to undertake concerning a gift of some precious books to that peculiar hermit, Robert d'Arbrissel. She says you will be away from here for quite some time. I don't know what to make of it and I can find no way to refuse, although I have wracked my brain trying to think up an excuse. Here!' She held the letter out to Benedicta. 'Read it for yourself.'

The letter was as the Abbess had summarised, and there was nothing more to be gleaned from reading it through, except that Benedicta was reassured to see that Countess Adela had not revealed that Benedicta had been sending spy reports to her for the past year.

'I wonder why she asks for me,' Benedicta risked, feigning a wondering expression.

'Indeed! That was my first thought. She must have countless minions who could complete such a task. She says she heard about you from her brother, King Henry, because *your* brother, Sir Haith, is at the English court. She says the King has recommended you to her as a woman of the utmost discretion and loyalty. Of course he is not wrong in that, although I hear the voice of your fond brother, Haith, speaking those words!' The Abbess twinkled her amusement at her friend.

Benedicta squirmed in her seat, hating to deceive the Abbess, the word 'loyalty' stinging her ears like the brush of nettles. Perhaps it would be good to be out of Almenêches for a while, to try to outrun her own perjury. Besides, the idea of a journey to see Chartres, The Well of the Strong Saints, and The Virgin's Holy Chemise, to meet with the great Adela de Blois in person – these were strong temptations. Benedicta hoped her confessor would not insist on a hair shirt when she got around to telling him that she was *so* guilty of lying. She luxuriated in the soft, red lambswool vest that Haith had sent her, which she wore concealed beneath her habit.

Benedicta settled at the library desk to decipher a letter from Haith and send him a reply, telling him of her planned excursion to Chartres. He wrote that he had been about the King's business, escorting a Welsh princess along muddy, potted roads to the betrothal of the King's son. 'She is the most beautiful and spirited person you would ever see, Benedicta, even in a rainstorm!' he enthused. Benedicta clicked her tongue in irritation. He had written to her about this married noblewoman before, but she wished he would stop blinking at someone out of his reach and find himself, instead, a nice Flemish girl to wed and make her a nephew or niece.

Her correspondence and her farewells done with, Benedicta took a last fond look around the cloister, stepped through the portal in the great doors and stood blinking on the other side of the walls of Almenêches. It was a few years since she had been outside, and she drank in the light, the smell of new-mown hay in the air, the sounds of birdsong and peasants calling to each other in the fields. The Abbess had arranged for a lay servant to accompany her to Chartres. He was a big lad, just coming into his full strength, arm muscles bulging. He stood holding her palfrey's head, waiting for her to mount. He will do, sure enough, she thought to herself. In any case, there would be little point in anyone trying to rob her on the road. All she carried with her was a brief letter from Abbess Emma to Countess Adela, and the thick travelling cloak and small dagger Haith had given her when he first heard she was 'gallivanting about the bandit-strewn countryside', as he put it. She had been on a few missions outside the abbey before, being the only nun entrusted with such external business, but it had been a while. She smiled to the young man holding her horse, took a deep breath, set her hands on the saddle and her small, booted foot into the stirrup.

4

Cumberworlds

The horses trod gingerly down the steep green bank towards the river crossing. Evening was drawing on and we would cross the Tywi and reach the monastery beyond for nightfall. We could hear the rush of the river but could not see it yet through dense willows crowding the edge. I leant towards Haith, to be heard above the sound of the stream. 'Will you stay …?' I began. Haith grunted and slumped sideways in the saddle towards me. I put out a hand to steady him. Arrows thumped into a tree close by. Haith's horse rolled its eyes in panic, readying to rear. Haith's face was contorted, his hand gripping the arrow shaft projecting from his shoulder. I pushed my horse closer still, grabbing his reins, pressed my knee against his. I kicked my horse on hard towards the water and yanked at Haith's panicking mount. '*Hold on*, Haith!' A blur of men armed with bows emerged from the trees but I did not pause. I knew the crossing here well. I gripped Haith's arm and heard him cry out in pain, but I kept the pressure of my knees on my own palfrey and urged both horses forwards into the water, swiftly up the bank, and into a full gallop across the open land beyond. Haith jostled against me, groaning.

The horses began to tire. I swerved into a thick copse at the side of the road, forcing the horses to stumble against tree roots and having to duck my head at low boughs until we were far from the road. I pulled up and jumped to the ground. Haith half-fell from the saddle into my arms, grimacing and groaning. 'Haith!'

I lowered him to the ground on his side, the arrow protruding front and back.

'Have we lost them?' he asked.

'I think so. They did not expect us to keep going.'

'Welsh … warriors?' he gasped, his face pale and sweating.

'Yes.' I took Haith's knife from the scabbard at his waist and cut his leather tunic and shirt from the wound. I cut off the arrow tip on the part of the shaft protruding from his back, doing my best to minimise the movement of the arrow in his flesh. I sat beside him, lifted my skirts above my knees and ripped two wads of linen from the hem of my shift. I cut a long white strip for a makeshift bandage to bind him together. Amelina would be angry at the state of my underclothes but she would be angrier if Haith, who had always been a favourite with her, did not survive. 'Shall I find something for you to bite on?' I looked around me desperately.

'No. Just do it, Nest.'

I stared for a moment into his eyes, stood, gently positioned one booted foot against his chest to steady us both, laid hold of the long shaft protruding from his shoulder and pulled as hard and straight as I could. Haith groaned and his eyes rolled in his head as he lost consciousness. I sobbed, stared at the broken, bloodied arrowshaft shaking in my hands. I threw it from me, wishing ardently that Amelina were here with me. 'Don't die, Haith, please don't die,' I moaned to his senseless face. Clumsily, around my shaking fingers, I stemmed the blood at the front and back of the wound with the pads made from my ripped shift, tying them in place with the long strip wound around and under his arm. Birds sang blithely, careless of us.

All the while, I was afraid the men would pursue and find us. Did they know who I was, or was this simply a random attack on a couple they presumed to be Norman? I decided we were as safe as we could be, concealed in the undergrowth, until Haith regained consciousness and darkness fell. I would easily hear anyone approaching us through this thicket. I looked at Haith's long sword. Could I wield it? I decided I would not have the strength and tightened my grip on his knife instead.

The sound of the birds died down and light began to fail. Was there some other course of action I should be taking? I stood and unhooked the skin slung from my saddle, taking a gulp of water and then held it dripping against Haith's lips. He opened one eye. 'We're alive then.' He looked terrible. Dark purple smears beneath his eyes were vivid against his pallor.

I smiled. 'I don't know whether to move or stay here.'

'It will get too cold. We can't be far from the monastery. If our attackers had pursued us, we'd know it by now.'

'The monks won't let us in at this time of night.'

'They will if you hammer hard enough and tell them you have an injured man.'

'Can you get into the saddle?'

'I can do what I have to,' he said, grimacing and leaning hard against me as I supported him to the horse. I held the horse steady and he pulled himself up with his one good arm. I mounted and leant to take the reins of his horse again. 'I can manage with one arm and my knees,' he said. Briefly, he placed his good hand on my arm. 'Thank you, Nest.'

I shook my head. 'It was just an arrow that needed pulling out.' I could hear the wobble of near-hysteria in my own voice.

We exchanged a long glance and then kicked our horses on to a slow pace.

The monks improved on the patch job I had done on Haith's wound and we were back on the road towards Pembroke in a few days. I had sent one of the older novices to Gerald to explain our delay.

We were a few hours out of Pembroke, when I saw Gerald approaching at the head of a unit of soldiers. As we neared I could see that my husband's face was etched with anxiety. His worry turned quickly to anger as we came to close quarters. 'My wife should never have been on the road without me, with just an escort of one man!' he shouted at Haith, whose face expressed his great remorse and distress.

'Gerald! You are shouting in the wrong place. Haith took the arrow and saved my life and there is no fault to be found here.'

He looked at us both chagrined, reached his gauntletted hand to mine and brought my hand to his lips. 'Yes. I apologise, Haith. Thank God, you were not harmed, Nest. Do you know who they were? The men of Owain ap Cadwgan, I'll wager.'

'I don't know. We did not linger for introductions. There was no indication who they were. Bandits perhaps.'

'They knew who *you* were,' he said. 'Come, let's get Haith to Amelina's ministrations, and you too Nest. Though you are unharmed, it must have been a frightening experience.'

It was wash day, and I knew Amelina would be down at the river with the other maids. Haith had healed and returned to court. I had discovered that I was carrying another child and Amelina was certain it would be a girl this time. I took little Henry's hand and told him we were going to see the cave and find Amelina. He had lately started to walk, or more accurately to run, since that was his principal speed. His balance was precarious and his progress reckless. Remembering our last expedition when he had tumbled on some steps and worn a green bruise on his cheek for days, and another occasion when I was obliged to pick up my skirts and pursue him across the courtyard and into the stables, with all the maids and soldiers laughing at us, I picked up a long, thin strip of woven cloth and wrapped it around my wrist.

'He is fast,' Amelina had declared, 'like a darting kingfisher!' Yes, fast and brilliant, I thought, trying not to remember his father.

I led him carefully down the steps into the curious vast cave beneath the castle, which was named The Wogan by the local people. Little Henry would not let me carry him anymore, so patience was required to allow him to clamber up and down obstacles on his short, unsteady legs. As soon as he reached the bottom of the steps, he was running full tilt, undeterred by the gloom. 'Be careful! The ground is uneven!' I let him explore, and told him that ancient people had once lived in this cave, long before the castle was built above it.

'Cold!' he said.

'Yes! Come.' I held out my hand. 'Let's look for Amelina now.'

We stood for a moment watching the women bending to their tasks at the river's edge. White sheets, shifts and nightgowns were draped across the rocks, being scrubbed, rinsed and wrung.

'Lina!' Henry shouted, and she looked up at us smiling, suds on her arms, sweat on her face and the tops of her breasts. Henry pulled me towards her.

'Don't tread on the clean linens,' I told him, 'or you will make more work for Amelina and she will be cross.' The other women called out affectionately to him, threatening to tickle him and blowing soapsuds from their hands to land on his nose. So close to the river's edge, I took my woven strip, tying one end under his arm and the other to my wrist. He frowned and pouted at me as I did it. If he fell in the water I might not get to him in time, before the fast current took him, swept him around the foot of the castle like flotsam, and carried him out to the grey swell of the cold sea.

'Are you planning to fish with Henry as bait?' Amelina laughed. 'It's a good idea to tether that boy, that kingfisher!' She kissed his cheek. We watched him poking his pudgy fingertip into a bar of softened soap. 'Taking a break!' Amelina called to the other women. She sat down on a flat rock next to me. Henry had found a gull on the beach to clap his hands at.

'I wanted to talk to you about Gerald,' I said.

'How was it with the King in Cardiff?' Amelina cut straight to the heart of the matter. She had taken care of me when the King had abandoned me, when I had to pass through my great distress and come to accept my life as Gerald's wife.

'It's done with. I told him to leave me in peace with my husband and he agreed to it.'

'Good. Gerald loves you dearly, Nest. It was wrong of him to allow the King to take you as his mistress, but he knows he was in error and suffers for it in all ways.'

'And yet, he did it. And gained position and land from it. We won't see eye to eye on this, Amelina. On Gerald, you are ever his champion.'

'People should be forgiven sometimes is all.'

I compressed my lips. I was not inclined to forgiveness in the main. I had found that if you forgave, invariably the offender would take the opportunity to give you yet more cause for offence.

'Things are good, aren't they?' Amelina asked. 'Between you and Gerald I mean.'

I nodded. 'Good. Just good.'

'You underestimate him,' she said. 'He has hidden depths.'

'I am well aware of his hidden depths.'

'No. No, you are not. I'm not talking about the Henry incident.'

'By that, you mean Gerald's great deception on our wedding day, I suppose. The fact that Gerald sold me over to the King for his advancement?'

'For his self-preservation,' she said, 'and I didn't notice you mourning it for long.'

'You forget yourself,' I told her, furiously.

We were both silent for a while, regarding each other, shocked at the violence of this unwonted disagreement between us.

'What other hidden depths do you mean?' I said, eventually.

'*Do* forgive him about Henry,' Amelina whispered gently, hoping not to rouse my anger again.

I shrugged. 'Well?'

'Gerald is no fool.'

'I know that.'

'He could have gone down with the Montgommerys, been attainted with his lord, Arnulf de Montgommery, and banished from the kingdom, but he survived it.'

'I know.'

That evening, I lay on my bed naked, my belly visibly swelling with the child. Gerald stood with his back to me, fully dressed, staring out of the window of my chamber at the full moon. 'Gerald, nothing happened between me and the King,' I said for the third time since my return to Pembroke. My husband had not lain with me since my return, but at least this time he had come all the way into my room.

'I wish I could believe that.' His voice was tight.

What cumberworlds these men were. I levered myself up and strode to him. I pressed myself against his back, embracing him, kissing the back of his neck where his fair hair curled. 'Do not insult me. I'm telling you the truth. The child is yours – you can see that. Yes, Henry would have taken me to his bed if I had allowed it, but I did not. I told him I was happy with you, here at Pembroke.' I pulled him around to face me and he came unresisting, but his eyes were closed.

35

'You've never been mine. You were always his.'

'Don't throw such falseness at me! You know *you* gave me to the King. If you can't trust me, if you can't believe me, then we should separate. I will go and live at Carew.'

I walked away from him but before I could reach the bed, his arms were around me. 'Nest! I *cannot* live without you.'

And so we were reconciled yet again. I was so happy, as I had told the King. And it was not enough.

The sun streamed into my chamber and I took the 'O sea-bird' scroll from my jewellery box to read it through, wondering again who had sent it. Sometimes, I confessed to myself, I hankered for another life. Instead of returning the poem to the jewellery box, I opened the lid of the large, carved chest where I kept all my parchment rolls. The chest was filling now with poems by Welsh bards, which I had commissioned. The world conjured by words was sometimes a nicer place to dwell in than the world conjured by the ploughs and swords around me. Carefully placing the sea-bird scroll where it could not be crushed, my fingers touched the soft, crimson leather of my journal. I had not looked at it or written in it since the day that I knew Henry had abandoned me. I lifted it out and smoothed my palm slowly down its cover. The cover was decorated with a rectangular frame, with interlacing patterns at the top and the bottom in bright yellow and blue-grey. In the middle, there was a drawing of a chalice with stems projecting, covered in leaves and fruits. I turned the small book over in my hands. Inside, its pages were made from smooth, creamy parchment and not the scratchy, hairy strips I sometimes had to resort to writing on for my daily lists and notes. I knew I could not bear to read what I had written at the height of my affair with Henry. I slapped my hand onto the last piece of writing so that it was concealed from my eyes. Giving me the journal, Henry had laughed at me, calling me 'his inky clerk'. I tried not to remember that day, how I had felt about him. I began to write, instead, on how I felt about Gerald.

I first met Gerald as one of the attackers led by Arnulf de Montgommery, who had fired my father's stronghold at Llansteffan. Gerald had escorted me, a captive, to Cardiff Castle and was kind to me in that terrible time. The curse I made against Bernard de Neufmarché, who murdered my father and older brothers, I had also placed upon the Montgommery men, one of whom I was certain must have been responsible for the awful death of my favourite brother, Goronwy, on the beach at Llansteffan. Gerald, kind Gerald, was the only Norman I had excepted from the curse.

For years, I could not bring myself to go to Llansteffan, although my mother had left it to me as my own land to command. My curse succeeded in bringing down the Montgommery men who had stolen my father's lands: Hugh, Earl of Shrewsbury, was killed by the Norsemen at Anglesey; Philip de Montgommery was imprisoned for treason and then died in the Holy Lands; Robert de Bellême had lost the earldom and been exiled; Roger de Montgommery was similarly disseised and exiled to France; and Arnulf de Montgommery, who had intended to marry me, was now a penniless lord in France. Yet, I was still not sure who, amongst Arnulf's men, had killed Goronwy and stolen light forever from my life by that act.

Amelina nagged me to recover from my aversion to Llansteffan. She told me it would heal my grief for Goronwy if I restored the broken castle. 'Don't you think so, my lord?' she asked Gerald, seeking his support for her encouragements, but Gerald remained stiffly neutral, refusing to enter into the discussion, leaving the room whenever my conversation with Amelina approached Llansteffan. He was still conscious, I supposed, of the ground between us that could turn swiftly treacherous. There was his jealousy at my affair with the King, which he had himself connived at in his ambition. There was the potential for antagonism between us at the Welsh dispossessions and the Norman aggressions. There were gulfs in our relationship where neither of us could stray. It was like loving a rose, trying to reach to the delightful scent, trying to embrace around the piercing thorns.

When I went down to break fast, Amelina was in the hall spooning medicine to a compliant giant of a soldier from the garrison as if he were my three year old. 'What are you giving him, Amelina?'

They both turned to me. The man's face was drawn with lines of pain, but he tried to smile nevertheless.

'It's poppy juice. For the toothache.'

'From your wise woman?'

'Yes. It takes away the worst of the pain, but he needs a tooth-drawer. This will only give temporary relief,' she told him. He stood, towering above her, clasped her hand with heartfelt thanks, bowed respectfully to me and left us.

'I've got water boiling to wash your hair after you've eaten,' she said, pushing the stopper of her medicine bottle down with force.

We returned together to my chamber and I closed my eyes, listening to the sound of Amelina pouring water from a jug into a basin. 'It's ready,' she said. I stepped out of my overgown and moved in my white undershift to the table where Amelina stood with the basin of water. A pungent steam rose from it, scented with cinnamon and liquorice. 'This will make that black hair of yours shimmer, I should think!' she said.

I stood close to the table, its hard edge against my rounding stomach and bent my neck, bringing my head with its heavy mass of hair as close to the surface of the water as I could. Amelina poured the warm water in rhythmical cascades over my head, pushing it down the length of my hair to the ends where they dangled in the basin. 'Are you done?' I asked, blinded by water, hair and steam. There was no reply. I fumbled for the drying cloth that I had seen on the table beside the bowl, but could not find it. I heard Amelina giggle. 'Amelina!' I said, irritated. 'My shift is getting wet. Stop playing games.'

'Such a crosspatch,' came Gerald's voice behind me. His arms slid around my waist and his body was close and warm against my back. 'You can leave us, Amelina.' I heard her giggle again and close the door behind her.

'Gerald, I'm wet and blinded.'

'Patience. I am not an expert at this maid's work.' He lifted the hank of my hair from the basin, wringing out the excess water, and wrapped the cloth around my head. 'You smell delicious.'

I raised my head with my eyes still closed. I had seen a girl with red-eye in the kitchen last week and I did not want to risk getting the spices in my eyes. Gerald turned me towards him and wiped my face with a soft cloth. 'There,' he said, delicately kissing one of my eyelids.

I opened one eye and smiled at him. 'Perhaps you would like to wash my clothes next, or sweep the hallway?'

'That is not what I would like to do next,' he said, touching the laces of my shift.

Gerald had sent out scouts to try to discover who the men were who had attacked Haith and I on the road from Cardiff. He was convinced that Owain ap Cadwgan had been responsible. He increased the patrols but the Welsh rebels could simply melt into the trees, slip out with the tides, ride up into the mountains. They knew their land and Gerald could get no grasp on them. Meanwhile, in the kitchen, Amelina and I listened to a travelling Welsh bard singing about the romantic Prince Owain of Powys and his brave quest to take the land back from the invaders.

Amelina had been wrong about the child I carried that year. I birthed another boy and Gerald named him Maurice, another Norman name. On hot summer nights, as I fed my new son, little Henry and William would sit with Amelina in my chamber, begging her for stories. 'Two little boys! Two little boys!' cried William. This was Amelina's story which always began, 'Once upon a time there were two little boys …' and then continued differently each time, as she would spin and weave the stories for them with her voice and hands and the theatre of her eyes and expressions. Tonight she began, 'Once upon a time there were two little boys and they knew a maiden named Mererid who tended the well of the great kingdom of Cantre'r Gwaelod.'

'The Drowned Court!' pronounced Henry, with satisfaction. He was an avid veteran of this particular story. William bit his lip in anticipation and I smiled to Maurice who stared up into my eyes.

'Mererid was in love with Seithininn who was responsible for closing the sluices of the city when it was threatened with flood waters.'

'What's sluices?' asked William.

'Kind of gates, to keep water out,' Henry told him. 'Stop interrupting.'

Amelina compressed a smile. 'Mererid and Seithininn loved one another so and one night they neglected their duties. Mererid took no notice of the water overflowing from the well and kissed and kissed her lover instead.'

Henry mimicked Mererid's kissing comically for us and William laughed loudly at Henry and at Amelina tickling him. 'Sshh! The baby's eyes are drooping,' I told them.

Amelina continued in a whisper. 'Seithininn thrilled to Mererid's embrace and turned his back on the incoming tide and the sluice gates that he should have minded. And the sea rolled in over the city, rushed down the streets, met the waters overflowing from the well.'

Henry swooped around the room, waving his arms, wobbling his head, pretending to be caught up in flood waters. William copied him. 'Did the two little boys save the city?' William asked, breathless.

'Alas, no. Nothing could save the doomed city and its drowned court. The waters grew higher and higher and the clothes and the tables and benches were washed out from the houses and tumbled in the waters in the streets, and the people fled to higher and higher ground and the water came on and on and did not retreat. The water washed over everything and everyone and drowned them all, though they held their heads above the water for as long as their strength held out. The king and all his court were drowned, and the lovers, Mererid and Seithininn, were drowned, and they all lie now beneath the waves of Carmarthen Bay.'

'Cheerful!' I remarked.

'No sense in lying in a story that's true,' Amelina said, grinning mischievously at the boys. 'But the two little boys swam away into another story. And now it is time for bed!'

Amelina prevailed on me with her urgings regarding Llansteffan and I began its restoration. Between us, Gerald and I were keeping our mason very busy. The plans for Carew, Llansteffan and Cenarth Bychan castles were spread out on the hall table as the mason talked us through them. Work on Carew was near enough finished. Cenarth Bychan would be finished before the end of this year. Llansteffan would be a while longer.

'They are all well fortified,' Gerald said with satisfaction. 'Owain won't be making any assaults here.'

'Owain is far away, busy with Powys and not at all interested in us,' I laughed at him. 'You worry too much about Owain.'

Gerald shook his head. 'He and his father are our greatest threats. With one face they treat with me and the other Norman lords as their allies and with another face they stoke Welsh rebellion.'

He was right, of course, but my own position was ambivalent at best on that. 'Despite the fortifications, these new castles will be comfortable, fit for habitation and not just for soldiers.'

He nodded.

'Yes, this is excellent,' Gerald told the mason. 'You can move your household to Carew now, Nest. It will be more comfortable for you and the children than remaining here at Pembroke.'

My youngest son, Maurice, was nearly a year old and would soon join the *conroi* of small boys rushing around the castles, headed by little Henry. I nodded reluctantly at Gerald's suggestion. Pembroke was a military garrison with few comforts, whereas Carew had been designed to be lived in. Henry, William and Maurice could play and learn there. Gerald was right, I *should* go to Carew, but I would miss the daily contact with him.

'I will come to you all often, don't worry!' he laughed. 'At least every week, as the duties here allow.'

'*Thrice* a week,' I bargained. Carew was a short ride from Pembroke.

'Done,' he said, moving towards me, and the mason coughed to remind us he was still there, rolling up his plans. Nevertheless, I pulled Gerald into an embrace, thinking how Carew would allow me more freedom to correspond with my Welsh contacts. Without the supervision of my husband, it would be easier to learn more about how the Welsh rebels fared in their contentions against the Normans, to find out if there was any news of my brother, Gruffudd ap Rhys, the rightful lord of this kingdom.

5

The Game of the Countess

Benedicta's journey from Almenêches to Chartres took her through the undulating hills of Normandy, past gnarly vineyards and blossoming white apple orchards, past shimmering pale green fields where young crops bent to the breeze. The servant from Almenêches left her at the gates of Chartres Palace with his good wishes. She watched his figure grow smaller and smaller on the road, her last connecting thread back to home. When she could no longer discern him, she turned to look with awe at the marvellous palace she had been summoned to.

She gave her name and business to the porter, and eyed the heavily armed soldiers. The porter ordered her to wait in the guard house. It was a long wait and Benedicta was famished. Her wimple and veil were hot and itchy about her face and neck. She fidgeted with them, trying to let a little air into her overheated skin. At last, the porter returned and conveyed her to a side door where a clerk met her. He, in turn, led her along an immensely long passageway and told her to wait again on a bench outside a pair of enormous ornately carved doors. Others waited with her, crowding the benches so that Benedicta could only keep one buttock firmly on the edge of the hard wood. There was a squeak, a creak, and a slender man opened the vast doors a crack, looked around the waiting room, and beckoned to Benedicta. 'Come, Sister.'

She stood, swallowing nervously, and slid through the slight opening between the high doors, and into the vast space of a lavishly decorated hall where more people crowded, waiting for audience with the Countess. At the far end of the hall two soldiers guarded another huge door. Benedicta supposed it must be the portal to Adela's inner chamber. The usher showed her to a bench near the guards. He bent to speak in a low voice, close to her ear, 'Adela, Countess of Blois, Chartres and Meaux, will see you soon. Remember that the Countess is a king's daughter, a king's sister.'

The 'soon' the man spoke of, turned out to be two hours more, giving Benedicta ample time to look at the decorations in the hall and the people milling around her. It also, unfortunately, gave time for her stomach to start rumbling audibly on its diet of nothing, and for her to grow more and more nervous, feeling a fraud sitting here. What could she possibly have to offer to so powerful a lady? Benedicta ardently wished that she was back at Almenêches, sitting comfortably with the cat purring and a glass of the abbey's wine in her hand.

She and Abbess Emma had been mildly scandalised by the erotic innuendo of a letter-poem Archbishop Baudri had written to Countess Adela. He asked her to give him a jewelled, fringed cope, saying that he was a naked poet without it. Benedicta had laughed at the image the poet conjured of himself composing in the nude. She had met Baudri once, in company with her friend Orderic, when she was staying at the monastery at Ouches. Although Baudri was aging, the features of his humorous, intelligent face retained the beauty of a young man. Benedicta had observed that this retention of youth in monks and nuns was quite a frequent occurrence, and no doubt the result of living a life of inaction, of uneventfulness. Baudri had written that Countess Adela was a queen to him, that he had seen her but been unable to look at her because her brilliance was like that of a goddess, and that his song would spread her fame from Cyprus to Thule, giving her life beyond the stars. Benedicta had been unable to suppress the desire that a man might write such words to her.

She could not stop herself from repeatedly glancing at the great door and its burly guards. To quell her anxiety, she recounted Baudri's letter-poem in her head. He had written that the walls of the Countess's inner chamber were covered in marvellous tapestries that seemed alive, showing the Flood with fish on mountain tops and lions in the sea. Baudri wrote of the decorations of the Countess's bed as if he had rolled in it himself. In Almenêches, Benedicta had longed to be in the marvellous palace of Chartres, but now that she was here she wished herself back in Almenêches.

'Sister Benedicta d'Almenêches!'

She looked up startled and saw the usher standing at the door, gesturing to her. The guards moved their spears. She stepped into the chamber and the doors clanged shut behind her. There was some distance to walk towards the noblewoman seated in state on a throne at the far end of the chamber. Benedicta took care not to trip on the muddied hem of her habit, marvelling at the floor mosaics that showed a map of the world with seas, rivers, mountains and myriad bizarre creatures. Reaching the edge of a long, polished table that was set before the Countess, Benedicta bowed her head.

'Sister Benedicta from Almenêches?' The voice was clear and rang in the chamber. A woman's voice accustomed to command.

Benedicta looked up at the red-haired woman. Countess Adela was in her early forties and had been seven years a widow. Her face was strong and comely. She had been married at seventeen to Count Etienne de Blois who had been twice her age, but she had, nevertheless, shared government with him from the beginning of their married life. She ruled for many years as regent for her young son, Thibaut, after her husband died in the Holy Lands. She dealt adroitly and firmly with the aggression of her Angevin and Capetian neighbours who had inevitably perceived a child heir as an opportunity, but one that *she* had not allowed.

Baudri had described Adela as capable of bearing arms as bravely as her father, William the Conqueror, if custom had not inhibited that. The strength of this slight woman was not in her physique but in her mind. She was renowned for having created a literary court around her, hiring singers and poets to praise her, to vaunt her rule far and wide.

'Yes, Countess. I am Benedicta.' The woman's black eyes were trained upon her and Benedicta hoped that the Countess could not see her muddy hem and shoes over the edge of the great oak table.

'Thank you for making the journey here. Bring food and wine,' she told a servant.

Benedicta was relieved at the last command, but then anxious that her table manners might not be adequate. Never mind, she was close to fainting with hunger. She hoped the servant would flit fast to the pantry and back. Benedicta sat on the stool indicated by the Countess.

'I have enjoyed your reports from Almenêches. You have a lively style of writing, Sister.'

'Thank you. I hope the paltry messages I have been able to send might be of some use.'

'Indeed they have. All information is of use in some way or another, Sister. Remember, it is not only the specifics of plots against my brother, King Henry, that are of value to us. We are also interested in the hopes and desires, the everyday activities of those who are his enemies. Something seemingly small and insignificant may give my brother the edge that he needs to keep the duchy safe from war.'

Benedicta glanced at the sumptuous bed beyond the Countess's throne. Baudri had written that the bed boasted a tapestry showing the conquest of England by Adela's father, Duke William; the comet predicting the conquest; the Norman fleet; the battle of Hastings; and the death of the English king, Harold. Benedicta did not see such a tapestry, but Adela's chamber was still the most splendid place that she had ever set eyes upon.

'You find me alone,' Adela said. 'When we dine in a few hours' time, my family and many others will be about us, so we will take advantage of our privacy now.' The servant placed two goblets of wine before them and a trencher with fresh bread and cheese. 'Please,' Adela gestured to the food. 'I know you must need refreshment before the usual dining hour.' She pushed an ornate silver handbasin across the table, and Benedicta dipped her fingers in the water, dried them on the linen, and ate as slowly and as quietly as she could manage. 'You must be curious about why I have sent for you, Sister Benedicta. I have need of an intelligent person to perform a task for me. My brother,

King Henry, assures me you have a wit as sharp as the crack of a whip.'

A smile flashed across Benedicta's face at such a description, which she swiftly suppressed, trying to keep her expression humble.

'I want you to convey a donation of precious books I intend to make to Robert d'Arbrissel's new abbey at Fontevraud.' The Countess paused for Benedicta to respond.

'I am happy to serve you, my lady, and honoured that you feel I can be of use in this matter.'

'I want you to spend time at Fontevraud, Sister, to find an excuse to stay there for a while.'

Benedicta nodded.

'You are probably aware that the abbey is favoured by the Angevin family and is a nest of repudiated and widowed noble-women of the families that are of most concern to us. I believe there will be a great deal more to interest us than what you have been able to glean at Almenêches.'

'I imagine so.'

'You may, of course, refuse this mission, Sister. I appreciate it is a lot to ask of you.'

'I am pleased to serve you and King Henry in any way I can,' Benedicta said, ignoring her misgivings. She could not see how she could refuse so great a lady.

'As you know, the religious community of Fontevraud is … controversial. I should not wish to send you unknowing into spiritual danger.'

I am already in spiritual danger, Benedicta thought, under-taking such spying. 'I heard that Robert d'Arbrissel has been suspected of,' Benedicta suppressed the urge to say heresy, 'unconventional views.'

'I can assure you, Sister, that he is a holy man. In particular, he is a champion of we weak women,' the Countess said force-fully. 'A most eloquent preacher. He was one of those forest her-mits, in company with Bernard of Tiron and Vitalis of Savigny. His preaching is a thunderclap that lights up a cathedral with its eloquence. He is an outstanding herald of Christ and an extraor-dinary word-scatterer. Yet, yes, there are some concerns about his theological position. I fear, Sister Benedicta, you may need to guard the whiteness of your soul fiercely when you are there.'

Whiteness of her soul? Was it not already blackened with duplicity? Oh, so much penance she would have to do.

'D'Arbrissel is known to practise and encourage *syneisaktism*,' Adela said, her expression eloquently steeped in abhorrence. 'I cannot send you into such danger without due warning.' Her voice lowered to a whisper and she leant closer across the table. 'He believes in the mortification of the flesh by sleeping amongst women.'

'I see.' Benedicta frowned and shrugged. 'Have no fear, Countess. I will not slip in that way.'

The Countess shook her head slowly. 'Do not be so certain of yourself, Sister. Always guard against your own lust and the lust of others.'

Benedicta snorted inadvertently and coughed quickly to try to cover the unseemly noise that had escaped her. The passions the Countess spoke of had never been roused in her, never plagued her. She knew from her readings that others, particularly religious men, often struggled with that sin, but she could not imagine it would present her with any real problem.

'You will remain at Fontevraud for some time,' the Countess instructed her. 'Later today, at the feast, you will see a storyteller who will act as go-between for you and me. His name is Breri. In a few weeks, you will set out to Fontevraud. I will send two men-at-arms to guard you and the valuable books I am sending.'

'I am honoured by your trust in me, Countess, and will do all in my power to perform this task well.'

'Good. Then my servants will convey you to a chamber where you might take some ease before the meal and change into a clean habit and footwear.'

Benedicta swallowed. So, the Countess *could* see over the table. Benedicta had no such clean clothes with her. At Almenêches the sisters were only issued with one set of clothes and these were then renewed every five years. Perhaps a servant could furnish water and cloths and something could be done to freshen her attire before the feast.

Benedicta was seated at one of the lower trestles but close, never-theless, to the high table, where Countess Adela conversed with her family and other noble guests. The hall was rammed with diners and rushing servants.

Another nun, seated next to Benedicta, introduced herself as Sister Lucie and explained who the people were at the high table. On either side of the Countess were her sons: Thibaut, the new Count of Blois, around nineteen years old, and Etienne, Count of Mortain, who was sixteen. Etienne was a big, freckled lad with a very loud voice; Thibaut was more slender and had an intelli-gent face, long hands and a merry laugh. Ranged on either side of these two young men were many young girls.

'Who are all those young ladies?' Benedicta asked her neighbour.

'Countess Adela's daughters are seated to the right of Count Thibaut – his sisters Matilda, Adelaide, Eleanore and Alix, and the Countess's nieces are seated to the left of Count Etienne.'

Benedicta frowned. 'Her nieces?' Benedicta knew that Adela's brother, King Henry of England, had one daughter named Maud, but knew of no others.

Her neighbour saw her confusion. She lowered her voice and brought her mouth close to Benedicta's ears. 'They are King Henry's daughters. The daughters of his mistresses.'

'Ah!' Benedicta counted five young ladies.

'The Countess is educating them all here and negotiating mar-riages for them.'

'Goodness! Nine marriages to negotiate, including her own daughters!' Benedicta reflected that, between them, King Henry and Countess Adela had accumulated a significant store of young women who could be used to confirm alliances.

'Yes,' Sister Lucie laughed, 'and those betrothals are a mere pin-prick in the business that Lady Adela concerns herself with.'

'And what do you do here, at the Countess's court, Sister Lucie?'

'I study poetry with the Countess. And games.'

'Games?'

'Yes. There is a small group of us, all nuns with the excep-tion of Lady Adela. We compose poems and songs, oftentimes in response to conundrums set for us by Baudri de Bourgueil. We weave words, literary morsels. Perhaps you will join our play for the short time of your stay? The Countess says that the one who is loved is conceived as a text and so we exercise the invocatory power of language.' Sister Lucie smiled.

Thinking of the handsome Archbishop Baudri and his suggestive poetry, Benedicta asked: 'Poems in Latin?'

'Yes, in Latin, but also in Langue d'Oil or Occitan.' Sister Lucie waved her fork gaily. 'Sometimes we play at satire, making our words salty!'

'I would be delighted to join your textual community,' Benedicta said, momentarily pleased at her own sophisticated remark, but then immediately anxious that her wit and knowledge might not be adequate for the game. How marvellous, she thought to herself, if she could in some small way swim in these swift currents, keep up with the effervescent passions of these intellectuals whose words she had read so avidly in the cloister.

A brown-bearded, rotund man sat down on the bench opposite them. A harp was slung across his back. 'Excuse me, Sister Benedicta, I wonder if I might speak a little privately with you for a moment, on an errand from the Countess.' His accent was strange. This must be the *ioculator* the Countess had told her about. Sister Lucie looked at Benedicta curiously but excused herself to speak with others in the hall now that the meal was concluded and people were beginning to move around.

'I will sing soon,' the man told Benedicta, 'so I must be brief. I am Breri. I believe the Countess has spoken of me.'

'Yes. I am pleased to meet you, Breri, and look forward to your performance.'

He looked up to a passing serving girl. 'Bring me a vase of wine, girl, and be quick about it.' He turned back to Benedicta. His cheeks were high-coloured and well-padded. He received his glass into a large hand and rolled the wine around the glass, taking his ease with an indolent and louche air. 'For now, our business is short, Sister. You travel soon to Fontevraud, and I will be a few weeks behind you on the road. I will stay in a nearby inn and contrive to fetch any report you have. It is safest if we deal with our tongues and not our styluses.'

49

Benedicta spluttered on her wine and looked again at Breri's face. Clearly his innuendo had been intended and he was pleased with its result. His eyes twinkled gaily at her.

'A little jest, Sister. Forgive me. It is my trade. All you need to know is this: the inn is on the road between Candes and Fontevraud and has the sign of a bear. You might leave a brief message there for me and I will meet you at the abbey under cover of dark to receive your report. Will that be satisfactory?'

'I am a novice at this creeping around,' Benedicta said. 'I suppose you are not, and so I am happy to take my steer from you.'

'Excellent. But do not use our actual names in any notes, Sister. I will term you ... .' He looked up at the ceiling and then back to her face, thinking. 'I will term you Ladybird. And you might call me Hawk.'

Benedicta frowned. 'I see. But I will ask for you by name at the inn, no?'

'Indeed, but it is with the written word we must take the greatest of care. Words in the air might be denied, or lost with the thrust of a dagger.'

Benedicta swallowed hard on the crust of bread she had been chewing and felt it rasp the tender interior of her throat. 'Thrust of a dagger?'

'No need to worry yourself,' Breri winked at her, 'Ladybird. Enough of business, now to play.' He stood and sauntered to the space before the high table and began to tune his harp. The noise of conversation slowly died down around him and an expectant silence grew in its stead.

Sister Lucie resumed her seat next to Benedicta. 'He is very good.'

Breri was a strange man from a strange country – Pays de Galles. Benedicta had never heard the like of his songs. He sang of the court of a strong king of the Britons and of his knights and, most particularly, one named Gawain. All eyes were upon Breri, and even the circumspect Countess leant forward, listening avidly. Benedicta marvelled at how far a story could travel, how far a thing could be told, and everyone in the human family could understand and feel with it, no matter what their origins were. When Breri's song concluded, the applause and shouted compliments were loud. Breri took his bows graciously and briefly before moving from the hall with a pronounced rolling gait and no glance at Benedicta.

On Sunday evening, Benedicta luxuriated in a tub in front of the fire in the small chamber allotted to her. Such physical self-indulgence, such privacy, was a rarity in her life and she relished it. The water was beginning to cool and she pushed herself upright, watching the water rush from her body. There was a long, burnished sheet of pale metal in the room, affixed to the wall, for looking at yourself. The Countess had many such new-fangled things about the palace: these mirrors, an abacus, clocks. Standing ankle-deep in the cooling water, knee-deep in the tub, Benedicta saw herself for the first time. She saw her pale hair, her smooth white skin. Her breasts were small and pink-tipped, her stomach flat, her arms and legs thin but muscled. Her hip bones jutted, angular. Her body was boy-like, she considered, unlike the rounded, fleshy bodies of women she had seen nurturing children. A tear trickled down her cheek and she wiped at it, telling herself it was probably water that had dribbled from her hair. If she had not been given to the abbey as a child, she could instead have been a wife, a mother. She stepped from the tub, rubbed the remaining water vigorously from her limbs and slid her shift and then her habit back over her head. It felt like stepping back into her life from some magical place she had momentarily slipped away to. It felt like putting her pelt back on.

She sat down to write to Haith who was currently at King Henry's court in England. She told him she was in Chartres on abbey business (which was almost true) and would be travelling on to the new abbey at Fontevraud. She told him she had been to hear the great theologian and reformer, Bishop Ivo, preach that morning. She wrote not a word of the Countess and her real reason for going to Chartres or Fontevraud, and felt a pang that now she must lie even to Haith. I must not worry him, she told herself, immediately finding herself out in yet another lie.

6

The Water Wolf

In my chamber at Carew, William stood with his head cocked to one side as Amelina dripped a pale yellow liquid into his ear from a screwed cloth, just as she dribbled sauces on a tart in the kitchen. I watched the slender viscous skein twisting around itself. William looked up at me without moving his head, comical in his sideways position. 'What's going on?' I asked.

'He has an earache. The wise woman prepared this camomile oil to ease it. We have to put two drops in each morning and two before bedtime. Stay still! Or it will go all over your tunic or the floor where it's no good for the earache.'

I crouched beside him and took his hand. 'I'm sorry to hear you have the earache, William. Amelina will make you feel much better soon, I'm sure.'

He grinned.

'Good, you can stand up straight now,' Amelina told him, and he careered out of the room in search of Henry and Maurice. Amelina and I raised our eyebrows at each other at the sound of a horse and shouts of welcome in the courtyard below. Amelina stood on tiptoe, peering from the window. 'A messenger wearing the King's livery,' she called back to me.

'What now?' I sighed. 'Things were just starting to settle.'

In the hall, I read the King's missive. 'Thank you.' I rolled it, handed it back to the messenger. 'Please take it to my husband at Pembroke but wait a moment while I write a note to add to it.'

'What is it?' Amelina asked.

'The King kindly informs me of his intention to arrive at Pembroke in one week's time,' I said, tensing my jaw. Henry wrote to me, at Carew, to announce his visit. Gerald would be offended at that. I wrote a short note, telling my husband I would follow the messenger the next day to put all in order at Pembroke for the King's visit.

'Pack up my things, Amelina,' I said. 'And your own,' I added, when I saw that the messenger was out of earshot. 'You are going on a journey with the boys.'

'To Pembroke?'

'No. You are going to take them to the seashore to learn how to fish.'

She gaped at me.

'I can't have my boy Henry here when the King arrives. He must be concealed.'

'But … yes, I can see that. But shouldn't William and Maurice stay? Won't Gerald be angry?'

'Probably. But it might enter the King's head to take one of Gerald's sons as hostage, if he cannot find his own. I'm not taking any risks. You know where to go?'

'Yes.' She had been to the old boathouse with me before. It was concealed in the cliff beneath Llansteffan castle and was only known to us. I had played there often in my childhood with my brother, Goronwy. Summer was advancing and it would be warm enough for them to camp there. My sons would be safe with Amelina for the duration of the King's visit. I would send one of my bodyguards with her: a Welshman I trusted not to betray my actions to Gerald or the King, or to any Welsh rebels in the area who might also be happy to capture the King's son, or Gerald's sons.

When I arrived at Pembroke, I let Gerald assume I had left the boys at Carew. 'Don't you think the King will want to see little Henry, Nest?' he asked.

'Unfortunately, that won't be possible on this occasion.'

He shook his head at me.

The castle bustled with preparations for the royal visit. Henry would soon arrive with an enormous retinue to house, feed and pickle in alcohol. 'Do you know why he is visiting?'

Gerald frowned. 'Well, if not to see you and his son, I hazard a guess that he wants to discuss strategy.'

'Can you be civil to him?'

'What choice do I have about that?'

'Gerald, keep him busy with strategy. Very busy.'

He nodded.

'And Gerald, you should come to my bed every night. Early.'

He took a deep breath. 'By Christ, Nest!'

'Hold your head, Gerald. Think of it as a siege that you are defending.'

We smiled grimly at one another.

I stood with Gerald at twilight on the battlements of Pembroke Castle watching the approach of the King's cavalcade along the road from Carmarthen. Behind us the river lapped softly at the stones of the castle and in the slant of the pale, evening sun, the towers and battlements were reflected almost perfectly in the slow waters. Ahead of us, on the road, churned a great crowd of people, horses, wagons, weapons, creating a maelstrom of dust, shouts and whinnies. As they grew nearer, Gerald and I began to discern faces and liveries and tell each other who we saw. The King's retinue included his bastard sons, Robert and Richard, grown to young men and trusted commanders; Haith; Richard FitzBaldwin; Walter of Gloucester and his son Miles; and Gilbert FitzRichard de Clare. We had heard rumours that the de Clare family were gaining great trust and prizes from the King. Gerald was anxious that the King might be coming to take away his office as castellan at Pembroke and give it to another of these Norman nobles.

When the cavalcade was at the gate, Gerald led me down to the bailey to offer them our formal greeting. The setting sun touched the top of the high battlements and dazzled me. The King dismounted. We greeted him hand in hand, Gerald bowing and I dropping a curtsy. Rising, I thought I could keep all formal but, as soon as I looked at Henry, his eyes were speaking to me of everything we had felt in our past. I looked away and mouthed the customary words of welcome.

Pembroke, with its garrison, was always a place dominated

by men, but now this maleness ratcheted up since none of the King's entourage were accompanied so far into Wales by their wives and, disconcertingly, even Henry was travelling without a mistress. For the first few days of the royal visit, I was busy supporting my staff in their efforts to billet the visitors. Henry had three horses with him and a full pack of hounds. The many nobles in his entourage were each accompanied with their own servants and horses.

My cooks and musicians performed well and the King applauded my arrangements. Gerald and I had decamped from the best room in the castle, which had been made even more lavish for the King. Gerald's anxious glances at me when we were in Henry's company were poorly concealed. 'You are doing well, husband,' I reassured him, knowing how much it cost him to keep a rein on his jealousy in front of the King.

'I wish I could be somewhere else,' he said. 'It was hard enough to imagine you with him at Woodstock and then recently at Cardiff. Now I have to have him drooling over you before my face.'

'Henry is not drooling, and I am not interested,' I reminded Gerald. 'Focus on discussing strategy. I will only be in the King's presence as much as I must be.'

On the third day, Gerald organised a hunt for the King. While the men were hunting, Amelina and I supervised the servants setting out a picnic. A small tent stitched from glinting tapestries was set up with food and drink laid on a trestle to keep it from the attentions of the sun and the insects. Two painted poles were planted before the open flaps of the tent and the King's banners flew from the pinnacles. A red cloth was set on the grass with silver goblets and plates, and ivory caskets brimming with sweetmeats. I would not have these Norman lords think they could call a Welsh court – my court – barbarous. Stools, benches, coloured cushions and baskets of bread were placed inside and outside the tent. My bard settled to tune his harp. Two kites circled high, keeping an eye on the proceedings.

When the men arrived, elated with their exertions, Gerald threw himself down on the red cloth next to me. Henry gave me a warm greeting, sat on a padded stool provided for him, and returned to a conversation they had evidently been pursuing on their ride, concerning Owain ap Cadwgan's killing of his cousins Meurig and Gruffudd ap Trehaearne. 'We will have trouble from that one,' Gerald said. 'He's a hothead.'

'Yes,' the King said, 'but he's acting on his father's policy, I'd say. The Trehaearne brothers were challenging Cadwgan's power in Arwystli. Cadwgan and Owain are ruthlessly stamping on any such challenges.'

'Cadwgan's taken a daughter of the northern king Gruffudd ap Cynan as wife too,' Gerald said.

'Yes, and it's all more of a power base for Cadwgan.'

'His position is strong,' Gerald responded. 'Perhaps too strong.' He glanced at me and coloured. He did not like to discuss the Normans' contention with the Welsh in front of me. Listening to Henry's remarks, I surmised his strategy was to enforce Norman overlordship in Wales with a light touch, without military intervention if he could achieve that. Perhaps, I reflected, that was the best I could hope for, for my occupied lands, for my people. If the King and I remained on fond terms I would at least be in a position to intervene with him on behalf of my Welsh compatriots should the need arise.

In the afternoon, I sat quietly at the hearth, embroidering, aware of Henry's gaze straying occasionally in my direction. The King was speaking to his scribe, Gisulf, about a survey of all the earls and barons. 'I need a list of per diems payable to each and every one of them in bread, wine and candles. Also, a list of exemptions from geld and *auxilium burgi* taxes.'

'I am about it, Sire,' the scribe said, taking himself off to begin his lists. It was impressive to watch Henry's *curia* in action. The work never stopped. His treasury and his officers travelled with him, and the business came to him wherever he was. My husband was only steward here, on behalf of the King. Henry kept Pembroke with its mint and its rich lands, and Carmarthen too, in his own hands.

'Where are your children, Lady Nest?' Finally, the King voiced the inevitable question that I had been waiting on.

'They are at Carew Castle,' I lied. 'It's more comfortable for a family there.'

'Ah, then perhaps you and I could visit them when my business is concluded here with your husband.'

'That is a charming idea, Sire, but I am with child, in the early stage, and my midwife advises I should not ride for these months.'

Henry stared at me, as did Gerald, open-mouthed, since I had not mentioned this pregnancy to him before now, and I had ridden to the picnic that very morning. The pregnancy was a truth, although nothing else was.

Henry smiled at me politely. 'Felicitations,' he said to Gerald, who closed his mouth up.

The King was pleased with Gerald's activities in Pembroke and with the building of Cenarth Bychan on the border with Cadwgan's lands in Powys. The whole area was bristling with Norman castles built or in progress now. Walter of Gloucester would be commanding the new castle Henry had ordered built at Carmarthen and Richard FitzBaldwin was restoring Rhydygors, which had been originally thrown up by his brother, William, one of the first invaders from Devon. Rhydygors had been destroyed by Welsh rebels and lain in ruins for years, but now its walls rose again.

I was intrigued to watch Gerald in the company of the King and his Norman peers. His vigour and intelligence were evident and he did well to conceal the anxiety I knew he felt, that the King could easily take everything away from him and give it instead to one of these other men. They were all men who were more important than the younger son of the forester of Windsor, all men that the King owed favour to.

'I hear you are restoring Llansteffan, Lady Nest?' the King's question broke suddenly into my thoughts.

'Yes. It is my land,' I said, more defensively than I had intended. The King had the power to command the destruction of castles if he had not given permission for them. All the Norman men gathered in my hall stared at me. To them, I was a Welsh cuckoo in *their* nest. 'I spent much of my childhood there.' The memory of my brother Goronwy, slain at Llansteffan by Norman invaders, lay unvoiced, heavy in the hall. They all knew of it. I had spoken of my grief at Goronwy's death often enough with Henry.

The King allowed a small pause before continuing his discussion with his commanders. 'You will arrange a garrison at Llansteffan when building there is completed,' he told my husband. 'Gerald FitzWalter has made an excellent suggestion that I am thinking to take up,' the King said, raising his voice to address everyone. 'He suggests settling a colony of Flemings nearby at Rhos, around the Cleddau estuary.' I heard this with surprise. Gerald had not mentioned this idea to me. The King gestured to Haith that he should join the conversation.

'There are many wandering Flemings,' Haith said. 'Many lost homes to flooding, like me when child. They always battle storms and tides in the Low Countries. Cannot hunt and exterminate the water wolf, you know! Homeless Flemings went first to Scotland but did not settle well, so now try here in Wales. Very loyal to King.'

'Some former mercenaries, I believe?' Gerald asked.

'Yes,' Henry said. 'They need land.'

Gerald nodded.

It was an ingenious suggestion by my husband. These Flemings would drive out the Welsh natives. They would have Gerald's back against Cadwgan. They would hold their gifted, their stolen land, ferociously against the Welsh. I said nothing. I could not. It was just another insult amongst many. I resolved to send a message later, warning Cadwgan about these incomers, these new land-thieves.

I was crossing the bailey at dusk when Henry approached me suddenly from behind, took my arm, and pulled me swiftly to the steps that led down into the Wogan watergate beneath the castle. 'Let's talk.' He clasped my wrist, leading me down into the cavern. The air, held in the grasp of the cold stone, was frigid. Water lapped at the rough opening to the river. Feeble light filtered weakly into the dank interior. Henry walked around, feeling the moss on the walls, exclaiming at the flint tools left behind by ancient inhabitants. I stood close to the bottom of the steps, wondering if I should simply flee from him. Completing his circuit Henry was suddenly very close to me in the gloom. I heard his breath, fast in his mouth. I was well aware that carrying the child of another man would do nothing to cool his ardour. I could make out the glimmer of his eyes, the jewel clasp of his cloak. 'So fertile, Nest,' he said, placing his hand on my belly, which was just beginning to round with the new child. 'Three sons and another child here.'

'So fat.' Warmth spread from the focus of his hand.

'I like it.' His hand slid swiftly down, coming to rest between my legs as if it had suddenly arrived home. He pushed at the fabric rucked beneath his hand.

'Sire …' I protested in a whisper, even as my body pushed forward, answering his hand. His mouth was on mine.

'Henry,' I panted, 'I need you to leave our son with me. Promise me that.'

'Yes, I promise.' He held my gaze and leant in to kiss me again. I succumbed to the desire coursing through me, as he pushed me back against the sharp, wet stones of the cave wall. I longed to repair the rejection and worthlessness I had felt when he had dropped me so unceremoniously. That festering wound might be assuaged if I would only allow this, but I knew I could not survive another encounter with the fire of the passion between us and the cold dowsing of it which I knew would inevitably follow, when he must return to his duties as king.

'Lovely Nest.' He caressed my cheek with the back of his fingers. 'I need to see my son, Nest.'

'I need you to leave me and your son in peace, Sire. He is well and that is all you need.' I slid along the wall, away from him, separating myself from the urgent pressure of his body.

He stared at me, silent for a while. 'I enjoyed our former wrangles, Nest, but I don't have time or spare energy for such complications now. I am your king.'

'You are a kind man who loved me and now you will kindly leave me in peace with my family.'

He broke into a hearty laugh. 'I always loved your resistance, Nest.'

'I am not a hart in the forest, Henry. I'm not going to get exhausted by the chase this time. I am not running from you to heighten your desire.'

'You heighten my desire whatever you do.'

'Henry, you left me. Abandoned me. Wrote nothing to me for two years.' The words had escaped from me before I could stop them. I had never meant him to know how much he had hurt me.

'Nest, as a man, I love you, and wish to do everything I can to protect you, nourish you, value you, as I know you deserve. You are my *axis mundi*, the centre of my world, but as a king I may have to act otherwise. It may sometimes seem otherwise.'

'A king who treats others as pawns at his disposal you mean.'

'All kings must do so, Nest.'

'King Philip did not cast off Bertrade in France. He suffered mightily for that choice. He made her his queen, nevertheless.'

'He put his personal feelings before his duty as king. His people suffered with an excommunicate king. Philip's relationship with Bertrade weakened his rule. You know what a heavy weight I carry, Nest, as king. It feels as if I am carrying Mont Saint-Michel upon my back at times. You helped me bear my burden for a while. Won't you help me again?'

He stepped close and probed his tongue into my mouth, holding me hard against him again. I put my hands on his shoulders and forced him away.

'Oh by the Lord's death, Nest! You know you want me!'

He was right, but I could not stand the grief he would bring me again. I would die this time if I let him use me and leave me for another woman. I swallowed and moved back to the steps, hearing the water lipping the rock. 'I'm leaving, Henry. My lord.'

He was silent behind me. I picked up my skirts with one hand, feeling the damp wall with my other, moving swiftly up to the bailey. I looked back and he still had not emerged. I wondered how many times he would try me and how many times I could hold out. At least he had given me a promise not to take my son.

The new influx of threatened Flemings arrived, driven from their homes by terrible storms that had carried away their land. These extra numbers of foreigners increased hostilities with the local populace. Gerald, with Haith's assistance, established their settlement at Rhôs. The Welsh complained that the colonists had been given all the best, fertile, low-lying land, whilst the native people were pushed further up towards the barren mountains. Gerald told me the Welsh referred to the Flemings scathingly as the 'down-belows'.

Many of the Norman magnates with lands in Wales came to visit the King during his stay at Pembroke, including Bishop Roger of Salisbury, Henry's main administrator, who was building a new castle not far up the coast at Kidwelly, and the Earl of Warwick, who held the fertile coast lands of the Gower, not far from Llansteffan. The Normans grew fast across the land like bindweed. My country was made the dwelling place of foreigners and a playground for lords of alien blood.

I sent to Amelina to return to Pembroke and bring the boys with her. After our greeting, she wasted no time. 'The King's still here then.'

'Yes. He promises not to take little Henry to court.'

'In exchange for?' Amelina challenged me.

I looked away.

'I've been having a bit of a dalliance too,' she said.

I looked back at her, exasperated, meaning to rebuke her for her assumption but her eyes were glowing with the excitement of her news. 'Tell me,' I said instead.

'A fisherman named Dyfnwal,' she said giggling. 'Very handsome! Strapping!'

'Did you tell him your stories of the Drowned Court?'

'Of course! He fishes the estuary at Llansteffan and is in and out with the tides every day. We imagined he and me as the distracted lovers who left the sluices open, who caused the disaster of the drowned court. I am awash with love, Nest!'

'Well, I hope you kept an eye on my boys in-between times.'

'Of course. You'll see.'

She was gone a few moments and I thought of the drowned court that was said to lie beneath the waves of Carmarthen Bay. The legend told that you could still hear the church bells tolling under the waves at times of danger. I thought I had heard the bells myself once, just before Llansteffan was attacked by the Normans and my brother, Goronwy, was killed. I closed my eyes, trying to picture his face. It swam to me vague and shimmering, as if underwater. The drowned court was the court of my father now – the Welsh Kings of Deheubarth – murdered and displaced by the Normans, by those I now loved: Gerald, Henry, my sons who were half-Norman in blood and fully Norman in their raising, except for the stories and the Welsh words I told to them. I looked up at the noise of Amelina at the door ushering in my three toddling boys.

'Mama! We have been battling Haith's water wolf with Dyfnwal!' exclaimed little Henry.

'Caught fish, mama!' said William.

I turned alarmed eyes to Amelina. 'Oh pish!' she said. 'You think I would let them drown or be in any danger. You know better. They've been paddling and learning to swim in the shallows with my lovely fisherman!'

'Haith says the water wolf stalks the land,' Henry shouted, his eyes large, his hands posed like claws, trying to capture my full attention. He put his two pudgy hands on either side of my face and stared into my laughing eyes.

'And is it true that you are with child again?' Amelina interrupted him, more concerned to catch up with what she had missed. 'The cook's assistant says you declared it in front of all and sundry in the hall.'

'It's true, I did, but it was useful to keep the King at bay.'

'Really?' she said, her voice sceptical.

'To stop him trying to make me ride to Carew to find his son at any rate,' I said in a low voice, so that little Henry would not hear me. He was busying himself with one of the dogs he was fond of. He had no idea that Gerald was not his father, that William and Maurice were his half-brothers. I would tell him in time, but not yet.

The King was delighted to become acquainted with his three-year-old son. It amused the King to create him Henry, Lord of Arberth, and to bestow those lands on him. He was delighted too with the rest of my brood. Little Henry and William tottered together around the bailey with their wooden swords and hobby horses demonstrating their fledgling fighting skills to the King, who laughed uproariously at them, ruffling their hair and rewarding them with sweetmeats that bulged in their cheeks.

Haith joined us for dinner on several occasions and discussion turned to the Flemings and their growing influence on trade. Tancred was building a castle at Haverfordwest, Lord Wizo was ruling in Wiston and Letard Litelking in Letterston. Odo de Barry, who held nearby Manorbier, was also of Flemish origin. Henry's Flemish plantation was swiftly and radically altering the character of the lowlands north of Milford Haven.

'But the relations of the Flemings are worsening with the Welsh,' I told Henry and Haith.

Haith nodded to me, his face a picture of theatrical concern. Henry merely smiled. It seemed to me that he meant to deliberately provoke the Welsh with his colonies of incomers, or at least to bolster the Norman colonists by it.

A week after Amelina's return from Llansteffan, she woke me with an armful of flowers and a whiff of fish. I sat up in bed and stared at her. Usually it was me who got out of bed first and had to shake her awake to her duties. 'You're up early.'

'I've got a visitor below,' she said, her eyes glinting with excitement. 'He gave me these flowers. And some fine fish.'

'I can smell the fish. You haven't brought them into my chamber?'

'No! I deposited them with the cook for dinner. I'd be grateful if you'd come to speak with him, Lady Nest.'

'Dyfnwal is it? From Llansteffan?' I swung my legs out of the bed and searched with my foot for a slipper.

'That's him,' she said, smug.

'Why does he need to speak with me?'

'Well, he won't tell me but he is insistent.'

'Do you think he has news of the Welsh rebels? Of Prince Owain?'

'Perhaps,' she said, hesistantly, drawing out the word as she considered this possibility. 'But I don't think it's that.'

'Well, you'd better get me dressed quickly then, so that I can clap eyes upon your paramour and see if he is as handsome as you claim.'

'He is!' she said, laying out my dress and picking up the hairbrush. 'He's cleaned up well, apart from a bit of a fish pong, but he says he can't tarry because of the tide.'

I entered the hall, curious to look at what the sea had washed to Amelina. Her Dyfnwal was indeed a handsome young man, dark-haired and brown-eyed with a dimpled chin and a large smile. He had slicked his hair and looked ungainly in his best clothes. It was still early and there were few people up and about as yet, mostly servants. I was pleased to see that someone had thought to offer him beer and bread.

He looked at me agape for a moment and then recollecting himself, he dropped to his knee. 'Princess Nest!'

'Please do stand, Dyfnwal. Welcome to Pembroke. You wished to speak with me?' I knew that I should tell him I was not a princess, I was simply the wife of the steward of Pembroke, a lady, but I knew that the Welsh held to my presence here in desperate hope for our lost kingdom and the royal line that I represented.

I indicated that he should sit and took my own seat, but he remained standing, looking awkward and uncertain. I smiled, trying to make him feel at ease. It was a pleasure to be conversing in Welsh. From the corner of my eye, I saw Amelina hovering at the foot of the stairs, peering around the edge of the doorway.

'It's, well, it's forward of me, I know.' He stopped and I waited.

'I've taken a great liking to your maid there, Amelina.' He jerked his head in her direction.

'Yes, I am greatly fond of her myself.'

'Well there's the trouble of it.'

I was growing impatient. 'Do say what you came to say, Dyfnwal. I understand you must get back to Llansteffan for the tide, for your next haul. Thank you for the gift of the catch.'

'It is my pleasure to bring a gift to you, my lady. Yes. Well. So, it's like this. I've a mind to be marrying Amelina.'

'Marrying!' Now I stared at him.

'Yes. She's a fine woman.' He glanced in her direction again.

'She is,' I said slowly, trying to recover from my surprise. I had not expected this. She had only been away for a few weeks.

'I know you won't want to be parting with her, lady, and I know she wouldn't hear of that neither.' He spoke in a rush. 'So, I'm thinking we could be married but she could stay with you mostly. I'm busy fishing six days a week anyway.'

I frowned. 'Well. If you were married you would want to see each other *sometimes.*'

'I expect you might allow it now and then,' he said, an expectant look on his face.

'I expect I might.'

He grinned.

'Have you asked Amelina herself?'

'No. Needed to be clearing the matter with you first. I know she wouldn't think twice about saying no if she thought she had to leave you.'

'Well, Dyfnwal, you'd best ask her and I wish you success.'

We turned to the doorway to find Amelina already half-way across the hall towards us and running helter-skelter into Dyfnwal's arms. 'Yes!' she declared breathlessly, the tops of her breasts wobbling above her chemise, under the pressure of his tight embrace.

The King stayed with us only a few days longer, and he and I did not repeat our caresses, but desire was there all the time in the way he looked at me. It was loaded in the tone of his voice. I had thought Gerald would not know, but evidently he guessed at something. His behaviour to me became politely strained again.

On the morning of the King's departure, the marshals had everything packed and ready, when it had seemed, only hours before, as if the great sprawl of the royal household could surely never be corralled. I stood with Gerald, my sons, and all our household on the steps of the hall to bid farewell. Henry bent his head to kiss the back of my proffered hand. In front of my husband, all contact had to be formal, proper, yet I felt the touch of Henry's lips, the tip of his tongue on my knuckle, his breath on my fingers, in every miniscule detail, as if we stood naked and embracing before the entire community of people crowding the courtyard. Henry looked up into my face with his liquid black eyes communicating his grief at leaving me. I could not trust myself to speak. He let go my hand and I felt as if my arms, the front of my body, were Carmarthen Bay with the sea rushing away from me, emptying, and never returning. It took all my force of will not to stagger at the power of my emotion. Henry and his household mounted and he gave the signal to move off. The great, shadowed gates of Pembroke Castle stood open like the yawning mouth of Jonah's whale.

Henry turned in the saddle to look back at me, and as he did so, I felt Gerald's stare, harsh against my cheek. I was not afraid of Gerald. We both knew I had only to mention a concern to the King, and Gerald would find himself, at the very least, relieved of his position and lands; at worst, lingering indefinitely in a dungeon or exiled. Yet I needed Gerald's good will. I might never be in Henry's presence again. He ruled a vast, unruly kingdom. Gerald provided me, and my sons, with his daily protection. I caught myself up at this mercenary train of thought. I cared for Gerald. Surely I *cared* for him, although it was hard to think about that as I strained for the very last glimpse of Henry. I kept my eyes dry and my expression clean of all the thoughts in my head and the tightening grief at my heart.

When the cavalcade was out of sight, I turned towards the hall, looping my arm around Gerald's elbow and turning him with me. 'Normality can resume at last,' I said gaily. I looked up, smiling at Gerald, but he did not turn his face to me. A muscle jerked in his cheek; his elbow stiffly resisted my touch. I pretended I had noticed none of this, and strolled to the hall with him. I did not chatter. That would certainly give him cause to suspect me.

7

Return to the Cloister

Benedicta's journey to Fontevraud was delayed by the gelatinous mire of the roads after the frequent spring showers. Yet summer was, at last, settling itself in and drying the fields. Countess Adela summoned Benedicta to an empty hall. She had been instructed to be ready to leave immediately so she was wearing her warm cloak and her few possessions were packed in the small leather pouch – the *scrip* – slung at her waist. A large wooden chest stood open on the table before the Countess, and Benedicta approached, curious to see inside. There were numerous books – large and small – studded with gold, silver and jewels. Benedicta could read a few of the titles gilded onto the book covers: Ovid's *Metamorphoses*; Marbod de Rennes' *Book of Stones* and his *The Figures of Speech*.

'Well may you gape, Sister Benedicta!' the Countess laughed. Benedicta closed her mouth quickly. 'A fortune in parchments but, even more, a priceless collection of ideas and words. Here is the key for the chest. Wear it about your neck.'

Benedicta fastened the thong around her neck and pushed the key inside her habit.

'Poetry is more than game, Sister,' Adela said suddenly, turning her gaze upon her with great sincerity. 'The world is changing and there are differing views. Some things are difficult, dangerous even, to discuss in a straightforward manner.' She lowered the lid of the chest and patted it. 'Take care of my freight of words.'

Benedicta nodded, not taking her eyes from the Countess's, so that she would see that she understood her meaning. She knew from her studies in the Almenêches library how poetry could provide a shield to a voice that might be considered dangerously close to heresy. Pope Urban's preaching, some ten years ago, had initiated a wave of moral censorship across the region and necessitated that intellectual debates were conducted with great circumspection. Poetry could be a kind of camouflage. Benedicta had read Ovid, Horace, Cicero. She had seen how writers such as Baudri and Marbod put those texts to use in discussing new values, new ideas that some conservatives might see as a challenge to the Church. Under the cover of song, writers, including some female writers, contemplated desire, eloquence, the place of women in society, the natural sciences. Poetry enabled hazardous play with the forbidden. Benedicta loved code, and she could not see why curiosity and a thirst to pursue knowledge should be perceived as a threat to faith. She wholeheartedly approved of such debates. She marvelled, nevertheless, that Countess Adela was able to skirt moral censorship so skilfully that she could be friendly with Bishop Ivo of Chartres on the one hand, who was one of the most ascetic reformers, and friends with Archbishop Baudri, on the other, who was at the forefront of this new, risqué, literary thinking.

'My brother, King Henry, is at war with the new king of France, Louis, after their recent dispute over the castle of Gisors, but Henry must return to England now for the betrothal of his daughter, Maud. The envoys of her husband-to-be, the German Emperor, are arriving even now in London. Whilst he is away, we are in great need of information. You can assist us, Benedicta. Fulk, the Count of Anjou, has died and the occasion of his burial gives us an opportunity.'

Benedicta was aware of the notorious Count Fulk who had taken and spurned at least five wives that she knew about.

'We need information on anything to do with King Louis, the new Count of Anjou, Amaury de Montfort, Robert de Bellême and the son of the deposed duke, William *Clito*.'

Benedicta wondered how the Countess felt about her eldest brother, Robert Curthose, kept prisoner now in England for so long, and his little son, William *Clito*, the Countess's nephew, under threat from his uncle, King Henry. The child was the greatest threat to King Henry's rule in Normandy and a rallying point for his enemies.

'The funeral of Fulk d'Anjou and the inauguration of his son means that all these people I have mentioned to you, that we must watch, are gathering in Angers.'

'You mean to send me there?' asked Benedicta, wondering how on earth she could possibly penetrate to the secrets of such exulted people.

'No, not to Angers, Sister Benedicta. Fontevraud Abbey itself will do for our purpose. Bertrade de Montfort is retired there. Her brother, Amaury de Montfort, and others of interest to us are likely to visit her.'

Benedicta knew of Bertrade de Montfort. Everybody did. She had been Countess of Anjou, was mother to the new Count, and had been Queen of France after the old king, Philip, notoriously abducted her from Anjou. Both she and King Philip had been excommunicated for their fornication. 'She is a religious now?' Benedicta asked hesitantly.

'So it is said.' Adela's voice was loaded with circumspect scepticism. 'She had no choice now that the old king is dead. Our new king, Louis, bears her no love since she displaced his mother.'

'I will do everything I can at Fontevraud, Countess.'

Adela regarded her with evident satisfaction. 'You are ready to leave?'

'I am, my lady.'

'Very good. There is a slight change in my plan. My son, Etienne, will travel to Angers to represent our family at the burial and the inauguration. He will travel with you as far as Fontevraud. Good luck, Sister Benedicta, and my thanks. You will see Breri in due course.' She signalled to her servant who opened the doors for two men-at-arms. Benedicta was by no means a tiny woman. She was taller than many other females, with a thin ranginess similar to her brother, Haith. Flemings need long legs – she always said, when people remarked on her height – to keep their mouths above the flood waters. Yet standing next to these muscled men-at-arms she felt like a miniature. They lifted the weighty chest easily between them and carried it out to the cart in the courtyard. Benedicta did not feel the pangs of lust for any man that she had met, but she was happy to admire a well-formed, fine-countenanced young man when she saw one.

Benedicta's unexpected travelling companion, Count Etienne, did not deign to talk with her overmuch. His exchanges with Benedicta were perfunctory and he made it obvious that a middle-aged nun could hold no interest for him. She overheard him telling the men-at-arms, who guffawed obligingly, that a woman in a nun's habit was an offence to nature. He had been educated at the court of King Henry in England and was a boy yet, at sixteen, but Benedicta could not find excuse for him in that. He was loud and selfish. She considered the disinterest to be conveniently mutual. Yet she could not fully maintain her defended demeanour when she overheard him one morning calling to the men, 'Where is that scraggly, underfed nun? Still snoring? We need to be up and on the road.' She knew that he spoke loudly deliberately so that she would hear, but she could not stop herself from feeling wounded by his words. All day, in the saddle, they kept coming back to her: scraggly, underfed. That was not what she had seen in the mirror at Chartres. Why should I care what he thinks of me? she asked herself, but the words rankled nonetheless.

Bereft of conversation, Benedicta entertained herself with looking at the wonders of nature. In particular, she loved the architecture of clouds, how they constantly formed and reformed, making a different skyscape to imaginatively gambol in, at every distinct minute.

In one village they passed through, the villagers were celebrating the beginning of summer. They had selected the prettiest girl in the village to be their Summer Queen. Benedicta, Etienne and the two men-at-arms tethered their horses to graze and rest a while. They sat on the grass at the edge of the village green, taking their ease after long hours in the saddle. The villagers offered them food and beakers of ale. They watched the 'Queen' – a twelve-year-old girl – enthroned in a wicker bower and crowned with a circlet of twining pink, yellow, and white flowers. A sceptre wound about with more flowers was placed in her hands, and the villagers danced before her on the green. Benedicta could not take her eyes from the pretty girl: her soft cheeks, clear eyes, the unblemished skin of her neck and arms and her light brown curls.

Benedicta listened with pleasure to the girl's excited laughter, and the villagers' singing. The sun was warm and bees hummed in the flowers, probing for early pollen. How Benedicta wished she could throw off her veil and wimple and twirl around and around there on the green, dizzy, her arms outheld in the sunshine. She turned to share her pleasure at the scene with her travelling companions and saw a look of unpleasant lust on Etienne's face, as he too stared at the Summer Queen.

A cloud passed over the sun and darkened the grass. The girl's smile disappeared. The pipes and the dancing continued but the villagers were growing uncomfortable at their presence here: three armed men and the careless privilege emanating from Count Etienne. Benedicta called to him, 'We should move on, Count, or we will not reach Fontevraud before nightfall.' Reluctantly he nodded and she was relieved to see him stand and give the signal for their departure.

Three days of riding brought the weary group late to the gates at Fontevraud. The high walls stretched as far as the eye could see in either direction. 'This is an enormous place for a bunch of discarded wives,' Etienne said with habitual churlishness.

'It would be best to show them respect I believe, Count,' Benedicta told him, 'since they will host us.'

He said nothing but his eyes glittered at her reproof although she had couched it as mildly as she could. Benedicta took a last look at a sliver of recumbent moon reflected in the river and glanced up at the original that curved bright in the brilliant pale blue twilight sky. One of the men hammered on the door to summon the porter.

'It's late,' the porter told them, 'and the sisters have already retired after vespers. I will call the guesthouse nun to tend to you and your horses, and no doubt Prioress Petronilla will greet you in the morning.' He closed the small grille in the door. Benedicta and the men dismounted and waited outside the gates. After a while they heard voices again on the other side of the studded wood.

'More!' they heard a female voice exclaim, presumably the guesthouse nun. 'Where am I supposed to put yet more of them? I've just seen the whole de Bellême and de Montfort entourages

71

bedded down in the stable hayloft and the lords themselves have had to make shift in amongst all the others in the guesthouse.'

Benedicta was startled to hear that de Bellême was already here. He was her quarry, but he would recognise and suspect her, if he saw her.

'Hush, Sister,' the porter told the guesthouse nun, 'they will hear your words.'

Etienne raised his eyebrows to Benedicta to indicate that they already did so.

'This is only a party of four,' the porter said. 'The lord will have to join those in the bulging guest house. His two men can wriggle in amongst the rest in the stable loft.'

'And the fourth?'

'The fourth is a nun so no difficulty there. I imagine you can show her to one of the spare cells?'

'Thank goodness for small mercies,' groaned the guesthouse nun, and the gates joined her with their own protest as the porter opened up for the visitors. The guesthouse nun presented them with an unequivocable welcome in her face that had not been present in her overheard conversation with the porter.

Benedicta kicked her palfrey forward to follow their guide and pass under the shadow of the convent gatehouse, wondering when, if ever, she might be out in the world again.

8

The Usefulness of a *Garderobe*

After the King's departure, Gerald did not come to sleep in my bed. My pregnancy was far advanced but he had shared my bed throughout when I carried our other babies. I had to find a way to repair this new rift in our marriage. When our daughter was born, Gerald kept his promise to let me give her a Welsh name and I called her Angharad. He was warm and affectionate to all our children including young Henry, but he continued cool towards me.

Amelina's wedding to Dyfnwal was set for the spring and she and I had been to visit Llansteffan on several occasions where she could see him and I could oversee the building work. News from the English court came in letters from Elizabeth de Vermandois, and Sybil de Montgommery wrote to me from Normandy. King Philip of France had died and been succeeded by his son Louis. Elizabeth wrote that Henry had betrothed his daughter Maud to Henry, King of Germany, and that during her betrothal ceremony, Princess Maud had to be carried by one of her knights because she was so small. 'Imagine it!' Elizabeth wrote. 'A child bride even younger than I was.' Sybil de Montgommery wrote that her new husband and life in Normandy were 'tolerable', but she missed me. Her daughter, Mabel, was in the Queen's household, waiting for the King to set a date for her marriage to Robert FitzRoy. Sybil told me in disgust that her former clerk, and my former tutor, Master Richard de Belmeis, had been ordained and was now Bishop of London, and still very close with Henry's queen, Matilda. 'So snakes thrive,' she wrote acidly.

Despite my numerous attempts, Gerald would not allow our conversation to approach the cause of our rift. In the hall, we behaved as affectionate man and wife. He sometimes caressed my arm and hand when we were in public but all affection ceased at the first step leading to my chamber in the solar. I busied myself with my children, with managing the household and my estates, but greatly regretted the loss of a warm relationship with my husband. At first, I thought he would thaw with time. After all, I had first come to him from Henry's bed. I was innocent of Gerald's suspicions, and yet not. 'Gerald,' I ventured one evening, deciding to take a direct approach, 'won't you come to my bed? I have missed you.'

'You need time to recover from Angharad's birth,' he said.

'I *am* recovered but still you leave me lonely. Is it the King? Is it about him?'

'Of course not.' He stared ahead at the scene in the hall of servants going about their business, clearing plates, refilling beakers. He stood.

'Gerald, please!' I whispered urgently to him, placing my hand on his sleeve. 'There was nothing between Henry and I when he visited. Nothing but the kindness of an old affection.'

'Of course,' he said, not looking at me, gently removing his sleeve from my hand, and walking away from me to speak with his sergeant about the patrol they were planning for the subsequent day.

The year wore on and there was no change in Gerald's demeanour. Would he keep me at arm's length forever? It was unjust that I should reject the man I loved and be rejected by the one I had chosen over him.

The winter was advancing into December and we were all installed in Gerald's new castle at Cenarth Bychan for the coming Christmas feast. I rolled from the nest of my bed reluctantly, tickling little Henry's cheek where he lay in the warm hollow that I had just risen from. He lay on his back with his arms flung out and his eyes screwed shut and crinkled (which meant he was awake). Lately he had taken to finding his way up the stairs and into my bed, complaining of bad dreams and a need to snuggle with his mama. I let him. After all, Gerald did not come to me, so my little son warmed me in his stead. 'Wakey wakey, up you get!' He snapped his eyes open, meaning to surprise me. 'You're awake already! I thought you were fast asleep!' He chuckled and I tickled him under the arm, poking him playfully until he rolled to the edge of the bed, planting his solid little feet on the cold floor. He shivered and I wrapped his cloak around him, made him sit back on the bed whilst I pushed woolly socks onto his feet. His legs were short, his feet broad and his toes splayed. The King's feet in miniature, I realised. Fighting around his wriggling resistance and cries of 'no, no', I planted several kisses on his forehead and cheeks. 'Go and find the nurse and get some warm clothes on.' He trotted out obediently. I looked at my own clothes rack with disinterest. Gerald no longer cared what I looked like. Perhaps I did not care either.

Amelina poked her head around the door. 'There's a visitor below, and the lord asks you to come quickly. Do you need help dressing?'

'No, I'll be there directly.'

She withdrew her head. 'Who is it?' I thought to call after her, too late. She was already out of earshot and rushing to her chores. I put on my pale grey gown trimmed with black fur and embroidery, brushed my hair swiftly, tied on a *couvrechef* and went to the stairs. I heard the voices of men at the table: Gerald and other voices I did not recognise, Welsh voices. I regretted my hasty decision not to have Amelina dress me. My hair was a little dishevelled to be greeting strangers, but there was nothing for it now. It would have to do.

Entering the hall, I looked with shock at the man standing in a shaft of sunlight from a high window. The winter sun slid sparkling fingers through his dense red-blond hair. I flushed, thinking guiltily of the 'O sea-bird' love poem amongst the papers in my chamber.

'Ah, Nest.' Gerald handed me to my seat. 'Prince Owain, may I introduce my wife to you.'

The boy I remembered was grown into a man. 'Lady.' He spoke in Welsh. He inclined his head politely and looked back to my face with interest. 'We met once before,' he told Gerald. 'At the court of King William.'

'That was long ago,' I said. Neither of us referred to the other occasion we had met, when he had hatched a plan for my escape from the Norman castle at Cardiff.

'Not so long,' he said, continuing to regard me so intently that it began to verge on rudeness.

Gerald, discomfited by Owain's staring, intervened. 'The Prince is here with an invitation, Nest.'

Owain smiled. 'An invitation from my father, King Cadwgan, and from myself. We would be honoured if you and your husband would share the Christmas feast with us in Powys.'

I exchanged a glance with Gerald to see what his intended response might be, and he gave me a slight nod to indicate that we would accept the invitation.

'How delightful,' I said. 'We are most pleased to accept.'

'Excellent!' Owain slapped his gauntlets, held bunched in one hand, against his hip. 'My father will be glad. And I am ecstatic,' he said, an amused smile hovering at the edge of his mouth.

He did not linger but was soon mounting and riding out again. I walked back arm in arm with Gerald into the hall. 'Well?' I asked him.

'Welsh treachery has masqueraded as hospitality before now, and I don't trust Owain, or his father come to that.'

'Yes. I felt a vein of humour at our expense beneath his politeness but King Cadwgan is an honourable man, I should think.'

'King Cadwgan is a wily, self-serving bastard,' Gerald retorted and I leant my head affectionately against his shoulder. Generally, Gerald's perceptions of his fellow men and women were accurate.

'You think we should find an excuse not to go? Perhaps it is because of Cenarth Bychan.' I had warned Gerald that Cadwgan would view the building of Cenarth Bychan, so close to the borders of Ceredigion, as a provocation. 'Indeed,' Gerald had retorted. 'And so it is intended.'

'There's something not straight about the invitation, for sure,' he said. 'I had planned for us all to spend Christmas together here at Cenarth Bychan. We can just go for one night and return swiftly.' He kissed my hand and left me to welcome the boys who came running into the hall with the nurse, who was carrying Angharad in her arms. Gerald ruffled each of their little heads as they rushed past him, excepting the nurse of course.

Amelina lined the boys up before her and I smiled at the sight of them obediently cleaning their teeth with twigs dipped in her fennel concoction. Maurice eyed Henry and William, doing his best with an awkwardly twisting, chubby hand, to emulate the movements of his older brothers.

Gerald and I rode across the wooden drawbridge into the gate-house of Gaer Penrhôs Castle near Llanrhystud on the frosty morning of Christmas Eve. We had a small, well-armed escort with us. The children were being looked after by Amelina at Cenarth Bychan, a little further south down the coast, a day's ride away. We dismounted in the courtyard and King Cadwgan, his young wife Euron, and Prince Owain came out to meet us. Cadwgan was nearing sixty years of age. He was not a tall man, but had a muscular stockiness and the bearing of a soldier. Gerald had told me that Cadwgan's queen, Euron, was his seventh wife. She was of an age with me. A servant led us to a fine room to deposit the few possessions we had brought with us, and to wash with a bowl of warmed water that stood waiting. I took off my green leather gauntlets and my fur-lined cloak that reached to the floor. A fire blazed in the hearth and we warmed ourselves, stamping the cold from our feet. Gerald took my hands and rubbed them between his own large palms. Then he surprised me, slipping the *couvrechef* from my head, stroking my hair and taking me in his arms. 'Nest.'

I heard desire in his voice for the first time in over a year. I took his face in my hands and kissed him for a long time, letting my body mould into the shape of his. Releasing my mouth to take a gasp of breath, I kissed his neck. 'How I have missed you.' We smiled at each other.

'We should go down, I suppose,' he said reluctantly.

I made a playful grimace. 'Yes, we have to.'

'But we will come back to this,' he said, kissing me briefly again and then leading me down the winding staircase, my hand in his. He stopped abruptly three times on the way down so that I stumbled against him and he turned and kissed me each time, smiling.

'I like this Christmas gift,' I whispered to him. I felt excited. At last he returned to me. I would not make a mess of it this time.

In the hall, the feast was prepared, the Yule Log blazed in the hearth, the bards were tuning their harps and voices, servants rushed to and fro with goblets and jugs, there was a mouthwatering aroma of roasted meat. The hall was hung with the lurid coloured banners of the house of Powys: a rampant dark blue griffin on a bright yellow background, his barbed tail curling tautly, red-tongued, red-eyed, his claws preparing to attack. 'Our honoured guests, please!' Cadwgan was indicating the two places beside him on the dais. Gerald handed me up and Cadwgan took my hand. 'My daughter!' he said. 'May I call you that? I have always thought of you in that way.'

It seemed odd to me to do so. I glanced at Gerald but his expression gave me no clues. Owain was seated next to me and I noticed again how handsome a man he was. His thick blond hair was shot with glints of red and gold. His blue eyes danced with a sardonic humour. We were immediately reminded, or Gerald was, that he was amongst the enemy, that it was Normans who had stolen Cadwgan's 'daughter' from him, since I had long ago been betrothed to Owain.

We sat down, and I prepared myself for more verbal sparring, hoping that was all we would have to contend with. Gerald's Welsh was very good by now and I was proud that he was one of the few Norman lords who made the effort to speak our tongue. I looked to the rows of people in the hall and saw that our contingent of men from Pembroke were not seated together. They had been spread around the room and none of them were close to the dais. And they were of course, all unarmed. All weapons had to be left at the door of a hall. I could not believe Cadwgan would offer us violence in the guise of this Christmas feast, but if there were any such attempt, I knew my husband to be an intelligent, valiant fighter. I had a knife in a leather scabbard strapped to my calf, beneath my gown, and there was a copious array of cutting implements on the table before us. A sudden sound of knives sharpening close behind me made me jump. Several servants, each armed with two long knives, flourished and scraped them against each other, preparing to carve the geese.

Cadwgan introduced us to his five younger sons who sat at the table with us. They ranged in age from fourteen down to Queen Euron's two small boys who were six and five years old. He would not risk violence with his family here. 'Two of my other sons, nearer to Owain in age,' Cadwgan told me, 'are hostages at the court of King Henry. They write that he treats them kindly and they learn a great deal there.'

'Oh yes,' I said, enthusiastic on a subject I knew well. 'King Henry and Queen Matilda have many young boys at court who are schooled well.'

'Not your own son, Henry, though,' Owain said.

Irritation flickered briefly across Gerald's face. Were they deliberately baiting us? 'No, our son Henry,' I responded, 'is learning his lessons well enough at Pembroke. This is a curiously designed castle.'

Cadwgan responded to my deliberate turn of the conversation by explaining that Gaer Penrhôs, which was a circular fortification, dated back to the times of the Romans.

The feast was splendid, and Cadwgan was a gracious conversationalist. He spoke to me of my father, of times when they had been friends and allies, although I knew there had been other times when they were bitter enemies. Now and then I caught Gerald's eye, and he smiled complicitly to me, the memory of our encounters in the stairwell evident in his expression. I looked forward to the night ahead.

The following morning Gerald and I rode out relieved to have put our heads into the griffin's mouth and that no ill had come of it. I was warmed by the sensuous memory of the night with Gerald. We had taken full advantage of our brief time together without the encumbrances of our children, our bustling servants, and Gerald's usually onerous duties.

At Cenarth Bychan the children were hopping with excitement in anticipation of their delayed Christmas gifts and feast. I liked this new castle. It was well made and comfortable. It occupied a good site on a headland with a long, sheer cliff face down to the river and a deep moat fronting the only means of entry.

I looked forward to resuming a full marriage with Gerald with passion, making up for lost time. Little Henry was chagrined to find himself banished from my bed back to the nursery. He pouted, and I tried not to see the replica of his father in his expression.

On the last night of the year, the children were finally all in bed and Amelina was quietly assisting the maids to clear the table and tidy the hall. Gerald and I sat comfortably in front of the fire drinking a last glass of wine before climbing the stairs, but we were both eager not to linger. 'Upstairs?' Gerald asked, standing and holding his hands out to me. I let him haul me from the chair, my weight suspended from his two hands. He pulled me close and kissed me long.

'Upstairs,' I laughed, 'before it's too late.'

In the warm chamber, I loosened my hair. I walked to the window that looked down over the river. With my back to Gerald I dropped my clothes to the floor, allowing them to puddle around my feet. I did not turn yet, as I felt Gerald push his clothed body against my naked back, and nuzzle my neck. I was about to turn to him, but in the gloom, I sensed, rather than saw, movement on the cliff face. 'Gerald, I think … .' I leant further towards the cold of the window. I could not see clearly, but something swarmed on the cliff. There was a sudden and very loud thud in the hall below. I turned frowning towards Gerald who held up a hand to me, listening. There were muffled shouts and then a piercing scream. Gerald reached for the swordbelt he had just unbuckled and flung a nightgown to me, and stalked towards the door. The sounds of grating metal, of clashing weapons, coming from below, were unmistakable. I slipped the white gown over my head moments before the door was kicked open. Gerald, dodged to the side and was concealed by the door that hung a little askew on its hinges. Two men stood in the doorway, blood dripping from drawn swords. I recognized Owain ap Cadwgan. He grinned at me. He had not yet seen Gerald concealed by the door and Gerald could not see them. I gripped the edge of the door and obstructed their entry. 'Wait!' I commanded, and Owain, to my surprise, hesitated on the threshold. I slammed the damaged door in his face and dropped the heavy bar across it, as best I could.

'What … who?' Gerald began, moving towards the door.

I held a finger to my lips to quiet him and stepped between him and the door. 'No!' I hissed. I couldn't bear the thought of him killed, hacked to pieces by their swords, and I was desperately thinking of my children, my Norman children. That was how these Welsh invaders would think of them. 'No, Gerald, I don't want you killed, please,' I pushed him backwards.

'What the hell … get out of the way, Nest.' Our tussling become serious and he would soon overwhelm me.

'No! Get out through the *garderobe* chute. That way you can attack them, take them by surprise. If you go out the door, you will just be cut down. How does that help me or the children?' I lifted my resisting hands from his shoulders abruptly. He nodded. Cenarth Bychan, as a new castle, had all the latest installations. The *garderobe,* in the alcove of our room, had a chute that opened out to a short drop to the cesspit below. There was violent hammering on the door and the wood began to splinter. 'Go now!' I hissed at Gerald and he turned. I heard the *garderobe* lid bang open and the squelch as he dropped into the mire below. Quickly, I went in, stared briefly down at him looking up anxiously at me, closed the lid, and hurried back into the room to see Owain stumble in across the shattered timbers of the door.

'Lady Nest! Do not fear. No harm will come to you. I am here to restore you to your rightful place, to your people. Please accompany me now.' He held a hand out to me.

'I am in my nightgown,' I said. 'I have to dress.'

'No time for that,' he said, 'and perhaps no need.'

I stared defiantly at him.

He handed me Gerald's heavy fur cloak that was hanging from the peg. 'This will do, and your shoes.'

He pointed at my thin dancing shoes in the centre of the pool of clothing I had slipped off so blithely moments before. I slid my feet into the shoes and walked with as much dignity as I could muster in a nightdress. I stepped across the splintered timbers at the threshold of my chamber. My children! What was happening with my children. I began to rush down the steps but Owain gripped my arm. 'No running away now, Lady Nest.' He walked down with me, retaining a painful grip on my arm.

In the hall, Amelina sat white-faced, holding the three boys to her and seated next to the nurse who was cradling Angharad. The baby was wailing inconsolably. Two men stood on either side of the pitiful group with swords drawn, and the boys were holding tight to Amelina's hands and knees. When they saw me, William and Maurice began to whimper. 'Don't be afraid,' I called to them softly, and as calmly as I could, I looked about me at the disarray in the hall. Tables and benches were overturned, serving maids were corralled by swordsmen in one corner. Two guards lay dead in the doorway and doubtless there were more dead soldiers outside. We had only a small garrison here. I counted fifteen men with Owain.

'Bring the children! Let's go!' Owain shouted. He pulled me with him and I looked back to see the men wrestling the children from Amelina and the nurse.

'No, no!' Amelina was shouting.

A soldier raised his sword, intending to break her grip that way. 'No!' I screamed. 'Amelina, let them go!' She looked at me aghast but released them into the rough care of the swordsmen surrounding her.

'No harm will come to them,' Owain assured me, but I trusted not one word he spoke.

'Henry, William, Maurice!' I called their names to focus their terrified attention on me. My brave boys stared at me, their eyes huge. One of the soldiers deposited Angharad in my arms and she fell immediately silent, her dark blue eyes trained on my face. The silence after her incessant wailing was a relief. I fought to appear calm for my children's sake.

Owain and his men hustled us out. I was lifted onto a horse that was snorting and pawing at the hard ground. The chill immediately pierced my cloak and thin nightgown. I looked to see what the children were wearing. 'The boys will freeze to death,' I shouted at Owain. They were each thrown up onto horses in front of three of Owain's men and, hearing me, the men wrapped their cloaks around my sons. I held Angharad tightly as Owain settled behind me. The cold saddle froze my naked buttocks and thighs beneath my thin nightgown. The heat of Owain's body warmed my back. I glimpsed a few men lying motionless in the gloom of the bailey. There was no sign of Gerald. A great hole gaped in the ground next to the gate. Some of the intruders had scaled the cliff from the river, whilst others had tunneled their way in. Owain gave a shouted command and we were suddenly out through the gate and riding hard. I closed my eyes and held onto my baby and the horse, trying not to think, to calm my mind for later.

Part Two

1110–1116

9

Discarded Women

Benedicta rose at daybreak with the bells tolling for the matins service. In the weak morning light she picked her way carefully amidst masons' materials that lay everywhere. From outside its walls, Fontevraud Abbey had seemed a vast, established enclave but it was still very much a work in progress. All here were under the dominion of Prioress Petronilla, since the abbey founder, Robert d'Arbrissel, had ordered that women should rule in this place. Fontevraud was astutely situated at the intersection of the three dioceses of Poitiers, Angers and Tours. When the building work was finished it would be the largest nunnery in all France.

Inside the great church, the chevet with transepts and crossing was complete, and the great nave was part-built. The masons had carved intricate twines and twists of stony fruit, foliage and vines. Benedicta marvelled at the soaring stone forest of the pillars and buttresses and felt how, in this church, humanity might reach to touch the divine, might meld with the glorious cosmos. She settled to the familiar prayers and murmured responses, glad to feel herself again at one with the generations of Christians who had come before her, murmuring her prayers in synchronicity with believers all across Christendom. She must try to focus on her pilgrimage to salvation and pray for Haith's, despite her earthly worries. Her concentration was disturbed by the sound of a suppressed male cough behind the grille. She looked up and fixed her gaze there. The territory of the church was carefully demarcated between the sexes and divided by a grille so that the sound of the soaring psalms penetrated, but not the eye (or aught else). The Countess's fears for Benedicta's chastity seemed quite misplaced.

Benedicta decided that she needed to make contact with Breri soon to make her report. Progress in her nefarious task for Countess Adela and King Henry had been accomplished swiftly. The Prioress had been delighted to draft Benedicta to her small coterie of educated nuns, to assist with the great business of constructing and running the abbey and its growing library. And it had been the Prioress who had suggested that Benedicta might also assist Bertrade de Montfort with her correspondence. As the nuns filed from the church, the sounds of the masons' hammers started promptly at the end of the service.

There was a flock of repudiated or widowed noble wives at Fontevraud: Ermengarde d'Anjou, the old count's sister, was Countess of Brittany but had left her husband and taken refuge at the abbey; Orengarde de Châtelaillon and Marie de Brienne, *two more* former wives of the old Angevin count were also here. How astute Robert d'Arbrissel must be to have put such emphasis on accepting repudiated wives and widows here, since they often came with substantial endowments to get them out of the way of fatigued husbands and daughters-in-law.

Many travellers had gathered at Fontevraud on their road to Angers. Amaury de Montfort, Bertrade's brother, was at the abbey guesthouse in the company of Robert de Bellême, intending to convey his sister to the burial of the old count and the inauguration and marriage of her son, the new Count Fulk V d'Anjou.

'Lady Bertrade,' the Prioress had told Benedicta, 'is in need of a draughtswoman to compose the set pieces in the formal parts of her letters, and she needs a reader of letters and instruments to assist her. I have heard from Sister Geneviève that you are well-read and can quote the Classical texts.'

'You flatter me, Prioress,' Benedicta said, 'yet it is true that I do have some learning and could offer this service to the lady.'

'I'm so sorry, Sister Benedicta, to take you away from your important work in the library,' Petronilla said, her face and gestures expressive of her apology, 'but I have no one else to spare. So few of us here are skilled in reading and writing, and those

88

few are fully occupied with the management of the building work and the day-to-day business of the community. And also, to be frank between us, there are some who can read and write but who lack the necessary social skills to deal with such a great lady as Bertrade, but I see from your time spent with Countess Adela of Blois that you are accustomed to the company of nobles and can comport yourself with dignity.'

Benedicta's work in the library gave her access to the writing implements she needed for her other 'business'. Although Breri had enjoined her to trust her reports for the Countess only to 'air', to the breath of words that might blow away in the wind and be denied, Benedicta was a committed scribbler. She had to put down at least some of her observations in writing to aid her memory and help her organise her thoughts into succinct and pointful reports. Writing was like breathing to Benedicta.

The library had stacks of small black wax tablets sandwiched between wooden frames. Benedicta took two of these tablets back to her bare cell, which boasted only a bed, blanket, small table, stool and chamber pot. It barely kept her warm in the chill of the nights but it did give her a requisite privacy. She settled down to transcribe her thoughts in miniscule script, using a book cipher. The book she chose to base her cipher upon was Ovid's *Amores*. She kept a copy in her cell, along with her Bible. She knew there was the risk of her cell being searched if she were ever suspected of spying, but she could eradicate the writing on the wax swiftly, with the blunt end of a stylus if necessary and certainly, she resolved, she would do so, after each delivery of information to Breri.

Building work at Fontevraud very ambitious, she noted down. *But for now, most accommodation very rough. Sisters refer to Robert d'Arbrissel as 'The Master'. Sing his praises day and night. He has been away travelling, preaching, for twelve years, so master only in name. Prioress Petronilla actually in charge. The religious men wear long beards and labour outside. Do not enter sections of the church reserved for nuns, except priest who hears confessions. Novices have their mistress or an elderly lay sister to keep guard on them, day and night. No signs of lewdness or co-habitation as suggested by rumours.*

Benedicta looked up and stared at the wattle of her hut. 'We are ordered by our Master to speak kindly and not swear oaths,' Prioress Petronilla had instructed her. 'We refrain from babbling and walk with our neck bowed and our face down.' The Prioress was a stately woman with a long face and sharp grey eyes. Petronilla was from the family of the lords of Craon and had been previously married to the lord of Chemillé.

Benedicta had become friendly with a young nun, Sister Genevieve, who said she had met The Master briefly, once, just before he left twelve years ago. 'Standing beside him in prayer,' Genevieve said, 'I was on fire. It was only through hard prayer and God's intercession, that I narrowly avoided the metamorphosis of my spiritual fire into carnal flames.' She stared with an expression of salacious horror at Benedicta who frowned. The man was over sixty years of age so how did he inspire such feelings? Although the priests did claim that age was no barrier to lust. Is there something wrong with me, Benedicta asked herself, that I have never felt this fire?

It was clear from what The Master had made happen here that he had a special pastoral message for women. Fontevraud gave welcome to repudiated wives, prostitutes, lepers and adulterers. 'His message is of especial power for those women who have done service in the unquiet of the marriage bed,' Sister Genevieve whispered, jerking her head in the direction of Prioress Petronilla.

Fontevraud was truly an extraordinary place. These educated, discarded noblewomen had lost their places in society, their wealth, their work of politicking and running great households. The Master offered them a meeting of minds; the intellectual, emotional, spiritual nourishment they craved and perhaps never met with from their husbands. Saint Benedict's admonition was to be stable, static, not wandering in the world, but she could not help but wonder at all that Robert d'Arbrissel might have seen and experienced on his journeys. She knew she should be content to contemplate the limited horizon of the small clearing in which she lived – either here or at Almenêches – with her eyes fixed on the distant horizons of the whole of Christendom, yet her eyes seemed to continually want to peer at what was over the next hill.

Benedicta had entered Bertrade's quarters, burning with curi-

osity to meet the woman who had been repeatedly excommunicated as the King of France's concubine, until the bishops had
eventually relented and acknowledged the marriage, and thereby
Bertrade's claim to be queen. Benedicta saw little evidence that the
lady was living the life of a religious recluse. Bertrade was dressed
in a nun's habit and wimple, but the cloth they were made from
was the finest and they were tailored tightly to her figure, quite
unlike the sack-like habit that Benedicta herself wore. The large
cross resting on Bertrade's shapely breast was splendidly jewelled
and threaded on a heavy golden chain. She was around forty years
of age, a few years older than Benedicta, but the small pale oval
of her angelic face was unlined and becomingly framed by her
wimple. She had large green eyes, a full-lipped small mouth, flawless skin, and wisps of yellow hair had carefully been made visible
at her temples. Benedicta found herself entranced at the sight of
this woman who had been reviled for years by so many church-
men across France. A fire leapt in the hearth, and two small dogs
luxuriated on cushions in front of it. Books, musical instruments
and trays of sweetmeats were scattered on small tables around
the room.

After a brief glance at Benedicta when she entered, and a nod
at the nun whispering in her ear, presumably conveying the information that Benedicta was here to take care of her correspondence, Bertrade did not deign to notice Benedicta's presence.
Instead, a servant made her welcome and set her to work at once
at a small writing table near a draughty window, where she was
instructed to prepare a number of letters for Bertrade's signature.
Benedicta set to work ruling out a sheet of parchment. She used
a sharp stylus to make prickings in the far outer margins of the
page and then incised a straight furrow from pricking to pricking
to guide her writing. When she had finished, her dry-point ruling
would not be visible to the reader, but it kept her writing straight
as she peered closely at the page.

When the first letter was finished and had been handed to Bertrade for her approval and signature, Benedicta set about preparing the wax for the seal. Bertrade was evidently still engaged in the
business of the region. Her correspondence directed patronage,
gave advice to her sons. The fact that she was no longer queen,

and that she had withdrawn to Fontevraud, had not left her powerless. Benedicta stole glances of admiration at Bertrade now and then, glances that grew from wonder at her beauty, which had always been renowned, to wonder at the shrewdness speaking in her letters, which Benedicta had not guessed at before. There had been rumours that Bertrade had brought about the assassination of Geoffrey d'Anjou to make way for her own son as heir to Anjou, and that she had attempted to poison Louis to enable her own son to ascend to the throne of France. An angel shot with iron then, thought Benedicta. A player behind a beguilingly pretty face. After two hours of working, Benedicta's neck and wrist were stiff, and the 'writing bump' on her middle finger was sore. She set her quill down for a moment and leant back to roll her shoulders. The door opened behind her and she heard male voices.

She dared not turn around. She was certain one of those voices belonged to de Bellême. She hoped the crowd of nuns and servants in the room would offer her anonymity if she kept her face turned to her work. The men's voices became muffled. She guessed their backs were now turned to her as they faced Bertrade and the fire. She allowed herself a quick glance. Yes. It was Bellême. She recognised his height, the set of him, his black hair shot with grey. The man standing next to him must be Lady Bertrade's brother, Amaury de Montfort. He was a head taller than Bellême and evidently younger. His hair was a thick blond, cut short to his ears in the northern fashion. Benedicta noted that he was narrow in the waist and loins, with broad shoulders and powerful arms. In the whole build of his body, she assessed, he was neither too slender nor overweighted with flesh, but perfectly proportioned. The two men spoke with Bertrade of their journey to Angers for the ceremonies. 'Be ready to leave after the prime service,' Lady Bertrade's brother told her. 'It's a short journey down the Loire to Angers.' Benedicta heard the brotherly affection in his voice, as he regarded his sister, and felt the familiar pang of missing her own brother.

'Your church here has lovely acoustics,' Amaury remarked.

'It does,' his sister replied.

'I thought I might die from ecstasy listening to the nuns sing evensong,' Amaury said, and Benedicta flushed with pleasure, thinking that she, herself, had been one of those voices raised in song.

'If you were ever going to die from ecstasy at the sound of women's voices you would have done so long ago,' Bertrade responded. 'Have you learnt if William *Clito* is safe?' Bertrade asked, her voice dropping close to a whisper.

Benedicta turned immediately to the desk and resumed her task. She held her breath in the silence that followed Bertrade's question, and imagined Amaury looking around the room to see who listened to this conversation. She kept her head down, intent on her jotting, grateful for her usually despised headveil, that hung over the edges of her face. 'We must be prepared to protect him from Henry de Normandy,' Amaury eventually responded in a low voice.

'It would help if we knew where the Count of Flanders stood.' Benedicta recognised de Bellême's voice. She did not dare to show any interest in the conversation and so had to imagine Amaury's shrug. 'Duke Henry means to win over Flanders with silver,' de Bellême said.

'Flanders may hold with us despite Henry's pieces of silver,' Amaury responded. 'And we can persuade young Fulk, my nephew, to support us with raids on Normandy. We are in contact with William *Clito*'s guardian Helias de Saint-Saëns. King Louis has determined on an aggressive policy over Normandy. He is not satisfied with the situation, that Henry gives him no homage for Normandy as he should.'

Benedicta's friend, Father Orderic, at the Abbey of Ouches, who was writing a history of the Normans, had once told her that unless curbed by the yoke of justice, Normans could be very unrestrained, and that another English historian, William of Malmesbury, wrote that without war the Normans hardly knew how to live. Did that explain why de Montfort and de Bellême felt compelled to contest King Henry's rule in Normandy?

'Henry has his bastard girls in legion, married off to our enemies,' de Bellême said, his voice laced with hatred. 'Even you, de Montfort. He thinks he has you in the palm of his hand, with this betrothal to de Meulan's daughter, whilst he seeks to advance the unjust claims of his own son, William *Adelin*, in Normandy and to crush the hopes of the rightful heir, his nephew William *Clito*. The prestigious marriage of his daughter Maud to Henry Emperor of Germany puffs him up further. He is rumoured to have sold the girl for an enormous dowry of 10,000 marks. The English must have been taxed to the hilt to pay for it. Might William *Clito* give homage for Normandy to King Louis since Henry has not done so?'

There was no voiced response and Benedicta did not know if Amaury had shaken his head or nodded. 'Temper your words, Robert,' Amaury said.

'It infuriates me that Henry holds Gisors against King Louis. *I* designed that castle! He has no right!'

'Peace, Robert. You are upsetting my sister's little dog with your passion.' The tone of Amaury's voice was deliberately urbane.

'We are not without friends at Henry's court or amongst those who have lands on both sides of the English sea. William Malet, William Baynard, Philip de Briouze, all stand with us,' de Bellême said.

Benedicta resisted the urge to let the stylus in her hand write down those names. She could not run the risk that someone would notice her sitting there in the gloom and come to look at what she was writing.

The more powerful and secure Henry became, the more de Bellême, de Montfort and d'Anjou regarded him as a threat to their own interests, their own frontiers. Besides if they could install William *Clito*, Henry's nephew, as a child duke, and later a duke who owed his rights to them, the boy would be pliable to their needs and demands. It occurred to Benedicta that these lords saw King Henry, despite his successes, as an upstart who was no better than them.

'We will take our leave of you until tomorrow, Bertrade,' Amaury said and Benedicta heard the men move towards the door. She glanced up to see de Bellême's back disappearing towards the stairwell and Amaury de Montfort making ready to follow him. She had not meant to make eye contact with either of them but, unfortunately, Amaury noticed her. He turned his gaze in her direction and Benedicta noted the fleshy beauty of his mouth and the intelligent dark green of his eyes. The razor had passed closely over his face, leaving a surface smoother than chalk. He looked very like his angel-faced sister. He smiled at her and her returning smile was automatic, unthinking.

Benedicta was astonished to find herself, after her thousands of days of quiet, dull repetition at Almenêches, in such a maelstrom of action. Whilst she was glad to be of assistance to the King and Countess Adela, she found herself moved by the pioneering spirit of Fontevraud and Prioress Petronilla. Benedicta had no time for those assumptions that all women are intent on tempting men into lust, which many clerics sermonised upon. Robert d'Arbrissel's mission to women was a breath of fresh air. The women at Fontevraud spoke of themselves as Robert's 'wives', his beloved ones, seeing themselves as living in spiritual marriage with him, as brother and sisters, as he helped them to reach the Kingdom of Heaven, no matter what their former lives had been, no matter what their sins.

'I heard that you were in the company of Lord de Montfort today,' Sister Genevieve whispered to her in the refectory. 'I've seen him across the courtyard twice.' Her voice was excited.

'Yes,' Benedicta said, modulating her own response to a neutrality but interested to hear what Genevieve might say.

'Handsome and charming, is he not?'

'As his sister, Lady Bertrade.'

'Yes. The two of them could charm the birds from the trees, so everybody says.'

'They *look* very fine,' Benedicta said, with circumspection, raising her eyebrows and Genevieve put her hand over her mouth to cover a titter of amusement at Benedicta's drollness.

Benedicta sat in her cell that evening contemplating her findings and sifting what she must convey to Countess Adela. She understood very well why de Bellême was an inveterate enemy of King Henry. They had been at loggerheads for years and the English King had convicted Bellême and his two brothers of treason, taken from them the Earldom of Shrewsbury, lands all over England and Wales, the vast riches that had accrued to the Montgommery family after the conquest of England. De Bellême's character, in any case, was well known to be cruel and belligerent. But she was perplexed at Amaury de Montfort. He had seemed urbane, intelligent, pleasant. He was, without doubt, the leader and stirrer of rebellion against Henry, but she wanted to understand why. A good spy should try to comprehend their quarry surely. She could not discuss the matter with Abbess Petronilla or Countess Bertrade, since that would raise suspicion against her. They would wonder why she was curious on this point. If she wrote to Haith or Countess Adela or put her question to Breri she would just receive their partisan view that Amaury was the King's enemy and raised rebellion against him. But why? She needed to know.

The following day she searched in the Fontevraud library for any documents that might throw light on her question, knowing, even as she did so, that she was hunting in the wrong place. Fontevraud was an Angevin foundation and close to the border with Aquitaine. There were charters and genealogies copied here pertaining to the noble families of those regions where Benedicta might hunt down *their* motivations and histories but that was no use to her. Amaury de Montfort was a Norman, or only just, since his lands were very close to the border with the French king. There was nothing in the Fontevraud library that could help her throw light on this perplexing man. She was frustrated in the matter.

A week later, Benedicta woke to a brilliant summer morning with a pale blue sky streaked with newborn clouds, long and wispy and pure white, and she woke with an inspired idea. Orderic. Of course! Why did she not think of it before. Her old friend Orderic Vitalis had many documents at his fingertips, collected from many great libraries, to fuel his history of the Normans. He had riffled through the parchment storehouses of Caen, Rouen, Le Mans, and so many more places. If anyone had an answer for her concerning Amaury de Montfort it would be Orderic.

She needed to write to him in cipher on such a delicate matter but she could not use her Ovid cipher. That would be too shocking for her shy, mild-mannered friend. She and Abbess Emma had spent several years living alongside Orderic, hosted by the monks at Ouches, after Robert de Bellême burnt down their monastery at Almenêches. Perhaps she could use another historian for the cipher. Orderic would be sure to have all of those books in his study. She looked again at the books at Fontevraud. Which one would also be in Ouches? She alighted on Dudo of Saint Quentin's *Historia Normannorum* and excited by the thrill of the chase, as any huntswoman would be, she sat down to write to Orderic.

I am working on a matter and would share some discussion of the text of Dudo with you, she wrote. Orderic might take this literally at first, but when he received her coded text he would understand, and she hoped he would burn this first key. She sent off this herald of what she hoped would be an illuminating exchange of letters with a travelling preacher who told her he was going in the direction of Ouches and would deliver her letter to Father Orderic. Next, she set about the more difficult task of writing her question to Orderic in cipher. This second letter was sent the following week with a merchant who was staying at the Fontevraud guesthouse on his way north. Now, she must wait impatiently for a reply. It could take months for Orderic to find the time to address her query, to research his answer. Then he would have to find a reliable courier. It was best that she put it to the back of her mind and thought nothing more of Amaury de Montfort and his motivations.

The Prioress needed to send a message to the Prior at Candes Monastery and asked Benedicta to call for Sister Genevieve.

'I could take the letter for you myself, Prioress,' Benedicta offered, thinking that she could leave a note for Breri. 'I am in need of some exercise.'

She concealed a brief note to 'Hawk', signed 'Ladybird', inside her red fleece vest and took the road to Candes, a busy trading centre at the confluence of the rivers Loire and Vienne. Benedicta revelled in such sights as she had been unaccustomed to during the last few months of her seclusion at Fontevraud. Boats, large and small, were moored at the wooden jetties. Men and boys unloaded sacks and barrels, while servants loaded goods onto donkeys. Fish traders called out their freshly caught wares, thumping mallets onto some still twitching fish as they did so. Reluctantly turning her gaze from the lure of the harbour, she made her way to the small monastery and delivered the Prioress's letter. Then she sought out the Bear Inn. Seeing a pole protruding from a house with a bushel hung about it she knew she had found the right place. She entered, swiftly found the landlord, and asked him to take her note. On her walk back, she worried at how on earth Breri was going to contact her without anyone knowing, so that she could deliver her cargo of information for the Countess.

Before sleeping, she perused her wax tablets, making sure she had all the information in mind that might be useful. Ovid's *Metamorphoses* was open on the table and Benedicta traced words and lines with a finger, retranslating back from the cipher. 'A lover stays up all night long,' she whispered to herself, quoting from Ovid's 'Love and War'. 'It is a lover's clever strategy to raid a sleeping foe/and slay an unarmed host by force of arms. Now you see me forceful, in combat all night long.' Hearing the words of the poem, Benedicta was astonished to find herself imagining Amaury's de Montfort's face close to her own, to imagine him raiding a sleeping foe, herself, forceful in … . She clapped a hand to her mouth and then to her eyes, not sure where best to place her defence.

With her eyes covered, she imagined Amaury with his back turned to her in Bertrade's rooms, his buttocks like firm, rounded hillocks. She slapped her palms down on the table to either side of Ovid's book. Her treacherous lips mouthed more words from another poem on the page before her: 'The girl entwined her ivory arms around my neck/and gave me greedy kisses, thrusting her fluttering tongue,/and laid her eager thigh against my thigh,/required my services/nine times in one short night.' Benedicta clapped *Metamorphoses* closed. 'Oh Lord, give me strength!' she cried out. She had heard the Countess speaking anxiously with Etienne and Thibaut about the charisma of Amaury de Montfort, and his power to suborn those who should be loyal to the King. Benedicta had never imagined that she would even look on him, let alone feel like this about him, imagine such things. She took out her rosary and bent over it with her eyes screwed shut for hours until it dropped from her weary hand and her eyes had closed in sleep.

Several days and nights passed and there was no sign of Breri. Perhaps she had missed him and it would be months yet before he passed this way again. Perhaps the Countess would deem her mission a failure. She went to midnight prayers and knelt on the cold stone, her head bowed, comforted by the thought that across the whole of Christendom, across the wide world, many others elsewhere were doing the same as she. She returned to her cell with her breath fogging before her and her cold fingers curled up inside her sleeves. She was startled by a low voice from a clump of trees beside the path. 'Ladybird!'

Benedicta looked behind and about her in alarm but saw no other person. She could just discern the glint of Breri's eyes in the gloom.

'I will follow you to your cell, Sister,' he whispered.

Benedicta swallowed. Now she was entertaining a man alone in her cell? Was there no end to her iniquity? She nodded and walked on swiftly, letting Breri slip inside the door ahead of her in the gloom.

He threw back his hood but retained his whisper. 'Greetings, Sister.'

'Greetings to you Breri. How did you get inside the compound? Are you staying in the guesthouse?'

'No. It's a large compound with a long wall.'

Benedicta regarded his portly form sceptically. She could not imagine him scrabbling over the abbey wall. Perhaps there was a gap somewhere or a fallen tree leant against it … .

'You have something to pass on to our dear friend, Sister?'

He meant the Countess. Benedicta had debated with herself what to tell, what not to tell, but how was she to know what would do harm, what would do good. It seemed best to simply tell the straightforward truth and leave the interpreting to the Countess and King Henry, and to God.

'De Bellême and de Montfort are plotting to support William *Clito*'s claim as Duke of Normandy against King Henry. I heard it confirmed with my own ears.'

Breri's eyes lit up. 'How on earth did you manage that, Sister?' His voice had lost its mocking edge and was tinged with a mild admiration.

'I am scribe to both the Prioress and Bertrade de Montfort. I was in the room for a conversation between de Bellême, de Montfort and his sister.'

Breri barked a laugh. 'Stupendous, *excellente*,' he said extravagantly in his Welsh lilt. 'I had no idea you were such a *superbus* spy. Yes, we have always thought that they conspired together, de Bellême and de Montfort. They shit out of the same arse, those two. Begging your pardon, Sister!'

Benedicta bit her lip and frowned at her shoes.

'And?' he prompted.

'They conspire with the new Count of Anjou and with William *Clito*'s tutor. They think the Count of Flanders may also support them, despite his treaty with King Henry.'

'You are a silver mine, Sister. Any other names mentioned?'

'They claimed to have support from William Malet, William Baynard and Philip de Briouze in England.'

'William Baynard,' Breri said, his voice alert. 'Are you sure you heard that correctly, Sister?'

Benedicta hesitated. What if she had it wrong and condemned a man unjustly. The King would verify the information, surely?

'That is the name I heard, yes.'

'This is of great value to the Countess, to the King. William Baynard has command of one of the three great castles of London and he commands the host of London. Not a person who should be counted amongst those disloyal to the King, eh?'

Benedicta made no response, her anxiety rising. She had hoped that it might be all rather something and nothing, but now it seemed of great significance.

'Did you hear any specifics of their plans?' Breri asked.

'No.'

'Very well then. Has that Robert d'Arbrissel gotten around to bedding with you yet, Sister?'

Benedicta flushed and yanked open the door of her cell. 'Please go,' she hissed.

'My apologies, Sister. I didn't mean to upset you. It's just the rumours.'

'He's not here at Fontevraud and there's no truth to those rumours.'

'If you say so. Nothing on the Earth moves faster than rumour, or travels less straight, eh, Sister?'

10

The Ransom

After several hours hard riding up into the foothills, we arrived at a hunting lodge. Owain lifted me and Angharad down from the horse. Inside the lodge, there was a separate room off the small main hall with a high, wide bed, and Owain told me to settle the children there. The men set about lighting a fire in the hearth in the hall but the place was freezing. We were frigid from the ride, our hands painful, our cheeks chapped red and flaky. I piled as many furs as I could find onto the bed and the three boys climbed in together, their teeth chattering, hugging each other for warmth. 'Henry, you are the eldest, and you will take care of your brothers now. We are on an adventure.'

'Yes, Mama.' He dropped his voice to a whisper. 'Will Papa come to get us soon?'

'Yes,' I whispered back, nodding and looking into each of their frightened faces. 'Very soon.'

'Mama, is Lina hurt?' asked William.

My thoughts flashed to Amelina's stricken face as she struggled to keep the children from the soldiers, and the horrible sight of the sword raised above her arm ready to swing down and sever it. I blinked the memory from my face, doing my best to look serene. 'She is well, William,' I told him, smiling into his eyes. 'She is with your papa, and soon you will be with them again.'

I sat on a stool, leaning my back against the side of the bed and fed Angharad, singing a soft song to calm the boys. Angharad stared into my eyes, sucking, blissfully unaware of her change of circumstance. Let Gerald be alive, I prayed silently and ardently. I laid Angharad in a makeshift cradle constructed from blankets on the floor beside the bed. By the time I laid her down, the boys were sleeping, tired out with stress. I smoothed the black curls on Henry's forehead and stepped quietly through to the main room to confront Owain.

He stood waiting for me, warming himself in front of the blazing fire. His men had disappeared, billeted elsewhere but no doubt within easy call. 'You should send the children back to Pembroke straight away,' I told him. 'My oldest son is the son of the King who will not brook risk to him.'

'You think I care about the Norman king? Don't you know that he is far away in Normandy? Send the children back you say, Nest, but not you?'

'You should send us all back, of course.'

He looked me up and down. 'It's warm in here now,' he said. 'Wouldn't you be more comfortable without that great cloak?'

My face was flushed but I shook my head. 'I'm fine. What do you mean by this affront? By coming in the middle of the night and stealing me and my children away like a thief.'

He was amused by my defiance. The firelight suited him, burnishing his thick hair, offering glimpses of the brilliant blue of his eyes. 'No thief, Princess Nest,' he said softly, greeting my anger with gentleness. 'I am a Prince of Powys. This heart pumps with royal Welsh blood, as does yours.' He slipped his own cloak from his shoulders and threw it to a trestle that was pushed up against the limewashed wall. 'My father's bard would tell you my lineage and your own.' He stepped close to me and began to circle me, as if we were dancers. 'Owain, son of Cadwgan, King of Powys, who is son of Bleddyn, King of Powys and Gwynedd, who was grandson of Maredudd, King of Deheubarth and Gwynedd, who was grandson to Hywel Dda, and he was the grandson of Rhodri Mawr, the Great King.' The sing-song of his Welsh was beautiful.

'Do you mean to mesmerize me like a lisping snake?' The relief of hearing and speaking my own language was enormous. For years, when I had first learnt French, I had struggled, unable to fully express my ideas.

He stood behind me and his laughter tickled my exposed neck where the black hank of my hair was gathered to one side and hung down the front of my nightgown to my hip. 'They told me you had a wicked sense of humour, Nest, daughter of Rhys ap Tewdwr, King of Deheubarth; granddaughter of Einon, who was grandson of Hywel Dda, who was grandson of Rhodri Mawr, the Great King.'

'Consanguinous lineages no doubt.'

He returned to stand in front of me. 'Ah, so you're thinking of marrying me after all, are you?'

All my life I had longed for a royal Welsh husband to save me from a string of Norman suitors and lovers, to give me my rightful place as a Welsh queen, to restore my identity to me. This man would have been my husband if the Normans had not invaded and killed my father. 'I am wed already.'

'That Norman nobody? I expect he's dead, don't you?'

The thought of Gerald lying dead and bloodied at Cenarth Bychan clutched at my heart but I kept my feelings from my face. He poured and held a beaker of wine out to me. I shook my head. 'I will retire now.'

'A pity,' he said, but let me go.

The following day we rode on further into the mountains. Owain gave me one of his tunics to wear over my shift and I cobbled together additional layers of wrappings for my children, but still neither I nor they were equipped for the cold ride and William and Maurice told me plaintively that they were hungry and freezing, whilst Henry gritted his teeth, suffering in silence. The soldiers muttered and I began to be alarmed at a growing sense that there was a lack of clear direction in Owain's plan. To these soldiers my children were Norman whelps. The Normans had shown no mercy to the Welsh and these Welsh warriors in their turn had no compunction to do any differently. All that kept us safe for now was my status and the ransom value of the King's son.

'Where are we heading to?' I asked Owain.

'Into the mountains.' His mood had turned sour with the increasingly bad weather. Snowflakes circled in the air and a bitter wind blew my hair into my eyes and pierced my cloak.

'Is there another lodge ahead? A village?'

'No questions!' he said, kicking his horse on abruptly.'

We came to another abandoned-looking building just before dark, this one in an even more ramshackle condition than the first. The soldiers had just succeeded in getting the fire to take and were warming some meagre supplies and a few rabbits killed in the woods, when we all turned to the drumming of a fast rider approaching. The man, jumped from his horse at the doorway and spoke rapidly and low with Owain there. A few of the men close to Owain, who could hear the words of the rider, looked displeased and stared in my direction. I took a deep breath as Owain came towards me. 'It seems that your husband, FitzWalter, lives. There was some uncertainty but it is confirmed now.'

I nodded, showing no emotion, and seeing no indication on his face of what this might mean. I kept silent.

'We have received a demand for your return and the return of your children,' he said, turning away from me, speaking in a low voice, as if speaking to himself. He walked back to confer with his men.

Although I could not hear what they said, their stances and the tones of their voices gave the impression that there was some dissatisfaction amongst them. I supposed that Owain had hoped that if Gerald had been killed in the attack, then he could take me as his wife, and the bards would sing of his prowess at besting the Normans, would make of us a new romance. What he had ever intended to do with my children, I could not think. It made no sense except to infuriate Gerald and the King and he surely had already succeeded in that. Although Henry was in Normandy he would soon know about our abduction and he would even now be giving orders for countermeasures. But would any of it be in time to save the lives of my children?

'The oldest boy! The King's son at least!' I heard one of the men shout at Owain.

I could stand the uncertainty no longer and I walked to the group of men, who turned to stare at me with hostility. 'What is it that you intend? I demand to know.'

'You demand!' Owain began, exasperated.

'Owain,' the man who had shouted patted the air in a conciliatory fashion, and Owain nodded to him. 'We are thinking to hand over the children in exchange for a ransom,' the man told me. They were hoping to avoid severe repercussions, was more the truth of it. 'An offer of ransom has been made.'

'From whom? On what terms?'

'Richard de Belmeis, King Henry's bishop and sheriff, has sent word that you and the children should be handed over to the Norman castellan at Cardigan Castle and a handsome ransom is offered for you. They offer the exchange at a place not far from here at daybreak tomorrow.'

'I didn't do this for a ransom,' Owain sneered. 'I'm not a merchant. I'll not lose face over it. I'd sooner hang them than return them.' He turned his back and stalked off. Several of the younger men followed him. The man who had spoken to me shrugged and looked anxiously at the remaining men. I returned to comfort the boys and to feed Angharad, my mind whirring at what this meant and what I could do, trying not to panic at Owain's threat. The older, wiser men, at least, knew that if any harm came to the King's son, and indeed to the family of the castellan of Pembroke, the Norman retribution would be harsh.

I set a sleeping Angharad down and told the boys to watch over her. I followed where I had seen Owain go and found him sitting alone in the cold hall at the long, scarred table. He was thumping his dagger repeatedly into the wood. He looked up at me, his eyes bleak. 'Well?'

'Will you accept this ransom offer tomorrow morning?'

'No.'

'What then?'

'I took you and I will keep you.'

'Will you let the children go to the castellan at least?'

He said nothing.

'Is it worth the retribution that you will bring down on yourself, on your father's kingdom?'

'Keep silent. I have not asked for your counsel.'

He was in a corner and he did not like it. It was not the outcome of his dashing raid that he had expected and now he sulked like a small boy who had not won a race. He threw the dagger from hand to hand, staring moodily at it. I could not leave the lives of my children in those hands.

'If I submit to you, will you hand my children over to the Normans in the morning?'

His hands stilled and he looked up at me. After a long moment of silence between us, he nodded his head.

'Give me your word,' I said, 'that you will return them unharmed.'

Lust hungered on his face, stopping his mouth. He nodded.

'Speak it.'

'I promise you, Nest. I promise you that I will return your children in the morning, unharmed. I promise you.' He stood swiftly and gripped my arms, meaning to embrace me, but I pushed him forcefully from me.

'No. Not now. When I see the children in the safekeeping of the castellan. I know his face.'

'Very well,' he said, his eyes intent, full of a suppressed triumph. I saw how he imagined that he could salvage something from this debacle, that he could bruit it about that the wife of the castellan of Pembroke, the Princess of Deheubarth, had given herself to him, how that would make him a hero in the eyes of the younger warriors.

Early in the morning I roused the children. I sat and fed Angharad again, longing to keep her with me but Amelina would find a wet nurse and they would all be safer returned to Gerald. I thought of him kissing me playfully on the stairs at Gaer Penrhôs and wiped a tear from the corner of my eye. I tucked a brief note to Gerald inside Henry's jerkin. 'Give this to your father,' I whispered in his ear. The short letter merely informed Gerald that I was well and glad Prince Owain had seen fit to grant my request and return our children to Pembroke. I could not run the risk of saying anything else that might jeopardise them if the note were discovered. I told them they were all going home to their father and I would follow soon.

We rode downhill again and emerged at the edge of the trees where a small unit of Norman soldiers were camped waiting for us. With relief I recognised Gilbert FitzRichard de Clare, who commanded Cardigan Castle on the King's behalf. My three little sons were deposited on the ground, ranged in front of the heavy Welsh warhorses, where they looked terribly small and vulnerable. I dismounted and carefully fitted Angharad to Henry's arms and kissed the top of his head. He was not yet five years old and barely strong enough to hold her. 'Walk carefully with her,' I whispered to him.

FitzRichard nodded to me, looking us over, seeing that we were all unharmed. He held up two bulging saddlebags and one of Owain's warriors kicked his horse forward, took the saddlebags and returned to sling them across Owain's pommel. We heard the chink of the coin within. 'Only the children!' Owain called to FitzRichard. 'Princess Nest of Deheubarth has opted to remain with her kin and countrymen.' FitzRichard looked at me in surprise but I kept my face expressionless. I saw him glance with uncertainty for a moment at little Henry. I knew that he would not risk the King's son in a skirmish with Owain's warriors. He nodded. I dipped my head and smiled encouragement to Henry and he stepped towards the Norman soldiers, holding his arms up awkwardly to keep his baby sister safe. His two brothers half-ran behind him, tripping on stones and over their own feet. Maurice, who was snivelling, looked back at me, and William dragged him by the arm to keep in step with Henry. I willed them on. Go, go! As they got close to the Normans, a hairy soldier jumped from his horse and took my daughter from Henry. 'Don't worry about the bairn,' he yelled to me. 'I've got three of my own.' I bit my lip, my eyes and mouth clogging with tears.

The children were lifted onto saddles and the horses wheeled away from me, with Henry bent round his saddle-companion to look back at me for as long as he could. I watched the road until the small cavalcade was no longer in sight. I turned back to Owain and a cloud passed over his face at something behind me. When I turned back to the road, I saw a messenger riding fast towards us. Owain took the scroll the messenger held out to him from the saddle. This messenger wore the blue griffin livery of Cadwgan. Owain read and frowned, turned his horse without speaking or glancing at me. Still clad in my nightgown, Owain's tunic, and Gerald's fur cloak I remounted and followed Owain.

11

Quandary

In her cell at Fontevraud, Benedicta set a flame to the wick laid in a small ceramic lamp filled with fat. When the wick burned steadily, she hung the lamp from a metal stand on her desk. The puddle of light produced was restricted, but she needed only a small area of illumination for the blank parchment before her. The flickering pool of light she sat in seemed to turn the darkness beyond to a deeper shade of black, to conceal the edges of the room and her narrow bed in the corner, where her headveil and wimple lay discarded. Everything, she thought, narrows down to this. Me, my thoughts, this blank page.

The study of Baudri's poetry at the Countess's court in Chartres and her own readings of Ovid's works had piqued her interest. She thought she might try her hand at writing something herself. She picked up her quill and dipped it in the brown gall ink she had made for the library supplies and wrote at the top of the page,

Under a waning gibbous moon,

She had spent some time looking at the moon this evening, as she did most evenings as she walked back after the compline service. She thought of the moon's shifts through its phases. Soon it would change to a waning crescent and then disappear altogether into black before emerging again with its waxing crescent, then waxing gibbous and then the splendour of the full moon. She thought of the full moon shining on leaves and grass, reflected over and over in the brook. She thought of Amaury de Montfort's face.

Benedicta shook her head. By what association? Why should she equate the full moon with him? The brilliant blond of his head perhaps. She frowned and returned to her poem. Under a waning gibbous moon. And now what? In the library, she had read about the Greek scholar, Pytheas, who claimed the ocean tides were controlled by the moon and she had studied a text by the Ancient Greek geographer, Strabon. He wrote that the sea swells with the rising moon and retreats with the declining moon. She pondered on the knowledge of flood-tides and ebb-tides, which had been so important for survival in her time as a small girl in Flanders. Bede wrote that the tide ebbed because the moon blew on the water.

It was hard to know the truth of the matter, she thought, but she had observed for herself the relentless to and fro of the waters, and the equally relentless roll of the moon from dark to light and back again. Now she imagined Amaury de Montfort lying on his back on a moonlit beach, rolling slowly onto one hip towards the sea to look at something before him. Was this a poetic metaphor that she should write down – moon – tide – Amaury?

In her imagination, Amaury now had his back to her. Was he looking at the swelling waves that might rise and cover him, listening to the rattle of the brown and white pebbles as the sea dragged them intermittently back and forth, back and forth? She imagined moving closer to the prone man, curious to know what he saw. As she moved closer in her mind's eye, she could see over his body, and she saw herself lying naked before him in the shelter of his broad back, the curve of his hip. She was the object of his gaze. Beyond her was the dark sea. 'Oh!' Benedicta put down her stylus, folded the parchment with its one paltry line of brown writing and stood up, looking desperately around her cell. Perhaps she should go out and walk before the midnight service, but perhaps she was moon-mad. Perhaps to expose herself to the moon would make matters worse. She was afraid to lie down on her pallet, afraid to close her eyes when even open they were determined to betray her.

The refectory was noisy with the clatter of plates and the low hum of speech. Benedicta sat alone, not wishing to gossip or speak to anyone today. She was perplexed. She pondered her experiences of Countess Adela's court where a woman exercised real power. Coupled with her experiences here at Fontevraud, where she saw the consequences of the injustices perpetrated against women, from the lowliest misused whore to the discarded noble wives, alongside the impressiveness of the rule of Prioress Petronilla and her staff of nuns – all these things gave her pause for thought. What was her own purpose? Her scope, her role? What could she achieve? The memory of her own naked, untouched body, reflected in the mirror at Chartres, floated into her mind. Unused and useless.

Benedicta shook the memory from her head, told herself she felt some zeal for her task as spymistress for Countess Adela and King Henry. It was an honour that such illustrious people should invest their trust in her. She believed, from Haith's accounts and her own observations, that Henry was a good King, was making all efforts to rule well for the people of England and Normandy. It felt good to have an endeavour that was necessary, that she could pursue with all her powers of observation and intellect. She must focus on *that*.

'Come to see me when you finish eating, Sister,' the Prioress told Benedicta at the morning meal. 'There is a letter for you.'

Benedicta smiled. It was likely from Orderic!

'The monk who brought this says it is from the monastery at Ouches,' Petronilla said, handing over the thickly wadded package to Benedicta and clearly curious about it.

'Yes. Father Orderic there was confessor to myself and Abbess Emma when we stayed at Ouches, after the destruction of Almenêches. We were there for two years or more.'

'Ah, yes. You keep in touch?'

'Yes. He is a historian and we write occasionally to exchange views on our reading matter.'

The Prioress clearly would have liked to be told more but Benedicta bobbed her head and left quickly, pushing Orderic's package into the safety of the tight sleeve of her underdress.

She walked briskly to the church for the terce service. After that she would have two hours before sext. Time enough. Leaving the church soon after, she made her way to the library and took Dudo's book from the shelf, concealing that in the more copious sleeve of her habit, and hurried to her cell. She needed privacy for the job of deciphering. She broke the seal and unrolled the parchment, looking at Orderic's spidery text tiptoeing many-legged across several sheets of parchment. Yes, he had understood her hint about the cipher. After an hour, she sat back from the labour of decoding and read Orderic's answer through in full.

Dearest Sister Benedicta,

You pose an interesting question and I have enjoyed hunting down an answer for you. I do not ask your reasons for posing this question but entreat you to take care and always to guard your soul in your endeavours.

I studied the genealogies and charters of the de Montfort family and know their history. The motives of men are never clear and straight but I hope that this answer will satisfy you. There are several grounds for enmity between these two men: King Henry de Normandy and Lord Amaury de Montfort.

First, they are close kin but in the eyes of Henry's family this should not be the case. Amaury is cousin to Henry through his mother, Agnes d'Évreux, who was cousin to Henry's father, Duke William (called The Conqueror or The Bastard, depending on your standpoint). Amaury's mother was abducted and forced to marriage by his father, Simon de Montfort. Henry's family continue infuriated at that and consider the de Montfort's claim to kinship with them, therefore, in great disfavour. The de Montforts, on their part, argue that they are descended directly and legitimately from Rollo (although in truth, Rollo and his descendents of Northmen had so many concubines it is hard to see how anyone might claim such a thing), whereas Duke William was the illegitimate son of Duke Robert of Normandy. You see, we are already swimming in the murky waters of old resentments, dear Sister Benedicta, and we have not reached the current generation yet!

Benedicta, leant back smiling to herself at Orderic's voice that she heard so clearly in his letter.

Second, When King Henry's father, Duke William, invaded England and made himself king there, Amaury's father was not amongst his supporters and so the family did not benefit, as so many other families did, from the invasion of my poor land.

Benedicta frowned at Orderic's own expression of alliances here. His mother was Saxon and his father a Norman clerk in the service of the Montgommery family, but he always thought of himself as English, as the underdog.

Amaury's father was one of the few Normans who gained no English lands and riches. I imagine there was some disgust at that.

Third, the seigneurs of the castles of Montfort and Epernon, close to the border with the French king, were vassals of the de Beaumont family who, as you know, abandoned their own allegiance to the French king in favour of King Henry. This left Amaury with a difficult decision. To follow his overlord Robert de Beaumont (known also as de Meulan), to the English court – where the de Montforts had no lands but might gain some – or to break with his overlord and keep his allegiance to the French court – where his sister's star was in the ascendant. Of course, he chose the latter, even though his sister's course was so fraught and is now done, and all her great power as queen is fizzled out with the death of her paramour, King Philip. Now de Montfort has recently jilted de Beaumont's daughter, Isabel, to whom he was betrothed long ago, and is negotiating a marriage to a princess of Hainaut so his alliances remain firmly this side of the English sea. And since that is so, he is a supporter of the dispossesed boy, William Clito, the son of the hapless former Duke of Normandy who languishes in King Henry's prison. I hope you are still awake, Sister! And I hope these are reasons enough for your probing mind!

She smiled and wished she and Orderic were in the same room, conversing, but this letter was nearly as good as that.

So it seemed that Amaury was out in the cold, in terms of the wealth that many Normans had reaped from the invasion of England. He was dependent instead on what the French King might choose to throw to him, and Louis had many other supplicants. De Montfort's only other choice would have been to eat his own gorge, to go cap in hand to King Henry, turn coat, as Robert de Beaumont and William de Warenne had done, and they had benefited so greatly from that. But Amaury had decided he would not do that. His enmity was fuelled by pride then? He felt that King Henry should treat him as kin. He saw others raised up to earldoms and counties, while he remained a plain seigneur and saw injustice in it since he was close kin to the dukes of Normandy, the counts of Évreux and a queen of France besides. He believed he was due more and that Henry was of a bastard line and an upstart. He is too proud that he has made a mistake with his allegiance and will not change it, Benedicta thought. How complicated men were. So she had reasons in plenty, but her question felt unanswered. He was still a most perplexing man.

At the Bear Inn in Candes, Benedicta was glad to see Breri's rotund form and cheerful smile as she entered the inn. She sat down opposite him. His cheeks were fat and stuffed like a hoarding squirrel. The innkeeper set a small jug of ale between them and two wooden goblets, and Breri poured for her. 'Sister Benedicta,' he said, 'I hope you are well.'

'Well enough.' She was impatient to get the business dealt with and return to Fontevraud, to her prayer and labour in the library.

'Well?' he asked. 'It's quiet today. We can talk here if we're quick about it.'

The year had been relatively calm until the summer. King Henry had been away in England for months seeing to matters in that part of his realm and leaving the administration of Normandy in the capable hands of Bishop John of Lisieux. However, the real defence of Normandy was entrusted to the King's sister, Countess Adela, to the network of spies that laced the duchy, including Benedicta and Breri. The situation for King Henry appeared to Benedicta to be quite positive. His daughter Maud had been betrothed to the German King at Easter in Utrecht and then she was crowned Queen in Mainz Cathedral in the summer. Eustace of Bologne had renegotiated the Anglo-Flemish Treaty with Count Robert of Flanders on behalf of the King.

Benedicta had felt some qualms when she heard that King Henry exiled William Malet, William Baynard and Philip de

Briouze for treason. He had acted on information *she* had supplied from conversations overheard at Fontevraud. It was the first time she had seen a direct consequence of her spying. William Baynard's command of Baynard's Castle had been given over to one of the de Clare family. Her deceit had directly led to the injuring of those three men – and based only on an overheard conversation. It had been bad enough acting as an informer at Almenêches with her friend, Abbess Emma, unaware of her treachery, yet now that seemed trivial. Now she must report on her friends and companions at Fontevraud, who were in many ways admirable and who had done nothing to injure her. Her spying was driving a wedge between Haith and herself since there was so much in her life she could not write to him about. She wished she could know for certain whether her spying was doing good or evil, whether she was simply seduced by her own need for stimulation or her vanity, a need to be of some importance.

William *Clito*, whose supporters upheld his claim to Normandy in defiance of King Henry, had survived childhood. In August, the King had sent Robert de Beauchamp, vicomte of Arques, to Saint-Saëns with orders to arrest the boy, but William *Clito* had been spirited away and nobody knew to where.

Countess Adela, through Breri, had asked Benedicta to try to find the whereabouts of William *Clito*. To betray three adult men to Henry's anger was one thing, but now she was asked to do something that might injure a child, a child who did indeed have the right to rule in Normandy, which his uncle Henry had usurped. She *had* overheard something pertinent, but should she tell it? She had debated with herself long into many dark nights, and often wished that she could simply return quietly to Almenêches and have nothing more to do with any of it.

'Sister Benedicta?'

'As you know, Breri, I am scribing for Bertrade de Montfort, and I have done my best in sifting through her correspondence, listening to conversations, but I can find no news of the Countess's nephew.' There, she had told the lie. She had no way of knowing whether her lie would protect the life and liberty of an innocent boy, or whether it would lead to more war and bloodshed.

Breri's cheerful expression fell. 'Nothing? No whiff?'

'There has been a great deal of talk of William *Clito* and his tutor, Helias de Saint-Saëns, of course, and Helias's betrayal of the King, but none of that talk has hinted at where they might be.'

Benedicta had heard Bertrade say, on at least three occasions, that they were fled to Flanders. Yet here Benedicta sat, those comments erased from her mind, presenting the sharp-eyed and razor-minded Breri with professions and expressions of ignorance.

'*That* is disappointing, Sister,' he said, holding her gaze, his face expressing a sour dissatisfaction.

She pressed her lips together and her eyes traced the meandering grain of the table.

'There is another matter we need you to look out for,' Breri said.

She raised her eyes to his face.

'We need proof of de Bellême's treachery – written proof. We think you are our best hope for gaining that, Sister.'

'I can't think how,' she said.

'I trust to your ingenuity, Sister. As does the Countess.'

12

Fire and Ash

Owain said nothing of our destination but there was a new purpose now to our ride. His father had clearly sent orders. I suspected that we were on the road to Gaer Penrhôs and only a few miles out from Cadwgan's castle. Owain directed us off the road and into the trees. 'We could ride hard and make Gaer Penrhôs before it is full dark, lord,' one of the soldiers called ahead to Owain. 'No. Something I have to do first,' Owain shouted back. 'We'll make camp at the lodge and ride into Gaer Penrhôs in the morning.' Again, I sensed disgruntlement from some of the men. We dismounted before another hunting lodge. Four men disappeared into the trees in search of supper. This lodge must be in frequent use since the hall was well-stacked with firewood and a good cooking fire was soon burning in the hearth. Owain took me by the wrist and led me into a chamber curtained off at one end of the hall where one of the men rose swiftly from lighting another fire in the small hearth there. He bowed to Owain and walked out without looking at me.

'Time for the ransom payment,' Owain said, smiling.

I had began to hope that the orders from Cadwgan would lead to my reprieve but clearly Owain had diverted from the direct route simply to take my promise from me. My stomach felt like jelly.

'It grows too hot in here already,' he said, throwing off his cloak. He whisked the cloak from my shoulders and I grabbed vainly at it, too late. He threw it on top of his own. He stepped

116

behind me, making me anxious that I could not see the expression on his face, the gestures of his hands, and could not prepare myself for what I might read of his intentions. 'Too hot by far,' he murmured behind me, his breath brushing the nape of my neck. Swiftly, he lifted the overlarge man's tunic up by the hem and pulled it over my head, leaving my hair in disarray. My nightgown beneath was unlaced and barely covered my breasts. I had left it so, while I had been feeding Angharad. I hugged my arms to me and began to pull the laces together with the shaking fingers of one hand. Owain reached over my shoulder and put his hand on mine as I fiddled with the laces. 'No need for that.' His voice was husky with desire.

My heart beat furiously beneath my arm as I held the nightgown closed across my breasts. I could see the dark patches of my nipples and the dark triangle of my pubis showing through the thin material. He stepped in front of me again, reached a hand to my cheek, stroking a lock of hair from my face. 'So beautiful,' he said. 'Nest?'

Gently he took my wrists, unprying them from their hopeless attempt to protect my modesty, holding my arms away from my body, staring at my breasts, my belly, through their thin covering. He dropped my hands, swiftly unbuckled his swordbelt, letting it fall to the ground with a clatter behind him. He untied the laces on his shirt and braies and pulled the clothes from him. I was breathing in and out swiftly, my breasts pushing at the fabric of my gown. I took in the unfamiliar details of his body. He was beautiful: young and lithe. A small scar followed the curve of one of his hips. His belly was flat and hard, his chest hairless. His skin was so white, it was almost translucent, except where he was heavily freckled on his arms and across his shoulders. His whiteness made his body look cold, like something blanched, found beneath a stone. He gripped me around the waist and pulled me to him and I gasped feeling the warmth of his unfamiliar body through my shift. He smiled, slid the loose nightgown from my shoulders, down to bunch at my waist, his mouth hungrily grazing on my milky breast. He pushed the nightgown further till it slid to my ankles, exposing me. He pulled a cloak from the pile where he had flung them, spread it on the floor, lifted me up as if I were a feather, set me down on the silky fur and entered me. I felt a kind of numbness, my mind trying to catch up with what had happened. His cries of pleasure were muffled against my neck and hair. My eyes were screwed tightly shut and a tear squeezed through at one edge and trickled coldly down the side of my head and into my ear.

I did not sleep. The fire was low and almost dead when pale light at last seeped through the window. Owain was sprawled naked on his belly on the fur-trimmed cloak he had spread on the ground before the fire; Gerald's cloak, I realized. I looked at the freckles spattered across his shoulders. His buttocks were firm and rounded. There were red raspberry patches on my breasts and sides where he had sucked at me. I was wet between my legs with him. I saw the shadow of a man cross behind the curtain and reached for my nightgown to cover myself. Owain mumbled, rolled over slowly, opening one eye and smiling slowly. 'Well ...' he said.

'*Yr wylan deg*,' I said to him in a voice that sounded dull in my own ears. 'O sea-bird ...' I expected him to take up the refrain, to complete the poem he had sent to me at Pembroke Castle, but he looked blankly at me.

Not him. He had not sent it. Then had it come from Gerald after all?

He reached for my breast but I moved out of his reach and stood. 'I need some proper clothes, Owain.'

He sat up, the rack of his stomach muscles rolling him easily from his sprawled position and he shook his head, laughing at me. 'As you wish, my lady. Your desire is my command. Soon, you shall have clothes.'

We rode into Gaer Penrhôs where Cadwgan stood waiting on the steps. His face was grim, but he greeted me courteously, glancing at my attire and then frowning at his son. A maid stood beside him. 'Gwen here will see to your needs, Princess Nest.' Should I demand my return to Gerald from Cadwgan? I did not know if the theft of me was Owain's sole initiative or the orders of his father.

An hour later, I walked down to the hall and took my seat

between Cadwgan and Owain. It was a relief to be bathed and wearing decorous clothing. Gwen had brushed my hair, sniffed at the smell of sex on me, and stared at the red marks on my body as I stepped from the lemon-scented bathwater. There was nothing I could do about that. Everyone would know I had lain with Owain, had dishonoured my husband. I would not weep in front of her, but I longed for the security of Gerald and knew I had lost him now for sure.

There was strain on Cadwgan's face, a scowl on Owain's, and tension in the air. We ate and made inconsequential and spasmodic conversation. I was famished. After the meal, Gwen led me to a cushioned seat by the fire. A bard strummed gently on a harp. Owain and Cadwgan remained in conversation at the table, and although I could not hear their words I could see what they spoke of Owain's gestures were dramatic. He threw his arms wide. Cadwgan looked coldly at his son. I surmised Cadwgan had not approved Owain's actions. Nevertheless, I supposed he would not undermine his heir, make him look a fool. Owain had put us all in an impossible situation. King Henry would be insulted, at least for Gerald and little Henry's sake, if not for mine, and he would not let the insult pass. Gerald was compelled to attempt to get me back and to take reprisals against Owain and his father. Cadwgan's position with his Norman neighbours, which he had played so carefully for so many years, was ruined.

After an hour of heated discussion, Owain rose and left the hall. Cadwgan came and sat close to me. 'I must apologise, Princess, for the inconvenience you have been put to.'

I raised my eyebrows at such a description, but said nothing.

'I am organising your return to your husband. As soon as I can,' he said, although there was an air of doubt about him as he said it.

'Was my husband injured in the attack on Cenarth Bychan?'

'The unfortunate … the unfortunate incident at Cenarth Bychan … .' Cadwgan reached for the right description. 'No.' He looked at me earnestly. 'I believe that Sir Gerald was not injured … physically.' He looked into my face. So, he knew. Owain had told him, or Gwen, or the soldiers accompanying Owain last night. I blushed and looked down at my hands.

'Your children are safely back there, I assure you, and you will soon follow them.'

'Thank you.' He rose and left me.

I worried at the question of whether I would be able to convince Gerald that nothing had occurred between me and Owain. I had not slept the night before, and the heat of the fire and the heavy meal made me doze. I woke with a start. I must have been asleep at the hearth for hours. The windows were dark and the day had fled. Owain crouched beside me, shaking my arm, Gerald's fur cloak slung across his shoulder. 'Quickly, silently,' he whispered to me, pulling me to my feet and wrapping the cloak about me.

'What?'

'Sshh.' He led me to the door and a view of two saddled horses in the midst of a small band of mounted men.

'But –'

'Sshh.' He hoisted me into the saddle. I looked up and fleetingly saw Gwen's face at the window above me, her mouth open, before Owain hauled my horse's head around. 'Grip,' he hissed at me. Automatically I did so, grasping the stiff leather of the reins between my fingers, bracing my legs tightly against the horse's flanks, just in time, before it lurched forward and we were thundering out the gateway and across the drawbridge at speed.

We rode away from the castle with the sea at our backs, up towards the foothills and then up, up into the mountains. There was no opportunity for conversation. The ten men who rode with us were amongst those who had raided Cenarth Bychan. The moon was a thin crescent sliver and the horses picked their way carefully along the steep paths in the dark. Black trees rose thickly on one side, and a sheer drop was barely visible in the gloom on the other side. After several hours of riding, I saw the outline of a few buildings ahead. We rode into a village, but many of the houses were in ruins, abandoned. A light shone in the window of only one small house, and we made for that.

Owain lifted me from the horse and I stumbled against him, every limb aching with the fatigue of the ride. 'Steady, Nest.' He took my arm and led me into the building. An old man and woman stood bowing a greeting to us. A fire blazed in the hearth and the woman set out wine and bread for us and for Owain's men. Outside, the men were stabling the horses. I heard the occasional neigh, a hoof striking the cobbles, men calling softly to each other in the dark. The old woman looked at me with shining eyes and patted my arm. She looked up into Owain's face with adoration. 'Gilda, my old nurse,' he said, laughing at her evident love for him. The old man, her husband, I noticed, did not seem so enamoured. Doubtless, if Cadwgan pursued us, they would suffer his displeasure.

'Owain, you need to tell me what is going on.'

'Sit,' he said to me brusquely, and pushed me unceremoniously down into a chair by the fire. 'Drink and eat.' He thrust a wooden beaker and a hunk of bread at me, and then reached for his own. 'No,' he said, after eating and drinking for a moment. 'I don't need to tell you anything.' He stood and went to speak to his men. The old woman smiled and nodded her head at me, her wrinkled upper lip slipping inwards to the cavern of her toothless mouth. After ten minutes, Owain returned and pulled me from the chair by the arm. His grip was hard and bruised me. 'Owain, you're hurting me.'

'Well this whole escapade is hurting me, I can tell you. In here.'

He thrust me through the door into a small room with a small bed. Evidently it was the sleeping place of the elderly couple. There was an unpleasant smell. 'I can't –'

'Stop whining,' he said. 'It's just for one night.' He pulled me towards the bed and began to undress me.

'No. I don't want to take my clothes off in here. There are fleas, lice.'

Owain laughed. 'Fleas! That's the worst you've ever encountered, is it? Keep your clothes on then.'

He pulled me down to sit on the bed, and kicked off his trews, retaining his shirt. He blew out the candle, pushed me back and lifted my skirts, preparing to get on top of me.

'No,' I struggled to push him from me.

'Keep still. I can't see what I'm doing in this pitch black. Stop aping the virgin.'

121

He slapped me lightly across the face.

'No!' I cried in a louder voice, wrestling with him.

'Christ!' He stuffed a wad of material into my mouth, his hood I guessed, and repositioned me with one hand, pinning down my wrists with another. He entered between my legs, forcing himself in, thrusting into me, crying out, careless that the old woman and man laying on the hard benches next doors, could doubtless hear him.

The following day we rode further up into the mountains of Snowdonia. I kept telling myself that I must think, must find a way but my mind refused to function. I could not think past the mere phrase: I must think. It was early spring and our path was frequently blocked by herds of sheep and goats and lowing cattle being driven up to the mountain pastures, coming from their winter stalls. Pigs, too, were being chased from their muddy sties in the villages and released into the woods to happily snuffle through the summer. The herdsmen and shepherd boys were leaving their winter homes in the valleys – the *hendrefs* – and moving up to their summer houses on the hillsides – the *hafods*. A great wave of goats and sheep crested the cliffs above the villages, making music with their bells, accompanied by the shouts of the herdsmen. In village streets, we had to stand aside and wait patiently as the herds moved up before we could continue our own journey, in their wake.

We rode into cloud and I felt the shifts in humidity on my skin. Turbulent streams rushed downhill and the sound of water was everywhere. The harsh sunshine cleansed the grubbiness I felt. Nevertheless, when I saw the blue-green of a high, small lake I asked Owain to stop and let me wash.

'It will be freezing!'

'Just for a moment. I need to wash my face and hands.'

He handed me down from the horse. At the edge of the lake, I dipped my handkerchief into the frigid, clear water and wiped my face and the back of my neck. Glancing behind me, I saw that nobody was looking in my direction. Owain was talking with two of the men. I lifted the front of my skirt and ran the cold cloth over my thighs and between my legs and dropped my skirts back down into position. Crouching, I cupped a mouthful of water. I looked out across the lake to the snowcapped mountain beyond and began to weep. I dipped the cloth in the water again, wrung it and spread it across my face, weeping into the wet cloth that was draped over my hands. I wept silently, my shoulders shaking. After a while I took the cloth from my face and stood up, smoothing down my skirts, and turned back to the waiting men and horses.

Owain hoisted me into the saddle, oblivious to my state. We continued on. I knew it was useless to question him in front of his men. I would have to wait until we were alone again, but there was no opportunity for several days or nights as we bedded down in abandoned barns, surrounded by the men. Owain held me with my back against his body and entered me from behind silently each night. I felt ashamed, like a cow tethered for the bull.

Eventually, we reached a village high in the mountains, where the men, women and children came out to watch our arrival. I heard the excited buzz passed from mouth to mouth. 'It's the Princess of Deheubarth.' 'The Prince of Powys has stolen the Princess from the Norman bastards.' Small boys ran alongside and ahead of us, repeating the news. The villagers pointed at me, and I heard murmurs of appreciation at my looks from both the women and the men.

'I need a head veil,' I said to Owain, who was riding in front of me. I felt exposed to the gawping and comments of the villagers.

He shrugged his shoulders and he called back to me, without turning in the saddle, 'I don't seem to have one of those about my person.' The two men to either side of him laughed appreciatively.

A young woman in the crowd, seeing and overhearing our exchange, stepped to the side of my horse, tugging at her own head veil. She handed it up to me and our hands and eyes briefly touched in sympathy. She stepped back, and pulled her rough, brown shawl up over her head.

I was shown to a comfortable house where a maid waited on me. Owain came to find me. 'Come, Nest. The villagers are holding a fire festival to greet Calan Mai.'

He led me to a great barn, where trestles were laid out with food and warmed drinks. The villagers were all gathering here with a great sense of excitement. A woman was lifted onto a trestle and sang. She had a pure, clear voice that raised the hairs on the back of my neck and brought tears to my eyes. She sang of loss. After a few minutes, some of the elders in the village began to join her song, in voices cracked with age, labour and emotion, and eventually the song swelled to include everyone there, including myself, in a great paean of loss and grief. We sang for Wales, and the song turned to defiance. All faces, including my own, ran with tears.

A small fire burnt at one end of the barn with a high pile of unlit torches before it. Many small children crowded together before the torches. An old woman – the oldest in the village, Owain told me – took the first torch from the pile and lit it, and then each of the children did the same, some of the littlest helped by their parents and looking rather afraid of their burdens. I thought, with pain, of my own small children and hoped ardently that they were safe now with Gerald. These village youngsters formed up a procession behind the old woman and walked out of the barn towards the centre of the village where a huge bonfire had been built. It was higher than the houses.

The old woman led the procession of children, with their flaming torches, through an opening at the foot of the bonfire, into the heart of the heap itself to set it alight. Then she hustled them all out swiftly, retreating from the curls of smoke. Everyone stood around the pyre waiting for the fire to catch. It was bad luck if it did not catch on the first attempt, and fuel at this time of year was hard to keep dry. We heard the fire before we saw it, a muffled rumbling from deep inside the pyre, then small licks of flame that ran swiftly, seeking each other, seeking the air, fanned by the wind, and then roaring bright up the whole great pyre.

The people bellowed with the conflagration and it warmed us and lit our faces and the inky black night surrounding us. Drums beat and whistles blew, voices were raised in song and people danced wildly, faster and faster around the flames. I flew in a dance, arm in arm with Owain, exhilarated. Might I be reborn with the May Eve? Could I leave behind my years with the Normans and become Welsh again, my Norman time cauterised from me?

Exhausted after a while, I shook my head as Owain continued

his whirling. I drew away from the dancing, a hand pressed to my side. I watched the embers running up into the sky and longed for my Norman husband, my Norman children, and for Amelina, and I knew that the little Welsh girl I had once been was gone. I could not find her in me anymore. I could not renounce my life with Gerald, which was my dear life now.

We stayed in the village for several months, but I could not discover its name from the circumspect inhabitants. They treated me with courtesy and kindness, but if I asked questions, they shook their heads and smiled apologetically. Everybody was loyal to Owain, or feared him. Some time into our stay, a party of Welsh warriors rode in, and at the meal in the hall Owain introduced me to their leader, his cousin, Madog ap Rhiryd.

'You're buggered, Owain,' Madog told him.

Owain laughed uneasily. 'Never that.'

'King Henry has put your uncle on your throne of Powys.'

Owain spluttered on his wine. 'What!'

'It's true. You've *really* angered King Henry, boy!'

'Henry's in Normandy.'

'And you think that stops him? That's too far for his reach? His instrument, Bishop Richard de Belmeis, has his orders. He released Iorwerth from prison and he's given him Powys. King Henry's new Normans at the castle at Cardigan – de Clares – they are hunting for you. You'll not be able to stay here. I'll help you all I can, but your father's powerless now.'

I noticed a certain relish to Madog's tone and wondered if Owain realised that Madog had ambitions for the Powys throne himself.

Owain frowned. 'My father is never powerless. He'll be cooking something. And so am I.'

'Oh aye?' said Madog sceptically.

The next morning, I woke nauseated, threw the blankets from me, rushed to an empty chamber pot in the corner of the room and spewed into it. 'What is it?' Owain called from the bed. 'Are you ill?'

'No, I am with child. Your child.'

'Really?' he beamed at me and I felt a wave of depression. 'Let's call him Llewelyn,' he said.

125

'I have to stay here,' I told him. 'I can't keep on with hard riding in the mountains in my condition.'

'We can't stay still.' He frowned. 'I'll think of something.'

Owain's thinking of something came to nothing. Despite my condition we were soon on the road again.

'What is your plan?' I asked him.

'Don't worry your head about it.'

I bit back an angry retort. King Henry had seen fit to worry my head about his business, and so too had Gerald, but Owain told me nothing.

We passed through several mountain villages, never staying more than three nights anywhere. We were moving back from the highlands of Powys, towards Ceredigion. We arrived at a village where a group of riders in Cadwgan's livery stood waiting for us. Owain scowled like a boy who had been caught red-handed stealing apples. Cadwgan's men entered a hall with us where a maid fussed around, making me comfortable at the fire. The men glanced at my swelling stomach. They sat some way off, talking with Owain. I decided I had had enough of being kept in the dark and edged my stool nearer so that I was within earshot.

'If her husband had died in the raid on Cenarth Bychan,' Morgan, the leader of Cadwgan's men, was saying, 'you could have married the lady, but –'

'You think I would marry her anyway,' Owain interrupted, in an astonished voice. 'A Norman whore? First the whore of one Norman – king or no, and then another.'

My hands stilled above the embroidery in my lap and I kept my eyes upon it but knew the men had turned to look in my direction.

'Hush, Prince,' Morgan said in an astonished tone. 'The lady hears you.'

The whole thing had been an assault on Gerald, against the Normans, and never a desire to rescue me, to have a royal Welsh bride, to ally with Deheubarth. I had suspected as much, but I had not really allowed myself to fully believe it until I heard him speak it. I stood up, flung the embroidery from me, swung my stool to the trestle where they sat, placed myself opposite Owain.

'What is it?' Owain's voice and face expressed irritation.

126

'Continue,' I commanded Morgan, fixing my eyes on Owain.

After a brief pause, Morgan continued to speak, addressing Owain. 'Your father has surrendered to King Henry and he has been deprived of all his lands. Your uncle Iorwerth rules in Powys.'

Owain scowled, looking at the table. 'Well, what am I to do about it?'

'Your father counsels you to hand the Lady Nest to us and we will convey her to her husband, then he suggests you seek refuge from the King's fury in Ireland. He believes, given time, King Henry will relent and pardon you and your father and the lands will be restored.'

Owain looked up. 'Hand her back in that condition!'

Morgan glanced embarrassed at me, his face flushing a blotched red. 'It makes no difference,' he said. 'These are your father's commands.'

'Very well,' Owain muttered in a low voice.

Morgan stared at Owain for a few moments and then turned to me. 'We will ride out at first light tomorrow, lady. Will you ready yourself?'

I nodded, not looking at Owain.

'We can go at a slow pace,' Morgan told me. 'Or would you prefer to travel in a carriage, my lady?' He was relentlessly courteous to me, making me feel the stab of Owain's words all the more. A Norman whore.

'I can ride, slowly,' I said. The thought of being jolted in a carriage on these treacherous mountain paths was not appealing.

I retired to my chamber early and sat, staring into the fire. It would take a few weeks perhaps to progress slowly back to Pembroke, to Gerald. And what would my position be there? As a married woman who had slept with another man, I would be judged complicitious whether I was willing or not, whether I had been coerced to it for the sake of my children's lives or not. I had heard of some married women judged to be fornicators who had been buried alive but most courts were more lenient and simply imposed a fine. Such things were seen as the woman's fault, unless she was a virgin. The most likely outcome of any legal proceeding was that *I* would have to pay a fine for allowing

Owain to have carnal knowledge of me. And how would Gerald react? I could not bear to think of it. He would take me back. The King would insist on it, probably. It was the best that could be done to save face for all of them. As if there were not shadows enough between Gerald and I from our past, now we would have to try to cope with this.

I did not want to return to Gerald in this condition. Perhaps I could persuade Morgan to leave me at Carew and ride on to fetch Amelina to me. He seemed a considerate man. Then I could birth the baby and return to Gerald after that. I could not give up the child that kicked against the hand I pressed to my side. Gerald would have to accept another cuckoo in his nest. But it would be easier for him to accept me if I did not arrive with a belly full of another man's whelp, if I did not birth that child in his earshot.

13

Helen of Wales

Satisfied with my plan to birth Owain's child at Carew and then return to Gerald, I decided to get some sleep before the long journey with Cadwgan's men in the morning. I took off my dress and climbed naked into the bed. Despite the cold season, I was hot at night and found it difficult to sleep with the growing mound of my belly in the way, whichever position I took.

Nevertheless, I must have slept, because I woke to pitch blackness in the room and an awareness of Owain swearing at having stubbed his foot against a table. 'Dammit! Nest are you awake?' he hissed.

'Yes.' I was groggy.

'Quick, get up. I can't strike a light. You'll have to fumble about and find your shoes.'

'But … .What?'

'Shut up. Just do it,' he hissed. He had reached the bed now and pulled me from the covers. 'You naked hussy,' he said, pausing briefly to stroke my swollen breasts and stomach. I batted his cold hands away from me. 'Here.' He found my nightgown and pulled it over my head, pushing it down over my swollen body to swing against my calves.

'But Owain …'

'Later,' he said. He pulled me by the arm towards the door.

Outside, there was a little light coming from a torch at the end of the passageway. He bent and slipped my feet into my boots, which he had found in the dark and carried out under his arm.

He pulled the fur cloak about my shoulders, tying the thongs together. It had long ago lost Gerald's scent.

Slowly, after my bewilderment of waking in the dark, I realised what was happening. 'No, no.'

He stared in my face. 'Keep quiet, Nest,' he threatened.

'Morg ...' I started to shout but Owain thrust a hand roughly over my face, slipped the scarf from his neck and tied it tightly around my mouth, gagging me. It tasted of smoke and sweat. He pulled me out into the bailey where two horses stood, held by his man.

'Are you sure you will go alone, Prince?' the man asked, hoisting me into the saddle.

'Yes, it's best. I don't want my father punishing you for my decisions.'

It is too late for that delicacy, I thought. Cadwgan would doubtless hold all his men accountable for aiding Owain's attack on Cenarth Bychan, and for their support of their prince on the run with me in the mountains. Owain grasped my horse's bridle and led us to the gate.

The man ran to open the gates for us, they squeaked in the darkness, and then we were out and across the drawbridge. I looked over my shoulder but the hall was dark and silent and no alarm was raised to halt our departure.

When we were some distance from the keep, Owain pulled the scarf from my mouth. I spat on the ground and he passed me a water bladder. 'Sorry,' he said. 'If I'd allowed you to shout, there would have been bloodshed.'

'I can't ride fast, Owain,' I croaked.

'I know, I know.'

Despite his reassurance Owain led us at a hard pace along a narrow path through the forest, and then we were descending. I knew better by now than to ask him anything. He never did me the courtesy of explaining his purpose to me. We rode for days, and I was exhausted. 'Owain, I will lose this child if we continue like this.'

'I have no choice. What would you have me do, surrender like a coward and be executed by your King Henry?'

Surely fleeing like this, against the command of his father, was the action of a coward? I remembered the courtesy of Duke Robert withdrawing from warfare against Henry because Queen Matilda was suffering with a difficult pregnancy nearby. The Duke was languishing in a prison now. I wondered where Henry was at this moment. Did he think of me? What would he think if he saw me riding fast, my big belly full of Owain's baby. I blinked. My hands on the reins were clenched so hard I could hardly flex them.

We came at last to a small village that looked out across the broad expanse of Ceredigion Bay. Owain left me in the charge of a family loyal to him. They watched me closely, like jailors, and I could barely gain a moment alone. There was no hope of sending a message to anyone, but who would I send it to in any case? What could I say? When Owain returned, some weeks later, his cousin Madog and many soldiers were with him, and they herded a small pitiful group of men, women and children chained together. 'What is this?' I asked the woman standing beside me.

'Slaves, bound for the Dublin market,' she said. 'Your lord will make a pretty penny off that.'

I stared at the captives aghast. I lifted the hem of my skirts and made my way down to the bailey. There was a stench of shit, sweat and fear coming from the group of prisoners. 'Owain!'

'Shortly, dear. Busy right now.' He sped past me.

I turned to one of the soldiers guarding the captives. Children with grimy tear-stained faces looked at me. A vacant-looking young woman with streaks of blood on her apron was being held up by a young boy next to her. 'Who are these people?' I whispered to the soldier. 'Where are they from?'

'They're from Llansteffan, lady. Your lord just made a very good raid there.'

'No! You,' I called softly to a small boy standing near the edge of the group. 'Are you from Llansteffan?'

'Aye, my lady.'

'But you're Welsh ...'

'Aye. Some of 'em,' he gestured over his shoulder to the miserable group, 'are Normans.'

'Lady Nest?' A man with a blood- and mud-smeared face jostled his way to the front of the group where one of Owain's soldiers threatened him with a sword. After a moment, I realised I was looking at Dyfnwal. Amelina's Dyfnwal.

'I will do what I can for you, Dyfnwal,' I promised him, in an ardent whisper.

I spun around, searching the crowd in the bailey for Owain. 'Owain!' My tone was peremptory. 'What is this?'

He glared at me. Grabbed my arm and pulled me into the stables, away from curious eyes.

'Do not dishonour me in front of my men, Nest, or princess or no, I'll give you a whipping.'

I clutched at my stomach, flinched at his words.

'I apologise,' I said. I needed him to answer me. 'It was thoughtless of me.' There was blood on his clothes, a streak on his neck, blood ingrained in the fingernails that gripped my arm. 'Someone told me these captives are from Llansteffan, from my land, but that cannot be true.'

'Your land! My land now, darling. Yes, they come from a raid on Llansteffan.'

'You took Norman and Welsh alike.'

'Aye.'

'You intend to sell even the Welsh into slavery?' I stared at him in disbelief.

'They are all collaborators. It's what they are fit for. I warn you, Nest, keep your nose out of my business and cease your questioning.' He dropped my arm and strode from the stables. I stared at his retreating back and at the captive boy and Dyfnwal beyond, who had watched our exchange. They returned my gaze with bleak eyes. I turned and moved back into the hall the other way. I could not face going past the group of captives again. What could I do? I was a captive myself.

At dinner, Owain, Madog and their men vaunted their success. They had slaughtered the Norman garrison at Llansteffan including the Fleming lord William of Brabant. I knew him. He was a great friend of Haith's. I felt as if I had stepped off the edge of a cliff into air, all reference points severed, and I was falling. Just falling. What was Gerald doing and thinking, knowing that I was with Owain, that Owain was raiding my lands? In the morning I heard, but could not look, when the soldiers moved the miserable crowd of captives out to the boats of the waiting slavers.

Madog was away the following day, and rode back into the bailey at a gallop, his horse skidding dangerously close to a small girl playing there. 'Owain!' he yelled. Owain came running from the stables and walked into the hall with his head close to Madog's, his arm around his shoulder. I moved from the doorway where I had watched Madog's arrival, and where they had passed me without a greeting. Keen to know what was happening I ignored their discourtesy and sat down next to Owain.

'Jesu, Owain, you've gone from bad to worse!' Madog exclaimed.

'How so?' Owain jutted his chin stubbornly.

'King Henry's taken great umbrage at your latest raid. He's taken Cadwgan to England in chains and Iorwerth is on his way here now. You'd better get out without delay.'

'Nest,' Owain told me, 'order the household to pack up and move off and get yourself ready to leave within the hour.'

I stood and moved to the stairs. I wanted to run, to get away, but how, when I was so weighted down both physically and in my mind by the inescapable bulge of my stomach. I cried tears of frustration, feeling betrayed by my own body. Owain waited for me to place his cloak around his shoulders when he came into the chamber. 'We'll leave now.'

'But Owain, do you trust Madog? Have you verified his report?'

'You talk nonsense, woman.'

'Richard de Belmeis sets your kin one against the other, with your uncle Iorwerth displacing your father. And Madog is also your kin who might stand to gain from your loss.'

'I did not ask your counsel.'

We were out on horses in no time and I turned in the saddle to look at Madog standing with his hands on his hip on the top step of the keep. 'Owain, did you tell Madog where you were heading for?'

He turned and looked at me and then back to his cousin standing there. 'I did.' He looked ahead, staring into space for a moment. 'Very well. We'll go a different route. In case.'

We reached the coast at nightfall and there was a small fishing boat waiting for us on the beach. When I understood that we were going to cross to Ireland, I was aghast. 'Owain, I can't. I can't cross the Irish Sea in a tiny boat, like this!' I gestured at my stomach. The fishing crew of four men, stood at some distance, watching us argue.

'Nest, you do nothing but complain. If it weren't for your brother, I swear I'd abandon you, leave you here right now.'

My mouth was open ready to continue arguing with him, but I closed it abruptly at mention of my brother and stared at him. 'What do you mean about my brother?'

'Just get in the boat. You will see him soon enough, God willing, if we survive the crossing.' He lifted my arm, pushing me towards the boat and I clambered in. He whistled to the crew and they came and hefted the small boat off its grounding and climbed in, their leggings wet to the knees. Owain sat next to me, his own trews and boots soaked.

'You should change your clothes.'

He laughed. 'Lord, my little princess, what you don't know about life. We'll all of us be soaked from head to foot shortly, I assure you.'

Alas, for once, he was right. The crew were skilled but the boat was perpetually rocked and with each deep tip of the waves, great gouts of water were sent over the sides of the ship and over us. The boat pitched and rolled and fell down high waves. The vessel was awash, our hair was plastered to our heads and faces, our clothes dragging on us like iron weights. For the first time, I was at sea where there was no sight of land. The grey swell surrounded the small boat on all sides, battering us, rising up, threatening to swallow us. The mast shuddered and the sail tore in the incessant gale. The lanterns were all doused. I shivered and spewed over the side, shivered and screamed as another large wave approached, gripped at Owain, and spewed. It went on like this in the darkness for hours and hours. Eventually, I must have fallen asleep with the exhaustion of it. I woke, my head against Owain's shoulder, blinking, unbelieving, at a blue sky and land before us.

There were men with horses on the beach, black outlines in the pale morning light. The men and Owain leapt from the boat again and hauled it, with me, onto the strand. Owain and one of the fishermen took a hand each and helped me step unsteadily onto the sand. I looked at the horses.

'Owain, I can't. I need to rest. I need to stay here a while.'

'You can't stay on a beach, dripping wet and freezing.'

'Then a cart. I can't ride.'

'Well, there's no option,' he said, hoisting me up and settling into the saddle behind me. 'We're not going far. I'll hold you. You're fine.' He slapped the horse's rump and we took off at a slow pace. The fishermen and their battered boat on the beach were soon out of sight.

We rode for half an hour and there were the walls of a city rising before us on the plain, with large corrals full of horses. 'Dublin,' Owain told me. There were many ship masts in the waters before the city.

We rode up the steep and aptly named Fish Street, which was lined with pungent fish market stalls. People stared at us in silence, the merchants with scales and weights in their hands, the customers with baskets brimming with iridescent fishtails and goggling fisheyes. I glanced at a child playing with a toy ship underneath one of the trader's tables. I thought I would drop from the saddle with fatigue. 'Here,' Owain gestured to a great doorway to one of the grander houses at the top of the street. He spoke with the guards and they allowed us entry. In the bailey, servants ran out to take our horses and help me from the saddle. 'Owain, I need to lie down. I am unwell.'

We entered the hall and two women took me by the arms and helped me up a winding stone staircase and into a small chamber where I collapsed onto the bed. The maids fussed around me, chattering in an unknown language. Irish or Norse, I could not tell. They stripped off my wet clothes, exclaiming at the great mound of my stomach. 'My child is coming,' I groaned to them but they did not understand me. 'Owain, Owain!' I cried out as loudly as I could. He appeared in the doorway, a beaker of wine in his hand and a flush on his face. The maids screeched and covered me with a sheet at sight of him. 'What now?'

'The child. The child is coming and they don't understand me.'

135

'Oh.' He stared at me nonplussed for a while, took a sip of wine, and then finally said, 'I'll find a translator … and a midwife.' He stumbled off, and I wondered if he would instantly forget about me. My waters broke and rushed out, soaking the dry nightgown they had just put on me, and the bed I sat on, so that there was no longer any need for a translator. A woman, a lady by the looks of her, came in and took charge. She issued orders and the maids ran out, returning swiftly with bowls of steaming water and clean cloths. Another woman, a midwife I supposed, came in, rolling up her sleeves. She washed her hands and positioned me on the edge of the bed. I clung to the bed strut like a woman shipwrecked, my body wrenched by contractions, faster and harder than anything I had known with the births of my other children. The women mopped my brow, filled the room with bunches of pungent rosemary and lavender, spoke soft reassurances to me in their language. I let out a first scream and then many more. The sounds of music, shouts and laughter from the men in the hall beyond died down into silence; the silence of listening. I could not care. Let them hear me screaming. My attention was all focused on the excruciating clench and twist of my muscles and the brief respites from pain in-between.

It was the longest labour I had ever experienced, going on into the following day, and then when the baby finally slid from me, purple and silent, the pains continued and the midwife and maids were exclaiming excitedly. The midwife held up two fingers to me. In my exhausted state, it took me a moment to understand her. The second baby arrived soon after his brother and with much less difficulty, and I lay back, panting on the pillows, my mind washed of everything. I could barely remember my own name.

Owain was elated. 'Two boys!' he exclaimed. I was too tired to respond. I had held my sons briefly and wept over them, but now they were washed and tucked up in the cradle beside me, head to toe, with Owain peering at them. 'Llewelyn and Einion,' he told me. He exclaimed at the boys' tiny fingers and perfect ears. He sat down on the bed, making me flinch at the jolt to my sore body. 'You don't look well, Nest.' I closed my eyes instead of responding. 'You need to look better than this for your brother.' I opened my eyes and stared at him. 'He's coming tonight,' he said.

I struggled to raise myself against the pillows. 'Tonight?' My voice was a croak, exhausted from hours of screaming. I reached for the beaker of wine on the table beside me. 'I can't … tonight. I need. …'

'What would you have me do? I can't put him off. He wants to see you and his nephews, and he and I need to talk strategy. How we will oust all these upstarts from our lands.'

I took another sip of wine and frowned. If my brother was relying on Owain as his fellow strategist, he had already lost. I was too tired to think. 'I will sleep before he arrives,' I said.

'Very well.' He patted my hand. 'I hope a few hours' sleep will revive you. You look like your own mother at the moment.'

I kept my eyes clenched shut. My own mother. An image of her in the attack on Llansteffan rose into my mind. I could not allow myself to react to his words. He patted my hand again but I pulled it away swiftly. I could not bear his touch or the rank sweat smell of him. 'Leave me,' I said on the verge on hysteria and heard him walk from the room, banging the door behind him and startling the babies awake. He was greeted by a rousing chorus of men slapping him on the back and shouting toasts in the hall beyond. The midwife resettled the babies, and I closed my eyes again.

I woke with a start to see a young man, no more than twenty, black haired, blue-eyed, approaching the bed, smiling. My brother Gruffudd. The last time I had seen him, he was a baby himself. He looked so like our father. I struggled to raise myself against the mound of soft pillows, and he hurried to assist me. 'Nest!'

'Gruffudd! I thought I would never see you.'

He hugged me as if we had known one another all our lives. 'Nest.'

'She's not looking her best right now … understandably,' Owain said behind Gruffudd, and my brother glanced at him, frowning, and then went to peer into the cradle.

'May I?' He beamed down at the babies, shaking his head in wonder. 'My nephews!' he said, looking up again at me.

Owain, tiring of familial mawkishness, told him, 'I'll be in the hall when you're through.'

Gruffudd sat gently on the edge of the bed. Despite the familiar lines of his face, his clothing and jewellery looked strange to me. Dublin was famous for its metal-work. He wore a large, silver Viking-style brooch, and rings and armlets decorated with the Norse gripping beasts.

'I wish I were not lying here for our first meeting,' I said, wiping my face.

'Why so? How wonderful to see you and suddenly two more in the family!'

I saw a cloud pass over his face and knew that he was thinking: two more bastards in the family. Did he see me a woman steeped in venery? 'Tell me about yourself. You are a friend of Owain's?'

'Yes. He and his father are here often. I've known him all my life.' There was a silence between us.

'You know what has happened?' I asked hesitantly.

'You mean with Owain … with your … husband?'

I nodded.

'I heard about it.' He looked embarrassed. 'It seems that Owain's plan went awry. He hoped you would be free to marry him after his raid, rather than … .' His words petered out.

Rather than this shame, he meant. 'Tell me about you.' I saw there was no profit in lingering on my own situation.

'After our father was killed, the King of Dublin took me under his protection and I am in the household of his son, Raegnald. This is his house.'

'Raegnald?'

'Yes, the son of King Thorkil.'

I stared at him, drinking him in, tracing every feature with my gaze. My brother. My family. All that remained of us. 'So you are a fighting man,' I said.

He nodded proudly. 'I am. And I mean to fight for my rights.'

I smiled but my stomach churned at his words. His rights. Gerald stood between him and his rights. Henry would defend against his efforts to take his rights. I wanted to ask him what support he had, what plans, but this was not the time. We fell to speaking of Deheubarth, since he had never been there. We carefully avoided mention of Owain, my Norman husband, or my current situation as Owain's hostage mistress, mother of his bastard sons. It was hardly to my credit.

'I am weary of exile, sister, and must return to my patrimony soon.'

'Gruffudd, you would do well to know clearly the situation in Deheubarth. The Norman lords have a strong grip on the land. There is a Flemish colony –'

'I know all this, sister.'

'Gruffudd, you are the only brother I have left. I would not lose you.'

'You will not.' He put his hand softly to my cheek. 'You need to rest now.'

'Gruffudd, do not underestimate the Norman lords in Deheubarth. They have become strongly entrenched in the years since our father died.'

He said nothing.

'Gruffudd, I heard of our brother Cynan's death at the hands of Bernard de Neufmarché, drowned in a lake after the battle where our father died. Goronwy was beheaded on the beach. He was thirteen years old. Then Idwal, they sent him to a dungeon in chains for many years of suffering. He died a few days after I was able to secure his release.'

'You did what you could. A woman has no weapons.'

'A woman has weapons!' I said to him fiercely, and he looked away from me. 'I do not tell you this litany of woes for your forgiveness that I could not save them. I tell you because I wish to save *you*. The Normans rule through fear and cruelty. They do what they must to keep what they have taken.'

'As will I.'

I closed my eyes. I was merely making him dig further into his position. He would have to find out for himself how bad the situation looked for him in Deheubarth. 'Will you do me one favour, Gruffudd?'

'If I am able,' he said cautiously.

'Owain raided my lands at Llansteffan recently and means to sell the captives as slaves here.'

'Yes, I know. He is giving me a quarter share since Llansteffan is my land.'

'Our mother left Llansteffan and Carew to me as my dower,' I told him.

He shrugged.

'Gruffudd, half of those captives are Welsh, not Norman.'

'What of it? They are collaborators.'

'My maid's husband is amongst the captives, a fisherman named Dyfnwal. Can you get him released for my sake?'

'I can't cross Owain. A young man will fetch a good price in the slave market.'

'Gruffudd, please. I ask this one thing of you. I will pay for him.'

'But what money do you have, sister?'

'I have this. I will pay with this.' I undid the clasp of the chain at the back of my neck and held Gerald's small silver cross out to Gruffudd. 'Please.' It had been the first gift Gerald had ever given me and I had cherished it for many years.

'I will try,' he said, taking the cross and studying it. 'If I can purchase him with this, I'll send him to you but I warn you, keep him from Owain's sight.'

I was able to rise from my bed a few days later and sat by the fire in the hall, with Raegnald and his wife, Owain and my brother. Slowly, I swilled wine in a wooden cup, mesmerised by the shifting reflections of pale sunshine on the meniscus of dark liquid. I had recovered my strength quickly after the births but as I revived, my tiny babies sickened. That morning, I had washed them in warm water with rose petals and salt with the help of the maids and done my best to feed them, but the midwife had insisted on calling a priest to baptise them immediately, and I saw from her dark looks that she thought they would die. The priest had arrived tolling an enormous, rectangular handbell, and added greatly to the growing sense of hopelessness with his gloomy face.

'They call you Helen of Wales in the streets, sister,' Gruffudd said, trying to dispel my dark mood. I saw Owain puff up at that. He liked that idea, that his sordid behaviour was somehow akin to a Trojan hero and I was a famous beauty from a Greek story.

'People in France drew the same parallel for Bertrade de Montfort,' I said, feeling argumentative, 'when King Philip stole her from her husband. None of these thefts came to good. They were merely excuses for war.'

I stared at Owain, and he stared back stonily at me, angry that I had punctured the notion of a romantic elopement. 'It goes to show that the beauty of some women must be blamed for many wretched things in the world,' he said.

'Must women always be unjustly blamed for men's choices and actions then?' I looked away from him and into the fire, too weary to argue, and not wishing to further embarrass my brother, who was caught in the midst of the miserable eddies of tension and growing dislike between his friend and his sister. I was sad to see how close in friendship my brother was with Owain. Gruffudd was addressed by Raegnald and all the men there as Prince, but I knew he would have a harsh fight to earn that title.

'Any news from Powys?' Owain asked Raegnald, who was reading a long scroll just delivered to him.

'Your cousin, Madog, has murdered his and your uncle, Iorwerth. Set his hall on fire with him in it,' Raegnald said with relish.

Owain smiled slowly. 'Iorwerth should not have presumed to take my father's throne. My throne.'

I looked into the dead eye of a fish shrivelling on a nearby table and put down my beaker with deliberation. I had met Iorwerth once, when I was still an unwed maiden, when Henry was besieging Robert de Bellême at Bridgnorth. The King had summoned me to his war camp, dangled the prospect of me as a bride for Iorwerth, a bribe for his support against de Bellême. Henry had hoped then to seduce me himself too, but I had kept him at bay. Iorwerth had seemed to me an honourable man, amongst so many who were dishonourable.

'King Henry has returned Ceredigion to your father,' Raegnald continued, 'on condition of his paying a fine of 100 pounds of silver and promising to have nothing more to do with you.'

Owain punched the air at the news of his father's restoration and laughed at the condition. 'He won't keep to that.'

Raegnald shifted in his seat. 'We should settle the matter of your sister,' he said to Gruffudd, who nodded gravely. I looked back and forth from their faces: Gruffudd, Owain, Raegnald. What were they talking about?

'Owain ap Cadwgan,' Raegnald's voice became formal, 'you are accused of abducting and ravishing Nest ferch Rhys, sister to Gruffudd ap Rhys.'

Owain shrugged. 'I cannot deny it with two sons crying lustily upstairs,' he said, with a wry smile.

'Why did you do it, Owain?' Gruffudd asked, an edge of anger in his voice. 'What was the point for you? You have dishonoured my family.'

'Nest was betrothed to me when you were in your napkins, sucking at the teat of your wet nurse!' Owain shouted. 'It was my right.'

Raegnald patted the air between them. 'Peace,' he said. 'I will have this business conducted calmly in my hall, and not in anger.'

'Look at her.' Owain gestured at me. 'It is plain that the fault lies with her beauty. See how ravishing she is. I could not think straight watching her pawed by Normans. One of *our* women.'

Gruffudd pursed his mouth and stared angrily at Owain.

Owain lowered his voice. 'A rape of her from her Norman husband was no worse than the rape of Wales by those very Normans.'

Gruffudd nodded his head and I dug my fingernails into the palms of my hands, staring at him, but he did not meet my gaze. Raegnald waited a moment to hear if there was any more to say between them.

'Owain ap Cadwgan, I order you to pay a fine of 50 solidi to Gruffudd ap Rhys in compensation. Will you shake on it?'

'50 solidi!' Owain exclaimed.

'I'll take nothing less.' Gruffudd spoke at last.

'Very well, though you'll have to take half next summer and not this.' Owain reached his hand to Gruffudd across my lap and they shook on their deal.

I stood and left the hall, not knowing where I was going but unable to stay in the hall with them any longer. I felt furious with Gruffudd that this cold negotiation was his only response to my situation with Owain. Gruffudd should have slain Owain! Did he realise how I had suffered? Did he care? I had been too slow, too stupid in it all. But I knew that Gruffudd's position was weak and he needed to keep any allies he had. I stood in the courtyard, looking around. Darkness was falling. I walked to the stable to check on my horse who had not heard my voice for days as I had birthed and cared for my sons. The warm scent of the horses and their steady chomping and shifting in the hay was comforting. I stroked the soft muzzle of my horse and looked into the dark of his liquid eye.

'Lady!' I swivelled to the hissed voice and saw Dyfnwal emerge from a gloomy corner. Gruffudd had been true to his word then.

'Dyfnwal! I am so pleased to see you out of that cage.'

He thanked me for rescuing him and wept for those others from Llansteffan that he knew well, who had been sold into slavery. 'They are gone on a ship already with Norsemen.' We grimaced together, looking into each other's faces in the gloom.

'There is a group of mummers in the house,' I told him. 'They are leaving in the morning. Stay hidden here tonight. I will bribe them to put you in disguise and take you away from here with them. Then you can make your way to a boat heading for Wales.' I would have to steal something for the bribe, I thought, but I would find a way.

'Let me take you with me, lady!'

'I wish I could come, Dyfnwal, truly, but I have two newborn babies who are fighting for their lives. I cannot leave them and they would not survive a sea journey.'

'Is there *anything* I can do for you, lady, when I regain Pembroke and Amelina?'

'Give word to her, and to my husband, that I am safe and hope to return home soon. Tell them, I *wish* with all my heart to return home.'

The youngest of my twins died the following day, and Raegnald's wife hurried the mummers from the hall, telling them there was no place for them amidst such grief. I sat before the fire, my face concealed in my hands in despair. Through my wet fingers, I glimpsed the actors and acrobats filing from the hall, one wearing headgear imitating a stag, another with the head of a dog, and a third in the guise of a rabbit. The dog, I thought, had something of the gait of Dyfnwal about him.

I waited until they were clear and then stood. 'Will you eat something, Lady Nest?' Raegnald's wife asked me. I shook my head and walked to the chapel to keep vigil for the soul of my son. My breath misted the freezing air before my face in the stony chapel. I prayed that Gerald would receive the message Dyfnwal carried for me and might find a way to bring me home.

The oldest twin joined his brother in death two days later. Unwilling to expose my misery to those around me, I clamped my jaw and told myself I could not weep. I was a numb stone. During my pregnancy, I did not know there were two of them rocking together in my womb, but I had sung to them, spoken with them. I had been alone in hostile circumstances and they had been my dear friends, my only confidants. Raegnald and his household were immensely kind to me, but I kept my feelings tightly bolted inside me. Owain's disillusion with me was now complete, and the only thing that made me glad in those black, silent days was that he avoided my company.

14

Blood and Wine

Benedicta loved the inexorable structure of her life at Fonte-vraud. She rose early in the morning for matins, then breakfasted, tended her herbs and pottered around tidying her cell. Then came the morning terce service, after which she undertook her scribing or library duties until noon, when she would attend the church for sext. Then the nuns took dinner and she gossiped in the refectory with Genevieve and Petronilla. The None service was mid-afternoon, and then she would do more work, write to Haith, and take supper. After supper, there was evensong. Then it was her nightly duty to cover the fire in the refectory with cold ashes and remove the log to keep the embers alive so that they could easily be revived in the chill morning. After all that, she could sleep peacefully, confident that her spying days were over, rising for compline and again for prayers at midnight.

The longer she spent at Fontevraud, the more Benedicta came to see how the community that was evolving here was a signal of many women's great dissatisfaction with the old rules and how so many of them sought for something else. They imagined other possibilities for women, other shapes for a woman's life. Benedicta realised she had also seen that at Countess Adela's court. She was living through momentous times.

All she had heard about Robert d'Arbrissel convinced her that he sought an equal society for *all* people who sincerely sought salvation, and especially for all women and the poor. Benedicta reflected, however, that the noblewomen he had left in command of Fontevraud did not quite share that aim and were busily, subtly, reframing it. They were not quite as interested as their Master in the rights of lepers, reformed prostitutes, and poor women.

Benedicta roused herself reluctantly from a deep sleep and realised that it was Sister Genevieve's voice outside her cell, Genevieve's hand knocking at the door. Benedicta stumbled from her bed and across the room, without tying the belt of her habit or finding her shoes. She yanked open the door, so that Genevieve almost fell upon her, with her fist clenched, readied for another bout of knocking. 'What is it?'

'So sorry to wake you,' Genevieve whispered. 'Petronilla asks that you come quickly. There is some emergency in the Countess Bertrade's rooms.'

Benedicta blinked, trying to gain some semblance of full consciousness, and staggered to where her shoes were neatly aligned next to the stool. She slipped her feet in, tying her belt, and looked around, hunting for her wimple and veil.

'Here we are.' Sister Genevieve held them out to her and made no remark on the fact that Benedicta was flouting the rules by sleeping without them. Her hair, by rights, should be covered at all times, even when she was alone and asleep; a rule Benedicta considered to be quite ridiculous. She had tried compliance and found that the wimple and veil twisted around most uncomfortably as she tossed and turned in her sleep, and often woke her with their heated strangling. In the middle of many nights she had pulled them, exasperated, from her head and neck, and flung them into the corner, until finally she had given up the attempt at obedience altogether.

'What colour is your hair, Genevieve?' Benedicta asked the other nun suddenly.

'Red. Sort of brown-red.' Sister Genevieve shook her head and hands, as if irritated with herself. 'We must be quick, now.'

The two nuns entered Bertrade's chambers, where Benedicta was astonished to see the lady's brother, Amaury, rather than the lady herself, and Prioress Petronilla. He was seated on the floor and the Prioress was kneeling beside him. They looked up at her entrance with Genevieve, and Benedicta saw a smile of recognition bloom on Amaury's face. 'I think I met you last time I was here, Sister,' he said to Benedicta, and winced.

Benedicta saw that one of his boots was off and his hose was rolled up above his knee, exposing a long, bloody gash – and a long muscular calf with an abundance of golden hair. The Prioress was dabbing at the wound with a wet cloth and wringing it into a bowl of rosy-tinted water.

'Ah, Sister Benedicta, thank goodness,' said Petronilla. 'Will you take over here?'

Benedicta had never been known for her nursing skills and she looked with bewilderment at the Prioress and the wet, bloody cloth she held out to her. 'It's just for a moment while I go to fetch you some writing materials. As you see, Lord de Montfort has suffered a mishap and needs to get word to those who are expecting him. Sister Genevieve is afraid of the sight of blood and is of little use here.' Benedicta looked up to see that Genevieve had turned her back to them and was facing the door, her shoulders trembling. When the Prioress had left, and Benedicta had pressed the cloth gently to the wound, she spoke to Genevieve. 'I think you should return to your cell. There is no sense in standing there quivering. You would do more good with your prayers.'

Sister Genevieve turned to thank Benedicta, blanched at the sight of the blood again, and rushed from the room. Amaury let out a small laugh and Benedicta smiled. 'You say well to your friend, Sister. Benedicta, is it?'

She nodded.

'Thank you for your ministrations, Benedicta.'

'How did you come by this wound, lord?'

He waved his hand. 'My horse was startled and I fell onto sharp rocks. A ridiculous accident. It's nothing really but I did not want it to fester. This was the closest place I could think of to get it tended. My sister is blissfully unaware that I am even here – sleeping the sleep of the innocent in her cot. The Prioress, as usual, has all in hand.' He smiled and Benedicta tried to avoid his humorous eyes.

'You must be in pain,' she said.

147

'Not now,' he said, meaningfully, as she held the cloth against the wound.

Prioress Petronilla returned and changed places with Benedicta, whilst Amaury dictated a short note, explaining his accident and delay. He mentioned no name and so Benedicta had no idea who the recipient of this note might be. She blotted and folded the small piece of parchment, handing it to Amaury's waiting servant. The servant was an unusually small man with brilliant red hair and a sword scar across his forehead that had left a thick bald section in the middle of his eyebrow. He thanked her, bowed to his lord, and left them. Prioress Petronilla drew Benedicta aside, looking unusually flustered. 'What is it?' Benedicta asked.

'By rights, the lord should be accommodated in the guesthouse but he is unable to walk there. He came straight here to Bertrade's quarters, because he knew it. I'm not sure what to do. We can't leave a man, even an honourable man as he doubtless is, alone here in the women's quarters, with so many young novices on the premises.'

Benedicta shook her head but could think of no solution to offer. She looked at de Montfort's leg. He probably could walk on it but doing so would open the wound again and lead to more bleeding. It was best to leave him where he was.

'Will you stay here, Sister Benedicta? Keep vigil until the morning. And then we can arrange to move him with the aid of some of the lay brothers. I am reluctant to wake yet more people on this account.'

Benedicta nodded. She felt some misgivings but could not voice them to the Prioress who placed such complete trust in her.

Amaury, meanwhile, had rested his head back on the cushions behind him, and looked as if he would sleep soon.

The Prioress patted Benedicta's hand in thanks and left the room.

Amaury breathed in and out gently. Since his eyes were closed, Benedicta was able to study the planes of his face. In the flickering light from the fire and the two candles burning in the room she allowed her gaze to linger on the rich golden brown of his brows and eyelashes contrasted with the yellow gold of his hair, the full sensuousness of his mouth. Two of Bertrade's little dogs sat on cushions nearby, softly snuffling in their sleep. The abbey was silent. Benedicta thought of the three hundred or so souls here, all sleeping soundly into the night. And here she was, as awake as she had ever been, looking at the real model of the man who had appeared in her fantasies and dreams so vividly for the last few years. He was, if anything, more beautiful than her imaginings. Benedicta felt a lunge of desire and looked away from him, desperately searching for something to distract her.

To the side of the room, the lord's cloak and saddle bags were thrown in disarray, evidently in the hurry of his arrival. She stood quietly and moved to tidy them, folding the fine black cloak carefully. One of the saddlebags was open and spilling its contents. She bent to pick up the fallen pages and put them back inside. De Bellême. She recognised the signature. She glanced quickly at Amaury. He slept. She opened the letter as carefully as possible, but heard the crackle of parchment loud in her own ears in the quiet room. She scanned the letter. De Bellême wrote to de Montfort of his intention to muster more support for the rebellion against King Henry in defence of the claims of William *Clito*. It was exactly what she needed for Breri, for the Countess. If she could give them this, surely she could sue for her release from any further spying duties.

'Sister?'

Benedicta, her back to Amaury, slid the letter smoothly back into the saddlebag, putting it down next to the cloak. 'I was just tidying your cloak and bag,' she said, turning to face him. 'Do you need water?'

Amaury was regarding her in a horribly alert manner. He did not look sleepy at all. 'Wine would be very pleasant,' he said, slowly.

Benedicta cast about the room. She knew Bertrade often kept a tall, silver jug of wine here, and finding it, she was relieved to see that the engraved lid was on so that the wine did not spoil overnight. She poured a beaker and handed it to Amaury.

'Won't you join me?'

She hesitated but then poured a little wine for herself and sipped at it quickly. Had he seen that she was reading the letter from de Bellême?

If Lord de Montfort would sleep, she could take the letter. He must be weakened by his injury. She poured another beaker of wine for him and for herself, smiling at him. He asked her about herself. 'You are Flemish, I think?' She told him about her childhood in Bruges, how she had been at Almenêches since she was six, was the library nun now, here at Fontevraud. The wine tasted very pleasant and they took some more. 'I enjoy Ovid,' she heard herself saying and bit her lip to suppress a giggle, when Amaury clapped a hand to his mouth to smother his laughter at this statement.

'Of course you do,' he said, 'I am beginning to see that nothing about you should surprise me, Benedicta.'

'Oh!' Benedicta was surprised to find that the tall, silver jug was empty.

One side of Benedicta's face was flushed hot as she knelt in front of the fire, regarding the man. Gently, he pushed her veil and wimple down from her hair and ran his hands over the golden stubble of her head, smiling. 'A beauty, beneath these black folds then, Sister? A brilliant butterfly emerging from its dull chrysalis.'

She felt the pull of the man as the sea feels the pull of the moon. She could berate him, push him away, but then the dangerous secrets he held that she needed for the King would remain hidden. More of her must be revealed, she thought valiantly, to get at them.

15

After Winter

'Lady Nest, you have a visitor in the hall.' I assumed it was my brother, but when I reached the bottom step and glanced into the hall I was shocked to see Richard de Belmeis standing waiting for me, looking very overdressed in lavish bishop's attire amidst scruffy hounds and scruffier soldiers. Over a pale yellow alb, he wore a richly embroidered darker yellow chusable with a high collar. The cincture at his waist was a thick twist of gilded cord. I felt a momentary disgust at the sight of him, at what I knew of his self-serving hypocrisy, and that he now took the status of a pious man.

'My dear Lady Nest!' he exclaimed. 'How glad I am to see you well.'

'Master ... Bishop Richard!' The servants had already offered him water to wash his hands and now a maid set a jug of wine and beakers down for us. I indicated a seat to the bishop and took my own beside him, keeping some distance between us. He slung one leg over the other and I was astonished to notice that he wore one green shoe and one red. I had never known him to be scatterbrained.

'You look well. Are you well? Unharmed?'

I did not know how to answer him. 'Do you come from ... my husband?' I asked hesitantly.

'From the King, my dear. I have been negotiating on his behalf with your,' he hesitated, 'your friend, Prince Owain.'

I suppressed my irritation at that description. 'Tell me your news, Bishop Richard, do,' I said, in no mood to be toyed with.

'You must prepare yourself for a voyage, my dear, and a home-coming.' He beamed at me. I looked down the length of the hall where Owain was standing with the houndsman. He stared moodily in our direction.

'Owain has agreed to release me?' I asked, not taking my eyes from Owain.

'He has!' Richard patted my hand. I moved it from his reach. 'I had to threaten him that bribes would be going to all his competitors in the other branches of the ruling house of Powys to encourage them to attack *him* and his father else, but yes, finally I have succeeded in persuading him.'

I never imagined that I could be overjoyed to see Master Richard, yet I turned to him now, smiling, but remembering to temper my pleasure under Owain's stare. 'When will we leave? I can be ready quickly.'

'As soon as you wish, my dear.' He swung his green shoe gleefully back and forth beneath the folds of his yellow robes and I frowned down at it. 'It's all the rage at the English court,' he told me smugly, jerking his head towards his parti-coloured shoes, 'but I don't suppose you have been able to keep up much with the fashions here, eh, Lady Nest?'

I gave no reply but made to rise, impatient for my escape. He touched my arm and nodded me back down to my seat. 'One more thing,' he said. 'You must be clear about the terms, the account of things we will give.'

'Tell me … .'

'If your sons had lived,' he made a brief grimace of sympathy in the direction of my face. 'My *sincere* condolences. But since that is not the case, we are able to take a different tack. It would be best, in law, and for the good repute of your husband, Gerald FitzWalter, and your king, Henry, if you are returned home intact as it were.' He paused and looked at me.

'Intact.'

'Yes. I understand that compensation has been paid to your brother. But if a suit of rape and abduction were brought against Prince Owain, for instance, in the court at Pembroke, this would be in nobody's interest, dear Nest. Least of all your own. That is the advice from King Henry.'

'I see.' I stared expressionless at him. 'I understand. I will ready myself to depart and swiftly.' I rose and left him, pressing my lips together, pressing my fingers to my temples.

An hour later, I stood before Owain, waiting for his deliberately delayed attention. 'I am leaving with the Bishop, Owain. Will you promise that you will see our sons' graves are tended to? Candles are lit for them?'

'They were my sons. Of course I will,' he said petulantly.

I stared at him, searching my mind for any words of farewell I should say to him, but I found none. I turned and walked back to the Bishop. I had to move quickly, without thinking, or I would fall down with the grief of leaving my babies cold in the ground here. 'We can go now,' I told Bishop Richard.

He looked surprised. 'No …'

'Tears?' I shouted at him.

'Baggage?' he offered timidly.

'No baggage,' I whispered, and moved to the door with him trotting behind in his rustling robes and stupid shoes.

'Certainly, well, let's see if the ship can be ready for us right away. Should we say some further farewells to the Prince, to our host? No …. I see.'

On the journey from Dublin to Pembroke, I ached for Llewelyn and Einon. A girl on the boat held a tarpaulin over us to conceal me from the men and helped me bind my breasts to soak up the leaking milk. We swayed and gasped at each dousing. The constant struggle to stay upright, not to be washed overboard, to still our chattering teeth, was exhausting. I took a bleak pleasure in watching Bishop Richard spew repeatedly over the side of the ship, and once, not getting to the side in time, over his red shoe.

Spring had arrived in Deheubarth. I looked for Gerald amongst the group of men and horses waiting for us on the beach, but did not find him. These were all unknown faces to me. One of the men dismounted to help me into the saddle. At my urging, we rode swiftly.

At Pembroke Castle, the household was out in force for my return, the courtyard full of avid faces, pushing and straining bodies crowded close together. At first it seemed as if they were all strangers, greedy for sight of me as if I were a baited bear, but at last my gaze alighted on a dear face. 'Lady!' Haith stood with his long arms open wide to me, his dense butter-colour hair, the laughing creases of his brown face creasing now for me.

'Haith!' I longed to walk into the welcome of those arms but over his shoulder I saw a small space cleared in the press of people, a space around my husband. 'I am so glad to see you,' I said to Haith in a low voice, brushing past the quick touch of his hand, to move to stand before Gerald. 'Husband,' I began, but was interrupted by the shriek of Amelina's voice.

'Make way! Get out of my way!' Her small hands levered apart the crammed shoulders of two people in the crowd like a blinking mole breaching a mound of soil. Her body wriggled with furious frustration behind her hands and face. Suddenly she was released from the press, bowling at speed towards me, colliding with my chest, her face burrowing into me. 'Nest! Oh, Nest!'

I kissed the top of her head. 'Dear Amelina.'

'I'm so glad to see you safe, my lady.' She drew a quick breath, readying to launch into her next speech.

'I am more than delighted to see you, darling.' I bent so that my mouth was close to her ear. 'But I must greet my husband first.'

'Oh, yes.' She relinquished me, stepping back, grinning irrepressibly, smoothing down the skirt of her dress, pulling at her bodice where it was threatening to reveal a great deal more bosom than was seemly.

I stepped close to Gerald, seeking for some privacy in the melee. 'My lord.' There were threads of grey in the blond curls at his temples. I lowered my eyes from the blank of his face.

He took my proferred hand, kissed it briefly, let it drop. 'Dear Nest.' There was no warmth in his voice.

I glanced up to his perfunctory smile. He kissed me softly on the forehead. I remembered the softness of his mouth on mine, on my neck, in love, when he had loved me. I looked into the dullness of his pale blue eyes. So, I had lost him then, at last.

'Amelina will make you comfortable,' he said. He bowed slightly and walked away. I stood looking forlornly after him.

'The boys are desperate to see you. Come on, Nest.' Amelina

tugged at me, her eyes looking after Gerald too. 'He will come around,' she whispered.

William and Maurice ran to greet me, and I dropped to my knees to embrace them while they chattered excitedly against my shoulders and hair. I held them close, looking over their shoulders to where a shy little girl with fair hair stood with a rather grubby doll in one hand and a *scopperil*, a spinning top, in the other. 'Who is that poppet?' I asked her softly. I reached out my hand to her and she toddled, smiling, to bump against her brothers' backs. She held the poppet up for me to kiss. 'You must be Angharad,' I said, as her tiny fist curled around my finger. I wanted to burst with tears at the thought of my lost baby boys, but I knew it would frighten the armful of children I had here. 'But where is Henry?'

'Gone away,' William told me.

I looked up in panic at Amelina. She gestured calmly with her hands. 'He has gone to train with Gilbert FitzRichard de Clare's household. Not far from here. Just up the coast near Cardigan. We can go and visit him. He is fast becoming a little man.'

I bit my lip to stop my welling tears. Two years lost with my children. The last two years I would have had with Henry as my boy still, rather than a fledgling warrior.

For my first few days back, I pled exhaustion and avoided dining in the hall with Gerald and the household. Instead, I luxuriated in the company of my children and Amelina and she caught me up with the news at Pembroke. 'So what happened?' she asked me eventually, when the children had left for their lessons.

How much was known? Bishop Richard had been the one to see me in Dublin with Owain. He knew about my lost baby sons and I could assume he would not keep this information to himself. He was not known for his discretion or loyalty. I sighed. 'What rumours filtered here?'

'We heard that you and Owain were wildly in love. The bards all sang of it if there were no Normans by. The Welsh Princess at last wrested from the invaders by the dashing Welsh Prince.' She looked at me expectantly.

'Did Gerald hear this?'

'He will have,' she said bluntly, shrugging.

'And is it known that I bore Owain twin sons?'

'No!' Amelina's eyes widened, but I knew I could not rely on her surprise at this information. Bishop Richard would certainly convey the news to anyone he thought should know it and that would include the King and my husband.

'They did not live,' I said baldly.

She stroked my dry cheek. 'And now?' she said, softly.

I looked at my lap. What was the truth of the matter? 'I love Gerald,' I said looking up at her, 'but I've lost him for sure.'

She said nothing. Gave me no reassurances.

'I was abducted!'

'Yes, of course.'

'It's not as if I left my husband willingly. I saved his life and my children's by my actions.'

'He knows that,' she said, grasping at anything that might help me.

I hung my head. 'I had no choice in the matter. A little part of me thought briefly what the bards sing – that Owain might be a romantic Welsh Prince, what I had longed for all my life, what I deserved, but I was wrong, Amelina.'

She raised her eyebrows.

'I was disappointed in him. Gerald is a hundred times more a prince than Owain will ever be. And this is where I belong, with Gerald, but now it's ruined.'

Amelina heaved another sigh. 'Give him time.'

I could not hide and avoid people forever. I went through the routine of dressing listlessly, putting on my best dark red gown, having Amelina brush my hair and plait it with slender pale red ribbons woven through it. My *couvrechef* was short and gossamer thin. My hair was visible beneath it and, treacherously, still black. It should have turned white with grief for my lost sons, for the trial of my time with Owain, for the knife cut through the love between myself and my husband. I took a deep breath and walked down to the hall. A hush fell on the clattering plates and chattering voices as I appeared at the foot of the stairway. I walked to the dais. Gerald stood and offered me his hand as I took my seat next to his. Before we sat he looked for a long time into my eyes, but he did not smile. 'Welcome, Nest.' We sat, and after a disappointed second to see if anything more would transpire between us, the clattering and chattering resumed. A servant poured wine for us both.

'Are you well?'

'I am, my lord. I am very glad to be home. And are you well?' I looked at him, trying to force him to stay in eye contact with me.

'Yes. All is well, now you are returned.'

But these were merely formal, empty words. I felt no warmth from him, and we struggled to continue further conversation. At least we had broken the ice.

Weeks passed. Gerald did not come to my bed, and I did not dare invite him for fear of rejection. He went doggedly about his business and was merely polite to me. The sun shone on Pembroke, on the river, and on the sea I could spy from the top of the walls, but between Gerald and I there was only perpetual winter, which would never be warmed again by the amber heat of long summer days.

The Norman power block in southern Wales had changed during my time away, with only Gerald and de Neufmarché now remaining from the Normans who had arrived while my father was still alive. Gerald told me that de Neufmarché was well past his prime and held his lands peaceably now. The King's new men in Wales, the new generation, were his son, Robert FitzRoy, who held Glamorgan; Gilbert FitzRichard de Clare, who held Cardigan; and his brother, Walter FitzRichard de Clare who held Striguil.

'I have to watch my back with these young men,' Gerald told me. 'They see Pembroke, Carew, Llansteffan, Cenarth Bychan, and they see castles and lands they would like for themselves.'

'You are not past your prime yet, husband,' I told him. 'There are plenty of wily strategems left in you.'

He smiled at my compliment. Sometimes it seemed there was no need for the Welsh to contend against the Normans, because in time they might devour themselves. Gerald did not speak directly of it to me, but I learned he had lost face over Owain's attack on Cenarth Bychan and the stories circulating of his escape through the *garderobe*. Henry had bolstered the Clare family in the region to shore up the disgrace Gerald had suffered, and they now inched their way into lands where Gerald had hoped himself to gain command and win title from the King. As if Owain's actions had not already done enough damage to the kingdom of Powys, Richard de Belmeis' 'negotiations' on the King's behalf, had wreaked further havoc in Powys. I feared that yet another swathe of Wales might fall into the Norman grip.

I decided to visit my son, Henry, at Cardigan Castle, with Amelina, and Gerald agreed to come with us since he had business with Gilbert FitzRichard de Clare. The busy days of harvest were in full force as we rode past the fields. Everyone was out working, young and old, striving to bring in the corn before too much rain or too much sun should beat them in the annual race and make them starve this winter. But the weather was temperate, and it looked as if they would win the contest this year.

We paused to look at the scene and rest our horses for a moment. We listened to the sound of threshing in a nearby barn, and the excited barks of dogs. Two peasants, a man and a woman, approached us. He was wearing tight breeches and a belted smock and held a wooden beaker to me. 'It's frumenty, lady, to celebrate the harvest. Would you take some? It's made by my wife, here. My new wife,' he added, speaking in Welsh and hugging the smiling young woman to his side. The frumenty was made from milk, wheat, raisins and spices and tasted delicious, as I gratefully told her. I took half and passed the beaker to Gerald and his eyes crinkled his thanks to me over the rim of the cup. He passed the beaker to Amelina and thanked the couple in Welsh. We set our horses on towards Cardigan.

Lady Adelisa de Clermont, de Clare's wife, greeted us and offered us water to wash our hands, and bread and wine were set before us. Lord Gilbert's brother, Roger, and his eldest son, Richard, were both fighting in Normandy alongside the King. We talked for some time of any news we had between us of events there. A short man with a large head of thick brown hair came into the hall and Adelisa called out to him. 'De Marais!'

He came to us, smiling. 'May I be of service, Lady Adelisa?'

'Yes. This is Nest, Lady of Pembroke,' she told him, 'Henry's mother.'

'Ah, yes, of course. I am deeply honoured to meet you, lady.' He bowed low to me.

'This is our Constable, Stephen de Marais. Will you ask Henry to come to us here?'

He bowed and returned with four boys close on his heels and Henry – my little Henry – thrust them all out of his way to get to me first. 'Mama!' I almost burst with laughter at the sight of him. He recollected himself. He slowed his pace and presented a very grown-up bow to myself, Gerald, and Lady Adelisa.

The three boys with him were the youngest de Clare sons: Gilbert, who was twelve; ten-year-old Walter; and Baldwin, who was close to my Henry's age of seven years. The four boys were being trained together in arms. Henry seemed quite at home amidst this group. His face was glowing like a beacon at the sight of me. Amelina clapped her hands in delight at him and after a brief look at Lady Adelisa to see that he had permission, he ran and kissed her cheek while she smoothed his hair and measured his arm muscles. Although I ached to hold him, I knew that my own caresses with him must come later, when we had some privacy. I must not puncture his dignity as a small man.

Gilbert and Adelisa, Gerald had told me, were from very high-born Norman and French families, but I was pleased to find Adelisa was a warm, affectionate foster-mother to my son and that they already had a friendly, joking relationship. 'We are honoured to foster your son, Lady Nest,' she told me. 'He is a delightful boy!' They all knew, of course, that he was the King's son. I realised that now he had left home, I needed to tell him about his paternity and felt great anxiety about how to tell him and how he might react. I talked it over with Amelina and we agreed there was nothing for it, I must simply tell him, before he discovered it from the careless words of a stranger.

I chose a moment when Henry and I were at last alone in the small chamber that had been allotted to Gerald and myself for our visit. Our hug was a long, close one. 'Mama! I was so afraid for you when that Welsh Prince stole you, and so relieved when I heard the news you were returned home to Pembroke and Papa. I prayed hard for you every night.'

'Yes,' I said, 'it was a terrible ordeal for us all.' I felt a sad tug at my heart that he should refer to Owain as 'that Welsh Prince' as if there were no Welsh blood in his own veins. He was being raised in Norman households and saw himself as Norman. When he came in the room, and rushed into my arms, he had thrown a leather-bound book onto the bed beside me. 'What are you reading here?' I said, pulling it towards me.

'It's a manual for fighting,' he said, enthusiastically. 'Look!' He turned the pages to show me two young noblemen crossing swords, assuming fighting positions. There were no words in the book, just these finely drawn illustrations. I knew that my sons must be fighters or monks, and I must harden myself to the terrifying thought of my tender boy one day parrying a real sword-edge rather than the blunt, wooden practice swords. I could only hope that he would learn these fighting lessons well.

'Henry, I have to tell you something, something that will be a surprise to you. Perhaps it will be hard to hear.'

He made his face serious. 'What is it, Mama? You are not going away again?'

'No. Not that. You know Gerald as your father.' His eyes widened but I had no option but to rush on. 'Gerald has loved you as your father, Henry, since you were a few weeks old. He loves you dearly, but he is not your father.'

'I'm illegitimate, you mean? I'm not Welsh, am I?' he said, looking aghast.

'You are the son of King Henry,' I told him quickly, 'who loved me before I married Gerald.' This was not strictly accurately.

'The King. King Henry?' He was silent for a moment and I waited. 'I liked him.'

'He is your father and acknowledges you as his son, just as Robert FitzRoy, Lord of Glamorgan, Bristol and Gloucestershire, is his son, and also your half-brother. It's why the King made you Lord of Arberth.'

'Robert FitzRoy?' he said, mulling that over, a look of admiration on his face. I knew that the parallel would help him to understand his position and that Robert would appear to him as a positive role model. He took the news with a small frown but seemed to make a quick recovery with his usual sanguine approach.

Amelina told me later that she had spoken with him about it, that she knew I had told him about his real father. 'He just said, very proudly, that Robert FitzRoy was his brother. It will take him time to absorb it.'

I was relieved to find no visible change in the affectionate relationship between Henry and Gerald.

At the meal, I noticed a tension between Gerald and Gilbert Fitz-Richard de Clare and guessed at its cause. Henry had strengthened the position of the de Clares in Wales because of Owain's assault on Cenarth Bychan and his abduction of me. The King and Gerald had both suffered injury to their reputations. Gerald had lost the King's confidence and now he lost real ground and prospects to de Clare.

Hoping to defuse the tension, I drew Gerald's attention to a conversation I opened with de Marais, the Constable, but unfortunately he then bored us both with overlong stories that were of little interest to us. He was a pedantic man with a patronising manner, a tiresome certainty that he was correct on every topic we tried.

At last, Gerald and I could escape from the meal to our own chamber. Gerald held the door for me to enter and then leant his back, laughing, against it, listening to the latch fall in place. 'I thought that de Marais would never shut up! That we must listen to him boring away into eternity!'

I smiled warmly to him and then felt overcome with uncertainty. Here we were, he and I, in a bed chamber together. We had been able to avoid that in Pembroke. I saw him looking at the bed and saw the same thought in his head. 'Nest, I can take a pillow, lay on the floor ...'

I stepped to him and put my hand on his chest. 'Gerald. I don't want that.'

He straightened up, his back still against the door. 'Perhaps it's best if I sleep in the hall. It will not be remarked. I ...' He was already half-turned to the door.

I gripped the bare skin of his wrist as he reached to the latch. 'Gerald. Please. Speak with me?'

'I can't,' he said, his back to me now.

'Please. Just words, Gerald. Please.'

He turned and looked at me. 'What can be said, Nest?'

I pulled him by the wrist now, walking backwards. There was a small table and two stools and we sat on them. A jug stood on the table and I poured a little wine into two beakers. Gerald picked his up and gulped it down. I refilled his beaker and took a sip from my own.

'We must speak of it, Gerald. Of Owain.'

'It would be best if we said nothing.'

'How? How would that be best?'

He said nothing, filled his beaker again and added a little to mine.

'I have loved you through it all, Gerald. I love you now.'

Still he was silent, his head bowed, staring into the tiny dark pool of his wine.

'I stayed with Owain when de Clare came to pay the ransom because I feared that Owain would kill our children. Owain was shamed by the whole incident. He had hoped that you would be killed and that then he could marry me. That would have seemed an honourable marriage by abduction to him. But you lived.'

'Indeed.'

'You lived because of my actions at Cenarth Bychan,' I whispered.

He looked up at me now. Looked into my face. And nodded. 'Yes. But I should not have escaped as I did, shamefully. I should have stood my ground and fought him.'

'You would have been killed if you had done so, and I would be his miserable wife now and our children would be in a shallow grave in the Welsh mountains.'

He held my gaze. 'I know you are right but I have lost face by it. It may be hard, impossible even, to recover my reputation amongst my peers.'

I felt as if our conversation was an attempt to sing a two-part melody from two different tunes that could never harmonise. 'When the ransom was offered, I suspected, I was sure, that

Owain would allow me and Henry, the King's son, to be ransomed, but that he would slay *our* children – William, Maurice and Angharad – as a way to make a name for himself in the songs of the bard, to impress his men with his zeal against the invaders.'

Gerald nodded. 'I am grateful beyond words that you have all survived it. All of you.'

I placed my hand over his. 'Can we … ? Gerald, my heart was never unfaithful to you.'

He nodded again and sighed heavily. 'It's hard, Nest. Give me time.' He stood, kissed the top of my head, took a pillow from the bed, and left the room. I closed my eyes, swallowing on my tears, gripping the edge of the table.

16

Hunting Ground

Benedicta tried to calm her mind as she packed her few possessions into her saddlebags. What had her nefarious activities got her into now? King Henry had summoned her to his court at Bonneville-sur-Touques. It would be delightful to see Haith, but she suspected that was not the reason for the summons.

Last year, the simmering divisions in Normandy had threatened to spill over the sides of the pot, and Benedicta regretted playing a part in it. At the beginning of the year, Robert de Meulan attacked Paris in retaliation for King Louis' raids on his lands. De Meulan captured the royal palace, broke the bridges, and pillaged houses and shops. In August, King Henry crossed to Normandy to support the Countess's son, Thibaut, who had come out against King Louis in a dispute about the construction of a castle at Allaines. As the year turned to autumn, Normandy was stormy with thunder, rain and war. Thibaut and other lords fought against each other, and against the French king, all along the banks of the Seine. Thibaut's brother, Count Etienne de Blois, had joined Henry's court. Robert of Flanders had been fatally wounded in the fighting, leaving a child heir, and his capable widow, Clemence, as regent.

King Henry had banished William, Count of Évreux, and his haughty wife Helwise, Countess of Évreux. They had gone into exile in Anjou where, Benedicta knew from Bertrade's correspondence, they were conspiring with Amaury, Robert de Bellême and Hugh de Chateauneuf-de-Thymerais. Hugh du

Puiset had been persuaded by Thibaut and Countess Adela to switch sides to Henry, and so the conflict flowed, back and forth. There was a rebellion in Anjou, and many suspected that it was engineered by King Henry, who had been slowly gaining friends in the lands close to Anjou and Maine by marrying off his numerous illegimitate daughters to win himself allies.

Benedicta had neither heard nor seen anything of Amaury since the night he had come to Fontevraud and she had stolen de Bellême's letter as de Montfort slept, after the heat of their embraces. Benedicta found that, whilst she regretted the deceit of stealing the letter, she had no such regrets about the loss of her virginity. On the contrary, if she never saw Amaury again, never repeated her transgression with any man, she would not regret it. She thought of the nonagenarian nuns surrounded by dust motes in the library at Almenêches Abbey and could only be glad that she had known desire and physical ecstasy.

About Amaury himself, she was not sure how she felt. She barely knew the man. He, no doubt, would forget her in a blink of an eye. Perhaps a nun was an unusual conquest for him, but doubtless there were many women loved and forgotten behind him as he made his shining way through life. She was brutally honest with herself. She knew she had no hopes at all with regard to Amaury, but her encounter with him had left her with other vague hopes and longings where before she had been so sure that she was impervious to such feelings.

Benedicta had reported to Breri that she knew from Bertrade's correspondence that William d'Evreux and his countess Helwise, who were childless, were determined to make Amaury their heir. Perhaps this was why Benedicta had been summoned by King Henry. She told Prioress Petronilla that it was her brother Haith who had urgently requested to see her. More lies. Benedicta was terribly anxious that if the extent of her spying were exposed to Haith, he might feel loathing for her and never speak with her again.

It was early November when Benedicta and her escort, a young servant lad from Fontevraud, arrived at the castle. She was exhausted by the four days' ride north. They had stayed at convents in Le Mans and near Alençon, and then at the great monastery of Lisieux. Now the five watchtowers and formidable walls of Bonneville-sur-Touques confronted them. This had been a favourite hunting ground for King Henry's father, William the Conqueror, and no doubt both the hunting and the proximity of his administrator, Bishop John of Lisieux, were the main reasons Henry held court here.

Benedicta was dismounting from her palfrey, her toe barely touching the cobbles, when she heard a commotion and turned to find herself confronting Robert de Bellême.

'You!' he said, instantly recognising her, as he had failed to do at Fontevraud. 'The sneaking sister from Almenêches!' His gauntleted hand went to the whip at his hip and he began to draw it from his belt.

Benedicta was quaking before him, her guilts coaelescing to reduce her to a kind of jellied thing. She heard Haith's shout. 'Bellême! What are you at? Leave that woman alone!'

De Bellême turned angrily to Haith, who was running across the courtyard towards them, his face a picture of anxiety, his straight fair hair flapping rhythmically at his ears as he ran and, Benedicta saw with dismay, his hand was on his sword hilt. 'Stay out of this, Fleming! I have cause to be angry with this nun. What are you doing here?' he turned back to Benedicta.

She could have asked him the same question. Her knees shook. She could not answer. Instead, she took gulps of air and stared in distress at Haith who reached her, took the horse's reins from her shaking hand and gave them to a groom. He placed his long arm across his sister's shoulders, gripping one shoulder reassuringly. 'She has cause to be angry with you, de Bellême,' Haith shouted. 'You burnt her convent to the ground.'

'She!' De Bellême pointed a finger at Benedicta, but whatever his accusation was going to be, it was interrupted by the arrival of King Henry. The crowd parted respectfully for the King, suppressing their delight at the expectation of witnessing either a nun whipped by de Bellême or de Bellême and Haith drawing swords on one another. Benedicta watched de Bellême damp down the fury that had risen at the sight of her. 'Sire.' He knelt to the King.

'What's going on here?'

'De Bellême was giving angry words to my sister.'

'This is not seemly,' the King told de Bellême, who rose and offered the King no argument. 'I will have no abuse of a holy sister at my court. Greetings to you, Sister Benedicta. My thanks for your attendance here.'

'Come with me, Benedicta, and I will get you settled,' Haith told her, keeping a protective arm around her as they moved past de Bellême.

'You would not have drawn your sword on such as one as de Bellême, would you, Haith?' she said in a nervous voice, as he helped her unclasp her cloak and she looked around, taking in her surroundings.

'Why not? For you, I would. I have faced him in battle often enough. As have you when he burnt your abbey,' he said, characteristically trying to lighten the tone of their exchange.

In the small chamber that Haith had led her to, Benedicta looked at two chests laying open with costly gowns displayed within them. More clothes were lain across a broad bed, and a small jewel casket stood on a table. 'You are billeted with Lady Sybil Corbet,' Haith said. 'But I don't suppose you will see much of her in this room.'

Benedicta nodded. She knew that Sybil Corbet was the King's mistress. Benedicta was bewildered by the enormous number of people rushing around the fortress, all seemingly intent on some great purpose. 'Is there an emergency?' she asked Haith.

He laughed. 'No emergency. Just the usual business of the King's court.'

'Such a lot of business!'

'Yes.' Haith sought to help her forget the terror of her recent encounter with de Bellême. 'The King has to keep a tight rein on everything in Normandy, but also England and Wales, and then there is all his diplomatic relations besides, outside his own realm, with the Pope, King Louis, Flanders, Maine.'

Benedicta wondered at Haith's descriptions of the King's officers. There were scribes, a Master of the Seal, justices, seneschals, chamberlains and butlers, chaplains and marshals. Benedicta saw that the King was perpetually working at a tremendous pace with

167

all these officials, and her awed respect for King Henry grew greater with her understanding.

Haith left her for a while to rest from her journey. She lay down on the bed but was startled awake and found herself looking at a small, young woman, very slender yet very pregnant and pretty. 'Oh, I'm so sorry,' Sybil Corbet said, her arms full of the clothes she had been tidying away. 'I was tip-toeing around, trying not to wake you, Sister.'

Benedicta sat up. 'Please, don't worry. I need to be awake now. I am pleased to meet you, lady.'

'And I, you. You are Haith's sister I understand, and I can see that in your face.'

Benedicta smiled. There was a knock at the door.

'Enter,' Sybil commanded.

An elderly and portly man stood in the doorway.

'Yes, what is it, Herbert?'

'The King commands your presence in his chamber, lady,' the man told her, and Benedicta noticed a moue of contempt on his face after Sybil had turned away from him and given her promise to attend the King.

'He's going to be my father-in-law!' Sybil whispered to Benedicta. 'Something of a grouch, don't you think? Let's hope his son is more pleasant; not that it matters really.'

Benedicta looked at her bewildered. 'Your father-in-law? You are marrying?'

'Yes, that grumpy man,' she gestured at the door, 'is Herbert, the King's chamberlain. I am to marry his son.' She smoothed her hand over her protruding stomach. 'It won't make any difference to my relationship with the King,' she asserted.

Benedicta was not sure how to respond to Sybil's confidences, and was relieved when the girl found herself a becoming gown and jewels and left the room. She did not return, and Benedicta, alone in the broad bed, was able to get an excellent night's sleep.

Her anxiety returned, however, the following morning when the court assembled, and she wondered what role the King might be expecting her to play here. Countess Adela and her sons, Thibaut and Etienne, were present, and the Countess gave Benedicta a warm smile when she noticed her in the crowd. Adela was still acknowledged as co-ruler with her son, Thibaut, and the relationship between them appeared to be comfortable, one of mutual respect. Etienne, on the other hand, could not entirely conceal his resentment at the power his mother wielded and his sense that this belittled him. Bishop John of Lisieux, the King's main deputy in Normandy, presided over the proceedings, with the King looking on. The Bishop announced that Robert de Bellême should stand to face charges.

'What! What is this? You think to insult me a second time!' de Bellême exclaimed. He ignored the Bishop and addressed the King directly who did not reply. 'This court has no right to charge me with anything. I am here as an envoy from France, protected by my status as ambassador.'

Now King Henry spoke – or thundered rather – and Benedicta flinched at his voice, resounding in the hushed hall. 'We do not recognise that as your status here, de Bellême. Here, you are *my* sworn vassal and you are forsworn. You are *my* vicomte for Argentan, Exmes, Falaise and you are in default.'

De Bellême opened his mouth in astonishment but found no words.

The Bishop took up the attack. 'You have rendered no royal revenues, no accounts. You have ignored three summons to the King's court to answer to this. You have acted against the interest of your lord over and over again.'

'The accounts can be rendered. This can be rectified. I refute your other charges and will not answer to such unfounded nonsense,' de Bellême said.

'We have copies of your treasonous correspondences,' the Bishop told him, splaying a sheaf of parchments on the table before him. With a sinking heart, Benedicta recognised one of the parchments as the letter she had stolen from Amaury. Benedicta had sent the letter to Countess Adela some time ago and it seemed the King had been able to garner other evidence against de Bellême from other spies.

'What is this?' de Bellême exclaimed, his voice laced with scepticism, as he approached the table for a closer look. Benedicta watched the colour drain from his face as he realised what he was looking at. He was condemned many times over in those letters.

'Benedicta,' Haith spoke close to her ear, 'isn't that your hand?' He was pointing at the parchment she had wrapped the stolen letter in, addressed to the Countess. It was amongst the pages on the table.

Of course Haith would recognise her handwriting. She had been writing to him all her life, since she was six years old. She desperately wanted to deny it but she knew that such a lie would only lead her further into a morass. 'Yes,' she admitted. 'I will explain later, when we are in private.' She did not dare to look at Haith's face, did not dare to see the loathing for her that must be etched there.

'Yet again, de Bellême,' the King said, 'despite my many forbearances towards you, *you* are a traitor to me. You were a traitor to me in England and you have continued a traitor to me here, in Normandy. John, Bishop of Lisieux, will take charge of the estates of Argentan, Exmes and Falaise on my behalf. You will be incarcerated at Cherbourg, to await my further disposition.'

De Bellême was swiftly surrounded by armed guards and seeing there was no use in resistance, he drew himself up with dignity. 'The King is a man of the greatest animosity and inscrutability of mind,' he declared. 'He only praises those whom he has decided to destroy utterly.' Benedicta turned her shoulder and avoided his eyes as he was escorted from the room, but she knew that he had turned his stare in her direction as he passed.

Benedicta dreaded the ending of the King's court session. She wished that it could go on forever with its interminable charters and announcements and calculations. To face Haith and try to explain herself would be a far greater trial.

They sat down to dine together in privacy in Haith's small chamber. She was surprised to see that he behaved and conversed with her as normal, as if nothing had happened. 'Henry tricked Robert de Bellême into coming to the court, with flatteries,' Haith said. 'That's it for the rest of de Bellême's life. He won't get out of that captivity.'

'It seems a shabby trick,' Benedicta said.

'Aye and one that de Bellême would have been happy to stoop to if he'd thought of it first,' Haith said pragmatically.

Although Benedicta thoroughly hated the man, she felt ashamed. Perhaps Haith had decided to ignore the question of her handwriting on the letter. She could lie. She could say she had been asked to make a copy and did not know what it was that she wrote. But no, she could not lie to Haith's face.

'So, it was your hand, Benedicta? On one of those letters that convicted Bellême?'

'Yes.'

'I saw the Countess give it to Henry yesterday. He was very pleased about it. To have written proof of de Bellême's treachery. But what part have you played in this?'

She looked him in the face now with an imploring expression and the words fell from her in a rush. 'I sifted through Bertrade de Montfort's letters at Fontevraud and told of anything of import against Henry. The Countess sent me there to do it. I feel awful about it, Haith!'

His mouth fell open in surprise. 'You were spying for Countess Adela? For Henry?' He was disconcerted.

'It was an awful thing to do. I allowed my vanity, my curiosity, to lead me deeper and deeper into deceit.'

He frowned. 'I admit, I am surprised at it. I had no idea you were about such things. And he did not speak of it to me. It has helped Henry,' he said slowly, evidently intending to reassure her, but she heard the perplexity in his voice, saw it in the way he looked at her.

'One letter there, I stole directly and sent it to the Countess.' She wanted to get the lies out in the open. But she stopped. She could not tell him, or anyone, of the greater sin she had committed to get the letter.

'Why did you do it, Benedicta?' he asked in surprise. She hated that she could see him reappraising her.

The excuses that it was vengeance against de Bellême, or care for King Henry, or loyalty to Countess Adela, all hovered on her lips, in her mind, but she closed her mouth up and said nothing. She realised that none of these reasons explained her actions, but rather that it had been a mixture of curiosity, a lust for danger and deceit, her lust for Amaury, that had driven her decisions. She could say none of this to her brother. 'I hardly know, Haith,' she stammered. 'I hardly know myself but I am trying to see, and hope that you will love me still.'

'Always,' he said, but his expression showed him still distracted. 'Be careful not to lose yourself, Benedicta.'

'Haven't you ever done something for him you knew you should not? That you regret?' she shouted.

Haith patted the air with his hands slowly to calm her. He frowned and looked down at his boots. 'I have. Yes, I have,' he said quietly.

For several days Haith and Benedicta wove around one another like wary fighters circling, getting the new measure of each other, but it was not in Haith's disposition to hold a grudge for long or to look anywhere except on the bright side. 'Good news, Benedicta,' Haith said, laying down his hat on the table, where she sat with a book. The graved laughter lines of his browned face creased to lend emphasis to his words.

'How?'

'The King says you are to stay with his court, with me!'

Her eyes widened. 'But, I should go back to Almenêches surely?'

'He has already written to the Abbess begging leave for you. Countess Adela has told him of your great learning and he wants you to educate some of the young ladies at court.'

'He has not spoken to me of it,' she said, feeling a confused mixture of delight to stay in Haith's company, at the Countess's flattery, and fear that this could only bode ill; that she would be drawn back into duplicity.

Haith looked crestfallen. 'I thought you would be pleased to spend time with me.'

'Oh, I am!' Benedicta hurried to reassure him. 'It's just a surprise is all.'

Soon after, de Bellême was sent across the English Sea and incarcerated in Wareham Castle. In response, his son, William Talvas, joined forces with the nephews of William de Mortain (who was still in King Henry's prison in the Tower of London, after the battle of Tinchebray which had taken place more than twelve years before). The young men rebelled against King Henry

172

but he stifled their rebellion, besieging and taking Alençon. He gave it to Thibaut de Blois, who in his turn, gave it into the care of his brother, Etienne de Blois. The King allowed de Bellême's son to continue as Count of Ponthieu, but his patrimony was much diminished. Reports held with certainty now that William *Clito* (still a mere ten years old) had fled to Flanders and to the court of the boy count, Baldwin.

17

Truce

'Nest! Quick!' Amelina was gripping the door jamb, her face lit with a huge smile.

I wove my sewing needle into the cloth in my lap. 'What is it?'

'There are visitors below. Welsh visitors!'

My thought went immediately to Owain. I glanced at a dagger in its scabbard on the chest and moved towards it. Amelina clapped her hand over mine as I reached for it. 'No! No need for *that*. Friendly visitors that you will welcome. Gerald is greeting them kindly even now and waiting for you.'

I frowned at her mysteriousness and followed her down the steps. A few children and a small band of men, marked as newly arrived by the dust and saltmarks on their clothes, stood in the hall with Gerald and several soldiers from the Pembroke garrison. They turned at the sound of our footsteps and I was overjoyed to see my brother, Gruffudd, amongst them. I ran to him and he opened his arms to greet me. I held his hand, swinging it and laughing, as I turned to Gerald, who laughed in response.

'I am glad to see you well, sister,' Gruffudd told me, 'and to make the acquaintance of your husband.'

'Your brother will be staying with us for a short while,' Gerald told me. I bit my lip. Was Gruffudd a prisoner? 'As our honoured guest,' Gerald added, seeing my hesitation.

'When did you cross from Ireland?'

'We arrived a few hours ago and came here directly.' Where else did he have to go? By rights he was King of all Deheubarth,

174

of all the lands that my husband and other Normans held for King Henry.

I glanced at the four, small children in my brother's entourage. 'Are they your children?' I asked, surprised.

'Yes.' He brought them forward one at a time, presenting them to me and Gerald. 'Anarawd.' He smiled shyly at me. 'Cadell. Gwladus. Nest.' To this last, youngest daughter, Gruffudd said: 'This is your aunt, Lady Nest.' My namesake and I looked complicitly at one another.

'Their mother?' I asked.

'She decided to stay home.'

So their mother was his Irish concubine. I doubted that it had been her decision to be left in Ireland without her children. Amelina, without needing word from me, bustled forward to take charge of them and make them welcome.

At dinner, Gruffudd talked of events in Powys, of Owain and Madog. I watched Gerald's face darken at the mention of Owain's name and steered the conversation elsewhere. My heart was heavy at the thought of Owain returning to Wales and being nearby.

That night, Gerald surprised me, coming to my chamber. 'Nest,' he said hesitantly. I had hoped that, after our conversaton in Cardigan, things might grow more intimate between us, but as soon as we had returned to Pembroke, Gerald had seemed unable again to cope with the complexities of our past. He had continued to be formal towards me. Now, I stepped quickly to the door where he hovered and took his hand, gently leading in him. 'I am glad to see you, Gerald. Please.' I gestured to the cushioned bench by a small table near the window where a cool breeze riffled a jug of pansies. He sat, looking awkward. I poured two beakers of wine and handed one to him. I gulped mine down fast. Now he was here, I was not going to let him go. I moved my stool close to him so that our knees were touching and I leant forward and took his hand. 'Will you speak to me of your day?' I asked him.

'Can I?' he said, the expression of his face and the tone of his voice were laced with a contradictory mix of challenge and beseeching.

He felt he could no longer trust me. Because of Gruffudd.

Because of Owain. Because of me, even. 'I hope so. I hope you will. I am your wife, your loving wife, despite everything that has happened, Gerald.'

He smiled briefly at me.

'Should we talk more of my time away? Would it help? I want more than anything to be fully reconciled with you.'

'No,' he said, swiftly, before I had even finished my sentence. 'No, I can't speak of it.' He looked away from me again.

'Very well,' I soothed. 'So we won't. Tell me something else.' Anything that would get him talking to me on a safe subject would be good.

'I doubt your brother intends to become a quiet farmer here, do you?' he said, going instead for the most difficult subject hanging between us.

'I don't know his plans.' He nodded, looking in my eyes. 'Perhaps Henry would be wise to offer him some lands, a Norman wife?' I said.

'I think you don't know your brother, Nest.'

'Perhaps not. Not yet. I spent only a few days with him in Ireland.'

Gerald looked away. Any mention, or approach to my time with Owain, was like a hot poker thrust at his heart. He must love me still then, but I must not rush him. He stood.

'You won't stay, my lord? My love,' I kept my voice neutral, but warm. I would not beg or wheedle.

'Not tonight.'

I reached up to his cheek and kissed him softly on the mouth. 'Good night then.' He hesitated, smiled, but walked from the room.

Amelina was right. He would come around in time. In the meantime, while I waited for Gerald, I spent time growing acquainted with my brother. Gruffudd did not say so directly, but he did not trust me either. He did not bring me into his confidence, but every day he spent with us I grew more and more certain that he was planning to attempt to retake his birthright. He rode out each day with the small group of Welsh and Irish men who were his entourage, assessing the lay of the land and the Norman defences at each place he visited.

'Why are you accepting my brother here?' I asked Gerald one night when he came to drink wine and talk with me as had now become his evening custom. He never stayed to climb into my bed, but he spoke with me, he kissed me goodnight. We were affectionate at least.

'I can keep an eye on him here.'

I smiled. My wily husband. But I reflected that if, no when, Gruffudd decided to make his move, my husband and my brother would be in deadly contention. I counseled Gerald several times to petition the King to make Gruffudd a land grant and he assured me he had sent word suggesting this, but no offer came from the King.

'Your brother's following grows,' Gerald said.

I did not like the way he eyed me for a reaction, the way his words were a mixture of statement and interrogation, so I made no reply.

'He garners sympathy as a forlorn, homeless prince. He is an inspiring, valiant figure. He has your beauty.'

'He is the blood heir of an ancient race of kings.'

'The older, well-established Welsh lords do not respond to the implication of his presence. They are well situated now, allied with Norman neighbours. They do not intend to risk that.'

They are bought off you mean, I thought, but said nothing. Bought off with scraps like dogs beneath the table.

'Younger members of the local Welsh nobility flock to him though. Hot-blooded fools.'

I knew that Gerald was deliberately trying to provoke me into making a statement of my views – or my knowledge. I smiled at him.

'He is beginning to be a threat that the King should know about.'

'You will do what you must,' I said. And so will Gruffudd ap Rhys ap Tewdwr I thought, not knowing whether to weep or triumph at that knowledge.

I walked across the courtyard towards the kitchen, intending to check with the cook if we needed more spices from the market, but I diverted from my path when I heard shrieks, giggles and bleats coming from the barn. I stood in the doorway, watching Amelina showing Angharad, and her cousins Gwladys and Nest, how to milk a goat, but the goat was not being cooperative. Streaks of milk on the floor and on their aprons, and three kicked-over buckets showed me that the milking lesson was not going well. 'We'll get there in the end!' Amelina shouted to me over the goat's back, holding fast to the horns while Angharad bent her little head, frowning at her work on the teats, and Gwladys and Nest held hands, laughing through tears as they looked towards me.

'Are you milking or wrestling that poor beast?' I called out.

Amelina momentarily lost concentration, the goat took advantage, struggled from their grasp, and bolted past me through the doorway. 'Oh goat's breath!' exclaimed Amelina.

'Perhaps you would do better to begin this lesson on a more pliant cow or a sheep?' I told her. 'Or at least, tie the goat first!'

I started as Gerald came up behind me, his arm snaking about my waist, and I quickly placed my hand on top of his to show that I wanted his arm there.

'What's this?' he said. 'Milking in progress but the goat had other plans?' We turned at the sound of horses at the gate and watched Gruffudd returning from one of his barely concealed reconaissance forays. 'There is bad news,' Gruffudd shouted across the courtyard to us, although his excited expression belied his statement. Gerald and I waited for him to dismount and we all moved together to the hall.

'Cadwgan has been killed by his nephew, Madog, at Welshpool,' Gruffudd said, as soon as we were seated.

'I am sorry to hear that,' Gerald said. 'He was a great and fair ruler.'

'Yes,' I said, hanging my head and thinking of the elderly man who had been kind to me on several occasions.

'King Henry has given the rule of Powys to Owain,' Gruffudd said abruptly. I took in a sharp breath.

'That is … surprising,' Gerald said, and swiftly shifted the conversation elsewhere.

What was Henry up to? Owain would give him and my husband trouble. Surely the King realised that. He could have given Powys to Owain's uncle, Maredudd ap Bleddyn, who would have been a much safer ally. Now with Owain in power, Gruffudd would feel more encouraged to make the attempt for his own kingdom. I frowned, perplexed that I could not speak of it either to Gerald or Gruffudd without being disloyal to one or the other. That evening, when Gerald came to sit with me, I made a determined effort to get him to stay beyond a conversation, and this time my blandishments and affection were rewarded with a return from him. He spent that night with me, and I was glad to be close with him again at last. But when we lay on our backs afterwards, our legs and fingers twined around one another's, staring at the waving reflections of moonlight on the water projected onto the ceiling, I knew that we were both thinking of Owain and Gruffudd and that there could be no speech of it between us.

18

Black-clad Life

'I had looked out upon the wide kingdoms of the Earth as if I were caught up in ecstasy, flying far and wide through words … . Now, however, I will return exhausted to my black-clad life.' Benedicta read Father Orderic's words aloud and looked up at him, her brown eyes brimming with pleasure. She put the parchment down so that she could bring her hands together to emphasise how much she enjoyed his writing. Orderic was pleased with her response and modestly tried to suppress the smile of satisfaction that crinkled the corners of his mouth. His tonsure ringed his bald pate in a narrow band, his eyes were rather close together, and he had large ears that stuck out from a long face. His thin neck rose exposed from his cowl, and Benedicta noted that one side of his chin was rather badly shaved. Orderic was no beauty on the outside, but he was all beauty inside, she considered, as she contemplated her friend.

'I would not wish to complain of my own "black-clad life",' Benedicta said. 'After all, I have seen a little more of the world than most other nuns. Yet there are areas of life, of experience, that are closed off to me.'

Orderic nodded. Like her, Orderic had come to monastic life as an oblate, as a young child.

'I wonder if I might speak with you, Father, about a matter that is troubling me?'

'Yes, yes, of course,' Orderic stuttered, a look of mild alarm entering his expression.

Benedicta had arrived at Ouches in February in King Henry's entourage. The King required her to stay in the monastery guesthouse whilst he went to Alençon to meet with the Count of Anjou, saying that he would have need of her. Benedicta acknowledged the King's order and wrote again to tell Abbess Emma at Almenêches of the continuing delay in her return. She was not sorry to spend more time in the company of Orderic.

When Haith came to visit her, she asked him to explain the King's command. 'Why does he have need of me? Do you know?'

'Henry wants to betroth his heir, William *Adelin*, to the daughter of the Count of Anjou. He has opened negotiations to make it happen.'

'But how will I assist?'

'The child, the Count's daughter, will come to Henry's court in England to be educated, and to learn the language and her duties under the tutelage of the Queen. She is a mere two years old.'

'She travels with a nurse, surely? With her own entourage of servants?'

'Yes, certainly, but most of them are also unable to speak English or to read and write. I persuaded Henry it would be wise to place you with the princess's household.'

Benedicta grinned at her brother. She had learnt a little English from his letters but she was by no means an expert in that tongue. Yet. She could learn it. 'Well, that is a delight! So, am I to go to England then?'

'Perhaps! We'll see. Let's not get ahead of ourselves. We have to see if Fulk d'Anjou will actually stand up to his promise and hand over his daughter and her dowry.'

Henry and Haith set off to Alençon to meet with the party of Count Fulk and Benedicta waited for news. King Henry had emerged the victor in the recent struggles against King Louis, the Count of Anjou, and the rebel Norman lords, including Amaury de Montfort. Fulk d'Anjou had given homage to Henry for the county of Maine and Louis had agreed to Henry's dominion over Bellême, Maine, and Brittany. Henry, on his part, had ceded nothing, and had still evaded giving King Louis homage for the Duchy of Normandy. The French king had lost substantial ground to the English king in this conflict.

Benedicta scraped at the residual hairiness on the parchment she was preparing for Orderic. She had shivered with Orderic through the cold winter, as they wrote side by side in the cloister, but now early flowers were trying to bloom, shoots were appearing in the herb garden, and spring was on its way. Benedicta had been able to give Orderic some scribing assistance in his work on the history of the Normans. The monastery of Ouches was on a small river called the Charentonne, isolated in a tangled forest on Normandy's southern march, and not so far from Almenêches. She went walking with Orderic in the forest collecting materials for their inks and seeing sometimes a silvan landscape, sometimes the choking smoke of charcoal burners and iron-ore miners. At the edge of the forest they looked out on a group of peasants at work in the fields making ditches and repairing the fences.

'What is it you wish to speak to me about, Sister?' Orderic asked, his cheeks tinged a little pink. 'I am not accustomed to taking confessions from female religious persons,' he warned. 'You might be wiser to consult with another priest.' Orderic's long pale face was inscribed with two lines on his cheeks, formed by worry or concentration. His head, ringed by his tonsure, was so white it looked as if it might be possible to see through to his brain beneath.

'Oh, don't worry, Father,' Benedicta interrupted. 'I don't have a problem with my black-clad life in *that* way. I would far rather spend time with a good book than a bad man.' Benedicta's laughed at her own joke, and crossed her fingers at her lie.

'Oh!' Orderic blushed a deeper shade of pink.

'No,' she said. 'It's spying that worries me and I needed to speak with you about it.'

'Spying!'

'Yes. I have been so employed by the King and Countess Adela. I passed information to them that I overheard concerning the King's enemies.'

Orderic frowned. 'But this is loyalty rather than spying surely. You are safeguarding the realm.'

Benedicta sighed. 'I wish it were that simple. I wish I were as innocent as you are, Father. I fear I have lost my brother's good opinion as a consequence of my actions.'

'Speak honestly with your brother. If you have lost his good opinion, you will regain it with honesty, for he loves you and you cannot lose that.'

Benedicta swallowed, hoping that Orderic was right.

'Perhaps, Sister, it is not only your anxiety about the honourableness or no of spying, or your fears for your brother's affection that concern you.'

Benedicta stared at him. He could not know about Amaury. Nobody knew. She hardly believed that it had happened herself.

'You have an enquiring mind, Sister,' Orderic said, tentatively, searching her face to see if he should continue. 'A thirst for venturing, even.'

Benedicta nodded, relieved. If it was just *that* he saw in her face, she was safe. 'I am nosy, you mean?' she laughed.

'Curious and adventurous, yes,' he said. He looked into her face some more. 'The religious life is not for everyone, Sister. It is possible to be pious also as a layman or laywoman.'

'I know that, Father.' Benedicta frowned.

'To leave the monk's or nun's habit is not to leave God,' Orderic said, looking meaningfully into her eyes. 'Each must find their own path to heaven in life.'

'I ... I have no thought of that, Father.'

He nodded slowly and turned their talk to the book she was currently reading.

In March, the King and Haith returned to leave the small Angevin princess and her household at Ouches. The King was evidently very pleased with the progress of his negotiations. The Count of Anjou had dowered the child with Maine, so at last that territory had been returned to Henry, and he was always happy to win lands by marriage rather than by war. The King and Haith rode out on campaign again to besiege the castle of Bellême, where the garrison was holding out against the King.

Benedicta diligently spent a few hours each day with the tiny princess and her nurse. The girl was known as Mahaut and had great brown eyes and glossy brown curls. She was Bertrade's granddaughter and kin to Amaury, and Benedicta could see something of their looks in the girl's small face. She was an affectionate child but there was little that Benedicta could do as a tutor with a pupil so young. The nurse herself had no capacity for learning, and the two ladies accompanying Mahaut seemed horrified at the notion that they should either read dusty tomes or learn the gruesome language of English.

Benedicta received a letter from Sister Genevieve telling her that Bertrade had left Fontevraud and was on her way to her own new abbey in Haute-Bruyères. She received a second piece of news with great sorrow. Abbess Emma de Montgommery had died at Almenêches. Benedicta wished that she had been with the Abbess at the end, had spent more time with her. She felt no especial pull now to return to Almenêches, and with Bertrade gone from Fontevraud and Bellême incarcerated, Countess Adela had no reason to send her back to Fontevraud either. Benedicta found herself both aimless and homeless.

19

London

Benedicta hugged little Mahaut to her, keeping them both warm in the fresh sea breeze. Although the boat rode up and down steep waves, Benedicta was enjoying the sea journey and did not feel at all sick. It must be her Fleming blood. Every Fleming, Frisian or Netherlander had reason to feel they were acquaintanced with the sea. They lived half their lives in it up to the knees, if not the neck. The Normans too had grown accustomed to traversing a transmarine domain. The sea was at the centre of the Norman lands rather than at its edges.

Haith bent to her. 'Are you feeling ill, Benedicta? The child is well?'

'I feel fine, Haith, truly. And Princess Mahaut is also well, aren't you?' She tickled Mahaut beneath her ear where it made her giggle. Benedicta was very fond of Mahaut, but she could not say the same for the child's affianced husband. Prince William *Adelin* was a spoilt, over-indulged boy, very different in character from his father. 'Is he like his mother in character?' Benedicta whispered to Haith.

'Not at all,' Haith whispered back. 'The Queen is pious, cultured and static.'

Benedicta laughed. 'You and your pronouncements, Haith! What do you mean, static?'

'If the Queen can remain in her chambers, excepting to go to mass, then she is happy. She has no desire for more.'

'If I had her wealth and freedoms,' Benedicta said, 'I would ride all over the kingdom, looking about me.'

'I know it!' Haith said, casting his eyes to the sky and throwing his long arms up in the air.

King Henry's truce with the Count of Anjou had led to a cascade of other reconciliations. Amaury de Montfort, the Count of Évreux, and his Countess Helwise were all pardoned for their revolt. Benedicta was glad for Amaury's sake. Henry and King Louis of France met for peace talks near Gisors and Henry agreed that his son, William *Adelin*, would do homage to Louis for Normandy, Maine and Brittany. Henry had won out and cut the ground from beneath his enemies.

Orderic had written that King Henry's fame flew through the four parts of the world, and Benedicta observed for herself that although the King certainly indulged his two great passions for women and hunting, he had a third passion and that was his work, his duty as king. His drive to enact his dominion, to set all to rights, set him apart from – and above, Benedicta considered – his two older brothers. The eldest, Robert, the former Duke of Normandy, had been a brave fighter and crusader but, all said, he was too indolent, too forgiving, to govern the unruly Normans, who required an iron fist. Henry's other older brother, William Rufus, had inherited the military zest of their father William the Conqueror, but Rufus was not interested in reaching peace with anyone, or in the administration of peace. Until his untimely death, Rufus had been happy to be perpetually at war. King Henry, on the other hand, curbed his capricious fellow Normans and sought peaceful resolutions. Benedicta still felt rather awed in his presence. There were aspects about the King, this great friend of her brother, which she was growing to like and admire. In turn, that made her feel a little better about her spyings and lyings.

After the ship docked at the English port, they rode to Winchester, where they stayed for one night and then they travelled on to London. Haith, Mahaut and Benedicta were to be accommodated in one of the King's fine townhouses, which fronted onto the river Thames. The ladies of Mahaut's household were used to the life of a great city, having grown up in Angers, but everything around her was a wonder to Benedicta. The King did not delay long in London, pausing a few days only to greet the Queen and then he travelled north on business, leaving Benedicta's brother with her for a while.

Mahaut's ladies, like the Queen, were happy to stay sewing and gossiping, finding out everything they could about the community in their new home. They made it plain that they had little interest in Benedicta's teaching and could see no point in becoming mistresses of Latin verse and literature. They were sceptical of Benedicta's value to their charge. 'The Princess Mahaut's business, Sister Benedicta,' they said, 'unlike yours, is to make babies and we assure you she will know how to do that when the time comes.'

Since there was little demand on her educative skills, after a few hours reading and writing each morning with Mahaut, she left the child in the Queen's chambers and travelled about the city instead, with Haith, as he went about his business. The King had allowed a palfrey for her use, and a river boat – as if she were a lady.

At Michaelmas, the great bell of Saint Paul's was ringing to call the citizens for the thrice-yearly Folkmoot. The citizens of London elected a sheriff and Haith had been proposed. 'I won't win. Not any chance,' he told her, but she waited at the townhouse, hopeful, to hear the outcome, pacing up and down, kicking her habit forward with each step, watching her crucifix on its long strand of beads swing back and forth.

At last, Benedicta heard Haith at the door and stepped into the corridor to see him hanging his cloak on a peg. 'Sheriff Haith de Bruges?'

'No,' he smiled wryly. 'I told you, won't win. London not keen on Flemings.'

'Why not? You are a good, honest, hardworking man,' she said, indignant.

'Easiest to show you.' He reached again for his cloak and plucked hers from its peg. He had bought the cloak for her when they arrived in London, saying her old mantle was shabby and threadbare. This dark blue cloak was a very fine one, too fine for a nun, Benedicta considered, but she slung it around her shoulders nonetheless, admiring every time the heft and hang of it, the intricate embroiderery around the clasp.

The King's house where they stayed was on Knichtrider Street, not far from the river, and in view of Baynard's Castle. Benedicta's nose was constantly assaulted by the scents of Saint Paul's bakery and the hops in the brewery. She glanced guiltily at Baynard's Castle as they passed. Her treacherous eavesdropping had deprived the Baynard family of it. As Father Orderic had advised her, she decided to speak with Haith about her sense of guilt.

'Don't feel that, Benedicta. If we had not discovered Baynard's treachery in time, it could have been disastrous for Henry. If Bellême, de Montfort and William *Clito* had mounted an invasion of England, then London could have easily been turned to their support and all would have been lost.'

She felt a little comforted by that.

'You need to realise what service you have done for King Henry, Benedicta.'

'Yes, perhaps, but there is no threat of invasion.'

'No, but there could be. Henry is a great King because he is never complacent.'

Haith led her down to Dowgate, where an important shipment of luxury goods was coming in. The ship's arrival was being overseen by the incumbent sheriff who ensured order and proper procedure. First, the King's chamberlain arrived to deal with the shipowner to see what was on offer that might be needed in the King's household. After him came the merchants of London. 'Now, see, here are the merchants from Oxford coming next,' Haith told her, 'and after that the men of Winchester. And last of all the foreign traders. Foreigners like you and me!' After watching the trading and order of things, Haith led Benedicta to the nearby cookshop, at Vintry, to get venison pies. Benedicta knew that she would never go hungry in his company. Haith was always hungry. 'Long limbs!' he laughed when she teased him about it. 'Big brains!' he said, touching her head. They sat together eating, watching the river. Benedicta would not have imagined, a few years ago, sitting in her cloister, that they could be so reunited, and here, so far from Almenêches. 'Are you missing your nunnery?' Haith asked her.

'In truth, not in the least.'

Everywhere they went, Benedicta heard the throaty burble of her own Fleming tongue and saw the wealth and great business of the Flemish merchants in the city. 'London trade is controlled by the men of Lower Lorraine,' Haith told her. There were other foreign merchants here: Frenchmen selling wine and whalemeat, Northmen selling timber and furs, but the Flemings were the largest group and the most prosperous.

The river teemed with fish and boats – small and large, so many that Benedicta wondered there were no collisions. In the middle of the city, the river was lined with great houses for the nobles who came to visit the markets, or attend the assemblies and the court when the King was present. Further downriver, the banks were lined with gardens and fruit orchards growing apples, pears and plums. They crossed the crowded wooden bridge, which was lined with the shops of armourers, tailors, cordwainers, saddlers, bakers and pepperers. They shuffled and apologised their way through the crowds. Her tall, big brother was the perfect companion in such a press of people. At the edges of the city were the less savoury activities: the tanners, fullers, butchers, and gongfermors.

During Lent, one Sunday afternoon, Haith took her to watch young men holding wargames. A swarm of youths, not yet invested with the belt of knighthood, wheeled in circles on horses, burst from the city gates in throngs, armed with lances and shields, and exercised their untried skills at arms. Despite the myriad charms that London held for her wide eyes, Benedicta noticed how Haith's conversation suggested that he was missing Pembroke and Wales. He frequently mentioned the Lady Nest ferch Rhys.

'Don't be putting your quick thoughts there, Benedicta,' Haith said, seeing the spark in her eyes, reading her mind. 'The lady is far above me and happily married.'

'If that is the case, Haith, then why do *you* put your thoughts there? If you hanker for what you may not have, then you will never get me a nephew or niece.'

'And that is my primary use, is it?'

'Of course!'

'And have you never hankered for what you may not have?' he asked, his face turning serious, and she felt the playful smile slip from her own mouth.

At Easter, naval tourneys were held on the river. Haith and Benedicta joined the spectators on the bridge. A shield was bound to a stout pole in midstream and a small boat was swiftly driven towards it carrying a youth standing in the prow who tried to strike the shield with his lance. If he struck, splintered his lance and kept his feet, he had succeeded, but very often a youth would strike and be jolted into the rushing river. Other youths were moored in vessels waiting to snatch up those unfortunates before they got sucked down and drowned. On the bridge and balconies of the houses, spectators laughed at the spills, or gasped and screamed if they knew the dunked young men and cared for them.

Later in the year, as winter came on and the weather turned to ice and snow, Haith presented Benedicta with a bundle of boy's clothing. 'How about you put these on and I show you some fun?'

'What!'

'Come on. Don't you want fun?'

'Is it seemly?'

'No.'

She blinked her eyes at him and then stepped into the kitchen to change into the clothes. She felt most peculiar in hose and breeches and was glad to cover it all with her long mantle. 'Do I get to know the mystery now?' she asked, presenting herself to Haith.

'No, but you better put this cap on to keep that stubbly head and your ears warm.' Shaking the maligned head, she took the cap from him and followed him from the house.

To the north of the city there was a great frozen marsh and Benedicta laughed with glee at the sight of skaters gliding, some with iron-shod poles in their hands and some being pulled on seats of iceblocks like millstones. Haith sat her down and tied animal shinbone skates to her feet. 'Do you remember doing this when we were small, in Bruges, with mother?'

'Oh yes,' she said, 'I do.' She grimaced, watching two skaters collide and fall on the ice.

'Remember, keep your feet apart and you won't get any scrapes or broken bones.'

Soon after Christmas, Mahaut was excited at the news that Queen Matilda and King Henry's daughter, Maud, who was eleven, had been formally married to the German Emperor Henry in Worms Cathedral. Haith watched the child bouncing up and down, from foot to foot, describing how she imagined her own wedding. When Mahaut left, after smacking a wet kiss to Haith's cheek, he told Benedicta: 'I just heard that there are plans to build a Benedictine nunnery in London.' He raised his eyebrows. He knew that she was concerned about her future, unsure what she would do when she was no longer needed to contribute to the care of Princess Mahaut. Benedicta nodded, her expression non-committal.

20

Three Kings

'You should know,' Gerald told me, 'that the King will be here within the week.'

I raised my eyebrows in query.

'He is not happy with the increasing Welsh opposition and has brought a vast army into the north to cow the Kings of Gwynedd and Powys.'

This much I already knew from my own sources. King Gruffudd ap Cynan had grown more and more powerful in the north. Owain was allied with the northern king, and had been harassing Gilbert FitzRichard de Clare in Cardigan. My brother had made no move as yet. Henry had been forced to act or see his Norman lords overwhelmed.

Henry's campaign had been meticulously planned and it was impossible not to admire his strategy. Whilst he had led an army into Wales from the east, Gilbert FitzRichard de Clare brought troops across the Severn from Cornwall and marched through our lands to the southern border of Powys, and, at the same time, Richard, the young Earl of Chester, and Alexander, the King of Scotland, had marched from the north. It had been a bloodless campaign and the Welsh commanders had submitted one by one, coming to terms of fealty with the King. Owain had been the last to submit.

'Henry's overlordship oozes everywhere,' Gerald told me, giving me his assessment of how things stood. 'Only a fool would omit the royal will from his political calculations.'

I said nothing. I had spent years in close proximity to Henry. I knew well enough who he was, how he was, but I had no desire to remind Gerald of that fact.

'The King is returning to Westminster but he wished to pay a visit to Pembroke,' Gerald said. 'He has invited your brother to meet him here.'

I hoped this might be a resolution for Gruffudd. If Henry would offer my brother lands and a rich Norman heiress perhaps they might come to terms.

When Henry arrived, I was momentarily shocked to see how his hair had thinned and greyed. The King was getting old. Our nine-year-old son Henry, was acting as squire in the King's entourage and looking very pleased with himself. The King presented Gerald and I with gifts of two beautiful horses. My horse was the purest white and had a very fine gait. I had never before seen such a beautiful beast. At dinner, we made conversation about the new Archbishop of Canterbury, the marriage of the King's daughter and the betrothal of his son.

'I have knighted King Owain ap Cadwgan,' Henry said, abruptly, 'and he has joined my entourage. Of course, I couldn't bring him here. He will accompany me to Normandy soon.'

Gerald could not suppress the look of fury that crossed his face at the mention of Owain's name. For an instant, I thought Henry might have taken leave of his senses or did not care about the terrible insult done to me and Gerald by Owain, but in the next moment I realised that whilst Owain, no doubt, thought King Henry did him a great honour for his valour and importance, Henry simply preferred to keep trouble right under his nose and within reach.

When Henry came to my chamber that evening, I was expecting him. I received him graciously and gave him a beaker of wine. He kissed my hand. He wore a heavily embroidered robe open over his nightshirt and his chest hair swirled at the neck opening, more grey than black now. He saw me looking there. 'A grey chest, Nest. You remember me in the days of black and wicked youth!'

'I doubt there is much change, Sire,' I smiled.

'Running in chainmail gets harder as you get older!' He

considered me for a moment. 'I believe you are rather happy here, Nest, with your Gerald FitzWalter.'

'I am, Henry,' I said quietly.

'Let's hope he can keep you safe this time then. I am weary, Nest. So weary.'

I swallowed.

'I am so rarely the man, Henry, now,' he said, 'that you knew, and ever the vexed king, Henry, *Rex Anglorum, Dux Normannorum.* I should have married you, Nest, then I wouldn't have all this trouble with these Welsh Princes. I hear you have been getting to know them, some of them, very well.'

'You would have had trouble with Scottish Princes instead, Sire,' I said, ignoring his last remark. I heard a sound at the door. 'My husband,' I said, standing.

Henry stood reluctantly with me. Gerald hesitated on the threshold. 'The King is retiring,' I told them both. Henry gave me a remorseful goodnight, and I gave him a grateful smile.

The following morning, my brother rode into the bailey with a well-schooled entourage of men. The King received him with as much ostentation as his chamberlain could muster from the resources of Pembroke. I was proud to see that my brother, too, comported himself as a king.

'I ask your fealty, Gruffudd ap Rhys,' Henry told him. I strained to hear what was beneath their words. I had watched Henry lie so well so many times before.

'I ask that you give me my rights,' Gruffudd responded.

'This territory was won in fair battle from your father,' Henry said. 'You ask that I give back what has been won now for many years.'

'I ask that you treat me fairly.'

'You are a noble and you require lands of your own.'

My brother waited.

'This is not a simple matter since all these lands are now in the holding of other lords. If you will be patient and keep faith with me, your overlord, I expect to reward you with lands that will satisfy you, Prince Gruffudd.'

'You offer me nothing now?'

'Alas, I cannot. Not immediately, but I am about it. I am a man of my word.'

A man of the art of creative delay, I thought anxiously, looking at my brother's face, because I knew this would hardly satisfy him.

'I will wait on your offer then.' Gruffudd turned on his heel and walked swiftly from the hall, his men keeping tight formation about him.

'Well!' exclaimed Henry, turning to Gerald and me. 'I believe he forgot to give me his fealty there!'

'I will wish him godspeed!' I moved swiftly to follow Gruffudd into the courtyard where he was already mounted and the gates were slowly opening for him.

'Gruffudd … Gruffudd! Wait a moment!'

'Sister?' His horse danced impatiently, turning in tight circles. He stilled it and leant down to me. 'That is your king then.'

'Gruffudd, I urge you, be patient as he suggests. He is a fair man.'

'Thank you for your counsel, sister.'

'Please … Gruffudd, consider –'

'Tell me, Nest, where am I to go? Where can I take my family? The only home I have is the mountains or the marshes. I can only feed my family and those who follow me if I raid.'

'Don't let us part in argument,' I begged him. 'Gruffudd, you have heard that Owain ap Cadwgan travels with King Henry to Normandy.'

He nodded.

'Gruffudd, do you trust Owain?'

He smiled. It was a nasty smile. I had seen it on my father's face when he spoke of Owain's father, Cadwgan. 'Owain has designs on Deheubarth himself, I hear,' he said.

'We both know him and we can both imagine there is truth in that.'

'Don't worry, Nest. I am not a fool. God keep you, sweet sister.'

My eyes clouded with tears at his words. He nodded to his men and they trotted smartly to the gate. I put one hand on my hip and the other to shade my eyes, watching him go.

King Henry had gone to Normandy, and King Owain of Powys with him. My landless brother, as far as I knew, was making camp in the mountains and I heard that his band of supporters, his *llu*, continued to swell in numbers, with young men flocking to him not only from Deheubarth but also from Ceredigion and elsewhere. Many older Welsh lords, had, as Gerald said, reached accommodation with the Normans, but those who were dispossessed and the younger Welsh nobility refused this submission and rode to join Gruffudd, so that the bards told how he flew the banner of all Britons now. He signified hope, not only for the Kingdom of Deheubarth, but for all the dispossessed Welsh nobility. These Welsh noble companions, the *kydmeithyon* of my brother, were not satisfied with *sarhaed*, with meagre compensations for the insults done to them. Instead they wanted Norman blood and they wanted land and dignity. Day by day, the bards' stories of my brother gave back hope to resistance where before it seemed to have burnt out. I knew that Gerald was keeping a watch on the situation and that there were many things he did not tell me.

I had been staying at Carew for a week with Amelina, my children and my nieces and nephews. I was heavy with child again. Gerald had been away this last week on the border of Ceredigion and I sorely missed his conversation.

'Nest!' My brother's voice in the courtyard below was urgent. I leant out the window and saw that his horse pulled a bier with a wounded man on it.

'Bring water and bandages,' I told Amelina and ran down. The man opened blue eyes and stared at me from the bier. 'Carry him inside.'

Once he was laid out near the fire, I saw that the injuries I could treat were minor: a shallow cut to his forehead that bled copiously but was soon cleaned and dressed, a few cuts to his arm. I looked with grief for him at the old injuries he carried that could never be repaired. His right hand had been cut off and the stump cauterized. His left foot had similarly been severed. He was a young man in his early twenties and I felt sorrow for him that he must live his youth with such disfigurement. Gruffudd's men brought in a crutch that the man was accustomed to move around with. His injuries had caused him to grow asymmetrical with pronounced muscles in his left arm and right leg, and limbs atrophied where the amputations had occurred. He must have been damaged in this way as a boy to grow so. I guessed that it was the work of a Norman butcher and I wondered at who he was or what he had done to have earned such harsh punishment.

'It's nothing,' he said cheerfully to me, as I dressed the wounds on his good hand. 'Just a few scrapes from getting through the cistern.'

'Well done, Hywel!' Gruffudd told him cheerfully, but his face was a picture of concern.

'He will be fine,' I told Gruffudd. 'Nothing serious here.'

'Apart from the maiming inflicted by your Normans, you mean,' Gruffudd said angrily.

I said nothing in response to Gruffudd's anger but looked back at the man, Hywel, for answer. Now that he was cleaned up, I could see he was handsome, with a cheerful smile, brilliant blue eyes and hair as black as mine.

'You don't recognize me of course. Why should you.' Unlike Gruffudd, he was all smiles and warmth.

'No … I'm afraid –'

'He's your brother, you idiot!' Gruffudd said, gripping my arm painfully.

I pulled my arm from his grasp, looking agape again at the young man. 'What do you mean? I have no other brother.'

'Our brother Hywel! He's escaped from Carmarthen Castle. I sent him in a concealed message and waited for him beyond the moat.'

'I don't understand.'

'She knows nothing of me, Gruffudd. Why should she?' Hywel did his best to calm Gruffudd down. 'Nest,' he looked seriously at me, focusing my attention, through my surprise. 'I was born in Carmarthen after the attack on Llansteffan.' He watched understanding dawn on my face. 'Our mother died birthing me.'

I shook my head in wonder. I took his good hand, gaping. 'Hywel! They did not tell me you survived. I heard only that my mother died and I was led to believe her child died with her.'

'No!' he shook his head laughing. 'Here I am, your little brother!'

I looked between them in wonder. Even Gruffudd had to cease his anger and laugh with me. 'I thought I was alone,' I exclaimed. 'I was alone for so many years. Now how rich I am!'

Gruffudd's face turned dark again. 'But look at what they've done to him. Look at it!' He lifted Hywel's stump arm and waved it at me.

'Do they pain you?' I asked him, gently taking the stump from Gruffudd and holding Hywel's arm.

'Not now. It was a long time ago.' He looked away.

'Who did it?' I asked, praying silently that it was not Gerald.

'FitzBaldwin, who commanded the castle at Carmarthen then. They were doing their best to wipe us out, eradicate the threat of the royal house of Deheubarth, but they failed, eh? Here we are, three of us!'

I took in a breath of relief that it had not been Gerald who had wielded a sword against the flesh of my newly found brother. I smiled at Hywel through my tears and did not voice my thought that a crippled boy, a woman married to a Norman and a king with no land were not much of a threat. I turned to Gruffudd. 'So Hywel has escaped from imprisonment?'

'Clearly,' he said abruptly. 'We need to get him out of here to safety before any of your husband's men discover it and return him to his dungeon or stretch his neck.'

'I wasn't in a dungeon,' Hywel said. 'There was no need. I had the freedom of the castle, but I've never been outside its walls before.' He looked around the hall, enjoying the new view, and then back to me, smiling. 'Nest's husband was always kind to me.' At his last words, I flinched. I felt as if the ground beneath my feet had suddenly become water. Gerald had known of my brother, Hywel, and told me *nothing*.

'Well?' Gruffudd recalled my attention. 'Do you have a suggestion for us, Nest?'

I suppressed the feelings about Gerald that were beginning to form and focused instead on my brothers' situation. I would return to thinking about Gerald's deceit later. 'It would be best to go north to the court of Gruffudd ap Cynan, the King of Gwynedd,' I told them. 'You would be out of reach there.'

'Why not to Owain's court?' Gruffudd asked. 'Powys is nearer. You could send him a letter asking for his patronage and care of our brother.'

'No. I don't trust Owain. Go to Gwynedd. I will have Amelina find you supplies. Her husband, Dyfnwal, has a boat at Llansteffan and he can take you past Pembroke Castle and up the coast. The Pembroke garrison know his boat and will not suspect him. I wish we could have time together, Hywel. Time to get to know one another, but if you have escaped without leave of the Norman lords, you should go immediately.' I looked at him with tears in my eyes and his own eyes filled.

'Your beauty was not overstated, my sister,' he said softly.

My acquisition of two brothers, when for so long I thought I had no kin, should have been occasion for joy and yet all I could think was that now I had two causes for anxiety, for distress.

'We will go north where there are yet more Welsh collaborators,' Gruffudd said bitterly. 'Gronwy ap Owain governs lands in Gwynedd on behalf of the Norman Earl of Chester, and Genllin ap Meirion Goch in Llyn acknowledges Chester as his overlord also.'

'Gruffudd ap Cynan is independent still. He will welcome you, surely?'

Gruffudd pulled a bitter face as if he tasted sour milk. 'Come, Hywel, we must shift from tree to tree, from rock to rock, we who should own this land. Your King Henry, Nest, gives me only a delay on top of another delay and promises like air. So much for your king's fairness and my patience, sister. I've heard not a word of offer from him. He plays me for a fool. He thinks me powerless.'

'King Henry is occupied in Normandy, Gruffudd. Give him a chance. I believe he will treat you fairly if you give him time.' I swallowed. In truth, I was not sure that I believed my words, or Henry's.

When Gerald returned to Pembroke, and then came to Carew a few days later, there was no indication that Hywel and Gruffudd had ever been here, and he said nothing of Hywel, although he must have heard about the escape from the Norman garrison at Carmarthen. I was furious with Gerald that he had known of Hywel's existence, so close by, all this time and never told me. What else had he lied to me about?

The King returned from Normandy in July and summoned Gerald to meet him at Chester, where he had lately arrived with the young earl, Richard, and his new wife, Matilda de Blois, Henry's niece. Since I was carrying a child, I decided not to make the journey. When Gerald returned, he told me that the King's mistress, Sybil Corbet, had been married whilst he was at the court at Chester.

'Married? To who?'

'To Herbert FitzHerbert, the son of the King's chamberlain.'

'I hope she will be happy and that he treats her kindly.'

'As far as I could see,' Gerald said, 'the King was still treating her kindly, despite the marriage.'

'I see.'

He coloured. He was hardly in a position to speak with superiority on that matter. 'What else occurred in Chester?'

'There was a constant procession of Norman lords from across all of Wales conferring with the King, giving reports of their regions, as I did. I suppose it is a difficult thing for him to span such a kingdom, from Normandy, to England, to Wales. He must spread himself thinly and look for the holes in his armour.' I wondered what report Gerald had given to the King concerning my brothers but did not ask. 'Gruffudd ap Cynan was there,' he added.

'Gruffudd ap Cynan?' I felt an immediate anxiety. Were my brothers threatened everywhere they went, hounded as outcasts?

'I don't know the details of the King's business with him. It seemed amicable.'

A few weeks later we heard that Gruffudd ap Cynan had betrayed my brothers' hideout in Llyn and had attempted to arrest them on behalf of King Henry. I wanted to exclaim at such perfidy but could not do so before Gerald. I suppressed my fury. 'Have they been taken?'

Gerald looked at me, not missing my use of the word 'they' or its implication that I knew that Hywel was with Gruffudd.

'No. They sought sanctuary in the church at Aberdaron. They escaped, and their whereabouts are not known. Your brothers are in open rebellion against King Henry now, Nest.'

'Do you think Gruffudd had any other options? Gerald, you should have told me about Hywel,' I said coldly.

He made no response to my remark concerning Hywel. 'Gruffudd should have stayed in Ireland. It will come to grief.'

I looked into his face. 'Gerald ... will *you* speak for him if it comes to that?'

'Yes, I will try,' he said.

My heart sank not only at the thought of my brothers' peril, but at the suspicion that my husband was lying to me. Suddenly, I felt that Gerald's ambition for position within Henry's regime would always take precedence over anything else, perhaps even over his affection for me.

Gerald was at Pembroke and I at Carew, as had become our pattern. Amelina looked around the door. 'Your brother, Gruffudd, is below, Nest ... with a lady.'

I raised my eyebrows but she shook her head. She did not know who the lady was. I stepped to the stairs to greet my brother and his companion.

The woman who turned from the fire was striking. She was a head taller than my brother and carried herself with great presence. Her hair was a thick, dark red cascade the colour and texture of a fox's tail. 'Lady Nest, thank you for receiving us.' Her voice was loud, assured. Her eyes were a reddish-brown and her skin was pale and freckled.

'Nest,' Gruffudd beamed at me. 'This is Gwenllian, my wife, Gwenllian ferch Gruffudd ap Cynan.'

'Congratulations,' I said greatly surprised. 'We did not hear of your marriage. How wonderful, Gruffudd.' I kissed him and the young woman. She was the daughter of the King of Gwynedd and my brother must have fared well in his negotiations there to have won such an alliance.

Gwenllian laughed. 'The news is coming fast behind us, dear sister, and my father is not best pleased.'

'Oh?'

'We eloped,' Gruffudd said. 'Or that is the story to protect Gwenllian's father.'

Gwenllian hurriedly put her fingers to his lips. 'You trust her so far?'

'I do.' Gruffudd said. 'My sister will not betray us.' He looked at me steadily.

I did not condescend to voice an assurance. 'Is Hywel well?'

'He is.'

'How has this come about? We heard that there was … enmity between you and King Gruffudd ap Cynan.'

Gwenllian and Gruffudd laughed. 'That is what we put about,' she said.

'Gwenllian's father gave us shelter as you said he would, Nest. I have raised and trained an army of good men with his support.'

I tried to keep the fear from my face.

'The Norman King Henry required that Gwenllian's father kill or detain me. Her father agreed to it, but we worked a trick between us.'

I looked at the floor. I could not believe that Henry would have ordered the killing of my brother but then it had been a long time. Perhaps I no longer knew him. Perhaps he no longer felt anything for me, no need to show mercy to my kin.

'A trick? What trick?'

'My father organised a fleet to smuggle us down the coast to Ystrad Tywi,' Gwenllian said, 'and he reported that he had attempted to take my husband but Gruffudd sought sanctuary in a church and then escaped.'

I looked between them, trying not to frown. They were a glamorous couple, and the dance of their hands upon each other's arms and cheeks showed clearly enough that there was passion between them. They were enjoying their illicit status. I ordered refreshments for them. 'We won't stay long, Nest,' my brother told me. 'Your husband might see fit to hand us over, or keep us here against our will.'

I could not disagree. Gruffudd wed to a princess from Gwynedd would only strengthen my brother's efforts to reclaim his kingdom.

'Where will you go now?'

'Best you don't know, don't you think?' Gruffudd said, and I coloured at his implication.

'Unlike the Anglo-Saxon thegns at Hastings, we have faced no single military calamity against the Normans and we possess the vital element of time,' Gruffudd declared, and I could see how many would be inspired by him. 'We have had time to withdraw, to submit, to calculate, to regroup. Now I am probing for the soft underbelly of the Norman position here.'

There is no soft underbelly! I wanted to shout at him, and yet, could he be right? Was there a possibility that he could be reinstalled as king here?

'We Britons are forced from our lands,' Gwenllian said, 'first by Romans, then by Anglo-Saxons and now by these Normans and Flemings, squeezed into ever smaller, barren lands. It is time to stop the flood of usurpers, to turn the tide back and drive them all into the seas whence they came.' Her expression was fierce and determined.

A part of me admired her, and another part of me trembled for the future, for Gruffudd and Gwenllian, for Gerald and my children. It was clear that Gruffudd's new wife would not counsel him to compromise, to live a quiet, peaceable life.

'We must act with the steel the valiant King Owain ap Cadwgan showed to his cousin, Madog ap Rhiryd,' Gwenllian announced. Seeing my frown of incomprehension, she said, 'Perhaps that news did not reach here before now. Owain took vengeance for the murder of his father, Cadwgan.'

I waited.

'King Owain blinded and castrated his cousin,' she said.

I said nothing.

'Owain was a strong king and acted well.' She stared into Gruffudd's eyes.

21

The Spyloft

Benedicta and the lumbering entourage of the royal household arrived at the Abbey of Saint Albans in driving sleet. The ride from London in the bad weather had taken the best part of the day, and every part of her body was frozen numb. She slid clumsily from the saddle, barely able to feel her own hands, and ran across the cobbles to the shelter of a doorway at the side of the courtyard. She stamped her feet and hugged her arms to her chest, hoping she would be given warm lodgings. The guesthouse was no doubt bulging with all the visitors for the King's Christmas Court and the consecration of the abbey, but as a member of the King's household there was a chance that she would be lodged somewhere reasonably comfortable.

Sybil Corbet, the king's mistress, who had lately borne him another daughter named Rohese, ran against Benedicta's shoulder, barging under the shelter and giggling. Soon, Lady Elizabeth de Vermandois and her daughter Isabel de Beaumont, were also crowding with them under the eaves. They had arrived earlier than expected and the monks were tardy in their reception. Eventually, Haith succeeded in hammering on the right door and the King's party were ushered into the dry warmth of the hall with the profuse apologies of Abbot Richard.

At the feast, Lady Elizabeth and William de Warenne were seated to one side of the King and Benedicta was seated next to Warenne. Elizabeth and Warenne did nothing to conceal their scandalous relationship. Their hands were constantly about one another. Twelve-year-old Prince William *Adelin* sat to the other side of his father and was entertained by their brazen adulterous behaviour, especially when Warenne went so far as to cup his hand to Elizabeth's cheek. Lady Elizabeth's elderly husband, Robert de Meulan, was suffering from very poor health and had entered a monastery earlier in the year. If Queen Matilda had been sitting with them, she would not have permitted such behaviour at her table, but she was very unwell after the cold ride from London and kept to her chamber.

The King was in a fine mood. He had extracted an oath of loyalty to his son from the Norman barons during his Easter court in Rouen. The French King, Louis, was still contrary nevertheless and had refused to accept the nomination of William *Adelin* as heir to Normandy, and continued to give his preference to William *Clito*. Benedicta's ears pricked up when she heard Elizabeth and Warenne complaining to the King that Elizabeth's daughter, Isabel, had been jilted by Amaury de Montfort who had married Richildis de Hainaut instead. Benedicta allowed herself the indulgence of a moment's memory of her brief hours with Amaury and, in the privacy of her own mind, she wished him well in his new marriage.

'Poor Isabel,' said Henry, knitting his brows, clearly not particularly interested in her tale of woe. Isabel herself was not present. She kept to her chamber, Elizabeth said, suffering the grief of de Montfort's ignoble treatment.

'It shows de Montfort's newfound allegiance to me is thin,' Henry said. 'De Hainaut is a family allied with Flanders, and with William *Clito*.'

'Elizabeth's *girl*,' Warenne said, trying to keep the King's mind on the track that he and Elizabeth were upon, 'is as beautiful as her mother, and de Montfort has lost himself a jewel there.'

'In truth?' the King said, his interest rising, as it always did on the topic of women's beauty. He was very probably, Benedicta considered, the world's leading expert on the subject. 'How old is the child?' the King asked.

'On the brink of marriageable age,' Elizabeth said. 'Isabel is fourteen.'

'Ah.' Benedicta watched Henry studying Elizabeth's admittedly spectacularly beautiful face as if he had never noticed it before. 'We should look about for a better match for her.'

'Indeed, Sire.'

Benedicta craned her neck to look up at the decorated ceiling of the abbey. The whole building was of an unusual design, built primarily with old Roman bricks and tiles from the nearby ruins of Verulanium. The walls, the Abbot had told her, were seven feet thick, and the crossing tower, with its four great pillars, reached for the heavens at one hundred and forty-four feet high. She moved slowly up the aisle taking in the large wall paintings under each arch: Saint Christopher, and then many small altars for other saints. It was the largest abbey in all England. Benedicta knelt at a small shrine to Saint Évroult, and took the latest strip of parchment from Orderic from inside her habit. He had taken to sending her extracts from his writing on a regular basis. Her mouth moved silently with the words written there:

The omnipotent Creator prepares those born on Earth and profitably teaches them in many ways, so that they might not fasten the anchor of their hope in the sea of this fragile world, nor fatally cling to transitory delights or gains. We do not have here a lasting city, as the apostle said, but we seek the one to come.

She was disturbed by two women from the town who stood close to her gossiping about the sexual activities of one of their neighbours. With a sigh, Benedicta rose from her knees and moved up the aisle in search of a quieter place to pray. In her nun's habit, she blended in with the many other religious men and women moving around and nobody took any notice of her. 'This way, Sire.' She recognised Warenne's voice and saw that he and King Henry were moving towards the saint's shrine. The two men were swathed in nondescript brown cloaks, as if in disguise. Benedicta's curiosity was piqued, and she swivelled silently on the smooth grey flagstones, away from the pew she had been heading for, and instead followed them at a discreet distance. What were they up to?

'Here.' Warenne stood at the side of a doorway in a wooden panel, allowing the King to enter before him. Benedicta hesitated, not knowing where the doorway might take her, nor if she was allowed to go there, but when she saw two monks pass inside, she decided to risk it, pulling her hood closer around her face so as not to be recognised. She found herself in a narrow, wooden corridor. Everyone was facing in the same direction with their faces close to the wooden wall. The King and Warenne were at the far end of the corridor, and the two monks were lined up alongside them, peering at the wall. There were only men here, but in her habit and cloak, she was not easily distinguishable from the monks. Curious, she stepped to the panel to see what they were all looking at.

The wooden panel was pierced here and there with small spyholes looking into the shrine of the saint. She had come across such wooden structures in other churches. They were a kind of false wall with just enough space for a person to stand behind, enabling the monks to keep an eye on visiting pilgrims and ensure that nothing was stolen. Since many such shrines dripped with gold and silver, it was an understandable precaution. Here, where they all peered, Saint Alban's shoulder blade was housed in a golden chest, raised up on an ornately carved stone base. The reliquary was draped with a rich red cloth and surrounded on all sides by tall candles. Whilst the two monks may have been keeping an eye on the relics, that was not the concern of the King and Warenne. There were only two people present in the shrine: Elizabeth de Vermandois and her daughter Isabel. Benedicta suspected that Lady Elizabeth was well aware of her audience, but the daughter was not.

Benedicta watched as Elizabeth stood behind the girl and took the hood back from her hair, arranging it neatly across her shoulders and then stepped to the side. The girl had her back to the wooden spyloft and all the peering eyes there received a very good view of the back of her head. Isabel's hair was a wonderful cascade of light brown curls, decorated with twisting strands of tiny pearls and sapphires that glinted in the light of the hundreds of candles illuminating the golden, red-draped shrine. Benedicta heard a low grunt from the King and one of the monks turned to look at him briefly, understanding what it signified but not daring a reprimand to someone who appeared to be a nobleman. Elizabeth then took her daughter's hand and very deliberately turned her sideways on to the spyholes, using the pretence of a bible studded with silver and jewels on a lectern that she wished Isabel to peruse. Isabel had a long slender neck, a small nose and neat ears. Her large eyes were the same unusual turquoise colour as her mother's. Benedicta had seen enough and slid from the spyloft quickly before anyone should notice her there. She walked swiftly down the aisle, fingering the pilgrim badge on her cloak. It depicted the execution of Saint Alban. Elizabeth and Warenne appeared to be pandering the girl to the King without a care for the proximity of the sacred bones.

Benedicta emerged from the great doors of the church into brilliant sunshine, was momentarily blinded and collided with someone who was about to enter the abbey. 'My apologies,' she bent to pick up a scroll that the man had dropped. He snatched it from her and she looked up into the face of the King's chamberlain, Herbert. She was a little taken aback by his angry expression and turned bewildered to a second man accompanying him. A small man with red hair. Benedicta looked with shock at the bald section of his right eyebrow. Amaury's servant. The man gave no indication of recognising her and he and the chamberlain moved on into the dim interior of the church. Benedicta hovered on the threshold trying to find a good reason why Amaury's servant should be in the company of the King's chamberlain but there was none. No *good* reason.

22

Salt-worn Lovers

When my son, David, was born, his care gave me some consolation for the fact that William and Maurice had reached the age when I must also send them away to train. At least, my daughter, Angharad, who was eight and a constant delight to me, would not be leaving. William and Maurice were going to join their brother, Henry, up the coast, in the household of Gilbert FitzRichard de Clare and the kindly Adelisa. I pulled William's collar straight and suppressed my tears. If they thought I was happy about it they would be. 'Your father and I will come to see you in a few weeks' time.'

My brother and his *llu*, his gathered host of Welsh nobles, had begun to carry out raids in Deheubarth soon after he visited me with Gwenllian. They had attacked Norman and Flemish settlers all across the region including a raid on the village of Arberth. People said that Gwenllian rode always at his side, her red hair flying like his banner. They attacked Llandovery Castle, which was held by Richard FitzPons, and tried to taunt the garrison to come out of the castle stronghold. Raegnald had trained my brother well. They burnt the bailey but could not breach the castle motte. It was a painful thought to know that my brother's Welsh warriors were often fighting other Welsh warriors who owed fealty to Norman lords. I saw from Gerald's stress that my brother was having some success, but he had no real base to fight from, having to attack and then always retreat back up into the mountains.

At Easter, Henry returned to Normandy and Haith arrived from London. Gerald told me he and Haith had orders to 'deal with' my brother, in cooperation with Owain ap Cadwgan and Gilbert FitzRichard de Clare, during the King's absence. The worst that I had worried about, that my husband would be in contention with my brother, was happening.

'Promise me you won't kill my brother,' I said to Gerald, and he stared at me, his face flushing from scarlet to white at alarming speed. I frowned. Had he planned to do so then? I thought I was asking him something that he could merely confirm.

'I promise you, Nest, that I will not kill Gruffudd, unless my own life, or yours, or our childrens' depend upon it.'

'If you are in combat with him, you could take him prisoner, could you not? Rather than killing him?' I floundered, confused by his reaction to my request.

'Absolutely,' he said firmly, trying to reassure me, seeing my rising panic.

'What is it, Gerald?' I could not understand the eddies and undertows of our conversation.

'Nothing. It's nothing.' He turned away from me.

We were both unhappy at the constant news of Owain operating close to our borders. He was in Henry's pay, had turned his coat and taken arms against the Welsh rebels, including my brother. 'Will you, ally with Owain?' I asked Gerald, but he shook his head and would not speak of it to me.

I arranged a spray of flowers in a vase on the small table in my room and heard the door creak behind me. I recognised Amelina's tread. 'What is it?'

'Lady!' she whispered.

I turned to her. Whispering signified something to do with Gruffudd.

'Dyfnwal asks that you come to Llansteffan directly and discreetly.'

'Tell me quickly.'

'It's Gwenllian, your sister-in-law. She is great with child and needs our help in the birthing. Dyfnwal's all a fluster at having her in his cottage.'

'I don't doubt it. Pack what we need. I will tell Gerald I am going to Carew and hope he is too busy to visit for a while.'

Standing outside Dyfnwal's cottage, we could hear that Gwenllian's birth pangs had already begun, and Dyfnwal squatted on the ground outside the door, wringing his hat between his hands in sympathy with the intermittent cries wrung from the woman inside the hut. He jumped up at the sight of us. 'Oh, thank God! She would not let me send for any woman from the village, fearing betrayal. I did not know what to do.'

We hurried past him and Gwenllian also looked relieved to see us. How hard it must have been, to lay here, thinking she must birth her first child alone.

The child was born soon after we arrived. She looked sickly and lay too quiet. Amelina exchanged a glance with me that meant she doubted the baby would live.

'Where is Gruffudd?' I asked Gwenllian. 'We should tell him you are safe and have birthed his daughter.'

She shook her head. 'I don't know exactly where he is.'

After a few days, the baby still lived and Dyfnwal helped us move mother and child to Carew under cover of a moonless night. Amelina smuggled them across the courtyard with a hood covering Gwenllian's distinctive red hair, and she took them up the stairs, settling them in my chamber. My steward roused from his bed and came to greet me in the hall, making no remark on the lateness of the hour.

When I went down to break fast the following morning, the steward told me a small group of pilgrims, who were on their way to Saint Davids Cathedral, asked a night's shelter. 'Yes, of course. Show them a place to sleep and see that they are fed. I would speak with one or two of them, as soon as possible.' I knew they had travelled from the east and thought it likely they had heard news of my brother.

A Welsh man and woman, husband and wife, presented themselves to me, thanking me for my hospitality. When the customary greetings, washings and dispensing of wine and bread were over with, they tentatively grumbled about the recent appointment of a Norman bishop at Saint Davids, testing the waters of my loyalties. 'Yes, Bishop Bernard will be another excellent source of information and control in Wales for King Henry,' I said, and impatiently moved straight to what I needed to know. 'I seek news of my brother, Gruffudd ap Rhys ap Tewdwr,' I told them. 'Have you come across any news as you travelled?'

'Aye, Lady,' said the woman in Welsh, leaning avidly forward. It seemed she was the spokesperson for this couple. She spoke in a low voice, conscious of the Normans around us. 'Your brave brother has driven William of London from his castle at Ogmore.' She looked at me with glee, her eyes wide, delighted to be the bearer of such big news.

'Ogmore? Are you certain?'

She nodded. 'All certain!' She tore another chunk from the freshly baked bread and passed it into her mouth, without taking her round eyes from my face.

William of London had been one of Robert FitzHamon's men. His castle of Ogmore was near Bridgend, near Glamorgan, which meant that my brother was threatening the lands of Robert Fitz-Roy and Mabel. Robert was with his father, the King, in Normandy, but his garrisons would brook no such affront to their grip on the land. They would pursue my brother relentlessly.

When the pilgrims had left me, I went upstairs to tell Gwenllian and Amelina the latest news.

'We will cast off the foreigners' yoke, Nest,' Gwenllian asserted, her daughter sucking at her breast. 'Many have joined us and the hope of all Welshmen is with my lord and your brother. Even the wildfowl of Llangors Lake testify that he is the rightful prince of south Wales!'

I ached that I might celebrate my brother's victory with her, but how could I, fearful as I was for him, for my husband and my sons? I envied the simplicity of her fury.

When Dyfnwal visited Amelina, he told us that the local Norman lords, including Gerald, had called a council of native chiefs at Carmarthen to discuss the threat from Gruffudd. 'Maredudd ap Rhydderch, Owain ap Caradog and Rhydderch ap Tewdwr attended,' he assured us. I gasped at mention of my uncle Rhydderch's name. I knew he had submitted to Norman rule as soon as my father had been killed years before, and yet I had not thought he would stay loyal to the Normans in the face of a challenge from his kinsman, from my brother. All these Welsh lords had each pledged men enough for two weeks' defence of Carmarthen Castle.

A week later my brother attacked at Carmarthen and we waited anxiously for news. Gerald returned weary from the fighting and stopped at Carew to tell me himself what had happened. Gwenllian and the baby stayed out of sight and earshot. Gerald told me that my brother had successfully breached and burnt the first ring of defences at the castle, but again had not been able to take the inner motte. 'He is defeated then?' I asked tentatively.

Gerald shook his head. 'He did not take the motte but he takes the hearts and souls of your countrymen, Nest, with his boldness. They flock to him. He commands a large host.'

A week later we learnt that Gruffudd was in Ceredigion where our kin had invited him: the nobles Cedifor ap Goronwy, Hywel ap Idwerth and Trahaern ab Ithel. It was unprecedented for men of Dyfed and of Ceredigion to band together in this way, since they were ancient enemies. The Welsh army burnt the Flemish settlement at Blaenporth and destroyed the castle of Ralph the Razo at Peithyll, who was the steward of Gilbert FitzRichard de Clare. The conflict was escalating. Now the Welsh army led by my brother was marching up the Rheidol Valley towards Aberystwyth. Through the agency of Bishop Roger of Salisbury, King Henry ordered a considerable force to be sent against Gruffudd, and this force included Owain ap Cadwgan, who was no doubt greedy for reward from the English King.

Before the conflict at Aberystwyth, my uncle Rhydderch swapped sides and joined forces with Gruffudd, which was another sign of how strong now was the hope and belief in my brother. The Welsh army, however, was repelled by the massed Norman forces. Gwenllian was relieved when we heard that Gruffudd had evaded capture and fled to the woodlands of Cantref Bychan. After some weeks, Gwenllian and her baby daughter were well enough to travel and she took her leave of me to journey in search of her husband. She refused my offer of sending a guard with her. 'I have no need of your servants, Nest. I cannot trust them. I will go to my man alone.' I layered her saddle and the baby's wrappings with soft furs and kissed

Gwenllian's cheek. 'Take care, my sister.' She returned my kiss and turned her horse's head.

'She is a brave one,' said Amelina, watching her depart and frowning.

'Yes,' I said, mirroring her frown. 'And perhaps too young to be so brave.'

'You were just as brave as her at her age.'

Amelina and I returned to Pembroke, where I hoped to keep any whisper of Gwenllian's recent visit to Carew away from Gerald, and to see if there was any further news of my brother. Gerald and Haith were out on patrol, searching for Gruffudd, and I sat in my chamber, writing up my journal.

'Nest!' Amelina's screech pierced my quiet afternoon.

'What is it?' I was already half-way down the stairs, calling out to her. Was one of the children hurt? My brothers?

In the hall, I saw Haith, dirty and bloodied, and when the crowd around the table cleared, I saw Gerald lying on it, unconscious and bleeding badly from a wound in his side. His face was white and still.

'No!' I gasped.

Amelina pushed past me with a small bowl in one hand and a jug in the other. We all watched her pour water into the bowl, set aside the jug, and gently balance the bowl on Gerald's chest. The hall fell silent and still as everyone there held their breath, waiting to see if there was any breath left in my husband. All eyes were glued on the meniscus of the water, on that small translucent circle.

The water trembled feebly. 'Yes!' Haith shouted, pointing.

'Quickly! Get him to the chamber, to the bed, and gently!' I commanded. The group of men unclasped Gerald's cloak and used it as a sling to lift and carry him between them.

I followed behind with Haith, whilst Amelina flew to fetch the castle surgeon.

'What happened, Haith?'

'We were in a skirmish with King Owain, lady.'

'Owain! But he is Henry's ally now, Gerald's ally?'

'That's not the way Gerald saw it, my lady. We came upon the Prince by accident and he had only a few men with him.'

'Owain wounded Gerald?'

'They fought and yes, Gerald was wounded.' He hesitated. 'Owain was killed.' He looked at me, evidently unsure how I would take this news, if the rumours of my enormous passion for the Welsh King might be true.

'Good,' I said, to set that record straight.

'Gerald's injury is bad,' he told me in a low voice. Haith had seen many battles with Henry and I knew that if he told me this, it was likely to be true.

The surgeon, when he came, was full of rheum and had to frequently pause in his ministrations to sneeze mightily. Amelina and I frowned together and stood as far from him as we could. He dipped a finger in Gerald's brilliant red blood and tasted it on his tongue. 'An excess of black bile,' he said.

When the surgeon was done, Amelina shooed him from the room. 'He is a walking miasma!' she said. 'He's probably killed all of us with his sneezings.'

Amelina and I cleaned Gerald's wounds, made him as comfortable as we could. I sat on a stool at his bedside with a bowl of water and a cloth, mopping the sweat from his face. He had regained consciousness and the surgeon had been cautiously hopeful that he would recover.

'I killed him for you, Nest. He's dead,' he said in a weak voice.

'Oh, Gerald, why did you tangle with Owain, and take such harm yourself?'

'Did you think that I would blithely let him pass me on the road then, after what he did to you, to us?'

'That is past, Gerald. I would rather have you safe and well. That is all that matters now.'

'Nest. I have things to tell you, to confess.'

'You have to rest.'

'No. Have to.'

'Amelina can bring a priest, Gerald, if you want, but you will regain your strength. Be easy. Rest.'

'No. Have to tell you. I betrayed the Montgommerys to Henry. It was me.'

I stared at him. He was delirious. 'No. Richard de Belmeis, the insect, did that.'

'Yes, Richard de Belmeis, but I helped him. I betrayed de Bel-lême and his brother Arnulf, the lord I swore my knight's oath to. I gave the King copies of the Montgommerys' treasonous letters.'

I swallowed. I could not envisage how such a thing could be true. How Gerald, my straight Gerald, my true Gerald, could have betrayed his own lord. 'You sought to be loyal to King Henry,' I said, searching for an excuse for him.

'I don't think you should be having this conversation now,' Amelina said, looking worried.

'No,' Gerald continued, staring relentlessly at me, 'I sought to keep Arnulf from *you*. I wanted more than anything that he should not marry you.'

'Then you did me a kindness, Gerald,' I told him. 'You have been my true husband, my dear husband, always –'

'No ...' he interrupted me. 'More. I knew about your brother, Hywel, maimed at Carmarthen, but I did not tell you. Could not. You would have hated me.'

'I know that, Gerald. I understand.'

'And Gruffudd ...'

'What about Gruffudd?' Gruffudd, was an adult. He had made his own choices in taking the fight to the Normans. I did not blame Gerald for that contention.

'I met him long ago in Dublin, when you were still a girl at Cardiff Castle, but I never told you.'

I stared at him. 'Why not?'

'You would have hoped then, hoped that you might be returned to your Welsh kin.'

I frowned slightly. This seemed devious, more devious than I thought Gerald to be.

'It doesn't matter now. Please, Gerald, just lay quiet and mend. We will speak of all this later.' I looked anxiously at blood seeping through the bandage on his stomach, and turned back to wipe his face.

'More.' His every word, every breath, was a gasp. 'Goronwy ....'

'Goronwy,' I repeated, my hand stilled.

'*I* killed Goronwy, Nest. At Llansteffan. It was me. I was the one who swung the sword that took his life.' He fought for breath through pain.

'You.' My breath stopped in my throat. My mind struggled to process what I was hearing. I felt I might fall from the stool I sat upon. The room span and contracted and expanded again.

'I'm sorry, Nest. So sorry.'

'Gerald, no … .'

'I was a boy myself. I was simply following my orders. I wanted to show I had the mettle for the act.' This was a long speech in his condition and he heaved for air for a longer time. I, meanwhile, could not speak, could not wipe his blood and sweat, could not bear what I was hearing.

'Forgive me, please, my love. I had no idea in that act that all my life with you would be tainted with the guilt of it. I could never tell you. I knew I would lose you.'

I put the cloth stained with his blood in the bowl and sat staring at him, my hands clasped tightly round one another in my lap, as if that might help me stay upright. Eventually, I found words. 'How could you live all these years with that lie between us, Gerald?' The biggest lie, after the lies he had told me when he married me and then gave me to Henry, the lies about my brother Hywel and Gruffudd. 'How could you?'

'I lived in horror with it, Nest. My whole life was formed that day. I killed a boy and fell in love with a girl and all was wrong and wonderful at the same time. No matter what I did, no matter what happened, I could not ever cease to love the girl.' His hand reached feebly towards me but I could not touch him, could offer him no comfort.

I stood and walked from the room, barely conscious of my actions. I walked straight through the hall, out into the bailey, desperate for air, to turn my wet face up to the grey sky. My thighs thumped against the well and I leant on the well brim, my arms spread wide to either side of me. I stared down at the deep, black water.

Stones crunched behind me and Amelina placed her arm around my heaving shoulders for some minutes, waiting for me to find calm. 'Can you forgive him, Nest? He needs you to forgive him.'

'What about what I need?' I whispered.

'Nest, please.'

'No,' I said. 'I cannot forgive him *that*.'

I kept away from the chamber where Gerald fought for his life, sleeping instead in the hall, rolled in my cloak and furs, my arm around my hound, staring at the fire, remembering, recasting my whole life. Everything was lies.

I heard the servants and the men-at-arms whispering, no doubt telling each other that I was a heartless bitch to abandon their master in his desperate state. From the corner of my eye, I watched Amelina come and go, up and down the stairs to the chamber, with bowls of water and bloodied bandages, casting her eyes in my direction now and then and sighing. Once, she came over and stood above me, hands on her hips. 'He's getting better,' she said. 'He won't die.'

I said nothing and she huffed and returned to her nursing.

After a week, Gerald's wound was healed enough for him to coming limping down the stairs. Seeing him in the doorway, I instantly stood and left the hall. I ran to the stable, buckled the saddle on my horse with speed and rode past Haith, who stood open-mouthed at the castle portcullis, as I galloped out. I rode to Carew and busied myself spending time with Angharad and David. I could not face a conversation with Gerald about Goronwy. I tried to tell myself that he had lied because he loved me, but that only made me want to push the thought of him away further.

Amelina followed me a few days later with urgent news. 'Nest, he's taken a turn for the worse again. You *must* come, now, without delay.'

I shook my head. 'I can't speak to him.'

'Nest, the wound has healed but he has some other sickness upon him now. I fear he will die, truly.'

I stared at the fire. It was a ruse. She had always favoured Gerald. Always persuaded me to him even when he had behaved so badly towards me over Henry. 'No.'

'Nest, please. Come for me, if not for him. My heart is breaking to see him die like this, with you unkind and cold to him.'

'Die?'

'I told you. It's not the wound anymore. In his weakened state, he's taken a sickness. He is coughing night and day. A great, racking cough it is. There's blood in his mouth and he is thinned to bones. Truly, Nest, you *must* come. He tosses and turns, now chilled, now fevered, and speaks only your name and moans of his guilt.'

'Then I must come.' Nevertheless, I moved slowly, reluctantly.

At Pembroke, Amelina flung herself from her horse and ran into the hall. I followed her more slowly and felt a chill at the back of my neck at the hushed stares of the servants. I was moving towards the stairs to the chamber, when Amelina came running back down breathless. 'He's worse,' she said, her voice tight, her face distraught. 'The priest's been. You'd best hurry.'

I climbed the stairs behind her to the chamber and saw that Amelina had spoken truly. Gerald was bone-thin and coughed violently over and over. I saw immediately that there was no hope for him but kept the knowledge from my face. I sat next to the bed but still could not bring myself to take his hand. He turned harrowed eyes upon me. This had always been between us, above Henry, above Owain. It was always Goronwy's death and Gerald's lies that had kept us at a distance from one another. I thought of my sweet brother and dropped my face into my hands weeping. I could not excuse Gerald for that killing.

'Nest, please.' He spoke to me as if the two weeks of my absence had not intervened. He knew my mind. Knew what I was thinking. 'It was my first fight as a knight. I wanted to impress Arnulf and rise in the world, prove myself. But Nest, I have regretted that act my whole life, every minute since.'

Yes, I thought, bitterly, there was always ambition lurking in Gerald, in the way he wanted me, in the way he gave me to Henry.

'I have suffered for it, Nest. I have paid for it. I made a grave error agreeing to "loan" you to the King because he could never really return you to me, could he? There was no truth in that notion.'

I looked up and saw Amelina looking at me across the bed, her eyes pleading with me. 'I forgive you, Gerald,' I said, my voice toneless.

Amelina glared at me from the side of the room where Gerald could not see her, shaking her head.

I cleared my throat. 'There were good years, Gerald.'

'You loved me sometimes.'

'Yes. I loved you.' I did not want our last words together to be words of rancour. There was a change in his face. He reached out his hand to me again and this time I took it. Pain and the struggle for breath contorted his features. 'I'm here Gerald, I'm holding you,' I said, salt tears spilling into my mouth. I watched the light dull and go out in his eyes. His eyes closed and would never open on me again. I fell over the bed, sobbing, remembering now, too late, how he had made my life bearable after the massacre of my family, during the early days of my time with the Normans. It was always the sight of his kind face that had given me hope, enabled me to carry on.

There seemed no liquid left anywhere in my body to summon up for more tears. Amelina's weeping, too, had given way to silence. We looked at each other across Gerald's body. 'I can't believe he's gone,' I whispered. 'Twelve years we were wed.' His dead face was a marble likeness of him, devoid of all his colour and vigour. A few more salty tears squeezed through my lashes and trickled to the corners of my mouth.

'We have to prepare him, Nest,' Amelina said, gently.

'No. I will do it.'

'We will do it together.'

'No.' I stood. 'I want to be alone with him.' I was too weary to say more.

She pressed her lips together, got up slowly and left the room.

Looking down at him, I marvelled at how quickly Gerald could cease to be the ingenious, humorous man I had loved and become instead this grey thing. I began to shake and stamped my foot at myself, taking myself in hand. Amelina returned with a bowl of water and cloths. 'Why don't we do it together?' she said gently. 'You will struggle to move him alone.'

Reluctantly, I saw that she was right. I pulled back the sheet from his poor body, all his strength emaciated so quickly to feebleness. I began to untie the laces on his nightgown, thinking of other times when I had done this in love, when the skin beneath had been silky and muscled, not cold and wasted as his limbs felt now.

'I want to wash him alone.'

'Very well. Call me when you need me then. I will bring a shroud.'

My mouth trembled at her word, 'shroud', but stolidly I dipped a cloth in the water, moving as if I were in a dream or under the sea. I worried at whether the water might be too cold for him. I washed him in long gentle strokes: along his arms, from his collar bones to his hips, along his legs. I washed his feet. I had always loved and laughed at his wide feet and their square toes. Memories of us laughing together, feeling ecstasy together, tumbled fast upon one another. I washed his hands that had touched me, lifted me from horses, passed me our newborn children in joy. 'Cleanse him with the water of Christ's side,' I prayed. 'He was a good man.' On balance, I knew it was true, despite the weeks I had spent locked in loathing at his revelation about Goronwy. I remembered everything he had loved me through: my affair with Henry, my abduction by Owain. His love had been true, unwavering, and deep as the ocean.

Amelina returned to help me roll the thing that had replaced my Gerald, back and forth into the cloth. We turned his body to and fro between us to get him first into a shift, and then into the shroud, as if we were dressing a child. How he would hate this, I thought, not to do something for himself. I looked with disbelief at his impassive face, felt the cold of his skin beneath my fingers. We tied the shroud at the neck and I couldn't bear to see him so: trussed, his arms that had fought, that had held me, that had thrown our children into the air, useless now in his death sack. 'I can't!' I collapsed onto a stool, closed my eyes as Amelina pulled the rest of the shroud around his head and face and closed it. How she could see what her hands were doing through the torrents of her loud tears I could not conceive.

23

New Quarry

'Nest, I think you should go down to the bailey.' Amelina's voice was urgent. 'The Welsh have arrived, and the de Clare household too, and it is looking ugly down there.'

Swiftly, I rolled the letter of condolence that I had received from Henry and stepped next to her to lean from the window, looking down on the many people dismounting and arriving. 'Henry writes that he has created Haith Sheriff of Pembroke and places me and my children under his protection,' I told Amelina and she smiled at this. One piece of good news. Haith had been my raft, keeping me afloat in a sea of overwhelming grief.

Gerald was to be buried today, and a truce was called between Normans and Welsh, enabling my brothers and Gwenllian to come to Pembroke to support me. My three boys had come from Cardigan with Lord de Clare's son, Gilbert. In the court-yard, my sons had just dismounted and the grooms were leading their horses to the stable. Henry was eleven and the image of his father, the King; William was ten and Maurice nine. William looked like me whilst Maurice had Gerald's looks and my gaze lingered on his face, on the way he stood, and I thought of how Gerald had looked when I had first seen him. My sons joined a group of other Normans standing in the courtyard who were gathering here to honour Gerald.

As Amelina had said, my brothers, Gruffudd and Hywel, were just riding through the gates, with Gwenllian and Maredudd ap Bleddyn, Owain's uncle, who had taken on the rule of Powys.

My brothers and Maredudd each had a small entourage of men with them. If Maredudd was inclined to seek a blood feud for his nephew's death, it was Gerald's sons, my sons, he must look to. On their part, the Norman lords of the castles that Gruffudd had attacked, had reason to seek redress in his blood. 'I must get them all into the hall and disarmed.'

I ran to the stairs and then slowed my pace a little to pass sedately through the hall where Haith was speaking with a group of Flemish lords who had arrived the night before. In the court-yard, I hailed my brothers, sister-in-law, and King Maredudd in Welsh and saw that the grooms and servants hurried to their needs.

I turned to the Norman group, switching to French. 'My sons, and my lords, you are welcome to Pembroke,' I smiled at them all warmly, trying to take their attention from the black glances they were throwing at the Welshmen behind me. 'Please, come into the hall.' They would have preferred to continue facing off against the Welsh across the cobbles of the bailey but could not refuse my invitation. I felt relief as swordbelts clattered in a pile at the doorway. Haith nodded to me conspiratorially. We had previously discussed our strategy for handling our contentious guests today.

Bishop Bernard had come from Saint Davids to officiate at the burial, and Bishop Richard de Belmeis had made the long journey from London, so that we had been obliged to delay the burial to await his arrival. Now I knew so much more of Gerald's association with de Belmeis in the betrayal of the Montgom-merys, Bishop Richard's presence made more sense, but in any case, he still held significant sway in Wales in Henry's name and would not miss this opportunity to assess the situation and report back to the King. Bishop Roger of Salisbury who held the nearby castle of Kidwelly, had written kindly, telling me he could not be present (he was Henry's main administrator in England and was busy there), but his castellan, Maurice of London, who also com-manded the castle at Ogmore, had come in his stead.

My sons' companion, Gilbert FitzGilbert de Clare, was doing his best, at sixteen years of age, to brazen out his youthful com-mand of Cardigan. His father was sick and likely to die and his older brother Richard was in Normandy with the King. The other Norman lords here were Robert FitzMartin; Miles of Gloucester, who held Carmarthen Castle for his father; Richard FitzPons from Llandovery; and Mael de Neufmarché. I exchanged a few words with each of them.

'I look forward to having you here for a few days,' I said to my son, Henry. 'I will go now to make your uncles welcome.' William and Maurice shifted their feet uncomfortably, and I saw on Henry's face that he did not like my reminder to him that Gruffudd and Hywel were his kin. When they were all seated, with beakers of wine, I returned to the courtyard and the Welsh.

'We won't enter,' Gruffudd told me in the courtyard, before I could open my mouth to speak. 'Or disarm.'

'Gruffudd, please ... .'

'No. We are here, Nest. For you. And because we all knew and admired Gerald FitzWalter. He dealt fairly with us when he could. But I will not enter the hall of Pembroke until the castle is surrendered to me, its rightful king.'

Anxious that no Norman should hear him making that claim, I rapidly gave orders to the servants who were bustling everywhere at my heels. 'Very well,' I said to Gruffudd, 'then I will send water and wine to you here.' The servants began to set up trestles in the bailey to seat the Welsh, and I looked at the sky, grateful that there was no rain. Maredudd gave me kind, temperate words, and I was relieved to find him more like his brother, Cadwgan, and less like his nephew, Owain. I said nothing of condolence to him for Owain's death. I could not put words of such hypocrisy into my mouth.

Gerald's burial was an occasion for grief, for my kin to offer support and kindness to me, but it was also an occasion for the Normans and Welsh to size each other up, to consider what might happen now in the vacuum left behind by Gerald's death. Gruffudd and Maredudd would see it as an opportunity. The de Clares and the Gloucesters would see it as an opportunity. And the King, I knew, would be thinking and planning, even though he was not here. He would act, through Haith, through his Norman lords.

The visitors – Norman, Welsh and Flemish – joined me at Gerald's graveside. No one tried to lay hands on my brothers, but the Normans and the Welsh eyed one another harshly over my husband's coffin. Angharad and Amelina with my three-year-old son, David, clinging to her hand, stood in the shelter of Dyfnwal's arms. David was too young to comprehend that his father would never return to play with him. Angharad and Amelina wept loudly, and I was grateful that their tears reminded everyone how we were here to grieve for Gerald's passing. My older sons stood to one side of me and my brothers and my sister Gwenllian on the other side. Hywel's stump arm was an unavoidable reminder of the violent past between the Welsh and Normans standing gathered here. I screwed my wet eyes up at the unbidden thought of my brother Goronwy's head rolling on the sand towards the surf on Llansteffan beach. At least my task of modulating the tensions between the visitors provided me with distraction from my grief, from thinking about how I had lost Gerald, how I had reason to hate Gerald.

As the priest intoned the words of the burial service, and I smelt the musty smell of the freshly dug earth, I forced myself to look around at the Normans edging Gerald's grave. Henry would soon think of giving me in marriage to one of these men. I was still of childbearing age, and he would not allow me to become a powerful symbol in Deheubarth for a Welsh husband. Henry had given Sybil Montgommery, aged thirty, in marriage to a fifteen-year-old lord when she was widowed. He had married his eight-year-old daughter, Maud, to the thirty-year-old King of Germany. I knew I could not discount anyone, young or old, except the married men and my own kin, from the pool of possibilities. Robert FitzMartin and Richard FitzPons had both recently married, yet the death of a wife in childbed was an ever-present danger.

Miles of Gloucester and Maurice of London were unmarried. As was Mael de Neufmarché. I quailed at the idea of being forced to marry the son of my father's murderer. Would Henry still feel any compassion for me in his decision? Gilbert FitzGilbert de Clare was a boy, a fledgling, to my thirty-five years. But I knew that would be no obstacle if Henry's strategems led him in that direction. The older brother, Richard FitzGilbert de Clare, was unwed and was perhaps a more likely prospect. He would be more than pleased to have his rule in Cardigan extended into

Pembroke, Carew and Llansteffan, and he had the ear of the King where they fought together now in Normandy. Looking round at them all, I had no doubt they would all have their bids already in with the King – their gifts and blandishments arrayed to net me. At least Henry could not give me to Richard de Belmeis now that he was a bishop. That was some great comfort.

I looked down at Gerald's coffin, and my eyes and mind clouded with tears at the so absolute loss of our life together. By custom, it was my brother Gruffudd who should have disposal of me as a widow, but in reality I was still the Norman hostage I had been since I was eight years old, since my father was killed.

Part Three

1117–1120

24

Tithes

Angharad and I emerged from Pembroke Chapel after mass and she took a posy of small purple flowers from the basket on her arm. 'What do you think of these, Mother?'

'Early gentian,' I said. 'They are lovely. He would have liked them.' I smiled sadly at the double cruciform of the flowers, realising that they reminded me of the small cross Gerald had given to me and that I had used in Dublin to pay for Dyfnwal's freedom. The flowers had four purple petals in a simple cross and another interior yellow cross, formed by their stamens. It was our habit to walk to Gerald's grave every Sunday after the service and place fresh flowers there. We lit candles for him too, inside the church, but I preferred our ritual with the flowers. It was more like him, to be outside in the open, under the sky, than to be inside in the darkened, hushed church.

I had been a widow for nearly a year, and silently thanked every messenger arriving with news that the King was still in Normandy. Whilst Henry was there, distracted with rebellions and wars, he could not be thinking of marrying me off. With my husband gone, by rights I should come under the protection of my brothers, Gruffudd and Hywel, but nobody knew where they were. Somewhere in the Snowdonian mountains. Since I owned my own lands and was still of childbearing age, it seemed unlikely that the King would allow me to continue 'unused' forever. My only alternative was to enter a convent in England, but that would mean leaving Deheubarth, leaving my children, Amelina, my life. I could not countenance that option.

Perpetually wearing black gowns and veils was depressing me, and I thought that the arrival of the spring gentians and other bright flowers must be a sign to take off my widow's weeds. I would do it tomorrow. They could not protect me in any case. Amelina had been stitching a new pale blue tunic for me with the bird's foot motif in silver thread at the neck and hem. I could wear a dark blue undergown with tight sleeves beneath it.

As we returned from Gerald's grave, Haith was waiting for us on the path. 'Hello, Angharad, Lady Nest. I wondered if you might stay and eat in the hall, before returning to Carew?'

I acquiesced gladly to his suggestion. Haith went about his work with dogged competence and was ceaselessly cheerful, often when he had no right to be, when he must search for ways to soothe the constant tensions between the Flemings and the Welsh. He often talked to me of his long days' work with complainants, calculations on his abacus, or a mountain of correspondence from the King's chancery and exchequer since he knew I was familiar with the business that Gerald had formerly carried out.

'How has the week been?' I asked him.

'Seems whole world is cup-shotten.'

I laughed. 'Tell me!'

'Not fit for lady's ears,' he said, but launched into his tale with relish nevertheless. 'Got drunks falling from windows, falling in river,' he counted them off against his long fingers, 'relieving themselves against respectable merchants' stalls like dogs! Mostly Flemings in that case, I must say.'

I laughed. 'Just drunks this week?'

'No. Look, I wanted to show you this!' He slapped a large tithe measuring bowl on the table. The wide, shallow bowl had two handles either side and was made from black leather.

I shook my head. 'A tithe measure?'

'Aye, but look close. See here?' He showed me how it had a false bottom. 'The villagers from Lamphey trying to short change the King.'

'What did you do?'

'Gave them a stern caution. Told them if I catch them cheating King again I have to hang them for it.'

'Taxes are high, Haith. Much higher than in the times of my father. What the King takes in taxes they cannot put on the table to feed their families.'

'These are troubled times. The costs of Henry's war in Normandy run high.'

'You can see why Welsh farmers and tenants might struggle to see the relevance of that for them.'

He shrugged, looked away at the tapestries decorating the walls, before turning back to me. 'Kingdom prospers under Henry nevertheless, as never before. No more Vikings or Irish warbands dare invade.'

I nodded. I did not want to be in disagreement with him and there was no arguing with Haith's loyalty to Henry.

He grimaced. 'Had to call an inquest for tomorrow for murdered man in Tenby. And there's been stolen horses and oxen ... .'

'A murdered man?'

'Likely killed by a neighbour. I've summoned citizens to hear evidence, but likely will end: neighbour needs to see priest.'

A hanging he meant. I closed my eyes briefly.

'Yes, horrible. I will have to send command to all to witness the hanging, if evidence damns him.'

'Must you?'

'Not you, lady. That's not necessary.'

I shook my head gratefully. 'Everyone in Tenby?'

'It's the King's orders. That people must witness punishments so they think two times before committing their own crimes. Keep order instead. And what about this reeve for a day election I have to go to at Llansteffan?' he asked. Now Angharad and I had to laugh outright. Haith, meanwhile, pulled comical faces at us. 'Not dignified! Maybe I ban it!' he said. The laughter lines incised on Haith's brown cheeks were looking more and more like the mark of a kite's claw these days.

When I had controlled my laughter, I told him, 'No, don't ban it, Haith.' Every year the peasants at Llansteffan elected one of the men among them to be the fake reeve for one day. Inevitably

231

the first proclamation was always that the actual sheriff should be pelted with rotten vegetables.

'So you say I must go and be pelted with cabbages and listen to this fake one make ridiculous fake proclamations?'

'It's important,' I told him. 'It's a way for them to let off frustrations harmlessly. Just fun. I think we'll come and watch and maybe throw a few soft apples ourselves!' I said, looking to Angharad for her agreement.

Haith had been away at Cenarth Bychan for a week, supervising repairs. He wrote to let me know that he was staying for a few days at Cardigan Castle where Gilbert FitzRichard de Clare had recently died and his son Richard FitzGilbert de Clare had inherited. Haith had to collect the *heriot*, the death duties, for the King. I hoped Haith would return soon with news of how my sons went on there but he arrived instead with my boys: Henry, William and Maurice, with Gilbert FitzGilbert de Clare. From my chamber window, Amelina and I looked down on Haith taking the steps up to the hall, two at a time, on his long legs. 'He's coming to you,' Amelina said.

I stood as Haith entered. 'What is it, Haith?'

'I come to give you notice, Lady Nest, in private, that your brother, Gruffudd ap Rhys, has been taken.'

I thought before the words came from his mouth that I would be able to bear myself with fortitude whatever it was that he came to tell me, but I was mistaken. I dropped down onto my stool.

'He is not injured,' he reassured me. 'We are riding to Kidwelly, where he has been taken to Bishop Roger of Salisbury, who will stand in judgement on him as the King's vice-regent. I thought that you would want to come with us?'

'Yes!' I stood again. It was thoughtful of Haith to take me and my sons to Kidwelly. It might help Gruffudd's case to remind the Bishop that Gruffudd had numerous kin who were loyal and dear to King Henry. 'Quickly, Amelina, make us ready.'

Haith smiled unhappily. 'Your sons are below.'

'Yes, I saw your arrival. I will be down soon. We will ride out in the next hour or so?'

'Yes.'

'I will be with you.' He turned to go. 'Thank you, Haith, for thinking of me. For your kindness.' He nodded and left me.

At Kidwelly Castle, I ran from my horse straight to the hall, not caring what anyone thought of my lack of decorum. I was appalled at the sight of Gruffudd, Gwenllian and their children loaded with chains, and standing before the Bishop and his steward, Maurice of London.

'I am come to plead for my brother, Bishop,' I exclaimed, out of breath, holding my hand to my chest, and Gruffudd turned towards me but did not raise his eyes to my face, shamed by his shackles.

'There is no need, Lady Nest,' the Bishop said. 'I have clear instructions on the matter from the King.'

I heard Haith, de Clare and my sons come into the hall behind me. 'Does King Henry give my brother his life?'

The Bishop nodded slowly. 'The King does not forget you, Lady Nest. Your brother will be treated fairly.' He ordered that the shackles be removed and I listened with relief to the clank of the chains being taken off. With deliberation, the Bishop informed Gruffudd and Gwenllian that King Henry demanded their sons, Anarawd and Cadell, as hostages. 'The King is prepared to offer you land, Prince Gruffudd ap Rhys, in exchange for your fealty and your promise of peace,' Bishop Roger said. 'He gives you Cantref Mawr, on condition that you take no more actions against the King's interests, and that you keep only a small household, for domestic purposes, and no standing army.'

I watched my brother's face as he struggled with the insult of it: to be offered such a small estate when he was the rightful king of all these lands. I saw Gwenllian nod almost imperceptibly and heard my brother speak the words of acceptance and submission. I knew Gwenllian would already be planning their next fight, and that King Henry and the Bishop would keep them under very close surveillance.

25

Mererid and Seithininn

I lifted the hasp and pushed back the dark, carved wooden shutter, looking from my chamber window onto the new day at Carew. A heron on the opposite river bank was disturbed and rose on its vast grey wings. It was early summer and morning mist still shrouded the distant hills and the village rooftops but had already burnt off from the river. It would be a hot day. A sapling close to my window was strung with a perfect spider's web that was just beginning to slack in the slight breeze. Beneath the water sliding over the weir, brilliant green waterweed acquiesced, perpetually bent and flattened with the flow. I heard voices but could not see who made the noise. I moved to the far casement and threw back the shutters. Amelina was below, near the well, rinsing the last of her wash in a bucket to peg out with the other lazily waving cloths. Haith sat on his horse, talking with her. They heard the creak of my shutters and looked up. I was still in my nightdress and stepped back from the window, blushing, although I doubted that much of me was visible to Haith from there.

As I rummaged in the chest for my clothes, I heard Amelina's footsteps come stomping up the stairs. She burst in, leaving the door ajar, rushed to the bed and bounced herself down upon it, holding a hand to her heaving chest. 'Let's go to.' She stopped, breathless.

'Why the rush?' I laughed at her.

'Sheriff Haith's waiting below.'

'He won't mind waiting for a while I'm sure. Let's go to?' I prompted her.

'Llansteffan!' The front of her chemise was wet from her laundry and one of her nipples showed through the thin cloth.

'Well, you'll need drying off first!'

She looked down at herself and shrugged. 'It's not *my* undergarments the Sheriff's interested in,' she said, looking meaningfully at my nightdress. 'He's on his way to Llansteffan and I thought we might accompany him. I'd like to go, Nest. I have some urgent news for Dyfnwal.'

'What urgent news?'

'I've started making him a warm tunic,' she said, lifting her legs up one at a time, and inspecting the toes of her boots.

I stared at the top of her bent head. 'Well, that can hardly be urgent, Amelina, with full summer coming on.'

'There are still chills in the early mornings and late evenings when he's obliged to ride his boat out with the tides,' she said. She stood and took over from me, laying out clothes for me on the bed.

I was not averse to taking a ride on such a fine summer's day and we were both soon more suitably attired. I went to greet Haith while Amelina found the stableboy to tell him to saddle up our palfreys.

'I hope I haven't made you hurry, Lady Nest,' Haith said.

'Not at all. A ride to Llansteffan is an excellent idea.'

The road was overgrown with new summer growth. Haith and I rode side by side with Amelina behind us. Yellow butterflies crossed the path ahead and white seed motes hung in the air. The sky was a flawless blue. I was in a confiding mood. I voiced my concerns to Haith about my widowed state and how Henry might decide to marry me off to somebody or some land- or power-hungry Norman or Welsh lord who might take it into their head to pay court to me. Haith expressed his sympathy with my dilemma.

'I suppose I should marry. It is the best course but I don't want to have my life controlled again, shaped for somebody else's purpose.'

Haith nodded, looked at the overgrown bushes. We reached a fork in the road and Amelina left us to ride towards Dyfnwal's cottage. 'Let's take the road to the beach,' I said, automatically turning my horse's head where I had ridden so often in my childhood. 'Do you think that I should let her go?' I asked Haith, looking at Amelina's retreating back. 'It seems unkind to keep a wife from her husband.'

'I think, this case, would be unkind to keep friend from friend. Dyfnwal knows that. If they live together all day, every day, maybe they not so fond.'

I laughed. 'Is that your view of marriage then, Haith? Is that why you have not taken a wife? You could not stand the sight of one person for so much time!' I was sorry to realise I had embarrassed him. He laughed but his face coloured and he studied the bushes with greater application. I turned our conversation to another, less raw subject, asking if he had heard lately from his sister, who I understood was a nun and in London with Princess Mahaut's household. There was evidently a great fondness between them and I enjoyed listening to Haith talk about her. I was surprised when the vista of the long, yellow beach suddenly opened up before us, not realising that we had made such progress already.

'Shall we gallop on the beach?' Haith said with enthusiasm.

Now it was my turn to be flummoxed. This beach was where my brother, Goronwy, had been killed. The last time I had seen horses galloping here it was the Norman invaders with their swords drawn bearing down upon us; it was Gerald (as I now knew) swinging his blade towards my brother's delicate neck. I looked at the sand twinkling. Little rills and pools left behind by the tide sparkled with sunlight. I stroked my horse's neck. 'Yes,' I said. It was time I replaced bad memories with good ones. I had learnt to ride on this beach with Goronwy. We had trotted up and down, side by side on our small ponies; he so sceptical that I could stay upright and not tumble to the sands in a bundle of aprons and frills he said, scoffing at me. I had proven him wrong, and had always been a good horsewoman.

With that memory in my eyes, I took off, giving Haith a surprise, kicking my horse into a sudden gallop, racing fast across the long, sunny stretch. I raced past the jagged, green shards of a shipwreck sucked down and embedded in the wet sand like the

ribcage of a cow rotting into the ground. It took Haith a while
to catch up with me, even on his big *destrier*, and then we raced
wildly neck and neck, my hair blowing in my mouth and eyes, my
knees gripping. At the high cliff, the beach ran out abruptly with
the turning tide starting to swirl back around the harshly serrated
rocks that were chiselled in green, grey and purple striations. We
were forced to pull up our horses. I stared silently for a while at
the layers of gnarled rock folded around themselves, mesmerised
by the relentless to and fro of the waters, the relentless erasure of
all traces of each day beneath the heavy grey swell of the water,
thinking of everything that it had covered over.

We dismounted to rest the horses. They were lathered with
white patches of sweat. 'There's a freshwater pond just up here.' I
pointed to a goat's path, barely discernible amidst the lush reeds.
'They can drink up there.' I led the way with Haith behind me.
When we came within sight of the pond, we let go of our bridles
and the horses ambled to the water's edge to bend their necks.

'If only we could do the same,' said Haith, looking at the unap-
petising green swirl of the pond.

'The spring is close by.' I took his hand and ignored his surprise at it, leading him through a small copse of trees and up a
slight rise. I, too, was surprised that I had taken his hand, but
decided it would be more awkward to let go now. Perhaps it was
an old memory of running here, hand in hand with Goronwy
that had prompted me to it. The spring was a beautiful sight with
a good run of pure water spurting straight from the rock into
a small, deep pool surrounded by boulders. We let go of each
other's awkward hands with relief and reached to the flow, cup-
ping mouthfuls. I swiped a little of the freezing water across the
back of my neck.

'Hot,' Haith said.

I unclasped my cloak and set it down and Haith followed suit,
soon resorting to stripping off his necktie and tunic too, and
standing in his white shirt and green trews. Looking down at
myself, I wondered if there was anything else that could decently
be removed. It was unbearably warm. I looked with longing at
the small stone pool. If I had been alone, I would have immersed
myself in the water. The horses ambled up the slope to join us

and stood in the dappled shade at the edge of the trees. We sat on the green mossed rocks at the edge of the pool.

'I was thinking to take off shoes,' he said.

'Good idea.' I slipped mine off and let out an inadvertant screech and laugh as I dipped one foot in the frigid water. The wet stones were slippery and I nearly lost my balance. Haith leant rapidly to grip my arm and the shoe he had been in the process of removing flew from his hand, plopped into the pool and sank.

'Drat!'

'You'll have to retrieve it,' I laughed. The horses swished their tails at the flies and chomped quietly on the grass. The air felt leaden, lazy. We sat gingerly at the water's edge, dangling our feet in the water to cool down. Peering at the surface, I thought I could see Haith's shoe below one of my feet. 'I think that's it there.' I leant a little, reaching with my toe to try and hook it.

'Careful!'

Suddenly, I slid fast into the water, finding no handholds to slow my fall, gasping at the cold, my skirts billowing around me, my headveil falling to float like a lily.

'Nest!' With a big splash, Haith was in the water beside me, holding my arm. The horses looked up briefly from their cropping to regard us.

'Don't fear!' I spluttered, 'I can't drown in here.'

'No, but you can turn into a frost candle.'

'A what?'

He dipped his head swiftly underwater and reemerged clutching his errant shoe, which he threw onto the bank. 'Frost candle. You say icicle.' He followed his shoe, hauling himself easily onto the bank with his long arms, but his bare feet slipped and slid on the rocks. Water poured from his trews and shirt. He held one arm fast around a boulder and reached another to me.

He hauled me out to stand before him, and shivering, feeling the moss between my bare toes, the weight of my sodden gown, I stepped close to him, put my hand on his chest and kissed him. It seemed as if the moment before I had been unconscious. There was no thinking. Then I was aware of my mouth on his, my tongue exploring his lower lip. 'Oh.' I stepped away from him. Should I apologise?

'My lady, forgive me.'

I looked up at him through wet lashes. 'It was me.' Words are impossible, I thought impatiently. I stepped close to him again, took his face in my hands, stood on tiptoe to kiss him again. Perceiving that there was no error here, no fault now, he responded, his tongue sliding into my mouth, his hands following the contours of my shoulders and then my breasts. We were both breathing heavily, plucking at each other's wet clothes. My gown dropped heavily to the ground like ripe fruit falling from the tree. The horses took no notice as we stood naked together in the dappling green. We lay on the ground and he slid his hands along every surface of my body, and I did the same to him, delighted by the long, solid planes of his arms and the contours of his muscled stomach. I touched my fingers to the scar on his shoulder where I had pulled out the arrow. I knelt above him and slid him into me, never taking my eyes from his face as I rose up and down on him. I cried out with pleasure and subsided on his chest. We lay heaving in synchronicity with one another, our breath gradually slowing, the sun warming my back and buttocks as I lay against him. Something just for myself, I thought. I have taken something I wanted for myself.

He caressed my shoulder. 'Your skin is white as the wave tops, and your dark hair rolls and ripples like the sea,' he said, twirling a strand around his finger. '*Yr wylan deg ar lanw, dioer,/Unlliw ag eiry neu wenlloer.* O sea-bird, beautiful upon the tides,/White as the moon is when the night abides.'

I lifted my head to look at him in great surprise. 'It was you!'

'Yes,' he said. 'I remember when I first met you in a boat on Thames. You were a brilliant, shining girl on your way to Westminster for the first time, before you were married.'

'I remember. You overslept that morning!' We laughed.

'No improvements,' he said. His face became serious again. 'Had to watch you come to Henry after your husband betrayed you to him.'

'Gerald did his best for me. He loved me.'

'Yes, and he was ambitious for himself.'

A tear escaped the corner of my eye. 'And you, Haith? You have no ambition?'

'My only ambition,' he said, touching a fingertip to my tears, 'is not to be the cause of this.'

We were silent for a while. 'I watched you fight your battles so valiantly,' he said. 'With Henry, with Gerald, with Owain. And must stand by, my hands hanging useless.'

'I never thought of any of it as fighting battles.'

'No?'

'Perhaps.'

'I got frantic when Owain abducted you. Begged Henry to send me in pursuit but we were in Normandy and the news was three months old at least. He said de Belmeis was a better course.'

'He wished to keep you with him.'

'Yes. I badgered every messenger for news of you. It's the only time in my life I considered disobeying the King. I couldn't understand how Henry and Gerald could be so calm about it. Henry simply said: "She won't be harmed", and Gerald did not reply to my letter.'

'You wrote to him?'

'Yes, seeking news of you, of the actions made to recover you.'

I pondered this and realised that Gerald had made precious little effort to rescue me. As far as I knew, he had sent no pursuit and no delegations to Cadwgan. My rescue had been wholly the work of Henry, through his mediator, de Belmeis. Gerald had just passively received me back. He had been shamed to have his wife stolen by a Welsh prince, and at his own escape through the *garderobe*. His shame and his anger had been stronger than his love or care for me.

How stupid I had been, all this time, not to see how Haith felt about me. How stupid not to see how I felt about him. 'Again?' he asked and I smiled, rolling off him and onto my back, opening my legs. His hand covered one of my breasts and he knelt above me, looking at me. I gasped as he entered me, as I had gasped at the cold water of the pool, and I gripped my two hands around his buttocks, pulling him harder and faster into me until we both fell still and silent again.

'Nest! Haith! Lady!' The crash of branches being moved about came from the copse below.

'Oh Lord! It's Amelina!' We had been lying there for hours. I had lost all track of time. The horses stood quietly, their bridles trailing, each with one leg resting on the tip of a hoof. I scrabbled for my clothes that had begun to dry in the sun but were still very damp and pulled on what I could with difficulty. I slung my cloak around me and turned back to Haith to see that he too had the semblance of decent clothing about him just as Amelina crunched up the slope and appeared next to the horses, at the edge of the trees.

'Lord! Nest! I've been worried out of my mind. The tide's come in and I saw the hoofprints on the beach. I thought the worst.' She sat down abruptly on a boulder, breathing heavily, her face flushed and sweating.

'You need not have feared. I've known the waters of the bay since childhood. They would not take me.'

'That's what Mererid and Seithininn thought,' she said crossly, frowning at Haith, taking in the fact that neither of us were wearing shoes.

'Mererid and Seithininn?' he asked, bewildered.

'Lovers who drowned here and the whole court with them!' she told him. 'I thought you had business at the castle.' Her tone was accusing.

'Yes. I must go there now. I'm very sorry, Amelina, that we have made you anxious. You are hot,' Haith said.

'Yes.'

'And bothered,' I said, not inclined to be chided by my own maid. 'So, did you give Dyfnwal his urgent news?'

'Yes.'

'That he is going to be a father,' I said.

Amelina and Haith both gaped at me in surprise. 'Yes,' she said.

'You think I would bear,' I hesitated at the count, thinking of my lost sons in Dublin, 'so many children and not recognise the signs?' I bent to kiss her cheek and Haith gave her his delighted congratulations.

'We should take better care of you, then,' he said.

I lay in bed with Haith, staring into the cracking fire, sated with lovemaking. After a very hot summer and a fine autumn, the evenings were beginning to draw in again and I enjoyed the sense of secret enclosure with him. 'Tell me about your homeland, Haith.'

'Flanders?'

I wanted to watch his mouth move, to hear his voice.

'Hmm. Well, it's long time since I been there. Was a small boy when I left.'

'But you remember something of it?'

'For sure. Remember how all life was about wrestling with water.'

'Because of flooding?'

He nodded. 'We had to always dig. Digging ditch to direct water, digging peat to burn and stay warm. Made embankments, dams, dikes. Shored up polders with planks, layers of seaweed and reeds.'

'What did the land look like?'

He pursed his mouth, thinking, remembering, and I smiled to myself at the sight of it. 'Peat mires, waterlogged and decaying plants and trees, lagoons, dunes, salt marshes, small streams fanning out, shallow lakes and swamps. During wet seasons great areas stood under water. Waterbirds came, delighted to find land turned to lake, make them new homes, but our homes washed away, were damp, inundated, everything always leaking and seeping.'

'You experienced bad flooding?'

'Yes. It's why we had to leave in the end. My mother had to send me and Benedicta away. No choice. We had nothing left. No home. She had worked for Queen Matilda, Henry's mother, and she wrote to ask for help. Queen took me into her household as playmate for Henry. Gave me education. She sent Ida, my little sister,' he said, smiling sadly, 'to the abbey at Almenêches. Maybe I cried as much water over *that* as floods,' he said, the smile-lines of his face crinkling. I traced the lines like the bird's claw with the tip of my finger.

'Ida?'

'It was her name before they made her a nun, made her Benedicta.'

242

'Were you afraid when it flooded?'

He nodded again. 'For sure. There were many strong storms.' He waved his hands to imitate the maelstrom. 'Storm-driven waves, wind-driven water, whipping sands, high tides crashing on shore, constant rain. Devastation and despair of floods. All our endeavours washed away.'

'Your description is making me feel waterlogged!' I exclaimed.

He laughed. 'Yes, the water wolf stalked the land. We tried to tame but never could vanquish that wolf.'

Haith had to make a journey to Carmarthen, and when he returned he came with bad news. He had received a summons from Henry in Normandy where rebellion was brewing with Henry of Eu and Stephen of Aumale, who were now both supporting William *Clito*'s claim. He read the letter from Henry to me telling of how conflict was building again with King Louis. Count Thibaut de Blois had taken King Louis' ally, Count William de Nevers, prisoner and had been waging war against Louis. Amaury de Montfort had suborned William Pointel, the man whom King Henry had left commanding the garrison at Évreux. Pointel had betrayed the citadel to de Montfort. The Bishop of Évreux, Audoin, who was loyal to Henry, had been forced to flee. 'The Bishop has vowed not to shave, until his cathedral is returned to him under the rule of Henry,' Haith told me, looking up from the letter. We exchanged an amused glance at the thought of the dishevelled bishop with an overgrown beard.

'If you must go,' I said, 'then I must have my tithes paid first.' I led Haith up to my chamber and took him to my bed. Afterwards, we lay in a shaft of sunlight that sparked his hair, lit the beautiful curves of his face and neck.

'Am wondering if there's a solution to your concern of being eligible widow, Nest.'

I raised my eyebrows.

'Why not marry Sheriff of Pembroke?'

'Marry you?'

'Ridiculous idea, sorry.' His face assumed a theatrical contrition. 'Was thinking could protect you from unwanted marriage. Make no demands on you. Just thinking that.'

I stroked my fingers deep through his thick golden hair, which was streaked with a few threads of white. 'It's a good idea,' I said.

He looked up, his eyes alight. 'Truly?' Then he grimaced. 'King won't be happy.'

'He owes me happiness. He owes you happiness. I would not marry you, Haith, because I need a husband who makes no demands on me.'

He grinned at me.

'It would be because I love you.'

'I will look for good time to speak with King about marrying you,' he said. I tried to keep the frown from my face, suspecting that this request would not be well received by Henry.

Haith had been gone from me only two weeks when I discovered that I was carrying a child. Amelina and I laid plans for me to conceal the pregnancy as it progressed. We let out the seams on my gowns so that they fell in voluminous folds to conceal the thrust of my belly for as long as possible, but the time came when this ruse would soon fail. I kept to my room for a month with a supposed chill and when the child was due we went to Dyfnwal's cottage. I birthed him there and he lay in a cradle next to Amelina's own small daughter. I named Haith's son, Robert. He was big, pink and squalling. With enormous delight, I let him grip my finger with his angry little fists.

When Amelina and I returned to Carew, we allowed everyone to assume that Robert was her child, a twin to her daughter. We sat together in my chamber when I fed him. There was a letter from Mabel FitzRobert waiting for me, telling me of the deaths of Queen Matilda and Robert de Meulan. The King, she wrote, had been unable to return from Normandy to be at the Queen's bedside, but he had ordered and paid for candles to be burnt for her soul in perpetuity in Westminster Abbey. I knew Henry would be miserable at these losses and I sent him a letter of condolence. Although his relations with the Queen had been more business than love, I knew he had respected her, been grateful for her counsel and support. The conflict in Normandy must be severe that he had not returned to see her in her last illness, had not traversed the English sea to attend her burial.

Soon after I received this letter from Mabel, another came from Elizabeth de Vermandois, Countess of Leicester. She confirmed my concerns for Henry, telling me that, with the rapid succession of deaths around him, he had told her, 'my friends die and leave me, Elizabeth.' She wrote to invite me to her wedding to William de Warenne.

Amelina packed my best gowns carefully into a chest preparing for my journey to London. 'Didn't even wait for her husband to be cold in the ground then!' she said, scandalised, and perhaps also intending some criticism of me.

26

A Murder of Crows

Benedicta set her foot unsteadily back onto the soil – or the jetty at least – of Normandy. This voyage had been very rough and, even standing on land, she was shaky with the nauseating roll of the ship. Haith had written to tell her that the King commanded her to bring Mahaut to Breteuil. She had frowned over the letter. Usually such a command would come directly from King Henry's chancery to Princess Mahaut and would merely mention Benedicta's accompanying the Princess as a side issue. Furthermore, Haith had sent the letter in their customary cipher, which they generally only used for personal exchanges. Nevertheless, Benedicta had implicit faith in her brother and since he told her to bring Mahaut to Breteuil, that is what she was determined to do. She told the Princess's ladies that it was a command from the King and ensured that they travelled with an adequate armed guard for the journey.

The day after arriving on the coast of Normandy, Benedicta and Mahaut were barely restored from their sea journey before they had to suffer the different sort of shaking motion of many long hours on horseback. Despite the discomforts of travel, Benedicta revelled in a sense of adventure, in going to encounter something never known before, but, as twilight fell, her thoughts turned more gloomy. Robert de Bellême had recently died in captivity at Wareham Castle. Although she and many others had suffered from his actions, she felt some pity for the man – so proud and active and reduced to pacing a small room, helplessly, for the last years of his life. Had she been right in allowing her actions to condemn him to that?

She was glad when they arrived at last at the fortress of Breteuil not long before full dark, exhausted and hungry, and she could leave her anxious thoughts on the road behind her. Haith greeted them in the courtyard and Benedicta saw Mahaut safely ushered to a comfortable room with her maid. Instead of receiving Benedicta in the hall, Haith suggested that she follow him to his private quarters.

As soon as they were alone, she turned a questioning face to her brother. He pushed a fine, lion-shaped aquamarelle towards her across the dark wood of the table. A serpent undulated along the lion's back to form a handle and a tail. She twisted the small tap in the lion's chest and trickled water into a bowl, rinsing her hands. She slid a damp cloth over her face. 'Do you mind?' she said, tugging at her veil and when Haith shrugged, she pulled the constricting cloths from her head and ran the damp cloth around the back of her neck and under her chin. 'It was terribly hot on the road.'

'You and your golden head, looking like a harvested field under a late summer sun! You are an immensely welcome sight, Benedicta, and you will bring salve to the King.' His face clouded at his concluding words.

'What has happened, Haith?'

'Take refreshments and brush the dust of the road away before you see the King and I will give you the details.' There was misery in his face.

'Are you well, Haith? Is the King injured.'

'Not physically injured. He has need of you.'

A servant knocked, entered, and set a bowl of thyme-scented pottage and fresh bread before Benedicta. She felt conscious of her naked head exposed before this unknown man. He bowed and left, closing the door behind him, the latch clicking into place.

'Everything started to deteriorate again after William d'Evreux died and King Henry refused the county to Amaury de Montfort,' Haith began. 'Henry tried his usual tactics with the wedding of Hugh of Gournay's daughter to Nigel d'Aubigny, thinking that would keep Hugh on our side, but his sister was no sooner married than Hugh walked out and declared himself in revolt against Henry, and others followed: Robert Giroie and Robert de Neubourg. It is Amaury, Benedicta, who has caused the sedition. Everywhere we look, in every direction, we see his animosity driving all towards chaos.'

Benedicta nodded, keeping her gaze down, not able to trust her features with the mention of Amaury. The ability of that golden-haired brother and sister – Bertrade and Amaury de Montfort – seemed almost magical in the way that they were so compelling for others – Bertrade leading the old King of France into such murky waters with the Church, into excommunication, and then Amaury ... .

'The King is in a bad state, Benedicta. I don't know what to do. I've tried to keep it from everyone, hoping he can recover himself. It's best if nobody knows of it, but it's been three days now and there is no improvement.'

'He is ill?'

'In his head, in his mind.'

Benedicta frowned. She could not imagine the King, who was usually so certain, so omniscient, in any state of mental feebleness.

'Some terrible things have happened and he is unhinged, unnerved by it all. There have been attempts against his life. He has nightmares. Talks to himself. I'm really hoping you can help me to bring him round, because if not, I do not know how to act next.'

'Perhaps you should have contacted the King's adminstrators, Bishop Roger of Salisbury and Bishop John de Lisieux?'

'I was hoping he would recover. To contact the Bishops seems a drastic step. I don't want to alarm everyone or undermine him unless there is no other option.'

'Why did you ask me to bring Mahaut?'

'He did command that himself, but then he was too distracted to dictate to a scribe. I thought the sight of her might cheer him.'

'That child would cheer anyone!' Benedicta said enthusiastically. She knew Haith was not given to exaggeration. If he was so anxious for Henry's sanity then he had good cause, and, if so, the stability of England and Normandy were under grave threat. So much depended on the King.

'We could apply to Countess Adela for assistance,' she said.

'Yes, that might be necessary. I would certainly trust the lady with such a delicate matter, but with her sons, I am not so sure ... they are in line for the succession ... .'

'Then it is Prince William *Adelin* who should be first to know if it continues so serious.'

Haith nodded, but the silent glance that passed between them expressed their mutual concern at the thought of the kingdom in the hands of that spoilt, unthinking boy.

'Perhaps, so,' Haith said. 'All I know is that the business of the court piles up around our ears because Henry is incapacitated and soon it will be apparent to all. Come into the hall and I will explain a little more, and then I will take you to Henry so that you can see for yourself. Help me make a decision what to do.'

Benedicta gripped his hand. 'Of course, Haith. I am glad you felt I could aid you. I will if I can.'

She moved to the door with him but he halted her, reached for her veil and wimple. 'Best cover that shimmering wheat stubble,' he said.

The hall seemed hung with misery, although Haith had said only he, and now she, knew of the King's parlous state. The few men and servants in the hall moved listlessly about and did not look up curiously at their arrival.

'Tell me quickly, Haith, what has happened here? Is there more?'

'Perhaps you heard that at the end of last year Etienne de Blois was ejected from Alençon by the people.'

'I had not heard it, but it does not surprise me.'

'Fulk d'Anjou responded to the invitation of the citizens of Alençon and took the stronghold, cast Etienne out. This was a bad turn for Henry. He must be able to trust his lords to hold what he wins with so much hardship. Then worse occurred when Henry's army attempted to take the fortress back and were defeated by Arnulf de Montgommery and Fulk.'

'Arnulf de Montgommery,' Benedicta said. 'He is Robert de Bellême's brother.'

'Yes.'

'And it looks bad for Mahaut's betrothal to William *Adelin* if her father has returned to contention against the King once again,' Benedicta said, frowning.

Haith sighed. 'We suffered heavy losses at Alençon, and Thibaut de Blois was badly injured. It was the first time Henry has ever been defeated. He worried that the tide had turned against him, that the Wheel of Fortune might drive him downwards. He has been trying to make peace with Amaury de Montfort, and failing. It is reported that Amaury is galloping all over the country exhorting all to revolt. He is working as an agent of King Louis against Henry and has a silver tongue. Even when Henry has made peace with these lords, Henry of Eu, Hugh of Gournay, Fulk d'Anjou himself, Amaury succeeds in charming them all back to sedition.'

Benedicta thought of Amaury's saddlebag and cloak slung in haste to the corner of the room at Fontevraud. She thought of her veil and wimple slung to the same corner, also in haste, and all that followed. She tried not to think of Amaury's tongue. Pressing her lips together in case a moan escaped her, she listened and nodded to Haith as if her mind were here in the room instead of galloping with Amaury, his arms around her waist.

'And now de Montfort has repudiated his first wife and married Agnes de Garlande.'

'Another wife!' Benedicta gaped. 'He only just married Richildis, surely.'

'Yes, the marriage did not last long, although Richildis bore him a daughter. Seems Richildis didn't suit or the Garlandes dangled the new wife and high office before his eyes, at any rate. But now neither the French King nor the English King are content with de Montfort.'

Well, Benedicta thought, I do not suppose that my worrying about him will do him any good. He is, for certain, a man able to take care of himself, and brazen enough, yes, to antagonise two kings, just as his sister, Bertrade, had set every priest across Christendom on their ears. There was something admirable about such a lack of obsequiousness.

News of the wars in Normandy had flown back and forth

across the English Sea, and Benedicta was aware of most of what Haith told her. As he spoke, she watched two small girls, finely dressed, enter the hall, led by two nurses. The girls both wore bandages about their eyes and Benedicta was startled to see that their small noses had been sliced and crusted blood showed there like tiny jewelled berries. She stared. Were they victims from Etienne de Blois' injustices? She turned back to Haith and his eyes were also on the two girls who chattered and laughed despite their injuries. His eyes were full of sadness, but he did not speak of the girls. Instead he continued with his tale.

'At the urgings of de Montfort, the King's daughter, Juliana, joined the rebellion against him with her husband, Eustace de Breteuil. The loss of Breteuil would have been crippling for Henry.'

Benedicta tried to scrub the query from her mind concerning Amaury's urgings to Juliana. What form might they have taken?

'Juliana tried to kill Henry,' Haith said.

'Her father?' Benedicta said, aghast. What could have happened to cause that? 'The King is a loving father.'

'She had reason.' Haith hung his head.

'Reason? Be more quick and full with your news now, Haith, that I might get about any help I can bring.'

He looked up smiling again. 'You are always a help. And impatient!'

'What reason could Juliana possibly have to attempt murder against her father?' Benedicta said.

Haith looked over to the two bandaged girls. 'Her daughters.'

'What?'

'Those girls are the daughters of Juliana and Eustace; Henry's granddaughters. They were given as hostages during the dispute between Henry and Eustace, in exchange for the young son of the steward, Ralph de Harnec. A terrible thing occurred, Benedicta. Eustace blinded the steward's son.'

'What? Why?'

'Speak low. I don't want them to hear us. Frankly, Eustace is a stupid man. Since he had blinded the boy, Henry had no option but to give up his granddaughters to the steward.'

Benedicta stared open-mouthed at him. 'No option?'

251

'The steward blinded the two girls and sliced their noses, maimed them as the law allowed,' Haith said in a whisper.

'The law! And *Henry* allowed that?'

Haith frowned, bit his lip.

'He has gone mad.'

'He had no option. He must adhere to his own laws.'

'He is *the king*.' Benedicta said. 'He always has options. His own granddaughters!'

'He is horrified at it. Out of his mind with grief and distress for the children, even for Juliana. He says he wants you to do what you can to help the children, but I believe you could do more to help him.'

'I don't want to help him.'

'Juliana tried to kill him with a crossbow but missed.'

'I don't blame her. What has happened to her?'

'Don't speak treason, Benedicta, please. That is not helpful. Juliana escaped. She jumped from the castle walls into the moat and got away.'

Benedicta said nothing, only gazing with compassion at the two girls who fumbled for their toys, sightless. She was horrified and disillusioned with the King. 'Haith, you should leave his service. You cannot serve such a man.'

'Please, Benedicta. Try to find compassion for him. He hates himself. Then there was the assassination plot against him from his chamberlain, Herbert, who has been a trusted servant for years. He was found standing over Henry as the King slept. Herbert carried a serrated hunting knife in his hands and was about to strike. It was just by chance that I wandered into the chamber at that very moment, to find a wine jug.'

Benedicta swallowed, remembering how she had seen Herbert with Amaury's servant in Saint Albans, and told nobody of it. Perhaps she was to blame. If the assassination attempt had succeeded. ...

'Is it known why Herbert wished to harm the King? Has he confessed?'

'His son is married to Sybil Corbet, Henry's mistress, and I suppose this is the cause of his murderous anger. We suspect

Amaury de Montfort had a hand in suborning him but have found no evidence of it.'

Benedicta compressed her lips. 'What father would wish to see his son married off to the King's leavings?'

'Hush!'

'You stayed the knife?'

'I wrestled it from Herbert's grip but you can imagine the horror of Henry awaking to such a scene taking place above his bed.'

Haith went to see if the King was able to receive her, and Benedicta sat, looking everywhere in the hall except at the two girls, contemplating this news. It cast her own actions into a different light. Henry and Adela, with their network of spies, including her, had corrupted so many people to deceit. She knew that it was her choice and she could not pass the blame to others, yet whilst Henry had seemed a good king she had been able to defend herself *to* herself, but now? Had she lied to friends, broken her vows to God, for the sake of a wicked man, a wicked king?

Despite her loathing and shock for what had happened to the King's granddaughters, a wave of pity swept over Benedicta when Haith led her into Henry's chamber. The King looked diminished. He was dishevelled and barefoot. She had never seen him anything but splendidly attired. There was a musty smell about him. 'He needs a bath,' Benedicta muttered to Haith's bent ear.

'I know but I can't persuade him to it.'

The King mumbled to himself, shivering and shuddering as if he had a fever. He sat on his bed surrounded by what looked like large jewels which he was prodding and pushing, rearranging on the quilt between his legs. An array of weapons was propped up against the sides of the bed – a sword, two short axes and a dagger sat on the pillow beside him.

'What's he doing?'

'Touching all his reliquaries. He has been collecting them for years. He hopes they can fend off the bad luck, the threat of death and damnation hanging over him.'

Benedicta sat down gently on a stool next to the bed. 'What have you there, Sire?'

'Fingerbone of Saint Barbara,' Henry said, holding up one golden container to her. She took it and examined the fine work. It was a diamond shape with four coloured jewels at each tip and a central white stone. Benedicta ran her finger reverently across the lumpen jewels and along the golden engraving. 'Saint Barbara, bless and cleanse Henry de Normandy of his sins,' she said, and kissed the central jewel.

'Kneecap of Saint Matthew,' he said, exchanging it for the return of Saint Barbara's finger.

'Perhaps a rather worn kneecap from a great deal of praying,' Benedicta remarked. Henry looked at her, his face clearing a little. 'You amuse me, Sister Benedicta. You are funny. And your brother.'

'Saint Matthew, bless and cleanse Henry de Normandy, I beseech you with the ceaseless prayers and hymns of a pious nun,' Benedicta said, kissing the relic, trying not to laugh with black humour at the King's plight and the notion that she was a pious nun.

Henry looked at her warmly and she returned his glance with a kindly gaze. 'Will you let me order a bath for you, Sire? Find you something to eat? And then some sleep would be a fine thing, no?' She had remarked the black circles beneath the King's anxious eyes. At the periphery of her vision, she saw Haith nod to her.

'I fear I have lost myself, Sister,' the King said, casting a haunted stare upon Benedicta. 'I tried to be a good king but I am an ogre. Everyone wants to kill me. Perhaps I should let them.'

27

Marriage

Our boat docked at Queenhithe. I steadied Angharad as the vessel lurched back a little from its collision with the jetty before settling again. 'We're here! Mama!' We had travelled with a small escort from Pembroke and one of the men handed first my excited daughter and then me to the shore. My nose and ears were assaulted by the cacaphony and stenches of London. It was some fourteen years since I had been in London. On my last visit here, I had been King Henry's most favoured mistress (but not his only one). Elizabeth de Vermandois and I had been young women together at court when she first began her affair with Warenne. Although affection had perhaps cooled a little between us over the years and experiences that we had spent apart, I had been fond of her and must see her wed, at last, to her love. I had left baby Robert and little David in Amelina's care at Carew.

Gerald had kept a townhouse in London for some years for his attendances at court or business with merchants and masons, and I made my way there. I had not set foot in the house before and was pleasantly surprised to find it full of brightly coloured tapestries and hangings, and with an elegant black and white diamond-tiled floor in the main room. Before the servants threw open the shutters, the sun pierced the regular slits in the carved wood, embroidering the room with slivers of golden light.

As soon as we had unpacked and seen that the house was habitable and provisioned, Angharad and I went in search of Elizabeth. We found her in her own townhouse embroiled in the preparations for the wedding. Her house was a great deal more splendid than Gerald's. Elizabeth was a Countess and Warenne was one of the wealthiest nobles at Henry's court. Angharad gaped and stroked at brilliantly vivacious silks, finely glazed pottery, cushions in yellow, purple and green. 'The glass is from Venice,' Elizabeth told her. Warenne and Elizabeth had been lovers for years and all had known it, including her first husband, de Meulan, and the King. I had once asked Henry why he had never made Elizabeth his mistress, since they were such good friends. 'She is beautiful and you like each other a great deal,' I said.

'Because I had you in my eyes, Nest,' Henry said. 'Elizabeth was a child. Still is. Whereas you arrived at court a wise woman, despite your youth. I admit to having many mistresses but my heart holds true to one woman at a time.'

Elizabeth's children surrounded her. Her sixteen-year-old twins, Waleran and Robert, greeted me. I had known them well at court as small boys and marvelled at how they had grown into young men. After the death of their father, de Meulan, Waleran was now Count of Meulan and Robert had become Earl of Leicester. They were identical twins, their faces impossible to tell apart, but their bodies were grotesquely divergent. Whilst Waleran was straight and tall, Robert had a hunched back. Yet it was Robert who had a sunny nature and Waleran who was dark-visaged and scowling. Her other children came to greet us: Hugh who was fourteen, and her daughters: thirteen-year-old Adeline, Aubree who was eleven, and nine-year-old Maud. Angharad, who was the same age as Aubree, was soon in avid consultation with the other girls concerning the role that the four of them would play as flower-maidens at the wedding.

At dinner, we discussed the rebellion in Normandy. 'Amaury de Montfort inherited the county of Évreux but King Henry refused his accession,' Warenne said. 'Amaury is a fixed supporter of the French king and of William *Clito* and Henry does not want Amaury sitting comfortably in one of the richest counties, slap in the heart of Normandy. De Montfort suborns many of the younger, disgruntled Norman lords.' Warenne told us of the young lords joining de Montfort in rebellion. Hugh de Gournay, Robert Giroie and Robert de Neubourg were amongst those named. I knew that Henry would take these betrayals hard since he had raised many of these young men at his court, hoping to keep their love by giving them his own.

We had all heard the reports that Henry had almost died not long ago in fighting at Laigle and we expressed our concerns about the events in Normandy. I lived in constant fear that I would hear of the death of one or the other of them: Henry or Haith, but of course I could not share the latter concern with Elizabeth and Warenne.

'If Henry should die,' Elizabeth said, 'Prince William *Adelin* is hardly able yet to fill the King's shoes.'

'He would be supported,' Warenne said.

'Did you know, Nest, that Etienne de Blois was ejected from Alençon for raping respectable women and showing no moderation or mercy?' Elizabeth asked me with a touch of saliciousness.

'Etienne of Blois has always worn the signs of being an immoderate lord. I hope this will give Henry pause in the rewards he heaps upon him. The mightier Etienne becomes, the less of a noble lord he is.'

Warenne nodded his head. 'Despite your absence from London for more than a decade, Lady Nest, you have been following the affairs of the court with your usual acuity.'

I smiled modestly and ignored the flattery. It did not take a genius to discern that Etienne de Blois was an unpleasant and ambitious young lord.

The following morning, I was in Elizabeth's chamber where her maid had laid out her wedding clothes for me to look and marvel at. 'But where is Isabel?' I asked Elizabeth. Isabel was her eldest daughter and I had spent a great deal of time with her as a baby and small child. Of all Elizabeth's children, she was my favourite. 'She is seventeen now?'

But her twin brothers are also 16yrs so how is this possible? See previous page.

'Yes.'

'I hope Isabel is not too disappointed over Amaury de Montfort?' I knew that de Montfort had thrown over his longstanding betrothal to Isabel to marry Richildis de Hainaut whom he had since repudiated and was now married into the powerful Garlande family who served the French king.

'Certainly not. Isabel is with the King in Normandy. At his side.'

I frowned. 'With the King … ?'

'In brief, you have to hear it sooner or later, Nest, the King loves Isabel.'

I stared at her. 'Isabel is Henry's mistress? She is a child.'

'She is a woman.'

'I do not understand why have you allowed that. Surely Isabel could have made a splendid marriage.'

'She *will* make a splendid marriage.'

'You can't think – Elizabeth, he won't marry her.'

Fury whipped up stormy in Elizabeth's turquoise eyes. 'Why not! I am descended from Charlemagne and the granddaughter of a King of France,' she reminded me unnecessarily. 'Why shouldn't he look to Isabel for a wife? She is young and fertile and will bear heirs to the throne.'

'He cannot take your daughter as queen when you are widely known as an adulteress, no matter how noble, and Isabel is herself known to already be his mistress outside marriage. The church would see these facts as taints that would disqualify any heirs the King might have by Isabel.'

Elizabeth turned her face from me. I clamped my mouth up. There seemed little point in arguing with her but I felt certain that Henry would not marry Isabel. There was not enough benefit for him in that. I was surprised that Elizabeth did not know Henry well enough to realise he would never allow Warenne to have that much power, or perhaps she knew it but chose to ignore it in her desires for her daughter.

She saw my disagreement even though I kept silent. 'You are jealous, Nest.'

'No.'

'I'm sorry. Isabel is seventeen and you are what, forty now.'

'Thirty-seven.'

'The King loved you once but he needs a young, childbearing woman.'

'I'm not jealous, Elizabeth and I am still a childbearing woman, by the way. I am fond of Henry and always will be but I am not jealous. I have not expected anything more from Henry for myself for a long time but I am concerned for Isabel. I am certain that he will not marry her. Why do you think he would? What political benefit is there for him in it? What necessary allegiance does your family bring to him?'

'You are wrong!'

I decided I could not, in politeness, continue this argument further in her house and I kept my thoughts to myself. I was appalled that she, as a mother, would countenance her young daughter bedding the King who was more than fifty years old.

Hearing our raised voices, Warenne sauntered into the room, and looked from one to the other of us. I kept my peace and so did Elizabeth. 'Lady Nest, I have a letter for you from Sir Haith,' Warenne told me.

'Some business concerning his work at Pembroke, I expect,' I said.

Neither Elizabeth or Warenne took any notice of correspondence between Haith and myself. To them he was merely a factotum and they had no suspicion of a relationship between us. I pushed the small roll of sealed parchment into the sleeve of my dress.

Back at my own house, I impatiently pulled at the small wax seal and unrolled Haith's letter. I read it rapidly. He wrote to tell me the King had refused permission for us to marry. I closed my eyes, quelling my disappointment, my fingertips touching his writing on the parchment as if I were touching Haith himself. He could ask again. I could ask when I got an opportunity to see Henry. It was not final.

When I returned to Amelina at Carew, I discussed the King's refusal of my marriage with her. 'When Henry returns from Normandy,' I said, 'I will go to court and persuade him to let me marry Haith'.

'Same persuasion methods as before?' she asked, archly.

28

On a Parapet

At Breteuil, Henry was slowly recovering and the extent of his collapse remained a secret known only to Haith and Benedicta. With reassurances and rest, he gradually grew able to appear in public again, at first for very short periods of time, which gradually lengthened each day. Benedicta schooled him to say, 'I have taken note of what you say and will consider on it,' instead of trying to make decisions when his mind was in such a welter.

It was a hard test for Benedicta and Haith to keep the King's condition from his extensive *curia*. There were so many cartularies and title deeds to keep in order. Luckily Robert, the keeper of the King's seal and the master of the royal scriptorium, was used to the King conveying commands via Haith. There were constant requests for decisions and signatures from the King's staff: Robert de la Haie and Robert de Courcy, his seneschals; Henry de la Pommeraie and William Fitz Odo, his constables. William of Glastonbury, Geoffrey de Clinton or William of Tancarville, his chamberlains, might opportune for an audience; or there were requests for decisions from Wigan, the marshal; Robert of Évreux, the treasurer; William d'Aubigny, the butler. Benedicta felt overwhelmed by the sheer quantity of the business that the King must usually conduct, even as she at least could approach it with a calm and stable mind. She found herself having to decide, on behalf of the King, how to take surety from the disturber of a group of monks, confirming a lord's right to receive the entertainment of a man and a horse from an abbot, and whether or not to allow a duel to be waged with champions in a dispute. Reports came from the king's justiciars concerning writs they had issued, sureties they had taken, pleas they had heard.

'I was thinking, Sire,' Benedicta told the King, as Haith assisted in dressing him, 'that I might write to Bishop John today, tell him you have had a coughing sickness that has set the work of your chancery and treasury back somewhat, and you would value his assistance for a few weeks.'

Henry nodded. 'Yes. Do that. I will not forget how you have helped me, Benedicta. You and Haith.'

Benedicta did what she could to organise the backlog of correspondence before the Bishop's arrival. After days of gentle dialogue with the melancholy King, she began to draw both the work and the man back into some order. It became possible to admit the King's chaplain, John de Bayeaux, to him without de Bayeaux noticing anything amiss. He was able to speak with his eagle-eyed courtiers now at least, without their noticing any great change in him. 'But the change will remain,' Benedicta said to Haith, 'underneath his usual demeanour.'

The King's granddaughters could never regain their sight, but between them, Benedicta and Henry ensured that they had every comfort to live as they must now live. Advised by Benedicta, Henry provided the finest music teachers for them, and since they were young, they swiftly learnt to feel their way around the castle, to cope with their physical change. Benedicta was pleased to see that Mahaut spent time playing and talking kindly with the girls, undeterred by their injuries. Eventually the bandages could be replaced with silken strips to match their fine dresses, but beneath the silk, their faces would always be a horrible mess of scarred and empty eye sockets. Tending to them, Benedicta felt again the conflicts of her situation. She admired, pitied, and loathed the King in equal measures. The balance was tipped because of Haith, and for Haith. And she had compromised her own honesty, her own vows for the King's cause that now seemed so soiled.

In the war between King Henry and de Montfort and William *Clito*, the tide turned again when the young Count Baldwin of Flanders died from a festering injury he had taken in the fighting the previous year. He nominated his cousin, Charles, as the new count of Flanders, and Charles was known to be sympathetic to King Henry, although not sympathetic enough to hand William *Clito* over to him. King Henry made peace with Fulk d'Anjou, and Haith told Benedicta in confidence that an enormous chest of silver pieces had greatly aided that conversation. At last, Mahaut could be married to the King's son, William *Adelin*. They heard that the Prince had just arrived on the Norman coast and was making his way to Lisieux for the wedding.

Benedicta travelled with her excited charge to Lisieux and to the cathedral of Saint Pierre in June. She watched the solemn procession of monks swinging censers and intoning prayers and saw Mahaut looking so small but so brave as she stood with her new husband before the Bishop at the altar, for the blessing. Her young charge was enacting such an important role in the peace-making, and Benedicta hoped that she could be of assistance to Mahaut as she prepared to become a queen. Benedicta, nevertheless, felt continuing misgivings at the temperament of the girl's new husband. Mahaut was twelve and William *Adelin* was sixteen, both young yet, and so perhaps there was hope that William would grow to be a pleasant man and a good king.

Mahaut's father, Fulk d'Anjou, left on pilgrimage to the Holy Lands after the wedding ceremony. Since the threats from King Henry's two neighbours – Anjou and Flanders – were now allayed, Henry hoped to reach peace with those rebels who held out against him, those allied with King Louis and William *Clito*. Henry did all he could to ameliorate the enmity against him, pardoning lords such as Robert Giroie, and restoring the fortress of Bellême to Robert de Bellême's heir, William Talvas. Despite Henry's efforts, Amaury de Montfort would not come to terms. Henry gathered his army again and Haith rode out with him, leaving Benedicta, Mahaut and the other wives and female kin of the King's commanders in the safety of the household of Bishop John in Lisieux.

Benedicta waited anxiously for news of Haith and King Henry, and, she admitted reluctantly to herself, of Amaury de Montfort. The Bishop of Lisieux was Henry's chief deputy in Normandy and everything that occurred passed across the Bishop's desk.

She should be able to follow events from here at least, rather than waiting in a nunnery for stale news that was months old.

'Benedicta! The Countess de Perche has some new songs, just copied for her,' Mahaut exclaimed, running into the chamber where Benedicta was peacefully reading. 'She invites us to hear them at a party in the garden this afternoon!' Matilda FitzRoy, Countess de Perche, was the eldest of King Henry's illegitimate daughters.

'Then we should find you something appropriate to wear, Mahaut.'

They chose a red gown that King Henry had given to Mahaut after her wedding, and Benedicta ushered the girl to the Bishop's garden where wooden benches had been set up in a square beneath the shade of a green canopy. In the centre of the square, perched on a three-legged stool, was the Countess's minstrel. Benedicta took a deep breath, enjoying the scents of the flowers and the sound of water trickling into marble basins. She looked around and found her gaze inadvertantly alighting on a life-sized, antique statue of a naked man. She had no idea the Bishop would have such objects in his garden and wondered if she should allow Mahaut to continue here.

'I am not sure these songs are fit for the ears of such young ladies, Countess,' the minstrel said, interrupting Benedicta's doubts about the statue. She saw that he was jerking his head meaningfully at Mahaut.

'I am a married lady and old enough for anything!' Mahaut declared, her face pink.

'Get on and sing us the songs,' Countess Matilda told him. Benedicta took her seat amidst the gaily dressed young ladies feeling like a black crow amongst jewels. The other guests were Matilda de Blois – Etienne and Thibaut's sister – who had lately married Richard, the young Earl of Chester, and Amice de Gael who was betrothed to King Henry's illegitimate son, Richard. All the young ladies' husbands and betrothed husbands, were like Mahaut's, with Henry and Haith at the battle camp.

'Stop swinging your legs, Mahaut,' Benedicta whispered. 'You are making the bench rock on the uneven ground.' Countess

Matilda was close to her half-sister, Juliana, and Benedicta supposed that she organised such entertainments to distract herself from her sorrow for her sister and her mutilated nieces.

'These songs are written by Peter Abelard, a canon at Sens and school master at Notre-Dame in Paris.' The minstrel cleared his throat. 'They are love songs to a young lady named Heloise d'Argenteuil.'

'Love songs, Sister!' Mahaut declared, clapping her hands. 'My husband is in love with me.'

'For sure he is, but sit quietly now for the songs, like a grown-up lady.'

'I have heard of this,' Matilda de Blois whispered behind her hands to Amice de Gael. 'Abelard and Heloise. It is a great scandal in Paris!'

'Abelard writes how first his aim was simply to seduce the lady,' the minstrel explained to them, 'to steal away her virtue in a cold and calculating act, but then he was caught in his own snares when he fell entirely in love with the young lady.'

Benedicta was lulled by the strumming and the minstrel's voice, the heat and the buzz of bees, and she allowed her thoughts to stray to Amaury. Real life was not a song. No cold seducer found themselves transformed into a hopeless and passionate lover – at least not her own at any rate.

There was a fair in Lisieux, and Benedicta went with Mahaut and Matilda de Blois to look at the wares. Benedicta loved the colourful melee of a market: the multicoloured awnings, the creative hawkers' cries, the cloths laid with jewels and shoes and belts. She took a deep breath and wished she had not done so. Mahaut held her fingers to her nose, pinching it closed. They stood next to a fish stall festooned with the scaley glints of tentacles and dead eyes. 'Urgh!' said Mahaut. 'Can't we move?'

'I'm trying,' said Benedicta but the crush of the crowd held them immobilised, keeping them at close quarters with the slither of a squid and the scents of the sea. There was a commotion ahead and the people squeezed together in the tight spaces between the stalls heaved this way and that, squashing them even further towards the slimey fish stall.

'What is it?' asked Mahaut.

'I can't see yet.' Benedicta pushed past a fat, sweaty man and backed up onto the church steps where she could get a better view over the heads of the crowd. The crowd had parted for the arrival of a royal herald. His horse's sides heaved for air, its mouth was flecked with white foam. 'I think it's news from the battlefield.'

'Oh I must know if my husband is injured or victorious,' said Mahaut urgently, and she and Matilda stepped up onto the steps beside Benedicta, craning to see what was happening.

'Citizens of Lisieux,' declared the herald in a stentorious voice, 'listen!' After the initial heaving and buzz of the first response to his arrival, the crowd fell silent. 'King Henry is victorious!' he declared. Mahaut smiled up to Benedicta. 'In the month of July, Henry's army sat in siege before Évreux, the stronghold of the rebel lords, Amaury de Montfort, and his nephews Philip and Florus, sons of Bertrade de Montfort, former Queen of France.' There were gasps from the crowd. 'The King's army broke through the defences of the city and burnt it to ashes but the citadel withstood them.' The crowd broke into loud conversations and exclamations at the awful reduction of the city of Evreux. Benedicta heaved a silent sigh of relief at the thought that Amaury had not been taken.

The herald held his hands up for hush, indicating that he had more to announce. 'The King then raised siege at Évreux and marched to meet King Louis of France in battle at Bremule, with the young prince, William *Adelin*, at his side.'

Mahaut bounced up and down in excitement at this declaration. Henry would have kept his heir well back from any real danger, Benedicta knew. She prayed, meanwhile, for the safety of her brother for she knew it was unlikely the herald would give any special note to Haith's fate.

'The French King is defeated!' yelled the herald and a great shout of approbation went up from all the people pressed there, and Mahaut joined in with the cheering and hollering.

'Hush! You are a princess, not a hooting peasant!' Matilda de Blois told Mahaut, but laughed as she said it.

When he could make himself heard again, the herald declared, 'King Henry's battleplans were wise, whilst the French king's attacks were reckless and disordered. William Crispin struck a blow to King Henry's head!' The herald was winding up the suspense for his audience but the merchants were beginning to mutter at this long-winded interruption to their business. 'Roger de Clare knocked Crispin from his horse and then must fling himself over Crispin's prostrate body to prevent the King's friends from killing that traitor. King Louis and the pretender, William *Clito*, evaded capture, turning tail so fast they left their horses behind them. Courteous King Henry sent King Louis' fine charger back to him, and William *Adelin*, following his father's polite gesture, returned William *Clito*'s mount to that lord.'

The herald's recital ended abruptly when a group of merchants anxious to keep their sales flowing without more interruption, offered to slake his thirst. Mahaut, Matilda, and Benedicta made their way back from the market, their servants loaded with purchases for the young ladies.

A few days later, Benedicta was reassured to receive a letter from Haith, telling her that he was safe and King Henry continued robust. He reported that Amaury de Montfort had not been present at Bremule and that whilst William *Clito* and William Crispin had fought alongside King Louis, a number of other lords had chosen to sit on the fence, or rather on a hill, where they could watch the progress of the battle, but stay aloof: Stephen of Aumale, Hugh of Gournay, Helias de Saint-Saëns. No doubt, wrote Haith, they would have swooped down to join the victory if the battle had gone in favour of Louis and William *Clito*, but instead Henry carried the day and they turned tail like roebuck bouncing white-rumped in the field.

In September, a group of travelling merchants arrived at the bishop's palace and regaled the Bishop and his guests with the latest news from the conflicts in Normandy. Amaury de Montfort, they said, had raised a huge army and marched on Breteuil intending to take it back for Eustace and Juliana, but this army was ill-trained. The Breton commander King Henry had left at Breteuil, Ralph de Gael, Amice's father, thumbed his nose at de Montfort. Ralph de Gael had emerged from the fortress and not even bothered to close the fortress gates behind him as he repelled the attack. Soon after, the valiant young commander, Richard FitzRoy arrived to give de Gael aid, and King Henry arrived a few hours later, so that de Montfort was forced to withdraw in failure. Doubtless the merchant knew that he was addressing an audience that included the kin of the victors and embellished his account to suit their side, thought Benedicta.

Vengeful at his losses, King Louis marched on Chartres and on Countess Adela. Benedicta was amused to hear how the doughty Countess had ordered the Virgin's Chemise to be taken from the cathedral and hung from the city walls like a banner before the army of the French king. Louis, confronted with the power of such a holy relic, turned his horse's head and ordered the withdrawal of his army.

Benedicta entered the hall, humming, feeling in a happy mood. Surely, with all this good news, Haith would return soon and they would all go to England together, she accompanying Mahaut to her new life at the English court.

King Henry's scribe, Gisulf, approached her. 'Sister Benedicta, may I have a word with you.'

'Of course.'

He sat down very close to her on the bench and leant even closer, speaking in an undertone. 'Sister, it is a rather embarrassing matter.'

'Oh?'

'I am in receipt of a letter of complaint written by Robert de Bellême to the King, shortly before he died. You know who I mean, Sister?'

'Of course.'

'He complains of his treatment. That he should be convicted on the evidence of a whoring nun.' Gisulf sat back to enjoy her reaction.

She struggled to keep control of herself, to deny him the satisfaction of seeing her shock at this announcement.

'Why do you speak to me on this matter?'

'De Bellême claimed he had the story from Amaury de Montfort. He names the nun, Sister, and gives quite a lot of detail about an incident at the blessed Abbey of Fontevraud. The story will not do the abbey's reputation a great deal of good, either, you can imagine. It is widely believed already by many to be a whorehouse.'

'I ask you again why you bring this matter to me and use such language in my presence.' Benedicta kept her quivering hands concealed within the long sleeves of her habit, and kept the fear from her face.

'The King has been greatly occupied and he has not had the time to give the matter his attention yet.'

Why would it be of concern to Henry, Benedicta wondered. Why would he care to what lengths she had gone to secure the evidence against de Bellême that he had needed. Benedicta decided that silence must be her best option with this odious man. She rose, pushing herself up from the table. 'It is no concern of mine.'

He clamped his hand over hers on the table, keeping her there. 'But it is, Sister. You know it is,' his voice was a sibilant whisper. 'Since the King is so busy, I thought I might show the letter to your brother first rather than worry the King with such a matter, especially since de Bellême is in any case dead now.'

'What do you want?' Benedicta rounded on him furiously. 'I have nothing.' Several of the servants looked in their direction, curious at her raised voice.

'I don't want silver, Sister. Amaury de Montfort thought that you had something. It is a little soiled of course now, but I am not such a particular, great noble as he.'

She stared at the man, horrified, and fled from the hall to the safety of Mahaut's chambers.

Benedicta awoke feeling as if she had slept for minutes rather than hours. Her head pounded and her mind was fogged with dreams of red-faced demons, their tongues protruding, their hooves drumming towards her. She left the bishop's palace at daybreak and moved across wet cobbles towards the nearby cathedral of Saint Pierre. She needed help. Would God still listen to her prayers? She looked across the courtyard to the church. The entrance was framed between two square and solid bell towers. The doorway was a great rounded portal with a series of arches, indented layer by layer, making visible the thickness of the wall into which the opening had been excised. Above the many-arched doorway was a vast rose window. Closing the creaking door behind her, she was relieved to find the cathedral empty. She looked at the three aisles, considering where best to take refuge. Alternating piers and columns marched up the nave in a sequence of arches towards the apse. Early morning sunlight was beginning to touch the exquisite stained glass. The thick massive walls, the ribbed stone vault, the twisted and decorated columns all gave her solace. She moved towards one of the side aisles flanking the nave, looking for the Lady Chapel.

The statue of the Virgin was ankle-deep in a sea of small red and white flickering candles. The air smelt of hot wax and seemed suddenly still, entirely silent. She sat on the bench close to the statue and raised her eyes to the Virgin's face. It seemed that even the mild romantic illusion she had allowed herself must be obliterated now that she knew Amaury had spoken of their encounter to de Bellême, had allowed it to be cast in the ugly words she had been forced to hear in Gisulf's mouth.

Benedicta had told herself at the time that she lay with Amaury that it was for the sake of King Henry, for the mission given to her by Countess Adela, but as time passed she had begun to wonder if she was being honest with herself. Had she, in fact, slept with him from lust, or even more likely from her primary sin, curiosity? Had she been motivated simply by the thought that there was something she could do and did not do her whole life? And where did this leave the state of her soul and her vocation? She prayed for guidance. The Virgin looked at her mildly. Benedicta did not feel outcast. She was relieved to find that she still felt at home here, in the church, under God's vault and his sky.

Making her way back to the palace, she encountered the Bishop at the entrance. 'Ah, Sister Benedicta, I have been looking for you.' His face showed excitement. 'You must prepare your charge for a journey. Pope Callixtus is to hold a council at Reims.'

'We are to meet the Pope?' Benedicta asked, her eyes wide.

'Indeed you are, Sister.'

On the following morning, the courtyard was full of carts, horses and people preparing to depart for Reims. Benedicta saw

Gisulf making for her and tried to turn her palfrey's head but the press of people and horses was so great there was no room for manoeuvre. Gisulf laid his hand on her horse's bridle. 'Sister, I am waiting for your response. Don't forget that I do send missives to the King and Sir Haith too, most days.'

She restrained the impulse to kick the man and satisfied herself instead with a light flick of her whip against his fingers so that he flinched and let go of her horse. There was movement in the crowd ahead of her and she kicked her horse forward without saying a word to the scribe.

The entourage of Archbishop John of Lisieux halted before the great double doors of the Palace of the Archbishop of Reims. They had ridden for four days beyond Évreux, crossed the border from Normandy into France and ridden on beyond Paris. The palace had a long frontage. Benedicta counted at least five turrets, all of a different design, and countless chimneys. The gateway had two moulded protrusions like eyebrows carved above it with fleshy vine leaves, bunches of grapes, fantastical beasts and angels. The horses started up again and they rode through the iron-studded doors into the interior courtyard. Looking up, Benedicta saw that the building had three stories and an exterior wooden balustraded walkway running around the top of the buildings in front of the diverse roofs, stone dormer windows and attics. Numerous doorways to the high turrets surrounded her. The vines, grapes and beasts motifs were carved in stone and wood everywhere, and joined by luxuriant cabbage leaves, cats and a naked figure riding a snail. Long gargoyles lay far above Benedicta's head, dripping water into the courtyard from the recent shower. She and Princess Mahaut were led up a high turret and shown into a fine apartment where the October draughts were kept at bay by billowing tapestries. Their chamber was adjacent to that of Mahaut's mother, Countess Ermengarde de Maine, who was here representing Anjou on behalf of her husband, who was in the Holy Lands. Mahaut was overjoyed to be reunited with her mother and with her younger siblings, Sybille, Geoffrey and Elias. The Countess gracefully thanked Benedicta for her care of Mahaut. After an hour of the excited chatter of four young children, Benedicta was relieved when Haith sought her out and drew her back into her apartment next door for some private conversation.

'What's happening?' she asked. There seemed to be quite an air of excitement and anxiety about the place.

'A lot! The Pope called this council primarily to come to terms with Henry, the German King and Roman Emperor.'

'The husband of our King Henry's daughter, Maud?'

'Yes, although she is not here but is Regent in Germany for her absent husband.'

'So the German King is here?'

'After a fashion. He and the Pope were due to meet to make peace between them at Chateau du Musson and the Pope's entourage were a few hours ago preparing to travel there, and Henry and I would have travelled with them. But we have just heard that the German Emperor has arrived with an army of 30,000 men. The Pope is not minded to go there now.'

'Who can blame him!'

'Indeed. Pope Callixtus is not inclined to trust his person to the tender mercies of a German army.'

'So now what?'

'Now His Holiness intends to continue the other business of his synod here and wait for the German King to disband his army and begin peace negotiations.'

'The citizens of Reims must be worried that the army will attack the city.'

'Yes, there is a good deal of anxiety about what the German King intends to do but with King Henry of the English and King Louis of the French here, it seems unlikely that he would attack. The business of the Pope's synod will begin in a few hours in the Abbey of Saint Remy. Will you attend?'

'Certainly, if I may.'

'Yes. All may come.'

'What is the business before the Pope?'

'He wishes to reconcile our King Henry with his brother, Robert, the former Duke of Normandy.'

'Is he here? Robert?'

'No. Henry would not release him from prison in England but

Robert will be represented by his son, William *Clito*, and by King Louis of France.'

Mahaut was content to stay with her family, so Benedicta went to the abbey in company with Haith and was astonished by the crush of finely dressed people there. Armed guards pressed at the crowd, keeping less finely dressed people, who wished for a sight of the Pope, outside the abbey. Haith was known to the guards and they were allowed through, finding a place to sit halfway up the nave. Benedicta turned to look behind her at the light streaming through the rose window, burnishing the stone of the church to great shafts of silver constrasting with the surrounding gloom. There was a murmur and shuffling from the crowd and Haith nudged her. Benedicta faced forward again to watch the Pope be seated in great state. The abbey was a sea of richly coloured fabrics – the reds, golds, greens of embroidered chasubles and mitres and the glint of jewelled croziers. 'So many clerics!' whispered Benedicta.

'The scribes say they have counted some five hundred archbishops, bishops and abbots.'

At the front, Haith pointed to where King Henry of England was seated with King Louis of France, Charles the Good, the new Count of Flanders and many other great nobles. On invitation from Pope Callixtus, King Louis stood and began a complaint against the English King and his comportment in the wars in Normandy and France, his usurpation of William *Clito*'s claim to the Duchy of Normandy.

From the shadow of the corner where she sat, Benedicta swallowed as she saw Amaury de Montfort step into a shaft of sunlight. Another tall young man was at his side, and she guessed this must be William *Clito*, the son of Robert de Normandy. He had something of the look of Henry about him. Amaury looked, if possible, more beautiful than her memories of him. Grateful for the darkened area where she and Haith sat, she thought it should be possible to get through these days without him noticing her. Perhaps even if he saw her, he would not notice her. She was merely one of many insignificant conquests no doubt.

When the arguments had been put forward by both sides, the synod broke for the day. King Louis no doubt hoped that the

Pope would rule in favour of William *Clito*, since Callixtus was uncle to Louis' queen. 'This is a very dangerous moment for Henry,' Haith told her. While they waited for the Pope's decision, Haith took Benedicta to see the cathedral and the reliquary containing the Holy Chrism which had been used to baptise many kings of France. Haith told Benedicta that Archbishop Thurstan of York had been consecrated by the Pope, which was an act carried out against the express wishes of King Henry. 'If the Pope rules against Henry and in favour of William *Clito,* would Henry abide by it?' Benedicta asked.

Haith shrugged. 'A year ago, I would have told you no. Nothing would induce Henry to surrender Normandy, but now, after his recent collapse and his fears for his soul, I cannot say what he would do.'

On the following day, the news broke that King Louis' plea had met with disappointment. The Pope required both kings to keep the Truce of God. 'Perhaps the Pope has looked well on a tall pile of English silver,' Haith whispered in Benedicta's ear. Haith, no doubt, knows that for a fact, she thought. So, no one was above corruption then on this sorry Earth.

The German King had made no move towards reconciliation, so the Pope solemnly excommunicated King Henry of Germany and his antipope in Rome. Soon after, the German army moved out of the territory and the threat to the city was over. Benedicta sensed the relief amongst the people she passed on the streets as a palpable thing. After two weeks in Reims, the business of the synod was completed and the Pope and all the visitors made ready to leave.

Mahaut's chests were packed for their journey back to Normandy in the morning and Benedicta sat looking at the full moon from the window. She felt too alert to sleep and stepped across the window sill onto the wooden parapet walkway. It was exhilarating to be so high up, to have this unencumbered view of the moon above and to able to look down onto the cobbles of the empty courtyard below.

'Benedicta?'

She knew the voice behind her right away. Amaury's voice. She considered simply running ahead without turning and slipping out of sight around a corner and then trying to find another open window that she might step through. But there was no knowing whose room she might be entering. There were few if any empty rooms in the palace at the moment. Speed would take him by surprise but to flee seemed a little ridiculous. She turned to face him but did not raise her eyes, looking down at his boots.

'It *is* you! How are you?'

Benedicta frowned to herself. She glanced up at him and then away again. He had been smiling – a warm, open smile.

'I am … greatly troubled.'

'I am sorry to hear that.' His voice was low and he moved closer to her in the confined space of the walkway.

She took a step away.

'What troubles you? May I be of assistance?'

She looked up at him, anger rising in her. 'Are you laughing at me?'

He frowned. 'Not at all. Benedicta?'

'You spoke of me to de Bellême.'

'Ah! That! It has come to your attention. I apologise. It was discourteous of me, but he asked how King Henry came by his letter. I realised how, Benedicta.' He paused and she lowered her eyes again. 'You tricked me, Benedicta, but I am not angry with you. On balance, I felt it was worthwhile … .' She heard the humour in his voice. '… even if it did turn the scales in King Henry's favour when I lost my ally, Bellême, to imprisonment, I could not regret a moment with you. Those memories still warm me on cold nights. I was most impressed by you, in so many ways, my dear Benedicta!' He held out a hand to her, palm turned up, but she made no move to take it. He sighed and let it drop back down to his side. 'De Bellême lost his liberty. I owed him honesty in the matter, but I meant no injury to you. Has such happened?'

'Yes. I am threatened with it.'

'Threatened?'

She looked up again and let her eyes trace his features. 'By King Henry's scribe, Gisulf.'

'Ah, him. I will run that creeping thing through and that will stop his mouth for you.'

'No! No bloodshed on my conscience. I am already so steeped in sin I can barely lift my face to God.'

'I will *threaten* him then. And make a donation to Fontevraud in expiation for both of us. I will take care of it, Benedicta.'

'You should not ... you should call me Sister.'

'Really?' he said, a smile of friendly amusement on his face.

'Why must you persist in this opposition to King Henry, Lord de Montfort? I would not wish to see you come to harm.'

'I am grateful for your care of me. If only I had possessed such a beautiful advisor long ago.'

'Do not flatter me, Amaury. Tell me why. I want to know.'

'I suppose I like to win. Conciliation and remorse are not in my nature.'

'So you let this need to win lead you by the nose, to your destruction?'

He shrugged. 'Or my triumph!'

'For no particular reason?'

'Reason? What particular reason do any of us really have for any of our actions? We alight on something, see it as our purpose, cleave to it for life, through thick and thin, and then as we lay dying we wonder why. And what if we had chosen differently? But if we have no such purpose we are lost, mazed, spinning without anchor.'

'I suppose there is some truth in that,' she said.

'What are your reasons, Benedicta? Your purpose?'

'Love,' she blurted. 'I act for love, I think. Love of God, of my brother, and ... yes, I would say love.'

He looked at her for a long moment.

'I envy you the simplicity and goodness of that,' he said.

But Benedicta did not feel simple and good. Deciding that his honesty merited her own, she added, 'And curiosity. I suspect that is mostly my reason for everything.'

Amaury laughed now with real delight. 'Well that is a very good reason, I would say.' His expression sobered. 'All I ask is that King Henry gives me my rights, my county of Évreux.'

'Forgive me, but that is disingenuous, surely. Your oath is sworn to the French king. Obviously, King Henry does not want a French ally in command of such a rich county, right

275

in the middle of Normandy, his own territory. You are King Louis' man.'

'I am no one's man, Benedicta,' he brought his face closer to hers, 'unless it is yours.'

She knew the untruth of his words very well and yet she thrilled to them. Suppressing a smile, she dropped her eyes reluctantly from his face, turned and moved swiftly along the parapet, meaning to make a circuit or at least wait until he had gone, to regain her own room, conscious of his gaze, warm on her retreating back.

29

Shuttle Diplomacy

Benedicta sat in a window seat in a pool of sunlight at the bishop's palace in Lisieux, reading the latest letter from Haith. Her copy of Ovid was balanced open at 'Love and War' on her knee and she traced one finger on Haith's coded letter and the other on the lines of the poem, deciphering it. Perhaps they should give up this ciphering, she thought, impatient to understand what he had written to her. The Truce of God between the kings had lasted barely longer than a blink of an eye. King Henry had returned to the attack and besieged de Montfort again in the Évreux citidel, which had already been weakened in the previous attacks and this time, Haith wrote, Amaury was forced to surrender. Benedicta quailed, fearing she would read of Amaury's death in the face of the King's *malevolentia*, but, Haith wrote that Amaury sued for peace through the mediation of Thibaut de Blois and King Henry had magnanimously pardoned the lord who had given him so much trouble. Benedicta took a deep breath, thinking it was probably an error on Henry's part to be gentle to Amaury, but relieved for Amaury's sake. No doubt, Henry thought he had much to atone for and sought any opportunity to do so.

Richard FitzRoy, Haith's letter continued, had come to intervene with the King on behalf of his sister, Juliana, and Henry gave pardon to his daughter and her husband. With their leader, de Montfort, at peace with the King, the other rebel lords soon came to Henry to offer their fealty. Stephen de Aumale, Hugh de Gournay and Robert de Neubourg had laid down their arms and enmity. As part of the peace negotiations, the King's illegitimate daughter, Alice, was wed to Matthew de Montmorency, the son of the constable of France who was King Louis' most important administrator. Haith wrote that King Henry had met with his nephew, William *Clito*, and offered him three counties in England. William had asked for the release of his father who had been imprisoned for thirteen years, but Henry refused and William *Clito* left without agreement reached between them. Although Henry is in the ascendency again, Haith wrote, with William *Clito* still unreconciled, there remains the likelihood of further conflict, but, prepare yourself, Benedicta, Haith's letter concluded, I am coming to get you, my indispensable sister. Juliana has decided to withdraw to Fontevraud with her daughters and King Henry asks that you and I escort them there.

Anything to be away from the scribe, Benedicta thought. He had not troubled her since Reims, and so perhaps Amaury had been true to his word and warned him off, yet she was glad to be away from the risk and to be returning to Fontevraud, to find, she hoped, her own peace.

Haith hammered on the great doors of Fontevraud and Benedicta remembered the time before when she had arrived here with Count Etienne, loaded down with the weight of the spying task she had to do. Now she returned with an even sadder freight: the Lady Juliana and her blinded little daughters. The vast doors creaked open wide to give entrance to the King's daughter and granddaughters, who were named Emma and Agnes. Benedicta described what she saw before her to the two girls. Many old friends were lined up to welcome them, including Sister Genevieve and Petronilla, who had recently been confirmed as Abbess. Their faces were wreathed with smiles that came and went and came again as they struggled with the sight of the blinded children and their unhappy mother. 'If anyone can help them it is Abbess Petronilla and this place,' Benedicta whispered to Haith.

Sister Genevieve led the way to the best chambers that had once belonged to Bertrade and Benedicta experienced her own tribulations. Naturally, this was where Petronilla would choose to house Juliana, but Benedicta was obliged to avert her eyes from the corner where Amaury's saddlebags and their clothes had been slung, where she had pilfered the letter. She was obliged to hurry even faster past the hearth where she had lain with him. 'I would be happy to return to the cell I stayed in before,' she told the Abbess, an edge of insistence in her voice.

The following morning, Haith was ready to return with the haste King Henry had required, and he took his farewell from Lady Juliana and then from his sister. 'You are sure you will stay here then, Benedicta?'

'Yes. It is the closest place to home for me now.' She might salve her sin with a lifetime of prayers.

'I will write.'

'Of course you will. Ovid, remember,' she whispered in his ear and he laughed.

True to his word, Haith wrote to Benedicta soon after his departure to tell her about King Henry's audience with Pope Callixtus at Gisors. Robert and Waleran de Beaumont, the twin sons of Elizabeth de Vermandois, had given a learned display of rhetoric and debated philosophy with the cardinals. The aetheling's court, though, wrote Haith, meaning all those young men gathered around Henry's heir, William *Adelin*, was in need of more educating, or perhaps less. The aetheling's court has always been a problem for kings, Haith wrote. Think on the trouble William the Conqueror had with his eldest son, Robert. Young men are impatient and uninformed and they see that King Henry begins to grow old and weary. Men who cannot win or do not deserve favour from the King find place and favour instead with the aetheling. He wrote that William *Adelin* and Waleran, in particular, were arrogant and ill-mannered to those members of the court who were not of Norman or French blood. William claims he will yoke all the English to the plough like oxen when he is king and Waleran laughs at those members of Henry's household who are not pure-blooded nobles (like me, Haith added), saying we are mere country bumpkins. The other young members of the prince's vivacious court, he wrote, include his half-sister, Matilda FitzRoy, Countess of Perche; his half-brother, Richard FitzRoy;

Richard, the young Earl of Chester and his new wife, Matilda de Blois, the sister of Thibaut and Etienne. Prince William is puffed up too far, too ill-advisedly, at being *rex et dux designatus*, Haith concluded. Benedicta was glad that they were using their cipher after all, and decided that, for Haith's safety, she had best burn this letter as soon as she finished it.

It is a pity, Haith wrote, that the identical Beaumont twins, the sons of Elizabeth de Vermandois, are so different in characters, as well as in body. Where Waleran's mouth is full of crass superiority against others, Robert is fair-spoken and fair-minded like his father. Henry has recently been greatly displeased to hear that Waleran arranged betrothals for his three younger sisters to men whose loyalty is suspect. Adeline de Beaumont is to marry Hugh, the Lord of Montfort-sur-Risle; Aubree de Beaumont is betrothed to Hugh of Châteauneuf-en-Thimerais; and the youngest sister, Maud, is betrothed to William Lovel. The challenge to Henry's authority seems all the worse, since the older sister, Isabel de Beaumont, is Henry's own mistress. But perhaps, thought Benedicta, that is what motivates Waleran de Beaumont to defy the King. Henry suspects this mischief is sown by Amaury de Montfort, wrote Haith. Benedicta blushed scarlet as her speeding glance recognised the Ovidian cipher for Amaury's name. Swiftly she touched the letter's edge to the candle, unsure if it were that flame or the heat of her shame that caused the parchment to ignite so swiftly and run blackening to ash.

As they entered the new year and celebrated Epiphany at the abbey, Benedicta was dismayed to receive a letter from Countess Adela requesting that she come to her at Chartres. 'There is much to do and I can think of nobody better than you for the task,' the Countess wrote. Benedicta had hoped to be left in peace.

She sat in the church for two days, seeking guidance from God, never moving and not taking food or water. Instead of growing easier with the passage of time, it grew harder and harder for her to reconcile everything she had done with the prospect of her future here, with her monastic life. Abbess Petronilla startled her, sitting down beside her. 'You have been in prayer a long time, Sister.'

Benedicta said nothing. Her throat was parched and she was not sure she could speak, even if she knew what to say.

'You are troubled, Sister?'

When there was still no response, the Abbess put both of her hands around one of Benedicta's and stood. Benedicta remained seated, her arm held aloft now by the Abbess. 'Come, Benedicta,' Petronilla said gently. 'Whatever it is, we can find balm for it through prayer. Come and speak with me about what troubles you.'

Benedicta rose reluctantly and went with the Abbess, who saw to it that she took some water and bread. 'Can you speak to me, Sister? Or would you prefer that I ask a confessor to come?'

'No!' Benedicta exclaimed. She could not bear the thought of having to confess her actions to any man. She wept. 'I have committed great sins, Abbess.'

When the force of her tears was spent, the Abbess spoke to her again. 'I know you, Sister Benedicta. I know that your heart is good. Whatever you have done, you will have done it for the sake of someone else, for someone else's good and not for your own.'

Benedicta shook her head. If only that were true. She told Petronilla about the spying on behalf of King Henry and the Countess, of how she had stolen de Bellême's damning letter from de Montfort's saddlebags, but she could not bring herself to voice the full extent of what had happened with de Montfort. 'You were commanded to it,' the Abbess said, hesitantly. 'You sought to serve the King.' Clearly she was shocked at Benedicta's revelation of such perfidious behaviour.

'You must do penance and confess. God will forgive you.'

Benedicta swallowed. It seemed unlikely that God would forgive her. Unlike Petronilla, He was aware of the full extent of her crimes. She explained that the Countess had required her attendance again and that she was reluctant to be drawn back into the intrigue.

'If the Countess commands it, Sister, you must go. Perhaps you can explain your qualms to her and she will understand and relieve you of any further need for lies.'

Oh, Abbess Petronilla, thought Benedicta, I thought you a knowing woman in this world and not so naive.

At Chartres, Benedicta was soon occupied, drafting correspondence for the Countess. She was surprised to encounter Archbishop Thurstan of York in the passageway. She watched the Countess, the Archbishop, and Count Thibaut at dinner, their heads together in close conference.

'I must take you into my confidence, Sister Benedicta,' the Countess told her the following morning. 'And I know that your integrity is beyond question.' Benedicta took a deep breath and kept her own views on that topic to herself, waiting for what the Countess wanted to tell her.

'You are perhaps wondering at the Archbishop's presence here?'

'It is an honour to be in his blessed company.'

'You have heard that my brother, the King, is angry with the Archbishop, has banished him from the kingdom.'

Benedicta felt it was best to venture no opinions in any directions.

The Countess leant towards her to whisper. 'My brother is well aware of Thurstan's presence and activities.'

Benedicta blinked. Was the Countess ensnaring an archbishop now in the perversions of her spy network?

'King Louis of France also believes, as does the world, that Archbishop Thurstan is in great disfavour with my brother, and so Louis gives Thurstan *his* favour, do you see? It allows King Louis to save face in making peace with us, if he thinks he is flouting Henry with his favour for Archbishop Thurstan.' The Countess sat back sighing with satisfaction with herself.

For the next month, the Archbishop, Count Thibaut and Cardinal Cuno shuttled back and forth, as the bobbin does on a loom, between the courts of King Louis and the Countess with messages and counter-offers. The Countess conveyed the progress of the negotiations to King Henry. In an ingeniously literal stroke, the Countess had scores of new looms moved into her great chamber to demonstrate this new technology. For days, the racket of the looms covered the sound of the whispered conversations and the missives dictated in low voices.

In June, the comings and goings of the negotiators and their offers and counter-offers resulted in a peace agreement between the two kings. King Louis granted Normandy to William *Adelin* and gave up his support for William *Clito*. It was a dazzling diplomatic triumph for Henry. Countess Adela began to make preparations to enter the convent at Marcigny. 'My son does need to marry sometime, I suppose,' she sighed, reluctant, to Benedicta. 'His wife would require the surrender of my titles and I would rather take my own time and initiative in that.' Adela would have far fewer obstacles and no trouble at all, Benedicta thought, in imposing her will on a flutter of nuns. Benedicta also made preparations to travel. She was to go with Mahaut and with Adela's daughter, Matilda de Blois, the Countess of Chester, to meet with King Henry and the young ladies' triumphant husbands at Barfleur.

Benedicta rose early with the sun and watched the dawning of a fair November day at the port of Barfleur. The squally winds that had bent the tree tops to and fro for the last few days had died down. Small clouds progressed slowly across the pale blue sky. Perhaps they would sail today if the fine weather held. From the window, she could see the quay and the three large ships waiting – the King's ship; a second ship that was still being loaded with his goods: barrels of wine, cheeses, fine textiles and ceramics; and a third ship – the new one – which would carry the Prince's household to England. She heaved a sigh of relief that the only sounds on this fine morning were birdsong and the waves chopping at the jetties. She had fallen asleep very late, still hearing the loud carousing of the Prince's court in the hall below. Even the King's requests for less noise and more temperance had only briefly quietened down the cacophony.

Benedicta's possessions were packed and waiting in a small canvas bag. She looked affectionately at the sleeping child on her cot. Mahaut was a beauty, and well might the Prince celebrate his marriage to her and his father's peace with the French king and Mahaut's father, the Count of Anjou. After all these years of war and strife there was tranquillity at last, a return to England and more time with Haith to look forward to. Benedicta had started to think that perhaps she would not return to one of the

Norman or French abbeys after all, but would instead seek a place in an English convent when the King no longer needed her at court. Mahaut was thirteen years old and it would be some time yet before her marriage with the Prince would be consummated and she could manage her own household. It was possible, too, that Mahaut might wish to keep Benedicta with her. No point in thinking too far ahead. She had not seen the loathsome scribe, Gisulf, about the court for some weeks, as the King had sent him on much business, but she knew this was merely a temporary respite. She had almost resolved with herself to tell the whole sorry story to Haith when they arrived in England. It seemed the only solution for her anxiety.

She bent to kiss Mahaut's soft cheek. 'Wake up, sweetness. It looks as if we may sail today,' she said in a whisper. Mahaut opened her light brown eyes and smiled lazily at Benedicta.

'Today. Really?'

'Yes, the weather is fair. I'm going down to the hall now to see if any decision has been made. Will you follow me down soon, Princess, and come to break your fast?'

Mahaut nodded her agreement and Benedicta turned to the stairs, speaking to Mahaut's maid as she passed. 'Dress the child in warm clothes,' Benedicta told her, thinking that she would need them if they went onboard ship.

In the hall, she looked for Haith but did not see his fair head looming above all the other mostly dark heads. Still late abed as usual she guessed. The King was seated at the trestle with his Italian shipmaster and a number of other men that Benedicta did not recognise – other ship captains, merchants and harbour-masters, perhaps. Her guess that they would sail today garnered more evidence. Benedicta sat with bread and a small wooden beaker of ale before her. She watched the King dismiss the men clustered about him and they moved out of the hall, full of purpose. Benedicta swiftly dropped her eyes to the trestle when she saw Gisulf arrive and sit beside the King to take the orders for the day. The horrid man was back already.

Mahaut came tripping down the stairs, her glossy brown curls bouncing on her shoulders. The King's expression brightened at the sight of her. Mahaut was a great favourite with him. He waved off Gisulf and beckoned to Benedicta to move her stool closer and sit together with him and the child. 'Sister.'

He kissed the top of Mahaut's head. 'Are you ready to see England again?'

'Yes, Papa,' she told him eagerly.

'You will be queen there one day, so pay heed to your lessons with Sister Benedicta. A queen must be learned. Is my Mahaut a good student?'

'Indeed, she is, Sire,' Benedicta answered. She looked up to the doorway at a dog's loud bark and saw Haith entering, stretching his long arms in the air above a dishevelled head of blond hair.

'Up with the larks as usual, Haith?' Benedicta said.

He smiled blearily, too semi-conscious to reply, and sat down beside Henry, searching the table for the ale jug. The King moved it and a beaker towards him.

'We sail today, Haith,' the King said. 'You go in the new ship with the Prince's household, as soon as you can get them up and ready after their noisome carousing last night. Sister, you and Mahaut will sail with me. We will go onboard in the afternoon and take sail before the light goes.'

On the dock, Benedicta stood saying farewell to Haith before leading Mahaut onto the ship. The child was hopping excitedly from foot to foot, looking all around her wide-eyed. A few of the Prince's household had emerged and were beginning to shift their horses and goods to the new ship, but many still tarried, the worse the wear from an excess of wine. Many small ships bobbed around the larger ships loading on goods and sailors. Someone, somewhere on one of the ships, blew a loud blast on a horn, startling everyone on the dock to laughter. 'I suppose we will have to wait for the next tide,' Haith told her, 'and will be some hours behind you. I will find you at my house.'

'Is the Prince up and about?'

'Yes, but sluggish, as are they all that were drinking and dancing until the cock crowed. Etienne de Blois says he is too ill to sail.'

'Ill with wine? He will recover in time, surely?'

Haith shook his head, frowning. 'I know he did not over-imbibe last night.'

'Some sickness instead, then?'

Haith shrugged. 'He looks fine to me.'

The King came onto the jetty in the company of his bodyguard and he paused to speak with Haith. 'I am aware I owe you a great debt, my old friend.' Mahaut took his hand and he smiled down at her and then returned his earnest gaze to Haith. 'You, and your sister here, have done me so many kind services they become impossible to count. When we reach England, I am determined to repay your kindness. You asked me a favour some time ago, regarding your marriage, and I denied you.'

Benedicta looked swiftly at Haith's face. What favour had he asked and not spoken to her of it?

'When we reach England,' Henry said, 'I will rectify this matter.' The King moved to board the ship.

Benedicta smiled happily at the sight of the joy on Haith's face. 'What does the King speak of?'

'Sister!' a sailor called down to her. 'We're loading the last of the barrels and horses and looking to cast off very soon.'

'Let's wait to see what the King intends when we reach England,' Haith said. Benedicta burned with a longing to know and wanted to press him further, but she was trying to school her curiosity, which had led her into so much trouble, so she stood on tiptoe instead, kissed Haith's lowered cheek, and hauled herself carefully up the slippery plank, clinging to the rope slung at the side to aid her. The boat slid smoothly from its moorings and she joined Mahaut at the stern, waving to Haith until they could no longer see his cheerful features. They pointed and watched the synchronised swoops and glides of the following gulls, like white handkerchiefs, that were mirrored in the white-crested waves beneath them.

'Let's go to the prow and watch for England!' Mahaut exclaimed.

'Very well,' said Benedicta, 'but move slowly. All is pitching and slipping.'

30

The Boy

Benedicta had settled Mahaut at court and made ready for Haith's return at the modest house that he had recently bought. It was good to be back in London. Two days after their arrival, she went to Westminster to meet Mahaut and expected that Haith would either be there already or arrive later that day. The vast stone hall felt chillier than usual and she wished she had worn her red fleece vest. Henry was seated, and many people crowded in the space as usual, and yet she sensed something different in the atmosphere. As she approached the King with Mahaut, she looked at the faces of the nobles and saw strange expressions there. Some bad news? People were grouped towards the sides of the hall, whereas usually it was hard to make your way through when there was so much milling and gossiping, pushing to get close to the King. Had something happened? Benedicta, without thinking, slowed her own pace, and Mahaut frowned at her, tugging her forwards.

'Ah, my Mahaut!' exclaimed King Henry, 'and Sister Benedicta. Welcome. I trust you are well settled after our voyage.'

'Yes, Papa. My chambers are lovely and Benedicta has filled them with flowers,' Mahaut answered him. The King beamed at her. He seemed his usual self. He had not noticed the odd tension in the hall, it seemed. Benedicta looked back over her shoulder. She had not imagined it. There was an uncommonly large gap in front of the King, and people's backs were turned as they huddled in small clusters, whispering low to one another. Benedicta caught the eye of Count Thibaut and her knees almost gave way as she read the expression of distress on his face. Something, something very serious. She watched Thibaut gently push a small boy in the direction of the King. The boy arrived before the long, burnished table where the King sat and reached a sheet of parchment across the breadth of the wood with a shaking hand.

'What's this?' asked Henry, kindly. He took the parchment.

The boy stared, mute.

'Nothing to say?' asked Henry.

'I think the boy, the letter, came from Count Thibaut,' Benedicta said.

The boy nodded and started to back away as the King looked down and began to read. Benedicta watched the boy's retreat but turned quickly at the sudden scraping of the bench against the floor and an animal sound emitted by the King. Henry's face had taken on a deformity, as if his skin had turned to molten wax.

Benedicta watched transfixed as the King dragged himself, half-falling, around the edge of the table, into the cleared space in the centre of the hall. The courtiers pushed themselves back further against the walls and into the corners.

'No!' The shout was ripped from the King's quivering mouth and cried out to the ceiling. He dropped the parchment to the ground and followed it there, bowing his forehead to the cold stone flags. The crowd shifted awkwardly in unison. All hesitated, trying to decide whether or not they should attempt to lift the King. Nobody wanted to touch him.

'Leave me here,' he whispered to the few who took tentative steps forward. 'Keep away from me.' He scrabbled at the hard, dry ground. Could he dig down into it? Find his son here? He was not there. He stopped scraping at the stone and turned his hands over, looked at red blood blooming vivid in the midst of pale brown dust on the fingertips. Whose hands were they? What could he do with them? He held them out in front of him like an offering. Was it his fault? It must be his fault. He was a sinner. He had done it. He looked up, anguished, through tears, at the carved teeth of the arched doorway yawning at him, ragged, jagged. Yes, he deserved it. He placed his bleeding fingers carefully on his thighs and small ovals of blood transferred to the beige cloth of his hose. He bowed his head down again onto the ground and began to grind his forehead in the dust. There was groaning. Somebody was groaning. An animal birthing, perhaps. Now he had the brown dust in his hair, in his eyes. His eyes felt hot and dry. He sat back on his heels and they were all hovering, starting to approach again. They would not leave him be. 'Leave me alone!' he shouted but they were coming towards him and would lift him soon, he could see it about to happen. Why couldn't they just leave him alone? He just wanted to stay here kneeling in the dirt, staring at the hideous stone archway. Just that.

Everyone stared at the King muttering and grovelling on his knees in the dust, for long, shocked minutes. Benedicta and Count Thibaut hurried to him, crouched beside him. 'Sire?'

'No!' Henry stared ahead unseeing. 'No!'

'Sire?' Thibaut asked again. The King's face was deathly white. Benedicta looked up and around at the ranks of horrified faces surrounding them. She looked down at the parchment and read there, '... with great sorrow, the loss of *The White Ship* and all aboard. The ship foundered against a rock just out of the harbour.'

Benedicta blinked. All aboard *The White Ship*. *All* aboard. Haith? Prince William? The young nobles of the Prince's court. Haith?

Count Thibaut gestured to a group of servants who hurried to help half-carry the King from the room. Benedicta stayed crumpled on the floor, her face in her hands, her world too collapsing around her.

The King sat staring into space and had transformed into an aged man. His hair was grey and thin, his face haggard. He had lost three children in the wreck of the ship: his heir, William; his first daughter, Matilda, the Countess of Perche; and his son, Richard. So many gone into the waters. Three hundred souls – passengers and crew. The King's greatest friend, Haith; Richard, Earl of Chester, who had been raised at Henry's court, and his wife Matilda of Blois, Henry's niece; Richard's half-brother Othuer, the illegitimate son of Hugh, Earl of Chester, and the two sons of Ivo de Grandesmil, all raised at court; Ralph the Red of Pont-Echanfray, the hero of the recent campaign, and one of the King's best military captains. All those young men and women floating down, down, their eyes open and unseeing, their skin pale as anemones. An unbearable litany.

Every moment of the day Benedicta wanted to lay down and die but she plodded on, one step, one breath, each filled with unendurable grief for Haith. She clung to the King's hand as much to comfort herself as to comfort him. Thibaut had brought the King one small piece of good news. His brother, Etienne de Blois, had not sailed with *The White Ship*, and lived still, although their sister, Matilda, Countess of Chester, was lost and Countess Adela was in great grief. Benedicta looked anxiously at the King, wondering if his sanity would hold under this extreme distress, wondering who amongst his enemies might strike first at his weakness. Perhaps she should write to Adela if Henry did not rally soon. Bishop Roger of Salisbury had come to court to take charge of business so it was just the King's mind that Benedicta had to worry about.

It did not take long for the news to spread across all Europe. The heir to the English throne was dead. King Henry had no heir. The alliances with Anjou and France were gone. Mahaut had lost her husband. The court buzzed with speculation about the succession. William *Clito* was now the most plausible heir, at least to Normandy. Or another of the King's nephews: Thibaut, perhaps. Or one of his surviving illegitimate sons might be legitimised. The eldest, Robert FitzRoy, was the obvious candidate. The King's own father had been a bastard. Yet many claimed the Church would not countenance that option. And Benedicta wondered what plans Amaury de Montfort might be hatching to take advantage of King Henry's grief.

After a week, news came of one survivor: a butcher from Rouen named Burold who had clung to a spar from the wrecked ship throughout the night. Haith would have said the Flemish word for butcher, a 'budger', Benedicta remembered, with another stab at her heart. They waited, hoping to hear of more survivors, but no more such news came. The families of the drowned tried to find the bodies of their loved ones but almost all had been swallowed by the grey swell of the English Sea and could not be retrieved. With Haith gone from the world, everything was gone from the world. Everything was just black.

The court was a bustle of coming and going, everyone desperate to hear a different story but as the weeks passed it became clear that the story would not change. They would not return. They were gone. Isabel de Beaumont arrived with her mother, Elizabeth de Vermandois, and Isabel attempted to comfort the King. The King's scribe Bernard was promoted to take the place of Gisulf who, too, had gone down with *The White Ship*.

Benedicta sat staring at the river from the window, thinking of how she had deceived herself, how she had not known herself, and now it was too late. She ignored a commotion at the door. Banging, barking, servants calling out. Someone else would have to deal with it. The maid tapped tentatively and put her head around the edge of the door. 'There's a visitor for you below, Sister.'

'I cannot receive visitors.'

'It's a lady!' the maid said, in awed tones. 'Come a long way by the looks and sound of her.'

Benedicta turned to the maid, frowning. 'From Normandy? From France?' Perhaps it was someone from Countess Adela but what lady would come here, to her?

'No, Sister. From Wales I reckon. She's got that accent, you know.'

'Wales? I don't know anyone in Wales.'

'I think you should come, Sister. She is weeping fit to drown us – well I mean ... not drown but ... says she knew your brother.'

Benedicta flapped her hands at the maid's faux pas and her graceless efforts to recover it. She stood and followed the maid downstairs.

An astoundingly beautiful noblewoman with black hair and large, dark blue eyes, stood wringing her hands in the middle of the room. The woman was tall with an exquisite oval face but that face was wet with tears and the sides of her nose and her mouth were puffed and red with crying. She was very finely dressed in a dark green hooded cloak with an intricate golden knot brooch at her throat, but she was smutted and smeared with the dust of hard travel. Another woman, her maid, also dark-haired, shorter and buxom, was tugging at her arm. 'Sit, Nest. Be calm! We don't know it.'

The tall noblewoman, snatched her arm back from her maid's grasp and turned to Benedicta. 'Tell me it isn't true, please!'

Benedicta dropped her gaze to the stone flags. 'Is it my brother, Haith, that you come to ask about?' She looked up again.

'Yes. Haith.' The lady's swollen mouth stayed open, expectant.

Benedicta noticed the delicate strands of tears and saliva between her lips. She put her hand on the lady's arm, and through gentle pressure and words, cajoled her into sitting. 'You knew Haith, my lady?'

'Knew!' The woman's mouth fell open again and her eyes welled anew. The maid fussed a handkerchief at the woman's wet cheeks, which she batted away. 'Oh, please, Sister Benedicta, tell me he isn't drowned,' she wailed.

Benedicta felt her own hot tears rising and took the woman's hand between two of hers. 'How did you know my brother?'

The woman snatched back her hand, dropped her face into her hands in her lap, unable to stay upright and wept loudly, her shoulders shaking. The maid put a protective arm around her heaving shoulders. 'My mistress is Lady Nest, Sister. She was a good friend of your brother. I am Amelina. We've come fast as we could from Wales. We were on our way here about another matter when we heard the news on the road and couldn't believe it. We hoped it might be scotched when we got here.'

'You also knew my brother, I see, Amelina,' Benedicta said, seeing the misery on the maid's face.

'Yes. We both knew him well, for many years, since we were girls.'

Amelina and Benedicta looked with great concern at the

engulfing grief of her lady, Nest. Benedicta ordered her own maid to stoke up the fire and bring wine and warm water for the guests to wash their faces and hands. She whispered instructions that the guest chamber should be made ready for them. By the time she resumed her seat, Amelina had succeeded in calming her lady a little. Nest sat upright, dabbing at her eyes, but each tear she mopped was replaced by two new ones. Amelina blew her own nose loudly.

'So, it is true?' Lady Nest said to Benedicta, visibly forcing herself to bravery, her mouth trembling. 'Haith drowned on *The White Ship*?'

'I fear that is it true, yes. I hoped for weeks that news would come that he had survived but only one survivor was found. The rest went down. Three hundred souls and my dear Haith.'

Nest stared at Benedicta, swallowing, her expression anguished. 'You look a great deal like him, Sister,' she said, when she could trust her voice.

'You knew him well?'

'Yes. I knew him well. I loved him well.' Nest stared at her hands in her lap.

Benedicta looked in surprise at Amelina and the maid nodded her head. 'They were deep in love, they were. Would have married if the King had let them. Greatly in love.'

Benedicta realised that this must be the Nest, the Welsh princess that Haith had written to her about but he had never spoken of a relationship between them, of love.

Nest sat upright again, long pale fingers wiping at the wet, delicate skin beneath her eyes. 'The Dogs have gone too far,' she whispered, staring at the fire. 'They have run amok and killed all and I have lost my Haith and poor Henry is broken into pieces. It is my fault.'

'It's *not* your fault *at all*,' Amelina said impatiently, and turned to answer Benedicta's bewildered frown. 'It's the Dogs of Annwn she's talking about. A curse she made against the murderers of her family: the Normans. But you didn't make no curse against Haith,' she turned back to Nest.

Nest struggled to recover some composure. 'Perhaps you are unaware that you have a nephew, Sister Benedicta.'

A great smile bloomed on Benedicta's face. She thought she had forgotten how to smile. 'A nephew?'

'He is called Robert. He is three years old and a bonny boy. I hope you will come to meet him at Carew.'

'Yes!' Benedicta laughed, 'Yes, I will.'

Part Four

1121

31

The New Broom

After the muted celebrations for Christmas and the new year, the talk at court was of nothing but the succession. Henry begged me to stay in attendance with him during the Christmas season and I could not refuse him. The King looked terrible: all the joy and strength wrung from him. His broad back hunched and I remembered his image of how he carried a great mountainous island upon it. He was still only fifty-three but looked twenty years older.

Benedicta suggested that Amelina and I stay with her in Haith's townhouse. I had given up the house that Gerald had kept in London some time back. Even if I had wanted to return to Wales, the season was too bad to allow for travelling. In truth, I had no idea of wanting to ever do anything again. I moved around in a daze, going through the motions of living each day.

The court waited to hear if the King would declare for William *Clito* his heir, or Thibaut de Blois, or even Robert FitzRoy. Elizabeth, however, had other ideas. She called upon me at Haith's house, bustling into the room, excitement writ large on her face, where I was sitting quietly with Benedicta and Amelina, sewing clothes for Robert.

I had heard rumours that Elizabeth was asserting Henry would remarry and father another legitimate son. For weeks after the news of *The White Ship* had come, Henry did not look capable of surviving the tragedy himself, let about remarrying and fathering more children, but slowly he had been recovering. Now he appeared almost his robust self, almost, but I thought he would never be quite the same. First the incident with his granddaughters, and now the loss of his children and all the youthful flowers of his court had broken something in him. He told me during a private conversation that a king must always be certain and he felt no certainty anymore.

'Nest! I have great news,' Elizabeth burst out.

I suppressed my stupid hope at her words. Every tall, broad back I saw in the crowd, I thought it might be Haith. Every high blond head. And each flash of hope ended in bitter disappointment, tasting of ash.

'What news?' I faltered.

'Isabel is bearing the King's son!'

I frowned at her. 'The King's son?'

'Well, of course, it could be a girl,' she said, 'but yes, the King's child. Gaiety will return to the world with that news, don't you think?'

Gaiety. No. I could not imagine what gaiety felt like. 'Henry will be pleased,' I said mildly.

'Pleased?' Elizabeth looked with theatrical outrage at me. 'He will be ecstatic. All is recovered now!'

'Not recovered, Elizabeth. Not all is recovered.'

'Well, no. Of course not, but you know what I mean.'

'Has Isabel informed Henry yet?'

'Yes. Just yesterday. And he was overjoyed, of course. My darling girl gives us all balm for the future. We are all summoned to the hall now, Nest. No doubt to hear this news and Henry's announcement of his intention to marry Isabel.'

I paused my stitching and stood, gathering my skirts about me. 'You should come too, Amelina and Sister Benedicta, if we are to hear good news from the King,' I told them.

Arriving at the hall, Elizabeth pushed and commanded a path through the throng of people until we reached the front and could stand looking at the seated King. 'Where is Isabel?' Elizabeth whispered to me. We scanned the crowding faces and saw no sign of her, but then I heard her voice behind us. 'Mama? What is it?' Elizabeth turned to look at her daughter in confusion.

'The King is making an announcement.' She frowned and turned back to look in bewilderment at Henry who stood up and the hubbub died down to silence.

'Thank you for gathering. I have momentous news and wish to share it with you all.'

We looked at him expectantly. Mabel stood with her husband, Robert FitzRoy, to one side, near the King, and Thibaut de Blois was close to them.

'We have all suffered great losses, great sadnesses for which there is no remedy,' Henry said. 'Only grieving memories of those we have lost. Only prayers for their souls. I have laid plans to establish a new monastery at Reading to honour our lost sons and daughters, our friends and loved ones.' He paused and scanned the crowd. 'I have decided to create two new Earls. My son, Robert, I make Earl of Gloucester.'

I smiled at Mabel, delighted that she would be Countess of Gloucester, Bristol and Glamorgan, inheriting the lands of her parents. Her mother would be proud to bursting and so was I. Did this mean that Henry would make Robert his heir?

'I create Ranulf, Earl of Chester.' Many of us in the crowd thought with sadness of the young Richard, Earl of Chester, and his wife, Matilda of Blois, lost on the ship. Thibaut de Blois looked down at his shoes, biting his lip at the thought of his drowned sister.

'We must have some hope,' Henry called out, raising his voice, 'some hope for the future. And so I have decided to take a new wife, a new queen.'

An enormous buzz from the crowd grew at this pronouncement. Elizabeth turned to exchange a smug smile with Isabel and pulled her forward a little more so that she stood at the front. Isabel was a woman now, and a beautiful one. She would make Henry a good bride and she would bear him new heirs. I looked at Henry and saw that, in the pause, his gaze had strayed to us: to Isabel and myself. He held my gaze. I had no expectations. I was nearing forty years in age. He needed a young brood mare now. Still, there was regret. I remembered how I had loved him, how once I had longed that he might make such a choice for me.

'I have been fortunate to secure the troth of Adelisa de Lou-vain, daughter of the Duke of Lower Lotharinga,' Henry said in a loud voice, shifting his gaze past me, past Isabel, past Elizabeth, to look out across the crowd, who greeted this news with claps and shouts of approbation.

I felt Elizabeth stagger against me. I heard Isabel utter a sur-prised 'Oh!'

'The bastard,' Elizabeth said, almost loud enough to be heard by Henry.

I pressed her arm, cautioning her. 'Let's move.' I gripped her and Isabel and tugged them away from the front of the crowd towards the side of the hall where we might recover ourselves in some privacy.

'You said you'd told him!' Elizabeth accused her daughter.

'But I did, Mama. Last night.'

'You told him about the child. That it was certain.'

'Yes. I told him.'

Elizabeth stared astonished at Isabel and then back to Henry. 'Well, I ... then ...'

'Elizabeth,' I cautioned, 'let's not have this discussion here, in sight of all these gossips. Let's retire to your room. If he is marrying the daughter of the Duke of Lower Lotharinga it's not something that has just happened overnight. He must have been negotiating this for months, perhaps even before the ship went down. Come!' I pulled them further towards the door. Isabel had her eyes cast to the ground and was snivelling a little. 'Keep your composure, Isabel,' I told her. 'Don't show your distress before all these others.'

Having done what I could to comfort Isabel and cool Elizabeth's fury, I returned to the townhouse, where another surprise waited for me. Amelina and I were astonished to see Benedicta stand-ing before us in a plain brown dress with a muted yellow mantle. Without the enveloping folds of her black habit I could see that she had Haith's slender ranginess. The yellow curls of her short hair and her wide mouth reminded me painfully of him.

'Sister!' Amelina exclaimed.

'No Sister,' she replied calmly. 'I have decided to relinquish my vows as a nun and to live as a pious woman instead. It would be best to name me Ida from now on. It was my birth name, before I entered the abbey. Ida de Bruges. I wondered, Lady Nest,' she turned eyes that were uncertain now onto me, 'if you might find a role for me about your household? It would be a comfort to me if I might find some purpose in helping to care for Haith's son. And I am lettered. I could assist with your business, your correspondence and so forth.'

Amelina gaped at her. 'This is a sudden decision.'

'No,' she said. 'I have been considering it for some time and now I have taken the leap, but with no living male relative I am in need of the shelter of some household.'

At last, I managed to get some words past my astonishment. 'There is no need for a role, Sis … Benedi … I mean Ida. You are my sister. You are kin. My son's aunt. You are already part of my household and always will be.'

'Thank you.' Tears sprang to her eyes.

Amelina gave me one of her surreptitious 'well I never' expressions.

'But Benedicta, Ida, won't you be pursued? By your Abbess, by the Church? Punishments for renegade nuns can be most terrible.'

'I fall between the cracks,' she said. 'I am an anonymous. Abbess Mathilde thinks I am at Fontevraud and Abbess Petronilla thinks I am returned to Almenêches. If you would conceal me in Wales from the notice of the King and the Countess, then I believe that no one will care one way or the other. I have not been honest with myself about who I am, what I hope for in my life. I believe I will serve God better as a pious lay woman than I ever did as a deceptive nun.'

'Are you sure you know what you are doing? You were safe in the nunnery. Living concealed like this, you will be in peril.'

'I don't want to be safe. I want to live my life.'

It seemed I had been right about the length of time that Henry's marriage negotiations had been brewing. The lady herself, Adelisa de Louvain arrived at court, fast on the heels of the King's announcement. They were wed a few days after her arrival

301

in London by William Giffard, Bishop of Winchester. Archbishop Ralph of Canterbury would normally have performed the ceremony but he had recently suffered a seizure that had left one side of his face paralysed and his speech impaired. Adelisa was an attractive young woman, descended from Charlemagne. In addition to her royal blood, her father had a powerful hold in the Low Countries and his men controlled a highly prosperous trade in London. It was, as ever with Henry, an astute move. Perhaps he was not entirely broken, after all. The main reason for Henry's choice, however, was of course the eligibility of a young childbearing woman.

Isabel had been dropped altogether. Isabel and her growing belly. I knew how she felt and did my best to console her. Elizabeth fumed but did not dare to berate the King. I allowed her to rant for a few days and then I told her the hard truth. Why would Henry make Isabel his queen when he could have a fresh girl in his bed, one who brought him a huge dowry and important new alliances? And furthermore, if the Church would not countenance the King making his eldest illegitimate son, Robert, his heir, then Henry knew that difficulties would be created over the child that Isabel carried, that everyone knew had been conceived outside of the marriage bed.

In June, the court prepared to move into Wales, and I along with them. Maredudd ap Bleddyn and three of Cadwgan's sons had taken advantage of the temporary vacuum of Norman power in Chester after the loss of the young Earl Richard on *The White Ship*. They had attacked two castles and slaughtered the garrisons. Perhaps they thought Henry's grief and his lack of an heir gave them an opening, made him weak. Henry acted swiftly and led a military campaign against them. Ida (I struggled every time to think of Benedicta with this new name) travelled in a covered wagon with Amelina and kept her face from anyone who might know her as a renegade nun. Henry's new queen accompanied him and he also commanded the presence in his entourage of Elizabeth and Isabel. 'Why do we need to travel to Wales?' Elizabeth asked him, her anger barely concealed.

'Because I command it,' Henry told her, serenely.

32

O Sea-bird

At Bristol, I parted company with the King's entourage and headed towards Deheubarth with Amelina, Ida and a small armed escort provided for us by the King. The journey took us along the shore of Carmarthen Bay and we stopped overnight in Llansteffan before making for Carew.

From the headland, Ida and I looked down on the shifting waters. From here it was possible to see the three blue talons of the rivers reaching up into the land. Water had taken Haith, taken my joy, yet I could not look on water itself with bitterness. Water still looked like joy to me. It was where we had first found one another, and now where I had lost him. Water was joyous and so was Haith, and everything about him had been engaged with water. One day I would join Haith in the swilling sea. I had written a last testament stating that I wished to be 'buried' in the waters of Carmarthen Bay and not in the ground. I imagined myself swimming to find him, lying on the sands and breathing life into his mouth from my own. Such fancies gave me some meagre consolation.

'See the wrack line?' Ida said, pointing at the scrawl of seaweed and driftwood left behind by the tide.

'Yes?'

'It looks like writing, doesn't it? Like the sea's diary.'

'Yes,' I smiled at her notion. 'We all struggle to leave our mark, our trace, just as the sea does. I keep a diary.'

'You do?'

I nodded. 'The traces of the past are all around us,' I said, looking at Llansteffan beach, the estuary of the rivers, the bay. 'The
land is a bumpy container of our memories. Nothing is ever truly
erased, it is simply transformed.'

'I suppose you are right.'

'There was an earthquake here once,' I told her.

'An earthquake?'

'Yes, the ground shook and rumbled. Timbers, roofs and
chimneys fell from buildings, rocks slid from the cliffs, but the
worst thing was the sea.'

'How so?'

'It swelled and heaved like the back of a great monster and a
great wall of water ran up the beach and kept going far inland,
swallowing the lower parts of the village. In its retreat, it sucked
everything back out with it – houses, barns, cows, hay bales, men,
women and children. There were just shattered ruins and shred-
ded timbers left behind and a terrible silence. The tide rolls back
and forth, back and forth, but time rolls on and on relentlessly
and cannot be undone or unravelled.'

I knew that the Normans who were here in Wales could not
retreat, could not go back across the Severn estuary and the English Sea. We each act and one thing leads to another and how are
we to know if we act for good or ill in the end.

Ida and I walked down to the beach, where I picked up a white
fragment and examined it. It must once have been a large shell
but it had been smoothed and smoothed, washed and planed by
the sea so that now its form was blurred almost beyond recognition. I slid my fingers up and down and around its white faces.
Everything is dilution rather than erasure, I thought. Nothing
is ever really lost although it may lose its shape. I drew a bird's
claw on the sand at the edge of the water with the eroded shell.
I watched the surf come in once, twice and a third time, gradually smoothing away my drawing to invisibility. *I* am not deleted,
I thought. We, the Welsh, we are not deleted. We cling on, we
transform. I stared out across the heaving waters of the bay. The
inevitability of the rising and the falling of the sea twice between
each moon, over and over, should be some comfort. Yet instead,

a powerful surge of longing for Haith rose and crashed over me like the neap tide breaching the sea walls.

Whilst Henry was in the field against the Welsh, we stayed at Carew, and I introduced Robert to his aunt Ida, much to their mutual delight. News came that the King had been hit a glancing blow from an arrow in Powys but had been uninjured. The kitchen girl came knocking at my door early in the morning and said Amelina was asking if I might come down to the kitchen to speak with her. 'And why can she not come to me?' I asked languidly, stretching my arms above my head.

'All covered in flour, she is, from head to foot,' the maid assured me, making me laugh at the vision of what I might find downstairs.

I put on an old gown and found Amelina in the kitchen making bread. I watched her knead the dough, mesmerised by her expert, rhythmical actions. The ends of her head veil were thrown back behind her shoulders to keep them out of her way and to cool her flushed face and chest. Her sleeves were rolled to above her elbows showing how solid and strong her hands and forearms were. A blue apron protected her gown from the flour. 'Thank you for coming, lady,' she said, without looking up from the fat roll of dough that was suffering an extreme pummelling between her fingers.

'Well?'

She set the dough roll in a circle of flour on the board, wiped her hands on her apron and looked up at me and then around the kitchen to see who was in earshot. 'Best go elsewhere,' she said, eyeing the cook and his assistants. 'I'll have to get the flour off my hands. Girl!' she called out, as she dunked her doughy hands in a bowl and carefully wiped the sticky mix from between her fingers. 'Get that dough into the oven!'

The maid walked swiftly to the table to obey.

I followed Amelina from the kitchen and out into the bailey where we sat on a bench near the well, a good distance from any possible eavesdroppers. 'Well? What is all this intrigue and subterfuge?'

'You know that arrow that was shot at the King?'

'Yes, but he is not harmed.'

'No, thanks be to God. But,' she lowered her voice another notch and tipped her head closer to mine, 'there's a traveller just arrived in the hall, a Welshman. He's a pilgrim going to Saint Davids. And he's saying it was Gwenllian that shot the arrow.'

I raised my eyebrow. 'Gwenllian? Gruffudd's wife?'

'Aye.'

'Has she been taken prisoner?'

'No. But the pilgrim says there were witnesses, credible witnesses, that said it was a woman, and some others that knew her by sight and said it was she.'

'It could have been any woman and she is maligned.'

Now Amelina raised her eyebrows. 'You think?'

I sighed. No. It *was* credible that it had been my sister-in-law, Gwenllian, and there was a harbinger in that of more trouble ahead.

In the wake of the news that Maredudd had come to peace with King Henry, I received a summons to attend the King at Cardigan and to bring my children, Angharad and David, with me.

'Why does he want you to bring the children?' Amelina asked, worried.

'I don't know.' I considered disobeying but there was a distance between Henry and I now, and a new hardness about him, and I did not dare.

When we arrived at the gates of Cardigan Castle, our progress was much hampered by an enormous herd of cows that were being driven in the streets and filled every space. Thousands of brown and white cows thronged and banged against one another, churning up dust and dirt, trying to raise their heads with frightened rolling eyes above the broad backs of the other cows. They milled about the gateway, lowing and shoving and trampling the ground to a morass. The soldiers cleared a path for our horses with difficulty and a great deal of shouting, pushing and switching of whips.

In the courtyard, the first person I encountered as I dismounted was the Constable of Cardigan, Stephen de Marais. 'Lady Nest,' he said, handing me down and looking red-faced and flustered, 'I wonder if I could trouble you to assist me? I am in urgent need of translation, with this fellow here.'

I smoothed my skirts and nodded to Amelina to take my children and belongings into the hall. 'How may I help?' I looked at the 'fellow' de Marais had indicated. He was a herdsman with an insolent smile on his face.

'I want to know what this fellow means by this, by bringing this great herd of cows here, to Cardigan. It is not what was agreed.'

I spoke to the lead herdsman in Welsh, having to raise my voice above the constant mooing and lowing all around us.

'He says it is the tribute from Maredudd ap Bleddyn, King of Powys, paid to Henry, King of the English,' I told de Marais.

'Yes, but why are they here, causing this obstruction?' His voice was peevish.

I spoke with the herdsman again and kept the amusement from my face as I translated to de Marais, 'He says he was told to deliver ten thousand cows to the King of the English and the King of the English is here.' I knew that Maredudd and the herdsmen had deliberately taken their orders over-literally, merely to cause disruption. To drive this vast herd all the way here to the west of Wales meant that the King's household would simply have to drive them all the way back, east across the country.

'What am I to do with them all here? They will need fodder and water to deplete the whole city, as if the King's court were not itself enough of a demand upon us here. Now we are overwhelmed by cows!'

I spoke with the herdsman again and could not fully repress my laughter this time, at his riposte. 'He says you'd best start eating them straight away,' I told de Marais, and picked up my skirts, walking swiftly towards the hall lest I laugh in his face, as the Welsh undoubtedly were laughing up their sleeves at the poor Constable. But then my smile slipped, when I reflected that annoying the Normans with a herd of cows was small consolation for everything that we had lost here in Wales.

People clustered in the hall before the King and his new wife. Henry was looking a little better. Queen Adelisa had a beautiful and intelligent young face. I thought that her glances at Henry suggested a real affection for him and I hoped she could help him with his sorrow and his burdens. My older sons were there: Henry, William and Maurice standing close with their friend, Gilbert FitzGilbert de Clare. I recognised Miles, the Constable of Gloucester and flinched at the sight of my father's murderer, Bernard de Neufmarché, who was there with his wife, Agnes, and their grown-up children, Mael and Sybille.

'I have been asked to rule on a dispute over the legitimacy of Bernard de Neufmarché's heir,' Henry announced. There was a surprised murmur, and both Bernard de Neufmarché and Mael de Neufmarché looked at the King and then at Agnes with expressions of shock and bewilderment on their faces. Clearly, they had received no forewarning of this ruling.

'I have been informed that you recently mutilated a Welshman in your household,' the King said to Mael.

'He was an adulterer,' Mael declared, his face still confused, trying to find his footing.

'Yes, an adulterer with your mother, Agnes of Wales, so I understand,' said Henry.

Mael made no response but his eyes were wide, his mouth open and his breath harsh in his open mouth.

King Henry turned to Bernard de Neufmarché. 'Your wife has admitted that Mael here is not your son.'

Agnes looked over at me. She had confessed her Welsh lover to me long ago, at the time of Mael's conception. Would I have to bear witness? Agnes was the granddaughter of Llewelyn ap Gruffudd who had been King of all Wales and she had been bitterly forced to the marriage with the loathed Norman, de Neufmarché. She told me when she was still newly wed, years ago, that she had tried and failed to kill her husband twice. 'Murdering brides are a rare breed, more's the pity,' she'd said, fiercely.

In the event, there were plenty of others who supported the assertions made concerning Agnes's lover and I was not called. After considering the evidence, Henry declared Mael illegitimate and disinherited. He declared Agnes's daughter Sybille to be the legitimate heir to de Neufmarché lands and titles and betrothed her to Miles of Gloucester. I doubted that Sybille was de Neufmarché's child either, but that would not signify to Henry, who simply wanted a man he could trust to take over from the aging Lord of Brecknock. I wondered what nefarious dealings Agnes had had with the King to bring this about to their mutual satisfaction. And I wondered at Agnes that she had seen fit to deal this blow to her hated husband, but at such cost to her son.

My curse of the Dogs of Annwn had finally caught up with de Neufmarché. He was old and sick and now he lost his heir. He had conquered vast lands and achieved vast wealth through cruelties and injustices, including the murder of my father and my half-brothers, Cynan and Idwal, but now he had lost everything and must watch it slide through his fingers like sand.

'Lady Isabel de Beaumont,' Henry called out, interrupting my thoughts. Isabel was standing with Elizabeth and myself, the child in her belly quite evident. She turned to the King in surprise at the sound of her name. 'Now what!' Elizabeth hissed under her breath.

'Lady Isabel, I have arranged a marriage for you,' the King said.

'What!' Elizabeth exploded.

'With the agreement of your guardian, of course,' Henry continued, ignoring Elizabeth's outburst, and glancing instead towards William de Warenne who flushed and looked away from Elizabeth's furious eyes.

I saw Isabel swallow. 'Be brave, Isabel,' I told her in a low voice. 'He will not be cruel to you.' I hoped that this was true.

'Gilbert FitzGilbert de Clare will take you in marriage,' Henry announced, 'and he will add to his duties, command of my fortress at Pembroke.'

Now it was my turn to stare at Henry, agape. At Pembroke?

'Lady Nest.'

Without thinking, I stepped forward, my heart beating hard. I had not expected any significant pronouncements about myself.

'You have brought your youngest children with you?' Henry asked me, his voice gentle.

'Yes.' Fear rose within me and I fumbled for my own so recent words to Isabel. He will not be cruel to you.

'I have arranged for your daughter, Angharad FitzWalter, to be betrothed to the son of Odo de Berry at Manorbier.'

I took a small breath. That was not a bad thing. 'Thank you, Sire.'

'And your youngest son, David, he is eight years old?'

'Yes.'

'I have arranged that he will go as an oblate to St David's Cathedral.'

'Sire,' I found my voice now, thinking to protest, but floundered without any real opposition in my own mind. Perhaps this was not such a bad option for David. Better perhaps than being a soldier frequently facing death, as my older sons did. I had often thought of my hands on Gerald's cold skin as I wrapped him in his shroud and trembled for my sons. But why did the King make arrangements for my children with such haste and without speaking with me about it in private?

'And you, Lady Nest, will be married to the Constable of Cardigan, Stephen de Marais.'

I closed my mouth. I stared at Henry. I felt rather than saw a shift in the group of people, as Stephen de Marais stepped forward.

No. I stared at Henry, pleading in silence. No, Henry. I could not voice my dissent.

'Your sons, of course, give their consent for this marriage,' Henry told me, holding my gaze. I shifted my stare angrily to my sons, who looked a little shamefaced but nodded their heads in confirmation. It was ludicrous that I could be disposed of like this on the say so of three beardless boys. I glared at William and Maurice but had to temper my angry expression, realising that, as usual, it was the King I should feel angry with. He did not intend to leave me available for exploitation by a Welsh Prince who might try to use me as a symbol for the Welsh resistance once more, or try to claim Deheubarth through me. My sons needed me to stay safely in 'their' Norman camp, and not 'stray' to the Welsh. My sons needed to be more Norman than the Normans because they were half-Welsh, they were mongrels. They thought of themselves as the sons of Gerald FitzWalter. They loved me but I was merely their Welsh mother and they were a little ashamed of that. And my boy, Henry. He did not flinch from my gaze as William and Maurice had. I had loved him so hard all my life. His eyes were liquid at the sight of me. No doubt I looked stricken, but he could not disagree with his father, either, he must be seen as a strong Norman lord in the Norman court. At this juncture, they must all betray me. They knew nothing of my love for Haith and my despair at his death. Only King Henry knew of that knife twisting in my gut, that sharp hook ripping at the corner of my tender blubbering mouth. I fought to maintain control of my expression, my stance.

I looked down, horrified, as Stephen de Marais took my hand. 'I am greatly honoured,' he said quietly.

'These marriages and betrothals will take place tomorrow morning,' the King declared. Queen Adelisa smiled serenely at him and they looked together back to all of us.

During the years of my influence as the King's mistress, I had rarely asked Henry for anything. All I had ever asked him for was to leave our son with me and to leave me in peace with Gerald. Surely I could ask him to excuse me from this marriage? I tried to gain an audience with Henry to ask that he would leave me a widow at Carew but he would not see me. I considered arguing with my sons but knew that if Henry was adamant for this course of action, they would not, could not, disagree with him. Fury, I should feel fury, I told myself, but oddly, I felt nothing. Since Haith was dead, perhaps it did not matter. Nothing mattered.

'He seems harmless,' Amelina said quietly, referring to de Marais, as she brushed my hair.

I thought I would weep but no tears came. I sat, impassive under Amelina's brushings and decorating. King Henry pronounced on us all but beneath his splendid show, he was weakened, and battling overwhelming grief for his lost children and all those young nobles of his court, their bones washed white on the sea-floor. Henry's back was against the wall and he was taking the actions he had to, to secure Wales, so that he could continue his struggle to pacify Normandy and rule England.

I was nearing forty and could not relish the prospect of doing duty as this wife. Yet I also had no desire to risk abduction by another Welsh pretender. I would manage de Marais. He had duties in Cardigan, and I would spend as much time as I could at Carew and Llansteffan with Amelina and Ida-Benedicta, and with my boy, Robert, and it would be a few years yet before Angharad would leave me to marry. 'Lady Agnes says her husband needs medicining, Amelina. She asked me if you might help him?' I did not look at myself in the mirror. I did not want to see this woman about to marry a man she could not care for. I would just think of other matters.

She shook her head and I raised my eyebrows quizzically. 'De Neufmarché! You hate the man,' she said.

'I do. I did. Yet I feel some pity for him now that he is brought so low and is aged, helpless in the power of Lady Agnes. Perhaps that is vengeance enough. If I am consumed with hatred forever, as Agnes is, then that hatred will consume me too.' I thought about how my curse, my revenge against the Montgommerys and de Neufmarché had not cured my grief for Goronwy, my father, my lost Welsh life. It could not restore Haith to me in happiness. 'If you can help de Neufmarché, I would not object to it.'

Amelina shook her head. 'Not likely. Have you seen the way he walks?'

I frowned at her, uncomprehending.

'He has a fistula. You know. Where the sun doesn't shine.'

'Amelina!'

'I'm not going near that. Riding with a wet saddle, I expect,' she added. 'He'll have to go straight to the wise woman himself for *that*.'

'Well, then,' I said, standing, and batting away her hands that were still primping and smoothing at my dress, 'let's go to the funeral of my wedding.'

I came last. We four couples stood hand in hand before Bishop Bernard of Saint Davids, King Henry, Queen Adelisa and the rest of the gathered court. My beautiful daughter, Angharad, had been betrothed to the boy, William de Barry, and was not displeased about it. Gilbert FitzGilbert de Clare had said the words of troth to Isabel de Beaumont and feigned not to notice her thrusting belly carrying the King's child as he did so. Miles of Gloucester had taken the hand of the new heiress, Sybille de Neufmarché, and had been well pleased to find himself suddenly heir to Brecknock and everything else that de Neufmarché had stolen in blood and anguish from my countrymen. Now, it was my turn. I stood with Stephen de Marais listening to the words marrying us, my heart sinking at the prospect, despite my arguments to myself and the stone face I presented to the world. I voiced my consent tonelessly for there seemed nothing else I could do. I thought I glimpsed Haith's face in the crowd, but I always thought so, every day, and every day I was wrong. So King Henry had created a new generation of Norman lords with a new stranglehold on Wales.

At the back of the crowd there was some disturbance. I glanced over to see the cause and saw Etienne de Blois step from the parting crowd. We had heard that he had disembarked from *The White Ship* before it sailed and so had evaded the fate of all of those other lost souls. So, he had made his way back then, perhaps sailing directly here to Cardigan to rejoin the King. Then I was astonished to see the tall, blond man stepping from the crowd behind Count Etienne. Haith!

I watched him bow to a beaming Henry and they embraced like two great bears, laughing in each other's faces, clapping each other's arms. 'News travelled that you were safe, nephew,' Henry told Etienne, 'but we all presumed *you* were lost. My old friend Haith! I am delighted to find you resurrected from the sea! Thank God, Haith! Thank God!' Henry gasped and spluttered through tears, as if Haith had just rescued *him* from drowning. The King indicated his delight to the gathered crowd, his eyes glancing and flinching from mine, as he remembered that Haith had asked to marry me and here I stood wed instead to this other man. Haith turned his gaze to me. My new husband held my hand firmly. Haith's smile stayed in place, suffused with sadness.

O sea-bird, I thought, looking at Haith with wonder, beautiful upon the tides, bright as a sunbeam.

Genealogy of the Dukes of Normandy/Kings of England/Counts d'Évreux/Lords de Montfort (up to 1121)

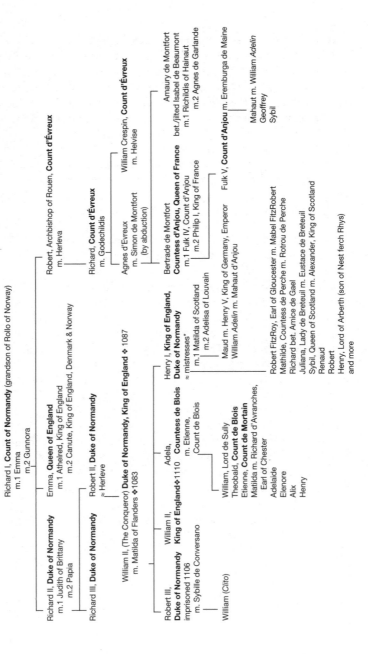

Genealogy of the Welsh Royal Families, early 12th century (up to 1121)

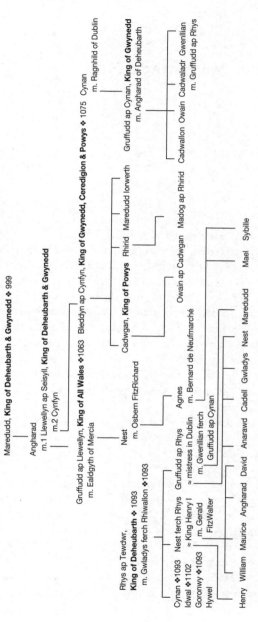

Maredudd, King of Deheubarth & Gwynedd ✤ 999

Angharad
m.1 Llewellyn ap Seisyll, **King of Deheubarth & Gwynedd**
m.2 Cynfyn

Gruffudd ap Llewellyn, **King of All Wales** ✤1063   Bleddyn ap Cynfyn, **King of Gwynedd, Ceredigion & Powys** ✤ 1075   Cynan
m. Ealdgyth of Mercia   m. Ragnhild of Dublin

Nest   Rhirid   Maredudd   Iorwerth   Gruffudd ap Cynan, **King of Gwynedd**
m. Osbern FitzRichard   Cadwgan, **King of Powys**   m. Angharad of Deheubarth

Agnes
m. Bernard de Neufmarché

Owain ap Cadwgan   Madog ap Rhirid   Cadwallon   Owain   Cadwaladr   Gwenllian
                                                                                                                m. Gruffudd ap Rhys

Rhys ap Tewdwr,
King of Deheubarth ✤ 1093
m. Gwladys ferch Rhiwallon ✤1093

Cynan ✤1093   Nest ferch Rhys   Gruffudd ap Rhys   ≈ mistress in Dublin
Idwal ✤1102   ≈ King Henry I
Goronwy ✤1093   m. Gerald   m. Gwenllian ferch
Hywel   FitzWalter   Gruffudd ap Cynan

Henry   William   Maurice   Angharad   David   Anarawd   Cadell   Gwladys   Nest   Maredudd   Mael   Sybille

Key to Genealogies

Genealogies are selective, rather than a comprehensive. I have not, for instance, listed Cadwgan's seven wives. Not all of King Henry's illegitimate children are listed. His known *mistresses in chronological order were Ansfride, Sybil Corbet, Nest ferch Rhys, Edith of Greystoke, Isabel de Beaumont and there were many others.
bet. = betrothed. m. = married. ≈ unmarried relationship. *Clito* and *Adelin* are designations meaning heir-apparent.

Historical Note

The stories of Nest, Henry, Haith and Ida continue in *Conquest III: The Anarchy*. This novel is based on historical research and on evidence concerning the real people and events that appear in it, although much is imagined beyond and around the evidence. Most of the events in Nest's life, depicted in this story, actually did happen. She was mistress to King Henry I and bore him a son, she was married to Gerald FitzWalter, castellan of Pembroke Castle, she was kidnapped by Owain ap Cadwgan and Gerald did escape down the toilet chute. She was married to Stephen de Marais and she probably had a son with Haith, the sheriff of Pembroke Castle. My task in this novel was to try to bring some emotional and psychological interpretation to her lived experience of those events.

Amelina and Dyfnwal are my inventions. Haith (named Hait or Hayt in the historical record) was Sheriff of Pembroke but his close relationship to King Henry, and his sister, the nun Benedicta, are my inventions, although King Henry and Countess Adela are known to have had a very effective network of spies.

The medieval writer John of Worcester reported that kings ceased to reign in Wales in 1093. He was referring to the death of Nest's father, Rhys ap Tewdwr, King of Deheubarth, who made a peace treaty with William the Conqueror in 1081 but was killed by the Norman, Bernard de Neufmarché, in 1093. We have a tendency, as Kari Maund points out of 'viewing history backwards, looking back into the twelfth century in knowledge of the events of the thirteenth century, rather than taking events of the eleventh century as a starting point' (1999, p. 68). The Norman conquest of Wales did not in any way resemble the swift conquest of England. For over two hundred years, from 1066 until 1283, when the last Welsh leader was killed, it was by no means certain that the Normans would succeed in subduing Wales. Even as late as 1400 there was a successful Welsh rebellion led by Owain Glyndwr. It took the Normans over 200 years to subdue and conquer the Welsh and in the period covered by this novel, many Welsh people believed that they might yet oust the invaders.

John of Worcester's assertion refers to the fact that after 1093 the Welsh kings were forced to acknowledge the Norman kings as overlords. Gruffudd ap Cynan, King of Gwynedd in the north, gradually took back his kingdom from the Norman invaders and Cadwgan ap Bleddyn, King of Powys maintained control of his kingdom for most of his long rule until his death in 1111. Both they and Cadwgan's son, Owain, were obliged to play a careful game of clientship with King Henry I whose campaign into Wales in 1114 was forceful and effective. King Henry succeeded in maintaining control in Wales through his careful distribution of Norman lordships and castles, despite the fact that he spent substantial parts of his reign fighting in Normandy.

The 12th century was a time of great turmoil in the relations of men and women. On the one hand noblemen such as Fulk IV of Anjou and Guillaume IX of Aquitaine engaged in serial repudiations of wives, and women such as Agnes d'Evreux (the mother of Amaury de Montfort) were married by kidnap. But on the other hand there were a number of notable female lords such as Adela de Blois and Clemence of Flanders. Robert d'Arbrissel's foundation of Fontevraud manifested a growing need to offer women both shelter and a sphere to exercise autonomy. At the same time, the Church was struggling to stabilise and impose their view of proper gender relations, with the abolition of clerical marriage and concubinage and simony. The Church's teaching on women, however, only bolstered cultural assumptions about their inferior position and character. I took inspiration for Benedicta's decision to leave the nunnery from the 16th-century runaway nun, Katharina von Bora, who married Martin Luther.

The *Conquest* series draws on the legend of the Engulphed Court of the sunken kingdom of Cantre'r Gwaelod or the 'Welsh Atlantis'. I have transposed the legendary Cantre'r Gwaelod from Cardigan Bay to Carmarthen Bay. A real earthquake was recorded in Pembrokeshire on 20 February 1247 (a little later than my fictional version, but it is possible that there was a record of an earlier one that did not survive). The 1247 earthquake was severe enough to cause damage to Saint Davids Cathedral.

The Welsh poem, 'O sea-bird', quoted by Nest on the first and last pages of the novel is from the poem 'To the Sea-gull' by the mid-14th-century Welsh poet Dafydd ap Gwilym, and so anachronistic in 1107 (Gurney, 1969). There was a Welsh bard, named Breri, singing songs about Gawain at the French courts (Weston, 1905). Nest's remark that 'my country is made the dwelling place of foreigners and a playground for lords of alien blood' is adapted from William of Malmesbury's complaint about the Normans in England (although he, himself, was half Norman) (1998–9, pp. 414–17). Benedicta and Amaury's quotations from the poems of Ovid employ translations by Jon Corelis (Corelis).

The wooden spyloft at Saint Alban's Abbey was built around 1400, so rather later than my fictional version in this story. In several places I have quoted from Amanda Hingst's excellent study of Orderic Vitalis's history of the Normans, the *Historia Ecclesiastica*, and from her translations of his work (2009). I have referred to Orderic's monastery as Ouches, since as Hingst points out, that was the name it was known by in Orderic's time. It was not until the late 12th century that it became more commonly known ast Saint-Évroult, after the name of its patron saint (2009, p. 142). Benedicta's admiration for well-formed men such as Amaury de Montfort and the men-at-arms who accompany her to Fontevraud owes a debt to Anna Comnena's description of Bohemond of Antioch in her *Alexiad* (1148).

Selected Bibliography

Brut y Tywysogion: Or, The Chronicle of the Princes, 681–1282. (1864) transl. and reprinted in *Archaeologia Cambrensis*, 10.

Ackroyd, Peter (2012) *The History of England: Volume I Foundation*, London: Pan.

Babcock, Robert S. (1992) 'Imbeciles and Normans: The *Ynfydion* of Gruffudd ap Rhys Reconsidered', *Haskins Society Journal*, vol. 4, pp. 1–9.

Bond, Gerald A. (1995) *The Loving Subject: Desire, Eloquence, and Power in Romanesque France*, Philadelphia: University of Pennsylvania Press.

Cawley, Charles (2014) *Medieval Lands,* http://fmg.ac/Projects/MedLands/Search.htm.

Comnena, Anna (1148) *Alexiad*, transl. Elizabeth A. Dawes (1928), http://sourcebooks.fordham.edu/halsall/basis/AnnaComnena-Alexiad.asp.

Corelis, Jon, *Translations of Selected Poems by Ovid*, https://www.poemhunter.com.

Duby, Georges (1985) *The Knight, The Lady and The Priest: The Making of Modern Marriage in Medieval France*, trans. Barbara Bray, Harmondsworth: Penguin.

Dyer, Christopher (2002) *Making a Living in the Middle Ages: The People of Britain 850–1520*, New Haven & London: Yale University Press.

Ferrante, Joan, ed. (2014) *Epistolae: Medieval Women's Latin Letters* https://epistolae.ccnmtl.columbia.edu/

FitzStephen, William (1990) *Norman London*, New York: Italica Press. Written around 1183.

Gravdal, Kathryn (1991) *Ravishing Maidens: Writing Rape in Medieval French Literature and Law*, Pennsylvania: University of Philadelphia Press.

Green, Judith A. (2009) *Henry I King of England and Duke of Normandy*, Cambridge: Cambridge University Press.

Gurney, Robert, ed. and trans. (1969) *Bardic Heritage*, London: Chatto & Windus.

Hingst, Amanda Jane (2009) *The Written World: Past and Place in the Work of Orderic Vitalis*, Notre Dame, Indiana: University of Notre Dame Press.

Hollister, C. Warren (2001) *Henry I*, New Haven/London: Yale University Press.

John of Worcester (1995–8) *Chronica*, ed. and trans. by P. McGurk, *The Chronicle of John of Worcester*, vols. 2 and 3. Oxford: Clarendon Press. Originally published in the 12th century.

Johns, Susan M. (2013) *Gender, Nation and Conquest in the High Middle Ages: Nest of Deheubarth*, Manchester: Manchester University Press.

LoPrete, Kimberly A. (2007) *Adela of Blois: Countess and Lord c. 1067–1137*, Dublin: Four Courts Press.

Malmesbury, William (1998–9) *Gesta Regum Anglorum: The History of the English Kings*, ed. and trans. R.A.B. Mynors, R.M. Thomson, and M. Winterbottom, 2 vols., Oxford: Clarendon Press, vol. 1. Originally published in the early 12th century.

Maund, Kari (2011) *The Welsh Kings*, Stroud: The History Press.

Maund, Kari (2007) *Princess Nest of Wales: Seductress of the English*, Stroud: Tempus.

Maund, Kari (1999) 'Owain ap Cadwgan: A Rebel Revisited', *Haskins Society Journal*, vol. 13, pp. 65–74.

Mortimer, Ian (2009) *The Time Traveller's Guide to Medieval England*, London: Vintage.

Rowlands, Ifor W. (1981) 'The making of the March: Aspects of the Norman settlement in Dyfed', *Anglo-Norman Studies*, 3, pp. 142–57 & 221–5.

Thompson, Kathleen (1991) 'Robert de Bellême Reconsidered', in Marjorie Chibnall, ed. (1991) *Proceedings of the Battle Conference*, Woodbridge: Boydell & Brewer, pp. 263–86.

Venarde, Bruce L. ed. & trans. (2003) *Robert of Arbrissel: A Medieval Religious Life*, Washington D.C.: Catholic University of America Press.

Weston, Jessie L. (1905) 'Wauchier de Denain and Bleheris', *Romania*, 34, pp. 100–5.

Wickham, Chris (2016) *Medieval Europe*, New Haven & London: Yale University Press.

A full bibliography of my research is on my website: https://traceywarrwriting.com.

Acknowledgements

I had the pleasure of living for some years in Pembrokeshire where this novel was first conceived. My experiences of Wales were enriched by my friends there, especially my muse, Bob Smillie, and my former neighbours, Andrew and Bodil Humphries. My friends and tutors on the MA Creative Writing at University of Wales, Trinity Saint David's also contributed to the delight of my encounters with south-west Wales.

My parents, Edward Warr and Maureen Warr, are both great readers and have been constant supporters in everything I have done, along with the rest of my lovely family. I am grateful to all my writing and reading buddies who have so enriched my engagement with text, including Jack Turley, Tim Smith, Mi Jung Seo, Gina Connolly, Anita Goodfellow, Ann Hebert, Karen Pegg, and all the members of the Parisot Writers Group in France. Writing this novel was significantly enabled by the Literature Wales Writers' Bursaries supported by The National Lottery through the Arts Council of Wales. My membership of the Historical Novel Society has been important in giving me a rich context for my work as an historical novelist. It is always a tremendous pleasure working with the staff at Impress Books and I am especially grateful to Richard Willis, Rachel Singleton, Laura Christopher, and Natalie Clark.